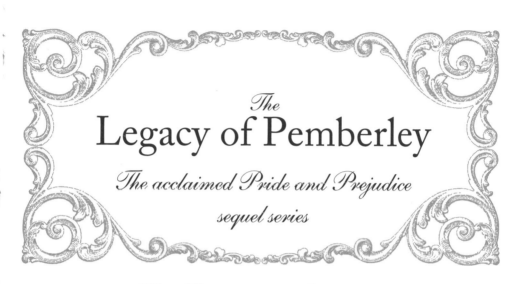

The Legacy of Pemberley

The acclaimed Pride and Prejudice sequel series

The Pemberley Chronicles: Book 10

DEVISED AND COMPILED BY
Rebecca Ann Collins

sourcebooks landmark

Dedicated to my husband, with love

The Legacy of Pemberley

is the concluding volume in

The Pemberley Chronicles series

by Rebecca Ann Collins

Many of the characters will be familiar to readers of the earlier Pemberley
novels, but inevitably, there are new faces and names.
For those who need an aide-memoire, a list of the main
characters is provided in the Appendix.

Foreword

To BE INVITED TO write a foreword to a book is usually both an honour and a pleasure, as it was when I was asked to do so for the fifth book in The Pemberley Chronicles series: *Mr Darcy's Daughter*.

This time, while it is still an honour, I am sad indeed that, with *The Legacy of Pemberley*, Rebecca Ann Collins proposes to "bring to a chronological conclusion" this charming and remarkable series of novels.

While we cannot quarrel with the logic of the decision—for as Ms Collins points out, the series spans a period of some fifty years, which in the life of a family and a community is a solid block of time—her readers will surely grieve over it.

Since the first volume, *The Pemberley Chronicles*, came into my hands, I have been absorbed, entertained, and continually surprised by the creativity and credibility of the author. It has been demonstrated in every following novel, in which she not only continues the lives of Jane Austen's characters with impressive authenticity but also creates characters of her own who fit quite seamlessly into Miss Austen's world. So much so that, occasionally, one has to stop and remind oneself that Cassandra Darcy or Jonathan Bingley are indeed not part of the original cast of *Pride and Prejudice*.

Even more importantly, she maintains the social and historical context of the period, preserving the manners and ambience of nineteenth-century

England to an extraordinary degree, creating for her readers not just another tale of Regency romance but a rich and rewarding experience.

All these remain true in this final episode of the series, in which Rebecca Collins brings us full circle to understand the true legacy of Pemberley. As with Miss Austen herself, Ms Collins shows that it lies not in broad acres and stately homes, material wealth, or political power, but in the deeply satisfying values and conduct of the men and women whose stories are told with honesty, affection, and humour.

Averil Rose
London
June 2005

Prologue

JUDE COURTNEY WAS CERTAINLY not the kind of young man whose conduct might be expected to provoke an outbreak of controversy around the breakfast table at Pemberley House.

Quiet, unfailingly courteous, and blessed with an amiable disposition, he was the least likely member of his family to cause consternation among his relations.

Yet, on a pleasant morning in early Spring, as Mrs Darcy read over a letter from Doctor Francis Grantley passed to her by her husband, she exclaimed and expressed her exasperation at the conduct of her young cousin.

"I cannot believe this. What on earth has possessed him? Surely, he must realise that in the present circumstances in which his family finds itself, this offer provides him with a splendid opportunity? To refuse it makes no sense at all," she declared, without any fear of contradiction.

Looking up from another document he held in his hand, Mr Darcy appeared to listen and comprehend, but withheld that immediate accordance that his wife clearly expected. His countenance gave nothing away either, which Elizabeth found rather vexing.

"Do you not agree?" she asked pointedly, "do you not believe that the offer of a scholarship for Jude Courtney to study theology at Oxford under the tutelage of Dr Grantley, with the prospect of a future position in the church, is one that is unlikely to be matched?"

On this, Mr Darcy readily agreed. "Oh, indeed I do. I cannot see that he could expect a similar proposition from any other source. There are not many people with Doctor Grantley's capacity or his inclination to make him such an offer," he said.

"Well then? Is it not unthinkable that Jude should refuse it?" Elizabeth persisted. "I had not thought him so lacking in judgment nor so incapable of discerning his own interest."

It was at this point that the controversy erupted, for Mr Darcy had just been reading a second letter, this from young Jude Courtney himself, in which he had explained in simple but unapologetic words his reasons for turning down what he acknowledged as a most generous proposition.

I have discussed this matter in great detail with Mama and believe I owe you and Mrs Darcy the clearest possible explanation for my decision, he wrote, and there was no doubting his sincerity.

Understanding his wife's frame of mind, Mr Darcy proceeded to read to her that part of Jude Courtney's letter that was relevant to the subject under discussion, having first asked for her indulgence. "I think, my dear, before you condemn him further, you should hear what he has to say on the subject. He writes:

"While I am deeply grateful for the kindness that has led Doctor Grantley to make this most benevolent offer and appreciate very much its value, I feel that it is not something I can accept at this time.

"It is not that I am in any way averse to the study of theology, but that I do not believe in my heart that I am a suitable candidate for this scholarship.

"First, I have not an academic or philosophical turn of mind, which can derive the most benefit from such study.

"Second, while my faith is strong and I am eager to help the many people in need I see around me, I do not believe that I can best help them from a position within the church. Indeed, were I to accept such a position in the Church of England, as might follow the course of study suggested by Dr Grantley, I should inevitably be cutting myself off from the poorest and most needy and neglected people in this community, whom I wish most desperately to help—for they are mostly people of the Catholic faith, who have little or no access to the services provided by our parish churches.

The exclamation that escaped Elizabeth's lips at this point, though rather unusual, did not prevent Mr Darcy from continuing to read:

"There is also the important matter of the care of my dear mama, for who would look after her if I were to go away to Oxford? Mrs Darcy and you have both assisted Mama for many years, as have my uncle Richard Gardiner and my aunt Caroline, and I must place on record my deep appreciation of your help. Yet, it is surely her children who must care for her at this time. It is a duty that my sister, Jessica, has carried out without complaint for many years, and it would be unfair indeed to expect her to continue to bear this responsibility alone.

"Perhaps at this point I should make it very clear that Mama has, in all our discussions of this matter, urged me to make my decision without taking any account of her situation; she insists that she is well able to manage here and I should do only what is best for myself.

Elizabeth interrupted, unable to contain her feelings, for it was exactly this matter that had been closest to her heart. "Why then can he not see that if Emily could be persuaded to come to us at Pemberley, where she could have the best of care, with no undue strain upon Jessica at all, every concern of his should be settled?" she cried, at which Mr Darcy held up a hand and proceeded:

"Besides, and perhaps most importantly, I find I have no inclination, no genuine calling to be a clergyman, and surely this should be the primary reason for accepting such a position. Were I to allow myself to be persuaded for financial reasons alone to follow such a course, I should feel I have practiced a most unseemly deception upon the church and those whom I seek to serve.

"I trust, sir, that in view of all these reasons, which I have honestly and openly laid before you, Mrs Darcy and you will understand and accept my decision.

"I have written in similar vein but not in as much detail to Doctor Grantley, begging him not to misconstrue my refusal and asking that he explain my reasons to his colleagues. I should not wish them to believe that

I did not fully appreciate the honour implied in the offer that had been made to me.

"Yet, I cannot help but feel that some degree of disquiet may follow, and I hope I am not presuming upon our relationship by asking that you reassure Doctor Grantley of my most sincere appreciation.

"I remain sir, most sincerely yours,

"Jude Courtney"

Laying down the letter, Mr Darcy looked directly at his wife. "How do you answer that, Lizzie? Is it not the honest account of a young man of integrity with a strong sense of duty, who will not place his own pecuniary interest before his principles?" he asked and he saw that there were tears in her eyes.

Elizabeth had no words to respond to her husband's question. She knew that Jude was perhaps her cousin Emily's most beloved child and so like his mother in character and temperament, the words may well have been her own.

Recalling Emily's early days in Derbyshire, when she had fallen in love with Paul Antoine and married him to care for him, knowing he was dying from tuberculosis, Elizabeth knew that Emily must surely have agreed with her son and nothing anyone could say would change Jude Courtney's mind.

Emily Courtney's memories of Pemberley went back many years, to her first visit there after her cousin Lizzie Bennet and Mr Darcy were married and everyone had been invited to spend Christmas at the family estate.

Arriving a few days before Christmas, Emily and her elder sister, Caroline, had become involved in the preparations for the traditional party for the children of the estate and the debut of the now renowned Pemberley Children's Choir. She recalled their great excitement as children, exploring the house and grounds.

But, above all, Emily's recollections were of an overwhelming sense of warm hospitality. Mr Darcy's generosity towards his tenants and servants had been no less impressive than the cordiality of the welcome extended to his guests.

It had been Emily's first opportunity to observe him closely, and it had secured in her mind forever every good opinion she had heard spoken of him. Mr and Mrs Gardiner had always held him in high regard, and everything she saw and heard at Pemberley had confirmed their judgment.

In the ensuing years, as her own family had been drawn closer into the Pemberley circle, with a business partnership between her father and Mr Darcy and later the marriages of her sister Caroline to Colonel Fitzwilliam and her brother Richard to Cassy Darcy, Emily was to understand more fully how very fortunate her cousin Lizzie had been to have married Mr Darcy. She experienced also the warmth and sincerity of his affection for her parents, extending to her sister and brothers as well as herself.

Emily's own close links with Pemberley had been forged in both good times and bad. She recalled Mr Darcy's opposition to the ruthless landlords, who enclosed acres of farm and common land, ousting families who had lived there for generations, and his protection of the persecuted families fleeing famine in Ireland. On each occasion, he had been steadfast in his determination to help the poor and powerless.

At other times, when disaster and disease had brought personal sorrow touching both Pemberley and her own small world, his kindness had been immeasurable, providing both comfort and practical help.

Through the years, Emily had grown to esteem and love the man who had stood for everything she admired and believed in, giving direction to the community in which she and many others lived.

Which is why she was finding it difficult to explain why this time, when it would seem to many observers that she most needed them, Emily had refused to accept the Darcys' invitation to move to Pemberley, where she could live in comfort and be well cared for. Almost everyone who was a member of her family, and many who were not, had expressed an opinion on the matter. For the most part, they urged her to accept the Darcys' kind offer; it was, they had said, the sensible thing to do.

Her brother Richard and his wife Cassy believed it was wholly in her interest and would probably be more convenient for Richard, too, since he would not have to travel the extra distance to Lambton in order to see her, which he did dutifully every day.

"It would be simpler and safer if you were with Mama and Papa," Cassy had said. "Richard would know that they could send for him if you needed him, and he would be with you much quicker. Besides, would you not be happier knowing he was just so much closer?" she had asked, to which Emily had responded with a smile that she hoped they would not need to trouble her dear brother too often, bringing tears to Cassandra's eyes. She, more than anyone else, knew how gravely ill Emily was and how anxious Richard was for her.

But Jessica had been the most persuasive.

"Dearest Mama, I know you wish to stay at Oakleigh, and I understand exactly why. Should you go to Pemberley, Julian and I will ensure that no one will interfere with your wishes or change anything at Oakleigh, except with your consent," she had said. Well aware of her mother's fears that Jude would be greatly disadvantaged if she left Oakleigh, Jessica had tried to reassure her.

But Emily had her reasons and did not hide her concerns. "It would not be fair for me to expect Julian and you to fight for Jude's rights, my dear, knowing full well that Robert and Rose will make every effort to reclaim what they feel is theirs by right. If I were to leave here, it would make their task easier. Your brother is gentle and easygoing, and they will persuade him that it is in his interest to allow Robert to manage the place while he works on the farm, and very soon, Rose will be the mistress of Oakleigh and Jude will be no more than a farmhand working for Robert. I could not in all conscience abandon him to such a fate."

Only when pressed by Jessica, who expressed her doubts that such an outrageous thing could happen, did Emily reveal that she had been visited twice by Robert already, once ostensibly to ask after her health and then again to put to her a "business proposition" involving Oakleigh Manor.

"On the first occasion, he asked very casually if I had made any plans for Oakleigh to be managed when I moved to live at Pemberley, as he assumed I would.

"When I declared that I had no intention of moving, he expressed his astonishment and claimed that he could not understand how I could refuse such a generous invitation from the Darcys.

"'Just think how much more agreeably accommodated you would be at Pemberley, with servants to look after you and every good thing available to keep you in comfort,' he said and added, 'My dear sister, we would all feel so much happier knowing you were there. Our minds would be more at ease. Why, only the other day, Rose expressed her deepest concern that you were here all alone with only Jude to assist you. Are you not fearful?'"

Emily had laughed even as she repeated her brother's words.

"At least in that he spoke sincerely, for I am certain that Robert and Rose would be delighted if I were to leave this place; I have no doubt it is their intention to gain control of it by one means or another."

Jessica was not unaware of the irony of the situation and cringed at the obvious hypocrisy of her uncle's sentiments.

"I cannot believe he would say such things, when it is generally known that he and Rose complain endlessly of having been cheated out of Oakleigh by some whim of my dear grandmother. What did you say, Mama?" she asked, and Emily had smiled as she replied.

"I assured him that I was not at all fearful and he should set his dear wife's heart at rest on that score, because there were many people here who could help me if I needed help. The tenants who have been here for most of my life I regard as part of my family; they would never abandon me," she had said.

"As for having servants to care for my every comfort at Pemberley, I told him how well Teresa and Jude looked after me, and now, with Nurse Nicholls coming in every afternoon and staying overnight, I have no need of an army of servants at all—they would only get in the way. Besides, I said, this is Jude's home and I cannot leave him alone," she smiled and added, "Robert did not appear to accept that at all well."

Jessica had not been altogether surprised, but had asked, "Do you believe they will try again to stake a claim to the property?"

Emily had nodded. "They have already—not openly but covertly. Robert went away, clearly disappointed, but returned a few days later with a plan. One he claims will ensure that the farm is well managed, while preserving Jude's rights to continue to live here. Their plan, and I am confident it is Rose's plan more than it is Robert's, involves moving me out to Pemberley, moving themselves into Oakleigh, and managing the farm to suit their own purposes. Oh, he was full of good intentions about respecting the rights of the tenants and making sure everyone was fairly treated, but I don't believe a word of it, Jessie," she had said and continued as Jessica had listened in astonishment. "No sooner than I am laid to rest, Rose will insist that it is essential to raise the rents and they will send the Mancinis packing. They are quite ignorant of the services Mr Mancini has rendered over the years and of the value I place on the kindness of his granddaughter, Teresa, who has cared for me with such loyalty that one might expect only of a child." Emily's voice was filled with the passion of someone who, being in many ways helpless, was determined not to surrender the last of her powers.

There had been tears in Jessica's eyes as she reached for her mother's hand.

"Dearest Mama, please do not think even for one moment that either Julian or I would wish to have you leave Oakleigh and move anywhere, if it is not your wish to do so. I had not known how determined my uncle Robert is to prise this place away from you and Jude. It is quite appalling that he should do so. Had I known, I should never have suggested that you move to Pemberley. You may be assured I will never do so again," she promised.

Emily had embraced her daughter. "Do not judge your uncle too harshly, my love; he is not a bad man, just a very weak one, and he has had the misfortune of marrying a woman of great ambition and determination. These are qualities that would generally be highly valued in a marriage of equals, but where one partner is weak and unable to resist the single-minded tenacity of the other, they can be quite dangerous," she had said, and seeing the confusion on her daughter's face, she had added, "Poor Robert, none of us foresaw this when he fell in love with Rose, so it would not be fair to blame him alone, would it?"

When Jessica had remained silent, Emily had continued, "You must not believe that I wish to deny Robert anything that is rightfully his. All I wish to do is to protect your dear brother Jude, who is the very opposite of people like Rose and Robert, and ensure that he has a home to live in when I am no longer here. Surely that is not too much to ask?"

Jessica, her voice very soft and tearful, had asked, "What does my brother say?"

Emily had smiled. "Nothing very much; he is concerned only that I do what is best for me and says he could live and work at Oakleigh, whatever happens, but I have no intention of leaving him so unprotected. I shall continue to live here in order to ensure that Jude has a home and some dignity, and can live as he chooses and marry whom he pleases."

Jessica had been taken aback by this last remark.

"Marry whom he pleases?" she echoed her mother's last phrase.

"Indeed. Is that so surprising?" her mother had asked.

"No, of course not, it is only that I had no idea he had anyone in mind," Jessica had struggled to reassure Emily, but her mother had smiled, and said, "Well, neither had I, until a day or two ago. But I do believe he has proposed to a certain young person, and if she accepts him, they shall marry and Oakleigh will be their home."

"And you have given them your blessing?"

"I have," Emily had replied, with a contented smile.

Clearly, her mother did not intend to reveal anything more about the identity of the lady, and Jessica was unwilling to pry. She had to be satisfied with the assurance that Emily thought they would be very happy together.

Leaving Oakleigh shortly afterwards to return to Pemberley, Jessica could not help wondering what this new element would add to the difficult situation that had developed around her mother's illness. Emily had asked that Jessica respect her brother's privacy and say nothing to anyone without his consent, and since Jude had not confided in her, it meant that she had to keep his secret, even though her own knowledge of it was incomplete.

"May I tell Julian?" she had asked, and Emily had replied, "Of course. I would not ask you to keep secrets from your husband, but until Jude has the young lady's consent and decides to announce their engagement, there is very little to tell." Jessica had agreed, but as she prepared to take her leave, she shook her head in bewilderment. She had no notion at all of her brother's choice of a wife, or even that he was proposing to get married at all.

It was most disconcerting indeed.

That night, after the rest of the family had retired to their rooms, Jessica revealed to her husband most of her conversation with her mother. "Mama is quite adamant that she will not leave Oakleigh; she is convinced that my uncle Robert and his wife will take advantage of her absence to insinuate themselves into Jude's confidence, but only to get their hands on his inheritance."

Julian was somewhat circumspect. "Can you be certain that it is your mother's intention to leave all of Oakleigh Manor to Jude? What of William and Elizabeth?"

"I think there can be no doubt at all of her intentions; she has said very clearly and on many occasions that Oakleigh was Jude's home. Besides, there is now a further matter to be considered—it would seem that Jude has advised Mama that he wishes to marry."

Julian appeared astonished. "Marry?"

"Indeed, he has already obtained Mama's blessing and waits only upon the lady's acceptance of his offer," said Jessica.

"And do we know the lady?" asked her husband.

Jessica could not hide her embarrassment as she replied, "We may or we may not; Mama alone knows who she is, and she will not tell any of us until my brother is ready to announce it himself. I am under very strict instructions to speak of it to no one except you, although there is not very much to reveal, seeing we do not know who she is or even if she has accepted him. So I must ask you, dearest, to be very careful not to mention this conversation to anyone, especially not to your parents."

Julian shook his head, unable to make anything of this new information. His young brother-in-law had thrown a completely new ingredient into an already complex situation.

"That should not be difficult, since there is very little to tell, but, Jessie, this is surely going to make a great muddle, is it not? In view of your brother Jude's previous unhappy experience, it would be best if this matter was not spoken of at all until he has the consent of the lady and, even more importantly, her family," he said a little apprehensively.

Julian was, as ever, anxious to avoid conflict, and he could sense that this was not a matter that would admit an easy resolution. His wife, being of a more practical nature, was unwilling to be panicked.

"I daresay matters will resolve themselves, dearest, if we keep our heads and do not become involved in an unnecessary controversy with my uncle Robert and his wife. It seems to me that Mama's determination to remain at Oakleigh, while it may not be in the best interests of her health or my peace of mind, should at the very least frustrate any attempts by them to take charge there. I have no doubt that she has made very sure that her will stipulates exactly what she wishes, and that should be that," she explained.

"It should, but we all know that isn't often the case. I wonder if my father is aware of your mama's intentions and concerns," Julian said, recalling that Mr Darcy had always been close to the Gardiners and had advised both Mr and Mrs Gardiner before they made their wills.

"I should not be at all surprised if he were," said Jessica. "I know he does not have a very high opinion of either my uncle Robert or his wife. It is quite likely that he has advised Mama on what needs be done to thwart their devious machinations, but knowing Mr Darcy, he would not reveal a word of it to anyone. And yet," she added, "he is unlikely to have been told Jude's secret. I gathered from Mama that no one knew but herself and the lady concerned."

Puzzled, Julian sighed, "Well, my dear, since neither of us knows anything more and both of us are sworn to keep secret what little we do know, in view of the lateness of the hour, I suggest we retire to bed." To this request his wife was quite happy to agree, and because it had been a rather long and tiring day, they slept late.

They came down to breakfast on the morrow to the astonishing news that Jude Courtney had ridden over to Pemberley very early that morning, to inform Mr and Mrs Darcy of his engagement to Miss Teresa Mancini.

END OF PROLOGUE

THE LEGACY OF PEMBERLEY

Part One

Emily's Children

Chapter One

ELIZABETH, WHOSE RECOLLECTIONS OF the disdainful diatribe her
engagement to Mr Darcy had elicited from Lady Catherine de Bourgh
were still clear in her mind, was in no doubt of the response that Jude
Courtney's announcement would provoke in similar circles.

Her Ladyship was no more, but there were others with even less justification for such prejudice who had espoused her ideas with alacrity, and they would
certainly find much to gossip about in the marriage of young Mr Courtney to
the granddaughter of an Italian flower farmer.

She had sat stunned as Jude had explained calmly and courteously that he
had his mother's blessing and that Teresa's mother and grandfather had given
their consent to the match.

The Mancini family had lived in the area for many years. They were
market gardeners and stall holders at Covent Garden, with close links to a
renowned restaurateur in London. None of these things seemed to concern Jude
Courtney, who had stated in a most matter-of-fact manner that his bride-to-be
was happier in her apron, working in the kitchen, than attending church teas
dressed in her Sunday best.

"She is kind and affectionate, and Mama loves her almost as much as I
do," he had said, adding, "Teresa is devoted to her care. We have both come to
depend upon her so much. I do not know what we would do without her." The

obvious honesty in his voice had convinced Elizabeth that his was no sudden proposal made on some romantic impulse.

She had been roused from her initial state of shock by Mr Darcy's voice, asking Jude if he had informed his older sister Elizabeth Harwood and his brother William of his engagement, to which she had heard Jude reply, "I have written to my sister today, sir, and Mama is writing to William, who is in the United States and unlikely to be back in time for the wedding."

Elizabeth had asked, then, if the wedding was to be soon, only to be told that Emily had urged that they be married as soon as possible.

"Mama wants to be well enough to attend. But it will depend on Teresa; she can name the day. For my part, I should prefer it to be sooner rather than later," said Jude.

Looking across at her husband, Elizabeth could not decide what he was thinking. His expression was serious but noncommittal as he listened and asked the occasional question. She wished she had some indication of his opinion, but Mr Darcy was giving nothing away.

After Jude had left them to proceed to Camden House, where he would inform his uncle Richard Gardiner and his wife, Cassy, of his engagement, Elizabeth attempted to discover what Mr Darcy thought of the match, but to no avail. He seemed quite determined not to comment upon the matter.

"But surely, you must have an opinion?" she said, frustrated by his reticence.

"I do, but at this stage, I intend to keep it to myself, Lizzie. I have no intention of saying anything that may offend young Jude and his bride-to-be, and more especially Emily. Expressing opinions that can have no possible effect upon the situation, except to cause misunderstanding and vexation, seems to me to be a waste of time," he replied.

Elizabeth's vexation increased. "Whatever do you mean? Surely you must either approve or disapprove of the match?" she protested, to which Mr Darcy responded with the kind of maddening logic with which she was quite familiar, "I need do neither, my dear, because it is of no direct consequence to me nor indeed to you. We are in no position to express approval or otherwise of Jude's choice of a wife, no more than you or I would accept that my aunt Lady Catherine had the right to interfere in our own affairs. We regarded her attempt to influence us as high-handed and arrogant. Why would this be any different, Lizzie?"

Elizabeth remained silent, remembering her resentment at the intolerable intrusion of Lady Catherine into her life and, even worse, her fury at hearing from Colonel Fitzwilliam that Mr Darcy had previously intervened to discourage his friend Bingley from courting her beloved sister Jane, causing, however unwittingly, a great deal of sorrow.

Whether arguments could be found to justify Jude's choice or not was not their business, and Mr Darcy had made that clear. By the time her son and daughter-in-law came down to breakfast, Elizabeth had accepted that, since he had obtained the consent of his mother, nothing anyone could do or say was going to change Jude Courtney's mind. Her own opinions would be as irrelevant to him as those of any other person.

Consequently, Elizabeth was able to break the news to Julian and Jessica in a quiet, unemotional manner that left them completely speechless. Nothing had prepared them for the news, and they were as astonished at Mrs Darcy's apparent acceptance of it.

Mr Darcy had retired to the morning room to read his newspapers, allowing his wife the opportunity to ask Jessica if she had had any indication of her brother's intentions. "Had you noticed, or has Jude given any intimation of his attachment to Miss Mancini?" she asked, and Jessica shook her head, still rather bemused by what she had just heard.

"Not at all; though I am aware that he has been much with her since Mama's recent illness. Teresa has been coming to the house to help care for her and Mama has appreciated it very much. She speaks highly of her kindness and warmth. She works hard and is also constantly cheerful, which Mama enjoys; it makes a welcome change from the dreariness of doctors' visits and daily medication," Jessica said.

She added after a moment's thought, "And, coming as she does from a farming family, Teresa is familiar with the work on the farm and does not appear to mind helping out when needed."

It was Julian who interrupted with a question. "But Jessie, while these qualities may equip her to be an exemplary nurse for your mama, how do they make her a suitable wife for your brother?"

Jessica shrugged her shoulders. "I am unable to say. Jude has never confided in me—and Mama, who has had the best opportunity to observe them together, believes they will be very happy. Perhaps he has told Mama that he loves her. What more can I say?"

Elizabeth could not help noting the strain on Julian's countenance. Having once made a disastrously unhappy marriage himself, her son would surely know the consequences of such a union, where with the very best of intentions, two young people may marry and succeed only in making one another miserable.

Elizabeth had another question. "Do you think, Jessica, that Jude's decision may have been influenced by his unfortunate experience last year with young Miranda Gardiner?" she asked, and Jessica was immediately alert to the possibility that this was so.

"It is possible and it may account for the secrecy he has maintained over this matter, but it does not account for his choice of Teresa," she replied, and Elizabeth had to agree.

The story of her brother's unhappy brush with romance had made no headlines, but Jessica was aware that the resulting hurt had been keenly felt both by Jude and their mother.

Some eighteen months ago, while Rev James Courtney was ill and their mother had been working hard to care for him and help his many parishioners, Mr and Mrs Robert Gardiner had decided the time was right for their two sons to be introduced to the cultural delights of Europe. Their youngest child, Miranda, had been left in the care of her aging grandparents, Sir James and Lady Fitzwilliam. The Fitzwilliams doted upon her, but lacked the energy and the imagination to keep her occupied through the day. Miranda was indulged but bored.

Discovering quite by chance that her cousin, Jude Courtney, had time on his hands and horses in the paddocks at Oakleigh, Miranda had begged to be allowed to ride over to Lambton and spend time on the farm.

The Fitzwilliams, with whom she was always able to get her own way, had welcomed the respite this provided them and consented, allowing the girl to go over to Oakleigh several times a week, where, in the presence of Mr and Mrs Courtney, they expected she would come to no harm.

Pretty, vivacious, and addicted to fun, Miranda had soon found herself able to get her own way at Oakleigh as well, for her cousin Jude had never known such a delightful friendship as he now found with his young visitor. Indeed, he had had no close contact with any young girl for many years. Miranda was particularly appealing, and he had made every effort to please her. Amiable and easygoing, Jude had acceded to her every request, maintaining by this means a blissful relationship, which in the case of two emotionally naïve and innocent young persons had led almost inevitably to the mutual perception that they were in love.

Whether by accident or design, neither had revealed their feelings to anyone else, and Emily, troubled and busy with dealing with her husband's ill health, had not noticed anything unusual was afoot. Miranda would arrive often quite early in the morning, escorted by a manservant, and would return at night accompanied by Jude. Emily neither saw nor suspected that there was any harm in it, and indeed there was not, unless it could be argued that the romantic illusions of youth were the source of evil.

The idyllic episode had ended with the return from Europe of Miranda's parents, who had been outraged to discover that their daughter had been spending a good part of the Summer at Oakleigh in the company of Jude Courtney, whose lack of style and *savoir faire*, in their opinion, ill qualified him to be a companion to their daughter.

Rose Gardiner had made no secret of her indignation, first venting her wrath upon her parents before declaring that Miranda's visits to Oakleigh Manor would cease forthwith. She had, however, not taken account of her daughter's inclinations. Self-willed and spoilt through the Summer by a high degree of indulgence and plenty of pleasant fun, Miranda had been in no mood to be compliant. Aggrieved that she was to be denied what had become a very flattering and agreeable arrangement, in which she called the tune and young Jude Courtney always obliged, she had refused absolutely to obey her mother. When her father had been applied to by his wife for support in the matter, Miranda had sulked, refused to eat or speak, and retired to her room, leaving Robert Gardiner looking particularly ineffective and foolish.

When at last she had been confronted by her mother, Miranda had declared that she was in love with Jude Courtney and wished to marry him, thereby causing even greater uproar in the household.

Turning upon her husband, Rose had demanded to know if he intended to let their daughter throw herself away on the youngest son of a poor clergyman, who had no profession or status, having chosen to work on the farm instead of acquiring an education.

"Just think on the prospect," she had said. "Miranda will be the wife of a labouring farmer, who spends all his spare time wandering around the villages in that ridiculous hat and boots, doling out charity to the indigent and lazy. Doubtless, he will expect her to accompany him, to visit their cottages, comfort their wives, and coddle their children, too."

Robert, to his credit, had tried to persuade his wife that it was quite likely that nothing at all would come of it, because both young persons may well change their minds, but Rose would have none of it.

"I shall certainly hope to change Miranda's mind, but I doubt that the Courtneys will wish to do the same with Jude. They are probably encouraging him in this, seeing a chance of improving his prospects by marrying a girl with Miranda's family connections. I'm afraid there is nothing for it, you must visit the Courtneys and make it clear that you will not give your permission for Miranda to marry their son, and since she is only sixteen, that will be the end of the matter. Meanwhile, I shall take Miranda to London and perhaps to Paris, so she can see what she will be missing if she persists with this ridiculous notion."

Robert's reluctance to do as she asked, knowing that Dr Courtney was gravely ill, had been worn down by the assiduous efforts of his wife, who had been joined by her mother, Lady Rosamund Fitzwilliam. Finally, he had given in and had visited Oakleigh Manor one Sunday morning to deliver the verdict of Miranda's family on Jude's first romance.

Despite his bumbling efforts to justify his intervention, neither Jude nor Emily had been convinced, and both had been left in no doubt of the tawdry reasons behind it. They never saw Miranda again.

Young Jude, bereft and humiliated, had confided only in his mother and sister Jessica, but had found later that the Fitzwilliams had spread the good news among their general acquaintance that Miranda had been saved from an imprudent alliance.

Throwing himself into his work on the farm and the charity work he did among the poor Irish families in the village, Jude had attempted to put the experience behind him. He had expressed no bitterness against Miranda or her parents, but Emily had found it very difficult to forgive them for the hurt they had inflicted upon her son.

"I do not suggest that Jude and Miranda would have been happy together—I seriously doubt that they would, and I am sure they would have come to that realization themselves before long and it is unlikely they would ever have married. But Rose and Robert were quite brutal in the way they proceeded, and it has hurt Jude very deeply," she had said to Jessica, which explained to some degree Emily's response to Jude's latest proposition.

"It is possible that Mama believes Jude has a better chance of happiness with a girl like Teresa Mancini. She is quite pretty, though not as beautiful as Miranda, with the additional virtue of not belonging to a family whose snobbery surpasses their compassion," said Jessica.

"And do you believe that this same snobbery, with which we are all familiar, will not now be marshaled against them? Is it likely that Robert and Rose, when they discover that Teresa Mancini is to be mistress of Oakleigh manor, will rest content?" asked Julian.

Neither Jessica nor Elizabeth could answer his question, but Elizabeth did remark upon the delicious irony of Rose and Robert realizing that Miranda, had she been permitted to marry Jude Courtney, would have certainly been the next mistress of Oakleigh Manor.

"The Fitzwilliams will be furious. They have always believed Oakleigh should have been theirs. My poor aunt Gardiner has been much maligned for having left the place to Emily rather than Robert. Well, they will have missed out again and will have no one to blame but themselves. Oh, I do believe there is at least some satisfaction to be had in that prospect. Do you not agree?" she asked with a mischievous chuckle.

Jessica and Julian had to laugh, and Mr Darcy, who had just come back into the room with a letter in his hand, had heard the last of their conversation and answered her question. "I certainly agree, and I always knew you would find a good reason to support the match, Lizzie," and before she could protest, he added quickly, "Now, do you suppose we could reach agreement on a much simpler matter? Who is to organise the first cricket match this year? I have had a letter from the club at Ripley suggesting a date for the first encounter between our teams. Darcy Gardiner is captain of our team, and Bingley is not as well as he should be. I feel it would not be fair to call on them. Julian, can we count on you?"

To the very great satisfaction of his parents, Julian Darcy rose, held out his hand for the letter, and said, "Certainly, sir, I should be delighted."

Chapter Two

THE NEWS OF JUDE Courtney's engagement to Teresa Mancini drew comment aplenty from around the district. Some, especially those who knew the young couple, were pleased, predicting they would be happy because they were both of an amiable and kindly disposition. Darcy Gardiner and his wife, Kate, had expressed their delight at the news. They had long hoped to see young Jude, whose devotion to his mother was well known, happily wed, and believed sincerely that by marrying Teresa, he was making certain of his future happiness.

"Unlike many other young women of her age, she is far less likely to be disappointed by the simplicity of Jude's life and is therefore more likely to make him happy," Kate had remarked, and her husband, who had known young Jude Courtney since childhood, had to agree.

"She is also a careful and intelligent young woman and so will assist actively in his management of the farm," he had added, sentiments he had previously conveyed to his mother with conviction.

Cassandra and Richard, who had been at first too surprised by Jude's announcement to comment, other than to wish him well, had gradually come to an understanding of the situation, particularly in view of Emily's obvious pleasure.

"I believe that my sister has known for some time of my nephew's attachment to Miss Mancini," Richard Gardiner had said to his wife as they prepared for bed. "She has shown no surprise at all and seems so thoroughly accepting of the match, I cannot believe she was ignorant of it."

Cassy had responded that Mrs Courtney was probably in the best position to see what was happening, and if she thought it was to Jude's advantage, it was quite likely that she may have approved and even encouraged the match.

"In fact, Darcy and Kate believe that Emily is so pleased because she knows that Teresa Mancini will help Jude manage the estate well and resist the devious plans of your uncle Robert and his wife Rose. Darcy is certain that when Emily is no more they will try again to obtain some part of Oakleigh Manor, and they say Teresa will not let them win."

Others, who knew them not at all, were unconcerned, seeing only a young couple who wished to spend their lives together. Jude, a shy but good-natured fellow, was well liked, and Teresa's open, pleasing nature had won her many friends.

But there were those who, with the least justification, expressed the strongest opinions. Among this last group were the family of Robert and Rose Gardiner and Jude's own sister, Elizabeth Harwood. In a letter to her mother, Eliza had pointed out what she considered to be the intractable problems created for her and her husband by Jude's impending marriage to an "Italian flower farmer's daughter."

> *Dearest Mama,*
>
> *Can you not see that this will be a subject for gossip and ridicule among those in our social circle, who will know full well that we may never be able to invite my brother and his wife to our home or introduce them into polite society in London? Mr Harwood is afraid that many of his business connections will be genuinely uncomfortable meeting them and wonders how they will get on without the kind of social intercourse that will be denied them.*
>
> *Mr Harwood feels that you should perhaps have alerted us when you became aware of what was afoot, and maybe we could have persuaded my brother to reconsider what is plainly an unsuitable connection for all of our family. It does seem that Jude does not comprehend that he has a duty to us all.*

Emily's reply to her eldest daughter was cogent and to the point. She wrote:

I think, dear Eliza, that your brother is as entitled to make his own choice of a partner as you were. None of us urged you to change your mind when your decision to marry Mr Harwood took you quite out of our lives to London.

Since then, your visits and letters have been few and far between, but your father and I have never complained. The young woman Jude has chosen is closer to me than you have been in all the years since you married Mr Harwood, and your brother has demonstrated his dutiful nature by the exemplary manner in which he has applied himself to the work on the farm and helped me with your father's parish duties.

When I had only Jude to help me during the long months of Mr Courtney's illness, I came to value his goodness and loyalty. Since I have been ill, I have had the benefit also of Teresa's kindliness and affection. If, as his widowed mother, I can say that, I doubt that you or any other person could credibly accuse him of not comprehending his duty to his family.

As to their lacking the benefits of what you call "polite society," dear Eliza, if they are happy here, then what need will they have of polite society in London? For my part, I long to see them wed and happily settled at Oakleigh very soon...

Emily did not wish to put Eliza down, but was determined not to leave any possible impression that she agreed with her on the matter of Jude's marriage.

From her elder son William, to whom Emily had written, there had been no reply. No doubt his concern was far more for his orchestra giving a series of concerts around the USA, thought Emily, who, though she never expressed it in words and would probably have denied it if asked, was rather disappointed in William's silence.

She wondered why he, a distinguished and accomplished musician, seemed to have lost connection with his family except on the rare occasions when he visited her at Oakleigh. When he had attended his father's funeral, he had seemed genuinely concerned about his mother's well-being and had expressed his desire to be of assistance to her. Since then, however, there had been only occasional letters. It was a matter that had disturbed both Mr and Mrs Darcy, and though Emily was accustomed to his long absences, it had troubled Jessica greatly.

"I cannot believe that my brother William has not found the time to visit since Papa's funeral. Mama must be hurt; I can see it in her eyes, though she will say nothing against him," she complained to her husband.

Julian knew how deeply she cared and tried to reassure her that William was probably very busy with his concert tours, but he knew even as he said it that Jessica was unlikely to be comforted. Her elder brother's odd behaviour caused her great distress.

Julian wished he could discover why William had become so distant from his family. A somewhat private and shy person himself, he found it impossible to approach his brother-in-law and ask for an explanation.

Frustrated, he decided to ask his nephew Darcy Gardiner to undertake an investigation to ascertain the reason William Courtney seemed disconnected from his family, in particular his ailing mother to whom he owed so much.

"Jessica is very unhappy, and I should like to be able to give her some credible reason for William's conduct. I am sure there must be some perfectly normal explanation," he had said and then added almost as an afterthought, "At least, I hope so. I cannot think of anything that should cause him to act so strangely. He has, as far as I am aware, no financial worries and, being single, cannot be troubled by the usual concerns that beset a family man. I must admit, Darcy, I cannot make him out at all."

While Julian had not wished to inquire too closely into the life of his brother-in-law, he had often wondered why William, who had been the brightest of the Courtney children and in whom his parents had invested so much of their hopes, had so rarely returned to their home to share with them his success.

It was a conundrum to which he had found no answer. He hoped that Darcy, who was well known for his tenacious pursuit of answers to problems, would have more success.

"I should prefer that you keep this matter to yourself, Darcy," he had advised. "It would not do for Jessica or Mrs Courtney to become aware of our concern."

Darcy Gardiner, whose discretion and integrity could never have been questioned, assured Julian that no one need know. "Fortuitously, we are going up to London for some weeks, during which time I shall do my very best to discover what it is that keeps William so occupied that he has no time to visit his mother," he said.

Then in an attempt to reassure Julian, he added, "There is likely to be a simple explanation, which, when we know what it is, will seem so obvious, we would feel foolish at having missed it."

Julian nodded and hoped he was right. However, unlike young Darcy, Julian suffered from a streak of pessimism, which made him uneasy. He was not at all sure the explanation would be a simple one, which everyone would accept.

❧

Later in the week, Mrs Darcy, anxious about Emily's health and keen to reassure herself that her cousin was being well cared for, travelled to Oakleigh manor, taking with her a basket of produce from the kitchen gardens and amply stocked pantry at Pemberley House.

Despite the sunshine, there was a persistent chill in the air, and Elizabeth was relieved to find Emily in the sitting room, which was always the warmest and brightest of the rooms in the house. It had been Mrs Gardiner's favourite room, looking out as it did on the sunniest corner of the garden with all her favourite roses. Elizabeth felt the tears sting her eyes as thoughts of her dear aunt crowded into her mind. She missed her and her uncle Gardiner terribly; their wise counsel no less than their sense of fun had lightened their lives for many years.

As she went to greet Emily, she was determined to be cheerful. Her cousin looked pale but reasonably well, and as they embraced, she smiled and said, "Lizzie, my dear cousin, it is too long since you have been here. I do hope you have come ready to stay to dinner? We have so much to talk about."

Elizabeth was taken aback. "Dinner? Oh no, Emily, I could not put you to the trouble. I wanted very much to see you and spend some time with you, but I must be back at Pemberley for dinner or they will wonder what has become of me and Mr Darcy will despatch the servants to find me. He is increasingly unhappy about letting me travel alone, even though I have assured him that I am perfectly able to look after myself and James is a scrupulously careful driver," she explained.

Emily laughed. "I can well believe it. Mr Darcy was always very particular about such things. Whenever Caroline and I visited you at Pemberley, he would insist that we were always escorted home by at least one trusted servant. I remember, Lizzie, that you used to joke about it when we first came to

Derbyshire. I recall you saying that it was a trait he had in common with his formidable aunt, Lady Catherine de Bourgh."

They laughed together, then, as once again the bittersweet memories of youth intruded upon them.

"Indeed I do remember it. I often teased him about it, but to no avail; he would insist that it was simply good common sense not to have young women travelling around the countryside alone," Elizabeth recalled.

Then, changing her tone, Emily spoke more seriously, "You are indeed fortunate, Lizzie, and so were we all when you married Mr Darcy. Mama used to say that she was once, for a little while, afraid that you were enamoured of Mr Wickham, of whom she had a rather poor opinion, but then Fate had decreed otherwise, and when Mr Darcy reappeared on the scene, Mama was certain he was the very man for you."

Elizabeth shook her head. "I must confess that my dear aunt was more certain of the outcome of our association than I was for a while; there were some very daunting obstacles to be overcome," Elizabeth said, and Emily laughed and provided the conclusion to her sentence, "…such as the objections of Lady Catherine de Bourgh?"

"Indeed, and certain unfortunate encounters we had been engaged in previously, in which neither of us had performed very creditably. I am ashamed even now to recall them. Then there was Lydia's elopement! Yet, in a strange way, it was the very stupidity of Lydia and Wickham that brought us to an understanding of our feelings for each other. Until that fateful day, when I believed I would not see him again, I never knew myself, nor comprehended the depth of my love for him."

"I am glad indeed that you did discover it, dearest Lizzie. Your husband has brought you great happiness and been as well a source of counsel and kindness to me and my family for so many years, and I do not know how we should have survived without him. Yet, he will say nothing of this and insists that we do not speak of his generosity. He is the finest person I have known, Lizzie, and in saying this I exempt no one save my beloved father, who would have said as much of Mr Darcy himself."

Elizabeth could hear the sincerity in her voice and, leaning forward to embrace her cousin, was shocked to feel how frail and thin she had become. Unable to help herself, she said, "Dearest Emily, will you not make both of us—Mr Darcy and myself—very happy by returning to Pemberley and letting us look after you?"

Emily looked into her cousin's eyes and, seeing the anxiety there, replied, "Lizzie dear, I can see you are concerned for me, but please let me reassure you. I know I do not have long to live, but I have no fear of dying. Remember that I have helped both my dear husbands to face the truth: that Death was not far away. The grief of losing them and Papa and Mama and your dear William has all come together for me now, to give me the strength to face what is to come. Have no fear for me, Lizzie. I am not alone here; Jude and Teresa and Nurse Nicholls look after me very well indeed."

Elizabeth held back her tears with great difficulty. "Will you promise me, Emmy, that if you needed us at any time at all, if there was anything Mr Darcy or I could do for you, you would send word?"

Emily could not ignore the intensity of her appeal. "Of course I would, Lizzie, why would I not? Apart from my family, no two people in all the world have meant so much to me as Mr Darcy and yourself. There, now are you content?" Elizabeth nodded and, holding Emily's hand, she could feel its warmth and strength.

They talked for an hour or more, and when she left to return home, Elizabeth was surprised to find that predominantly, she was feeling not melancholy but a sense of enlightenment, as though Emily had opened her eyes to something her own anxieties had concealed.

Back at Pemberley, the Bingleys were expected to dinner. Elizabeth had only time enough to bathe and dress before the maid ran upstairs to announce that Mr and Mrs Bingley had arrived. Going downstairs, Elizabeth was relieved to see that her brother-in-law, whose health had been a source of some concern over the Winter months, was looking and sounding much better than before. While he and Mr Darcy were engaged in conversation, Elizabeth took the opportunity to tell her sister Jane about her visit to Oakleigh.

"Did Emily speak to you of Jude's engagement?" Jane asked, and Elizabeth was quick to respond, "She did indeed. Emily is convinced that Jude and Teresa Mancini will be very happy together; she insists that they love each other dearly. Jude claims apparently that the girl had refused to accept his offer until she could be assured of Emily's approval. She feared the censure of his family and, though she loved him, did not wish to be the cause of a rift between him and his mother. Emily says Teresa wept when she gave them her blessing," said Elizabeth, and Jane, always tenderhearted and easily moved, was close to tears herself.

"Oh Lizzie, if only there were some way to help dear Emily. I think of her every day and cannot help but wonder at the cruelty of Fate… How much she has suffered…"

"And yet, she is so full of courage and spirit, she puts me to shame," countered Elizabeth. "She will not let you feel sorry for her and will insist that life has brought her many blessings. Indeed, I confess I went to Oakleigh expecting to come away deeply dejected, because there is no doubt that she is dying, and she knows it."

Jane's eyes had filled with tears. Leaning forward, Elizabeth took her sister's hand in hers. "But Jane, Emily is astonishingly honest, and her understanding of her situation is so lucid, it is not possible to be melancholy in her presence. Sad, yes, but never doleful, because she will not let you be so. I did so wish that you were with me…" she said and felt her sister's fingers tighten around her own. Jane's concern for her beloved husband's health had cast a shadow over much of the previous year, and clearly, she was not yet relieved of the anxiety.

"I wish I had Emily's strength, Lizzie; I do worry inordinately about Mr Bingley's health, and I know I should be able to deal with it better, but I cannot bear to think of losing him. After all these years, how should I live alone, Lizzie?"

Elizabeth drew her close. "Oh, dearest Jane, I am sorry, I should not have been so thoughtless. But you must not let your anxiety overwhelm you, my dear; Bingley seems a good deal better today than I have seen him look in many months. Tell me, has he taken the advice about not riding out in the cold every morning?" she asked.

Jane nodded, dabbing at her eyes. "He has, but only because Doctor Gardiner insisted and Jonathan, when he was here, supported his advice very firmly."

"I should never have thought my dear, amiable brother-in-law could be so very stubborn!" said Elizabeth, shaking her head and lightening the mood as the gentlemen returned to the room and the footman entered to announce that dinner was served.

Chapter Three

A MILD SPRING FOLLOWED by a warm Summer gave Emily Courtney a somewhat longer lease on life than had been expected, but in the end, having fulfilled her wish to see her son married, she faded quickly, leaving many grieving, not just among her family and friends but throughout the district, for Emily had spent much of her life in their service. They came from miles around, from the villages of the parish and the moors that surrounded it, to say their farewells.

Frank Grantley, the new rector of Kympton, asked the gathered congregation not to mourn the death, but rather to give thanks for the life of this most exemplary woman, before she was laid to rest between the two men she had married, each of whom she had deeply and selflessly loved.

Jessica, standing at the graveside, read the identical inscriptions, one old, the other quite recent—*dearly loved husband of Emily*—on the headstones of Paul Antoine and James Courtney; she wept, remembering what each man had meant to her mother. From everything her cousins Jane and Elizabeth had told her, Paul Antoine had been the great romantic love of Emily's life, and following his death, she had grieved for a very long while. Yet, from all Jessica had seen in her life at home, there had been such warmth in the relationship between her parents that she had envied them. They had seemed to share so much, their thoughts often coincided, and they would complete each other's sentences, providing a source of amusement for their children.

❧

On the morrow, the family gathered for the reading of Emily's will, and her lawyer, Mr Fitchett, arrived on the hour. Seeing the large number of relatives, he smiled in a curious fashion and went into the library, where he opened up his briefcase and laid out the relevant papers on the table. When he was ready, he invited them in and proceeded to read the preamble to the will in a dull sonorous voice, seemingly calculated to put everyone to sleep. People struggled to stay awake in case they were mentioned and missed it and would then have the embarrassment of having to ask.

William Courtney had arrived that morning, having missed the train and his mother's funeral. Eliza Harwood and her husband had stayed over after the funeral, eager to discover whether their two children were beneficiaries of their grandmother's largesse. Jessica was seated in a corner of the room, tearful and quiet, with Julian beside her, while Jude and his wife sat to one side of them. Emily's elder sister, Caroline, and her brothers, Richard and Robert, sat in the front row with their wives. Julian whispered to Jessica that he thought Rose looked as if she anticipated good news. To which his wife replied that she could not think why.

"I cannot believe that she can have any expectations," she said, "when she has consistently complained about Mama inheriting Oakleigh. It is unlikely that even someone as forgiving as my mother would forget that; besides, your mama believes Rose has plenty of money and has no need of more."

Mrs Darcy, who had been rather distraught at the funeral, did not attend the reading of the will nor did her sister Jane. Becky Tate and her sister Catherine had also left to return to Kent that morning. Mr Darcy sat alone beside the door, as if ready to leave at a moment's notice.

Having completed the initial formalities, Mr Fitchett took up the will, which seemed amazingly brief in comparison to the number of people who appeared to have expectations of it.

The will was not the formal sort of document they were accustomed to. Indeed, it was more in the nature of a letter from Emily to her relatives. It began with expressions of appreciation to all those who had helped her over the years, naming them and thanking them individually.

Proceeding to her family, she mentioned her two elder children, Elizabeth and William, to whom their mother left sincere congratulations for, she said, they had been so successful each in their own way, they no longer needed her. She wished them and their families even greater success in the future. This declaration brought a gasp of disbelief from Eliza Harwood and a derisive snort from her husband, but no more.

To her younger daughter, Jessica, Emily gave heartfelt thanks for the care and affection she had received and bequeathed to her all of the jewellery that had been gifts from her father, Mr Gardiner, as well as one thousand pounds from the proceeds of the sale of her first husband's farm in France, to be used for the education of Jessica's daughter, Marianne.

Finally, to her youngest son Jude, whom she described as the kindest and best son a mother could hope for, she left the entire estate, including the manor house, the woods and farmlands of Oakleigh, and the tenancies within its boundaries. She did, however, urge him to continue to support the poor and needy as she and his father had done; for the rest, it was his to do with as he pleased.

The only other bequest was to Mr Mancini, the flower farmer, whose five-year lease on a piece of land was extended to a lifetime arrangement on the same terms, in appreciation of his invaluable and unstinting help.

Concluding the reading of the will, Mr Fitchett wished the gathered ladies and gentlemen good day and closed his briefcase with a loud snap. Some of the family members remained seated, apparently still stunned by what they had heard, while others rushed out into the hall and thence into the drawing room, where cook had placed plates of refreshments and drinks on a table.

Jude stayed to talk to Mr Fitchett, while Jessica left the room with her husband. William and Eliza stood starkly alone in opposite corners of the room, and most of the others clustered around the table with the food. Many of them had little to say, but they could all eat and drink and so made for the safest place in the room. Most conspicuous of all, in full, formal mourning, were Robert and Rose Gardiner, whose look of absolute fury was plain for all to see. Obviously bitterly disappointed, they did not seem to care who knew it. When invited by Jessica to take some refreshment, Rose declined with barely concealed contempt and flounced out of the room, swishing the train of her fashionable black taffeta gown as she went. Neither she nor Robert had expected to be beneficiaries of

Emily's will, but they had talked of the possibility that she might leave something to her two nephews.

"I would have thought that simple family loyalty would have sufficed to persuade her to set some small amount aside, perhaps enough to buy them a young colt or a tour of Italy?" she argued, and weakly, Robert agreed that his sister had been remiss to ignore the boys' entitlements.

"To leave them out altogether, to make no mention of them, as though they did not exist!" Rose complained, irked above all by the implied insult of being ignored. "I do not mind a jot for myself, I had no expectations, but for you, her brother, and for our two boys, I am indeed offended. I should be a most peculiar wife and mother if I was not," she insisted.

That the boys were amply supplied with everything they needed and more besides seemed not to signify. That Emily's situation had been infinitely more straitened than their own was of no account. Only one thing mattered: they had been left out of her will, and Rose was angry. Worse still, Jude Courtney and that woman had got most of it.

Complaining to her mother, Rose declared that she firmly believed Mr Darcy was once again the guilty party. "I am convinced he has had a hand in shaping Emily's will, just as he advised Mrs Gardiner to cut dear Robert out and hand Oakleigh Manor over to Emily. Else, why was he there, observing us no doubt to see how we responded to the news?"

Lady Fitzwilliam was not quite so sure. "He may have been there to see how well Julian and Jessica were treated; it is more likely, I think, that Emily was influenced by that Italian man and his granddaughter that Jude was the right person to inherit the farm."

Rose was unforgiving. "If that was the case, she was a greater simpleton than I believed her to be, because Mr Mancini and his granddaughter will soon push poor Jude out of the way and run the place as they see fit. It will be such a waste. And what about our two boys? Was it too much to expect that their aunt would remember them in her will? Eliza's children got nothing. Jessica's daughter was the only grandchild mentioned; she got a thousand pounds! Hmm. I wonder why the baby girl deserved a thousand pounds and our boys nothing!"

Lady Fitzwilliam had no answer to this puzzling question. She could not fathom why Emily had not seen fit to bequeath something to her nephews, she said. "Surely, it's only natural?" she argued. But Jessica recalled very clearly an occasion when Rose's boisterous boys had thundered around the house, playing at being soldiers, ignoring her appeals for quiet because Dr Courtney was recovering from a severe attack of bronchitis. "I do remember Mama saying she had not met two more selfish and uncaring boys than young Joshua and Jeremy Gardiner, adding that she knew also from whom they had inherited their disposition," she said, to which her husband replied, "Unlikely, then, that she would consider it necessary to leave them anything in her will."

At Pemberley that evening, the Darcys and their immediate family gathered for a quiet dinner in a somewhat sober atmosphere. Richard and Cassandra, who had been thanked in Emily's will for their unfailing care and concern, were sad, but accepting of the fact that she had lived far longer than had been expected.

"I had been afraid to hope that she would live to see Jude married," said Cassy. "When Richard told me how very ill she was, I feared it would be a matter of some weeks."

Her husband nodded. "Yes indeed, as a physician I could not explain it. It was as though her determination alone kept her alive," he said.

"She was certainly determined to make her intentions abundantly clear in her will. I did notice that Robert and Rose looked put out," Julian remarked and Cassy interrupted, "I cannot think why. Surely they did not expect to benefit?"

Julian went on, "I was going to say, particularly when they heard of the extension for life of Mr Mancini's lease, which must be galling indeed."

It was at this point that Mr Darcy intervened quietly. "Galling to Rose and Robert, perhaps, because they have no notion of the value of Mr Mancini's services to Emily's family."

"Indeed," said Richard, "Emily owed her life to him last year, when he came into the house with logs for the fire and found her collapsed upon the floor. Had he not raised the alarm and carried her to her room, we may well have lost her then. I went to his house to convey my thanks and that of the rest of our family. I did tell Robert at the time, but I doubt he took much notice."

Mr Darcy and others around the table recalled the incident well. It was after that scare that Teresa Mancini had started to visit Oakleigh to help Jude care for his mother, so she would not be entirely alone at any time.

"It should not surprise that Emily saw fit to reward Mr Mancini by extending his lease," said Elizabeth, and her husband added, "It would not surprise anyone, if it was more generally known that in the course of the last two years, Mr Mancini has kept the family at Oakleigh supplied with most of their provisions of fresh food."

"Fresh food?" Elizabeth exclaimed, clearly astonished.

"Certainly," said her husband. "He brought them regular hampers of food, everything from vegetables, fruit, game, poultry, honey, wine, and other good things from his produce, for which he would take no payment at all, because he knew of the straitened circumstances in which the family was placed after Dr Courtney's illness. Emily told me herself; she was uneasy that he took no money and asked me to see him. I did and offered to pay him, but he would take nothing. He said letting him lease the land for his flower farm had given his business new life, and he had prospered as a result. He was only thanking Emily for her kindness to him, he said; he wanted no money for any of it."

Elizabeth could not believe her ears, and none of the others at the table seemed to have any knowledge of it. "And this was before Jude's attachment to Teresa was known?" she asked.

"Oh yes, well before. Emily told me of it while Dr Courtney was still living—although he was very sick at the time," replied Mr Darcy.

Cassandra asked her husband, "Did you not know of this, Richard?"

Richard Gardiner shook his head, "Absolutely not. I knew Mr Mancini did many jobs around the farm, chopping logs for the fire, mending fences, and such, but that he was supplying my sister's family with groceries, no, I did not."

"Jessica, did you not know?" Elizabeth asked. "Did not your mama say anything to you?"

There was no need for Jessica to answer; the tears that coursed down her cheeks were answer enough, as she shook her head and reached for her handkerchief. Pushing her plate away, she said through her tears, "No, I cannot believe that while I was here with Julian, enjoying the best of everything, my parents and my brother were living on the charity of Mr Mancini. I knew he was a kind man, but I had no knowledge of this. I knew they had little money, but I did not know it was as bad as this." She sobbed and as her distress increased, Julian rose and helped her from the table, his grave countenance revealing his response to what they had heard. The others were shocked into silence.

Then Richard Gardiner turned to his father-in-law and asked, "Do you mind, sir, if I ask when you learnt of this situation?"

Mr Darcy answered, apparently without any reluctance, "Not long after Dr Courtney's death, your sister sent for me to ask for some advice about her own will. She wished to make some minor changes; she told me then that she was concerned that Mr Mancini's lease would soon run out and she wished to make it a more permanent arrangement, which could not be changed no matter who owned or managed the estate after her death. She knew even then that she was not likely to live very much longer, and she was quite open about it."

"And did she give you any reason for wishing to extend his lease in this way?" asked Richard.

Mr Darcy was quite emphatic. "Not at first, but when I insisted that I had to know why she was doing it, or I could not advise her, she decided to tell me. Mr Mancini had learned that there was little money for groceries, probably from the servants, and had begun to bring them small amounts of produce and then more and more until it seemed he had become their main source of supplies. Though she had tried to pay him, he had always refused to accept money, she said. I was shocked, of course, and asked her why she had not applied to me or to you or Caroline, but you know her answer—she declared that she had taken enough help from all of us for many years, and at least with Mr Mancini she could recompense him in a way in which she could not repay her family. The lifetime lease was her way of thanking him for all he had done for them over the years," he explained.

Richard's solemn expression and the tears in Cassandra's eyes obviated the need for words. Elizabeth too was so moved she had risen from the table and made to leave the room, when Mr Darcy said softly, "So you will understand now, Lizzie, why I was quite unable to say anything at the time Jude announced his engagement to Miss Mancini. I was taken completely by surprise, and knowing what I did, anything I said could have been misunderstood and given deep offence."

Elizabeth nodded, understanding exactly. "But you are pleased with the way things have worked out?" she asked.

Mr Darcy was unequivocal. "I am. I do believe it is in the best interests of young Jude, and I think Emily knew this, too. His future security and happiness were all she wished to ensure, and as far as we can tell, she has achieved her aim. Mr Mancini has much regard for young Jude, and Jude in turn respects his skills and knowledge as a farmer. With his wife's affection and sound common sense, I believe, like Emily, that they will not only be happy, but will do well together at Oakleigh. We none of us can hope for much more," he said.

Chapter Four

ELIZA HARWOOD HAD NOT made any arrangements to travel to London that afternoon. It was awkward because she had hoped to be asked to stay on at Oakleigh or perhaps even Pemberley, but disappointingly, no invitation had been forthcoming. Indeed, it had seemed to her as though the Darcys were pointedly ignoring her. Mrs Darcy had barely spoken with her at the funeral, and except to ask if she knew why her brother William had been delayed, Mr Darcy had said not a word to either of them.

Soon after the reading of the will, Mr Harwood had declared his intention to take advantage of the offer of a seat in the carriage of a new acquaintance, a businessman he had met at the Royal Inn, leaving Elizabeth and her maid to take the train on the following day. Temporarily embarrassed, Elizabeth was spared the indignity of looking for a room at the local hostelry by Robert and Rose, who invited her to stay with them overnight—an offer she was delighted to accept.

She could not have known that Rose would use the occasion almost exclusively to bemoan the injustice of Emily Courtney's will and how very hard-done-by her family was.

"I have no complaint on my own behalf. I know only too well that Mrs Courtney had no particular affection for me," she had said in a self-righteous little voice. "It is for my dear husband and sons that I am concerned. They surely deserved better. I cannot comprehend how they could have been dealt with so harshly."

Writing later to Anne-Marie Elliott, Jonathan Bingley's daughter, who had written to condole with her on the death of her mother, Eliza complained of the acute discomfort she had suffered as she had been forced to listen throughout dinner and afterwards to a recital of Rose's woes. Eliza wrote:

Rose is of the opinion that Mama decided quite perversely to insult her family by ignoring her sons in the will. "It was as though she had made up her mind to say to us, 'There, your sons do not exist, they are of no consequence to me whatsoever...'" she said, and I could see that she was deeply distressed and nothing I could say would make any difference.

That it was my own mother she was slandering did not appear to signify at all, nor was she at all concerned that neither I nor any of my children had gained any benefit from Mama's will. Mine, being her grandchildren, would surely have a far greater claim upon Mama than her nephews. But it seemed to me that Rose's only concern was to impress upon me the wholly unbelievable notion that Mama had been deliberately manipulated by Mr Darcy, against whom she has a deep prejudice, and while her husband, my uncle Robert, did not always agree, he has become so weak a man, he did nothing at all to defend Mama against his wife's accusations.

For my part, I have no proof of any malign intent on the part of Mama or Mr Darcy, though I must admit, it does seem to me that the Italian flower farmer, who plays such an important role at Oakleigh these days, and his granddaughter may well have exerted some undue influence upon her. They have had more time with her than any member of her family except my youngest brother, Jude. Doubtless, Mama's serious illness and my brother's fascination with the young woman must have made their task easier. It is not too difficult to see that, in these circumstances, a young man may be persuaded to agree to anything.

Anne-Marie could not mistake the bitterness in Eliza's words. She took the letter along when she went to Netherfield Park on the morrow. Parliament was sitting and her husband, Colin Elliott, was at Westminster, affording Anne-Marie an opportunity to spend some time with her father, his wife, Anna, and their children. Their two sons, Nicholas and Simon, liked nothing better than playing with Anne-Marie while her own daughter, Joanna, was adored by her grandfather. The warmth of their personal relationships and the easy conviviality of the atmosphere at Netherfield had a special attraction for Anne-Marie, whose childhood had been constrained by her mother's inexplicable allegiance to Rosings and Lady Catherine de Bourgh!

"How I hated those formal afternoons at Rosings Park with Lady Catherine holding court, telling Mama what she should and should not do, while we struggled to balance plates of cake and cups of tea on our laps, under her disapproving gaze. Ooh!" she would say and shudder at the memory.

Arriving at the house with little Joanna and her nurse, she was greeted by Anna and Jonathan with the news that Anna's cousin Becky and her new husband Mr Contini were soon to arrive for a short visit.

"We had been expecting them at Easter, but the sudden death of Mr Contini's mother took them to Italy and then, of course, there was Emily's funeral in Derbyshire, all of which has delayed their visit," Anna explained.

"So, they are arriving today?" Anne-Marie was delighted. "Oh, but it has been well timed from my point of view; I have heard so much about Becky from Colin, and Papa speaks so highly of his friend Mr Contini, I have been eager to meet them," she said as they took tea on the lawn, watching the children at play. "I have met Becky, of course, most often at family weddings and funerals, when one has so little time for any conversation. She is very elegant, and I know she used to write, as Marianne Lawrence, and I understand from Papa that she intends to buy a printery and publish the work of other women writers."

Anna nodded. "Indeed she does. Jonathan has recently approved the purchase, and I believe there is only the matter of a suitable manager to be settled, which is another reason for this visit—Becky is keen to get the business started as soon as possible," she said.

When they had finished taking tea, Anne-Marie produced Eliza Harwood's letter for Anna to read. Perusing it quickly, Anna was left aghast at its contents and tone.

"My dear Anne-Marie, I can scarcely believe this. Not only does it expose the complete hypocrisy of Robert and Rose Gardiner, whose blatant selfishness is quite shocking, it reveals also Eliza's own prejudice and small-mindedness in her criticism of Jude's wife and Mr Mancini, accusing them of exerting undue influence on Emily."

Anne-Marie laughed. "I find it passing strange that Eliza Harwood should censure anyone on that score; she has never been above using all her powers of persuasion to influence persons. Yet, no doubt she has a very short memory on those matters, and now that her own fortunes or those of her children are affected, she disparages others who may seek to do the same. Not that I believe for one moment that Emily Courtney was open to such influence; she was far too principled a woman to allow that."

Jonathan, who had joined them, having despatched the children indoors, heard the last few words of her sentence and asked lightly, "And who do you speak of in such glowing terms, my dear? Do I know this paragon of virtue?"

When he learned the truth, however, his expression became a good deal more serious. As he read the letter Anne-Marie handed him, he looked visibly shaken. Returning the offending document to his daughter, he remarked, "I have rarely seen such uncharitable sentiments set down in writing. I am very sorry for young Jude Courtney; unless his wife is a strong woman and supports him in resisting the efforts of these people, I have grave fears for his future. His mother may have hoped to leave him a reasonable inheritance, but Robert and Rose will not rest until they have tried every possible means to prise Oakleigh away from him, and to that we must now add the considerable weight of the Harwoods' grievances as well. I am not surprised at the former, their greed is well known; we are all well aware of Rose's ambition, but Eliza? Her husband has a thriving business and makes plenty of money, not always in the most legitimate ways, it must be admitted, but they cannot want for anything. Why then does Eliza complain that her children have gained no benefit from Mrs Courtney's will? What advantage can she possibly gain by depriving her young brother of part of his legacy? It is not as if Oakleigh is some great or profitable estate like Pemberley or Ashford Park; it is a modest property that survives upon the hard work of those who farm and manage it. I am truly unable to comprehend the motives of those who would…"

His sentence was cut short by the arrival of a hired carriage bringing their visitors and the voices of Simon and Nicholas calling out to them from an upstairs window. Everyone rose and went out to welcome Mr and Mrs Contini to Netherfield.

After dinner that night, as Anne-Marie obliged with some music to enter-tain their guests and Mr Contini spent time in conversation with his friend Jonathan Bingley, Becky and Anna sat together and inevitably, the question of Emily's will and the consequent recriminations arose.

As one of Emily's closest and most loyal friends, Becky was unable yet to speak without emotion of the funeral, and to Anna's surprise, she claimed to have no knowledge at all of the will or the furore it had caused among some members of Emily's family.

"Because Catherine had to return to Kent almost at once, we left Pemberley very early, before the will was read and anything was known," Becky explained, "but Emily had made it plain that Oakleigh was to be Jude's home. It was what she indicated to me when we last met. Once that had been decided, I did not believe there was much more left to bequeath to anyone clse. I had understood from Jessica that there was very little left of Emily's own inheritance."

Anna agreed, "I do believe you are right, Becky; she gave much of it away, but there were some other arrangements that aggravated her brother Robert and his wife. I understand from Jonathan that Robert had put before Emily a proposition for him to manage the estate, while allowing Jude and his wife to make their home and continue to work there."

"What as? Farmhand and cook?" asked Becky scornfully. "I cannot believe that Rose, were she to get her foot in the door at Oakleigh, would let them sit at the same dinner table as her family. Ever since her father succeeded to the family title, the Fitzwilliams have given themselves such airs, no one is good enough for them. Mrs Darcy, who was once a friend of Rose's mother, Rosamund, admits she finds them quite impossible."

Anna laughed; she too had heard tales from her mother-in-law Jane Bingley of the sudden elevation of the Fitzwilliams and its strange effect upon them. Becky continued, "Emily knew what would happen, she was much wiser than many people thought, and she was determined not to let them cheat Jude out of his inheritance. Which is why she asked Mr Darcy to find her a good lawyer, who would advise her how she could ensure that no one would be able to subvert her wishes, as expressed in her will."

Anna's eyes widened. "So Mr Darcy *was* involved, then?" she said, and by way of explanation, related the gist of Eliza Harwood's letter.

Becky was astounded. "Of course Mr Darcy was involved, but not as they would have you believe. Emily asked for his help, and I understand he recommended a very thorough lawyer, well known to his family, to advise her. Mrs Darcy says that it was imperative this was done, because Emily was very afraid that her brother Robert and his wife would not rest until they had got their hands on Oakleigh. And as you can see from that letter, Emily was right to be cautious," she declared.

Anna was too astonished to comment, but Becky added that Eliza Harwood's interest was probably different to that of the Gardiners.

"She has no need of any part of the property," Becky said, "but if the talk among their circle in London is true, her husband is neither the kindest nor the most faithful of men. Eliza, who is unhappily dependent upon his generosity, may have hoped to gain some degree of independence by inheriting something from her mother."

Anna was surprised to hear this, but recalling that Becky did once have friends in very high places and assuming she had heard some gossip about the Harwoods during her sojourn in London, she had to allow that there may have been some truth in the story. But, unwilling to pursue the matter, she decided to let it drop.

It was late and their guests were tired. Anne-Marie begged to be excused and left them to go upstairs to bed, and the rest of the party soon followed suit. But Anna could not sleep without acquainting her husband with Becky's extraordinary tale. She expected Jonathan to be as taken aback as she had been and wondered how Becky could have heard of the supposed misdemeanours of Eliza Harwood's husband.

"Who could have told her, even supposing that they were true?" she asked and was amazed when Jonathan said casually, "Oh, they are certainly true; it has been well known for some years that Harwood is no model of fidelity. He is a businessman of wealth and influence and keeps the company of those who use their money and position to secure not only their commercial interests but their private pleasures as well. I have been told Mr Harwood has an apartment in London, which is frequently the venue for some quite riotous parties and with such evidence, I daresay, one is entitled to draw the obvious conclusions."

Seeing the astonishment upon his wife's face, he added, "And if you are about to ask how I know all this dearest, well, it was Anthony Tate who told me. He knew Harwood well; he didn't like him and once threatened to expose him, but desisted out of sympathy for his wife and children, who would have shared in the disgrace, had he done so. And that, my love, should also answer your question as to how Becky knows. No doubt it was common knowledge in their circles; Tate would certainly have told her."

Anna could scarcely speak, so appalled was she by his revelations. "I am shocked, horrified—Mr Harwood presents himself as a pillar of the community, Anne-Marie has told me how he once had political ambitions."

Jonathan smiled as he lay back on the pillows, regarding his wife's face. "Indeed he did, and that was when Tate threatened to expose him. He told me he would never permit a man like Harwood to hold public office, as long as he lived. It was not only his private peccadilloes, Tate believed he was a fraud and a cheat in business as well," he said, and Anna asked, "But, Jonathan, how do we know that it is all true and not something fabricated by his enemies, who would wish to damage him?"

Jonathan drew her into his arms. "Dearest, I know how reluctant you are to think ill of anyone, but in this case, I do believe the evidence is clear. Anthony Tate was not my only informant. There is another quite impeccable source. About two years ago, my mother and father spent some time in Bath, when Papa was ordered to take the waters and recuperate after a bout of influenza. They stayed with my aunts Louisa and Caroline, remember?"

Anna remembered it well. "Indeed I do, and Caroline Bingley was, at the time, hopeful that she had attracted the attention of a certain retired admiral? Am I right?"

Her husband laughed. "You are; sadly for Miss Bingley, his attentions did not outlast the season. Also, he did suffer badly with the gout, which may or may not have been regarded as a serious disadvantage. However, Mama did spend quite a lot of time with my aunts and the admiral in all the best places in Bath, and on several occasions, she saw Mr Harwood there and not, I fear, with his wife. In truth, he was seen with two quite different women, each of whom he appeared to favour with his undivided attention and money. My mother was shocked beyond belief, but Miss Bingley and Mrs Hurst assured her that this was quite a common occurrence. Harwood apparently was a regular visitor to Bath, but never with Mrs Harwood."

"And when did your mama tell you of this?" asked Anna.

"Oh, not long afterwards," he replied. "I visited them in London to ask after my father's health, and still appalled by what she had seen and heard, she told me all about it, which of course confirmed everything I had learned about the man from Anthony Tate."

After a short silence, Anna, still seeming rather confused, asked, "Jonathan, why did you not think to tell me about this at the time?"

It was a question he had not anticipated, but he answered it without hesitation. "Because, my dearest Anna, you had brought so much that is good and beautiful into my life, I had no wish for us to speak of something as ugly as Harwood's appalling behaviour. Besides, it was of no consequence to us at all. We could have no influence upon the situation, and I particularly wished that Anne-Marie should not hear of it; she may have been very upset. You will recall that she was once quite close to Eliza Harwood and used to think very highly of them."

"Do you think Eliza knows? If she does, how can she bear to continue in such a marriage?"

"She must know, almost everyone else among their general acquaintance does, though they will not tell her. But there is little she can do about it. Her husband, it seems, does as he pleases. He is a man of some wealth and consequence, and she is completely dependent upon him."

Anna's voice was very soft, almost despairing, "Poor Eliza, what a dreadful life."

Jonathan nodded. "Yes indeed. Now I think you will understand why I did not wish to tell you about it at the time. I knew it would distress you."

Anna turned to him, her troubled eyes softening. "Yes, I do understand and thank you." And there was no more to be said on the matter.

The following morning brought first some unwelcome rain, followed by a fine, bright afternoon, which called for a drive out to Hatfield House. "You must see it," Jonathan had insisted, and Aldo Contini had agreed that such an historic place, situated so conveniently in the district, could not be missed.

"It would be like going to Florence and not visiting the Palace of the Medici," he said, partly in jest, which caused both Anna and Becky to warn that while Hatfield House was steeped in English history, it could not boast of the opulent grandeur of the Florentines. For Anna and Jonathan, it brought back many memories of their first meetings and the happy days when he had come into Hertfordshire and decided to purchase Netherfield Park. It had been a fateful decision, which had had many unforeseen consequences for both their families. Becky, always sensible of such matters, could not help noticing the genuine warmth of their affection for one another.

Later, as they relaxed in the shade of a mighty oak, Becky recalled her conversation with Anna on the previous night, concerning the situation of Eliza Harwood.

"Poor Eliza, how utterly unsupportable must her position be," she thought, but some of her natural sympathy was diluted by her knowledge that Eliza had quite deliberately decided to marry Mr Harwood, on very short acquaintance, after discovering that his family was well connected and owned a great deal of property in the south of England.

"Eliza, unlike Jessica, was never happy in Derbyshire," Emily had told her. "She would tell us all that one day she would marry a man rich enough to own an estate in one of the southern counties, and so she did."

"And do you believe she is happy?" Becky had asked.

"It is not what I would have chosen, but Eliza is not a romantic young woman. She will find satisfaction where she can. She has a fine house, plenty of money and servants, she wants for nothing; perhaps she is happy; she has never admitted to being otherwise," Emily had replied.

Becky had never discovered if Emily knew what a high price her eldest daughter had paid for her fine house and estate in the south of England. Happy in her present marriage to a man of only modest means, but with a wealth of affection and regard to offer, Becky felt a cold shiver travel down her spine as she contemplated Eliza Harwood's unhappy fate. How very different was the situation of Emily's younger daughter Jessica and Julian Darcy. Whenever she had encountered them, Becky had been aware of the intimacy of their relationship and the warm sincerity of their feelings of mutual affection and esteem.

Having failed in his first marriage to Becky's daughter, Josie, mainly as a consequence of his single-minded dedication to his research, Julian appeared to be devoting himself with the same intensity to securing the happiness of his wife and child.

While her sister had sought status and wealth, marrying an aspiring businessman from a wealthy family, Jessica's happiness flowed from the love of her husband and daughter and the fulfilment she found in the work she did at the parish school at Pemberley. They would never be wealthy, for Julian refused to take any more than his agreed allowance from the Pemberley estate, having signed away his inheritance to his son, Anthony, yet they were deeply in love, and even a disinterested observer could tell which of the two women enjoyed the greater degree of contentment.

Chapter Five

W ILLIAM COURTNEY HAD NOT made a good impression upon the Darcys. He was handsome, talented, and a distinguished musician—everything that should have counted in his favour— but when he failed to arrive in time for his mother's funeral, everyone who knew Mr and Mrs Darcy and their great affection for Emily Courtney knew also that her son had earned their lasting displeasure.

He had, however, been present for the reading of the will and did not seem particularly perturbed or disappointed that his mother had left him nothing more materially significant than her congratulations on his present success and good wishes for his future.

When his sister Eliza Harwood had complained about her children being left out of their mother's will, clearly expecting him to express similar dissatisfaction, he had surprised her by declaring that as far as he was concerned, he had not expected a penny.

"I think Mama and Papa spent enough on me through the years I was studying music. I am well able to support myself and have no dependents. I had no expectation of receiving anything more. In fact, I am glad Oakleigh Manor has been left to Jude, because he is best able to make the most of it; the rest of us know nothing about farming. Jude, I am told, loves it; he wants no other life."

Eliza had appeared puzzled by this apparent magnanimity, pointing out that one did not have to till the soil and milk the cows oneself; there were tenants and labourers who would do the work, drawing a sharp retort from her brother that he did not fancy being an absentee landlord anyway.

On the afternoon following the reading of the will, William Courtney presented himself at Pemberley to call on Mr and Mrs Darcy. It was one duty his mother had impressed upon him. "If it were not for Mr Darcy's generosity in paying for your education, your father and I could never have afforded to send you to Oxford. You must never forget what you owe them. They are very proud of your success, and through you they celebrate the memory of their own dear William, of whom they had such great hopes, before he was so cruelly taken from them," she had said.

William Courtney was very much aware that the Darcys, especially Mrs Darcy, saw in him a reflection of their young son, whose name he shared. William Darcy had died in a foolhardy escapade when he was scarcely sixteen years old, destroying a life full of promise and a prodigious musical talent. Ever since it had become clear that Emily's young son William had a similar gift, Mr and Mrs Darcy had been eager to assist in its development and applaud his success.

As for William Courtney, he had felt impelled to do his best and succeed in his chosen field, not only for himself and the expectations of his family but for the memory of his cousin William Darcy and his parents who had never ceased to mourn the loss of their son.

Arriving at Pemberley that afternoon, he was shown into the saloon and plied with refreshments until Mr and Mrs Darcy appeared. Their greeting, initially rather reserved, confirmed his belief that he had incurred their disapproval, and he set about trying to explain the reasons for his late arrival, with a tale of a tardy cab driver and a missed train, but it soon became clear to him that they appeared not to find his excuses credible. While Mr Darcy seemed unwilling to discuss the matter, Elizabeth asked poignantly if he had not thought it appropriate to travel down a day earlier, especially in view of the fact that he had not seen his mother since his father's funeral. The implication of the question was clear, woundingly so.

Perhaps William's downcast eyes and disconsolate expression had some effect on Mr Darcy, who intervened to comfort his wife and say, "Lizzie, my dear, please do not distress yourself again about this. I am quite sure William has contemplated that possibility and realised that had he done so, things might have been different. Besides, I do not believe that Emily would have wished that questions of attendance at her funeral should cause such pain and grief to those she loved very much."

Elizabeth nodded and dabbed at her eyes, while Mr Darcy offered William a glass of sherry. Feeling a good deal worse than when he'd arrived at Pemberley, William had tried desperately, over the next half hour, to make conversation, but sadly, failed to do so, except in the most superficial terms; not even the mention of his very successful concert tour of the eastern United States excited their interest sufficiently to elicit any significant questions about his work or his future plans. He left, wishing them well, but feeling that he had forfeited their affection and respect; it was, for William, who was generally of a friendly disposition, a particularly depressing sensation.

As he was leaving Pemberley House, a young man walked up from the park towards the house, accompanied by a boy. As they approached, the man smiled and quickened his step; it was then William recognised his cousin, Darcy Gardiner. They shook hands and Darcy introduced young Anthony Darcy.

"Julian's son?" William said, surprised at how grown up the boy looked.

"Indeed, and the next master of Pemberley," Darcy replied. "Anthony and I have been doing the rounds of the park; he is learning fast."

William remarked that there must be a great deal to learn, and the boy smiled and replied that there was, but it was all very interesting. As they stood together, they did not notice that Mr and Mrs Darcy were watching them from one of the windows. Neither spoke, but both were aware of the deep sense of disappointment they felt about a young man for whom they'd had great affection. They could not hear their words, but clearly William and Darcy appeared to be having a perfectly amiable conversation. Elizabeth sighed, wishing things were different.

Before they parted, William asked after Darcy's wife, Kate. Recalling that their wedding had been another family occasion he had missed on account of being out of the country, he apologised and invited them to visit him whenever they came to London.

"I expect to be spending quite some time in London this year, before I leave for a series of Winter concerts in Europe; I should be delighted to see you and your wife," he said, and young Darcy Gardiner, quite charmed by his famous cousin, agreed that the pleasure would be mutual.

"Well, send me word when you are in town. If you give me some notice, we might arrange for you to have seats at one of my concerts, if your musical taste runs to that sort of thing," he said, and Darcy responded, "Indeed it does, Kate plays the pianoforte and enjoys music very much. I am sure she would like nothing better."

"Well, there you are then," said William, handing Darcy his card. "I shall look forward to hearing from you." He then shook hands with them, entered the waiting vehicle, and was driven away, leaving his cousin more than somewhat baffled.

Later that evening, Darcy Gardiner and his uncle Julian Darcy fell into conversation as they waited for the ladies to join them before dinner. Julian had previously expressed his concerns about William's often inexplicable behaviour, and the two men had discussed the possibility that there may be some simple explanation.

"He has invited us to visit him in London, and as you know, Kate and I are to travel there quite soon," Darcy told him.

"How very opportune," said Julian. "Perhaps you should accept the invitation as soon as possible, before he changes his mind or his travel plans."

Darcy looked surprised, as much at his tone as his words. "Why? Do you really believe that is likely? Why would he? His invitation sounded quite genuine," he said.

Julian was somewhat sceptical. "It may well have been at the time, but as we have found in the past, Cousin William is a rather quixotic character. He does the strangest things, and it is not often possible to explain his odd behaviour. If you believe, Darcy, that it was a genuine invitation, then my advice to you is take it up expeditiously. It may offer an opportunity to discover something more about our distinguished cousin, which may not arise again."

The arrival of the ladies interrupted their conversation, but later, when they were seated at dinner, the subject came up again when Kate Gardiner, addressing Mr and Mrs Darcy, asked, "And how did you find William Courtney today, Mrs Darcy?"

Before Elizabeth could answer, Mr Darcy, sensible of her feelings on the matter, said, "He appeared surprisingly untroubled by questions about his late arrival for the funeral, and though I was unimpressed by his explanation, I would not go so far as to suggest that he had no tender feelings for his mother. He clearly feels some degree of guilt at not visiting her before her death."

Mrs Darcy's silence signalled her own disapproval, but Cassandra spoke up. She had met and observed William Courtney at the reading of the will, she said, and didn't believe he was unfeeling or cold-hearted at all.

"When I spoke to him about his mother, he thanked me and said he and their entire family owed a debt of gratitude to those of us who had cared for her. He made mention of Papa and Mama and Richard, of course, but as I have just told Jessica, he had very special thanks for her and Jude. He said they had done everything for their mother that he had not and for that he was very grateful to them."

There was a moment of silence and then, Julian said, "But, Cassy, surely the material point is he never made any effort to see his mother, even after he was informed by Richard that she was dying. It is easy enough to thank those who cared for her, and so he should, but it was surely his duty to visit her, to give her that last comfort, do you not agree?"

This time there were tears in the eyes of all the women, and when Jessica left the room sobbing, Mr Darcy said he felt they had all suffered sufficiently for William Courtney's sins of omission and needed some respite, making it quite clear that as far as he was concerned, the subject was closed.

It was reopened, however, when Darcy and Kate returned home that night. Kate, noticing that her husband had been rather quiet after the contentious conversation around the dinner table at Pemberley, asked as they prepared for bed, "Do you suppose, my dear, that Julian Darcy is right about William Courtney? I thought his judgment rather harsh. I hardly know William at all and would not wish to proffer an opinion publicly, but he did not seem to me like a man without deeper feelings. I cannot believe that he had deliberately stayed away when his mother was ill, could you?"

Darcy's answer was quite categorical. "I certainly could not. William had just spoken with me on the steps of Pemberley House; he was leaving, having called on Mr and Mrs Darcy, when I arrived with young Anthony and he was most gentlemanly and cordial. He asked after your health, apologised for not having attended our wedding on account of being on tour in America, and has invited us to visit him when we are in London next month."

Kate expressed her astonishment. "William Courtney invited us to visit him?"

"Indeed he did and in the most gracious and friendly way. Look, he gave me his card—here it is—and asked me to send him word when we would be in London. What is more, he said he would try to arrange for us to have seats at one of his concerts while we were there."

"What did you say? Did you accept?" Kate was wide-eyed.

"Of course I did, I said we would be delighted. I told him you play the pianoforte and would like nothing better than to attend one of his concerts. Was I right?" Darcy was smiling, and Kate hugged him.

"Of course you were, dearest, I cannot imagine anything I should enjoy more. I have heard so much of his talent and yet never had the chance to see a performance. It would be a wonderful opportunity. Do you really believe he would arrange tickets for us?"

"I believe he would," Darcy replied. "Why bring up the subject, if he had no real intention of pursuing it? He has no reason to do so. I am only his cousin; he has no need to impress me with such promises or favours. I am inclined to believe he would keep his word, although Julian seems to think otherwise."

Kate seemed surprised. "Julian? Does he know about it too?" she asked.

Darcy pulled a face. "I'm afraid he does; he came upon me while we were waiting together for the ladies to come downstairs, and I told him about the invitation."

"And what did he say?"

"Oh, he was rather sceptical, as I would expect him to be. Apparently Jessica is particularly upset about William not visiting their mother before she died, and it is understandable that Julian would share her feelings, I suppose," Darcy said.

"That is certainly understandable and even justifiable in the light of William's past conduct, but why should Julian also believe that William would invite us to visit him in London without meaning to keep his word? It would be a most ungentlemanly thing to do, and we have no evidence that he is such a person," Kate argued.

Darcy nodded. "None at all. You are absolutely right, my love, but I am afraid Julian seems convinced there is something more to William's strange behaviour than meets the eye."

"Does he? In what way?" asked Kate.

Darcy was noncommittal. "I doubt that even he knows; he simply feels there is something about William's behaviour that is not right. I believe it is just a suspicion; he has suggested that I should make some enquiries when we are in London."

Kate was outraged. "What? Darcy, you cannot agree to that! Not if you intend that we should accept William's invitation, which you have as good as done. It would be the most duplicitous thing to do, and I certainly would not advise you to do it. Indeed, I should not feel comfortable accepting any invitation from William, under such circumstances," she said firmly.

Darcy knew she was right. He was deeply troubled himself and wished he had said nothing to Julian about his conversation with William. It had complicated the situation, and now, if his wife were to insist that they decline the invitation, it would make matters worse. It was likely that William Courtney would conclude that Darcy and Kate had been influenced by his grandparents and the rest of the Pemberley clan not to accept his hospitality. Yet, to do so while following Julian's suggestion that he should make some investigation of William's conduct was unthinkable. It was a false position that he, on reflection, found quite abhorrent.

When he spoke, after a few moments, thought, his voice was grave. "You are quite right, my love, it would not be possible for me to do as Julian asks while accepting William's invitation. It would place me, both of us, in a most invidious position and could likely cause a great deal of damage within the family if William were ever to discover the truth. I shall tell Julian so tomorrow. I am sorry if he thinks I have squibbed it—I did originally agree—but that was before I had met and spoken with William and accepted his kind invitation. I'm afraid I shall just have to tell Julian I cannot do it."

Kate was thoughtful. "Do you have to? Is it not possible to say nothing now? Avoid discussing the matter until we are back from London, when you could say to Julian that you noticed nothing untoward at all. At least that way you will not lay yourself open to an accusation of hypocrisy. Darcy, I am wary of these private investigations into people's lives, they are high-handed and intrusive and can often cause trouble between the parties concerned," she said, adding in a more confidential tone, "As you well know, dearest, I have myself been a victim of the kind of intrusion that often allows malice and misunderstanding to be used to destroy a person's happiness or indeed their very character. Were William ever to discover that you were involved in such an enterprise, and we have no evidence that he is engaged in anything that warrants such an investigation, we should be badly compromised and probably lose his friendship and respect forever."

And her husband knew that every word she spoke was sound common sense. It was one of the qualities he most admired in her. Agreeing that she was right and it was best not to say anything more about the matter to Julian, he declared that he would make no further mention of it to anyone.

Kate, never inclined to push her husband too far, smiled and said, "I think that would be very wise, dearest. I do not believe that it would be fair either to you or to William for you to undertake such a mission. I am quite sure, too, that Mr and Mrs Darcy, if they knew of Julian's suggestion, would not be comfortable with the proposition. It would not be considered proper and would place you in a most unhappy position. I think you are quite right in deciding not to proceed with it."

Her husband, delighted with his wife's approval, relaxed and held out a hand to her. "Thank you, my dearest Kate; what should I do without your excellent understanding and judgment? I am sure I should be quite at sea. I confess I have been troubled by the matter and wondered how I should deal with the situation. At least, we can now make arrangements for our visit to London and our meeting with William with a clear conscience," he said. To which she replied with a bright smile, "And we can enjoy every minute of it."

Chapter Six

THE ARRIVAL IN THE district of a Mr Wilson Croker went almost unnoticed at the time, probably because it coincided with the celebrations following upon the victory of the Camden and Pemberley cricket team over their traditional rivals from Ripley.

It is quite likely that Teresa Courtney was one of a few people who had seen the stranger drive up the road in a smart little vehicle, alight at the boundary of Oakleigh manor, and survey the surrounding countryside. With little interest in the cricket, she had remained at the farm, intent on getting on with the task of preserving fruit, while Jude and some of the young men had gone down into the village to watch the match.

Carefully preparing a basket to gather the ripe fruit, Teresa had gone out to the orchard, when a man she had never seen before had alighted from his gig some distance from the farm gate, which opened onto the lane that formed one of the boundaries of the property. She had observed him at first without much interest, as he strode along the laneway for a fair distance, with a notebook in hand, stopping from time to time to write in it.

For all she knew he could have been an itinerant artist or a man from the council—neither interested Teresa at all. She was more concerned about ensuring that the plums she was intending to preserve were unbruised as she gathered them into her basket, sampling them for sweetness and wiping her hands on her apron.

The man, who had clearly seen her when he first arrived, returned after some time and barely threw a second glance in her direction before getting back in his vehicle and driving away.

Getting on with her work, Teresa soon forgot about him, but she did remember to mention his appearance to her husband when he returned home in time for dinner. Flushed with the success of the home team and keen to sample the contents of the jars on the kitchen table, Jude Courtney greeted his wife with more than the usual affection and seemed at first disinterested in the stranger, but when she described the man and his vehicle, he began to pay more attention.

"He was very smartly dressed, that is all I could see from where I stood in the orchard, and he had a very stylish hat that must surely have been made in London. He saw me but did not even trouble to tip his hat; I was picking plums, and he probably took me for a servant," she said, laughing, which caused her husband to look across the table at her and say, "If that is the case, he cannot have been from the district. Everyone around here knows you and your grandfather. He must have been from Derby or Birmingham. I wonder who he could have been and what he was doing up here. Who could possibly be interested in this part of the country?"

Having thought for a moment, he asked, "What did he look like?"

Teresa laughed again. "I did tell you, my dear, I did not see his face clearly, but he was fashionably dressed; he had a notebook in his hand and was writing in it; it seemed as though he was looking at the farm and the land around it. He walked all the way up the hill towards the woods and back again," she said.

Jude was somewhat disturbed, but unable to put his concerns about the presence of a stranger in the area into words. He was aware that on previous occasions agents from the big towns and even as far afield as London had made approaches to his late grandmother and even more recently to his mother, wanting to bid on the property, offering them considerable sums of money for the holdings.

Oakleigh Manor with its salubrious surroundings, its fertile farmlands, pastures, woods, and trout stream was, despite its moderate size, clearly a valuable asset. Since their marriage, Teresa had worked hard to get the house scrubbed, cleaned, and tidy, while Mr Mancini had spent many hours restoring the grounds and fences around it. Both of them took great pride in their work and soon had the old place looking like it had been before, a desirable if modest estate. With Mr Mancini's help, Jude hoped to get the home farm production up again to where it would support the family. There was of course the problem of capital. Following his mother's death, not a lot of it remained and some would have to be found to get the farm working again.

"Are you quite sure it was not one of your grandfather's friends come to look over the flower farm?" he asked, and this time Teresa put down her spoon and took her preserving pan off the stove before answering, "Surely, my dear, I should recognise my grandfather's friends. I have known most of them all my life, and if it was one of them, they would have spoken with me. No, this man was not anyone we know, believe me; he was a total stranger, and yet he seemed very interested in our farm."

Not being of a generally suspicious nature, Jude Courtney did not appear too deeply troubled but was, nevertheless, sufficiently concerned to make a mental note to draw the attention of his cousin Darcy Gardiner to the matter of the stranger, when he saw him at church on Sunday.

Thereafter, he turned his attention to his wife for whom his feelings grew stronger every day. With both his parents being continually busy with work in the parish, Jude had grown up with his sister Jessica for company; since she had left home to live at Pemberley and teach at the parish school, he had missed the consistent care and affection she had shown him as a boy. Following their marriage, his wife Teresa had brought warmth and affection back into his life, and he returned it in full measure.

Darcy Gardiner, in the midst of being congratulated by all and sundry on the victory of his cricket team, was rather surprised at the seriousness with which his young cousin approached him after church on Sunday. Although his tale of a well-dressed stranger surveying the land around Oakleigh and taking notes on the previous afternoon, while most of the village was at the cricket match, did sound extraordinary, Darcy wondered if Jude wasn't jumping at shadows. But his wife Kate, listening to Teresa's story, was prepared to take it much more seriously than her husband. Her Irish antecedents made her rather suspicious of strangers, particularly well-heeled ones, looking over her land and, she declared, anyone whose interest was benign would not have missed the opportunity to talk to one of the local people. That the man in a stylish hat had apparently ignored Teresa, while looking over Oakleigh and its environs, Kate found deeply disturbing.

"Darcy, I do believe you should make enquiries in the village about this man. A stranger of such a description cannot have passed through unnoticed; he must have hired the vehicle or rented a room or eaten a meal somewhere. Someone will know his name or his business," she said with such certitude that Darcy had to take her concerns seriously.

Promising Jude that he would make discreet enquiries, Darcy tried to reassure Teresa and urged her to remain observant in case the stranger returned to the area.

"You are quite right to have been concerned. With the parlous state of agriculture in England, there have been several reports of agents from Birmingham and Manchester moving into these parts looking to purchase likely properties, but I would not have thought that they would be interested in a place such as Oakleigh Manor. It is quite clearly a working farm requiring too much hard work for their clientele, who are mainly the recently rich looking to acquire a country estate to improve their social standing," he said.

"If that were all, I should simply tell them that Oakleigh is not for sale," said Jude, shrugging his shoulders, but Teresa was not quite so easily reassured and welcomed Darcy's pledge that he would discover the identity and motives of the stranger in their midst.

"I am not happy that this man should be wandering around our farm, without a word to us to say what his business is," she complained.

Kate, too, was uneasy, and while she urged her husband to make enquiries in the village, she was determined to do likewise. The two couples parted, and while Kate urged Teresa to be vigilant at all times, Darcy, sensing her unease, promised to return with more information as soon as he could find it. He did not expect it to be very difficult—if this stranger was as conspicuously dressed as Teresa had described, then someone in the village must remember the man.

Unhappily, he was to be proved quite wrong.

Despite making many and varied enquiries in and around the village and even as far as Kympton and Pemberley, he could find no one who could remember the man he described. When he mentioned it to his parents, Cassandra and Richard both reminded him that there had been reports of brokers from London looking for land for developers, who planned to build new mansions in the countryside to satisfy the demands of those whose newly acquired wealth had not bought them the genteel status they craved.

"Stranded outside the circle of society they would like to enter, they are trying to buy their way in by acquiring some of the trappings of the country gentleman's way of life. The very first of these is a country house and its accoutrements," said Richard, adding, "I think you should talk to your brother-in-law, Mr Carr."

When Darcy looked surprised, his mother explained, "Your sister Lizzie has told us of the innumerable offers Mr Carr has rejected from agents who want to buy part of his land. This man could be one of them, although I cannot think why he would be up near Oakleigh; there is not a lot of land one could build on there."

"Unless he has an interest in the land on Oakleigh Manor," said Darcy, and both his parents nodded sagely.

"Which is a possibility I would not discount," said his father. "Your uncle Robert has been promoting the idea for years, but your aunt Emily would never consider it."

Darcy's eyes widened in astonishment. "I think I should call on my brother-in-law as soon as possible. There may be more to this than meets the eye," he said, rising from his chair and preparing to leave.

While Darcy Gardiner planned to call on his sister and her husband at their farm, it was Kate who claimed the first sighting of the stranger. On a visit to Derby, seeing a familiar figure descending the steps of the council chambers, she stopped to ascertain the identity of the gentleman. She was surprised to discover that it was Robert Gardiner, accompanied by someone who fitted exactly the description of the man Teresa had seen, right down to his well-cut suit and stylish hat! They descended the steps to the pavement and stood talking together, looking at their watches, clearly waiting for someone to join them. Kate withdrew into the doorway of a book shop, preparing to disappear within if they appeared likely to move in her direction. Very shortly, the two men were joined by another, who alighted from a hired vehicle and crossed the street, and the three walked up the road and out of sight.

Kate wished she could have followed them, but sensibly decided that she could not do so without attracting their attention. Determined to discover the identity of the man with Robert, she went up the steps into the council chambers. There, she would find a young man, Sam Chiswick, who owed his education and position to her father, for whom he had worked for many years before moving to improve his prospects by taking a job as a clerk in the council. Out of both affection and a sense of loyalty to her father, he had maintained an association with their family, and Kate hoped he would help her now.

Pretending she was there to make a routine enquiry, she sought him out and asked if he could discover the identity of the man who had just been in with Mr Robert Gardiner. She insisted that it was a private but very important matter. The young man was eager to assist, but told her he had to be discreet, which meant she had to wait, which she willingly did, inconspicuously taking a seat on one of the public benches in the waiting hall. Scarcely had she sat down and taken out her book, when the man himself raced up the steps and into the main office, looking exceedingly disturbed.

Kate was very glad that his companions had not thought to follow him in, for then Robert Gardiner would surely have seen her there, and since he was not accompanied by his wife, he may even have felt free to be civil and may have tried to make conversation, which would have been very awkward indeed. As she watched, pretending to be reading her book, the man reappeared with young Sam Chiswick, still agitated and speaking loudly, declaring that he was lunching with Mr Robert Gardiner at his club and if the missing item was found, it should be immediately returned to him. He was most insistent upon the importance of recovering his property. As Kate watched and listened in amazement, young Sam Chiswick nodded and bowed and agreed to do his very best to find the missing article and return it to the owner.

Presently, the man departed and Sam Chiswick approached Kate. "Begging your pardon, ma'am, but I believe this is what you are looking for," he said softly and held out to her a slim tooled leather wallet, which held a number of cards. Kate could not believe her eyes. "Indeed, how very clever of you to find it, Sam," she said, and quickly extracting one of the cards, returned the case to him. "Now, you can make an even better impression, by racing down to Mr Robert Gardiner's club and returning this valuable item to the gentleman, who should be very grateful for your efforts." Sam bowed and declared that he was about to do just that, once he had obtained his supervisor's permission to do so.

Kate, smiling, thanked him again and left, unable to hide the supreme satisfaction she felt. She could hardly wait to get home to give her husband the news. The name on the card read Wilson J Croker, broker and developer. The address was an office situated on a smart street in London. The question now was, Whatever was he doing with Robert Gardiner? It was a question that might have been answered quite simply if only Kate had been able to be present at a dinner party that had been held in Derby some days earlier, at the home of one of the richest men in the county.

Sir William Bilson owed his wealth and his knighthood to the phenomenal success of his scrap metal and rubble business. It had started life as a dust and rubbish collecting operation in the slums of Bolton and Bury with two rag and bone carts and two dustmen, which had eventually spread its tentacles all over the Midlands, sucking up the detritus of industry and turning it into gold—or at least the equivalent of money in the bank. The mansion he had had built for his family in Derby, well away from the dumps of industrial debris that made him his money, occupying as much space as a small village and consuming infinitely more resources, stood as a symbol of the success of this modern alchemist.

On the night in question, Sir William and his wife, Lady Florence Bilson, were entertaining two newcomers to the district. They were Mr Wilson Croker and his accountant, Mr Pipes. The former had been introduced to Sir William by a business acquaintance in Liverpool, and the latter always went along as an essential attachment to his employer, for Mr Croker hardly went anywhere unless there was some opportunity for doing business. The two men were a study in contrasts: Mr Croker was young, handsome after a fashion, genial, and exceedingly well-dressed, while his companion was middle-aged, plain, dour, and wore a suit that must have been made at least a decade ago. His entire demeanour was odd to say the least.

In the company gathered at the Bilson mansion were several local dignitaries and socialites of varying degrees of importance in the community. They included the mayor, his wife and some members of the council, a local member of Parliament and his wife, a county lawyer, and two civil engineers with their wives, as well as Mr and Mrs Robert Gardiner and their pretty young daughter, Miranda.

Unbeknownst to most members of his family, but actively encouraged by his wife, Robert Gardiner had begun to take a great deal of interest in the building industry. Disappointed that he had not been entrusted with the control of his father's Commercial Trading Company, which now flourished under the management of his sister Caroline and her son, he had hoped to inherit the family property, Oakleigh Manor. When, however, that too had slipped from his grasp, Robert, in a fit of pique, had decided to sell his shares in the family business and invest the money in what was becoming a booming new enterprise: building mansions for the newly rich.

Although they had neither wealth nor influence on such a scale as would have warranted their inclusion in the Bilsons' guest list, their connection to two of the most renowned families in the county, the Darcys and the Fitzwilliams, gave them the necessary cachet. That and the fact that while Robert was not known for his business acumen or quick wit, his elegant wife was a most entertaining purveyor of county gossip, had seen them invited to many a social function.

Conversation around the dinner table was for the most part of a general nature. Predictably they began with the weather and the health of the Queen, and progressed to topics like the imminent collapse of British agriculture and the possible bankruptcy of many individual farmers. Almost everyone had a view on such matters. However, when it came to buying land cheaply as a consequence of the agricultural recession, there were not as many people prepared to offer an informed opinion. Sir William pointed out that there were bargains to be had if one knew where to look and, turning to Mr Croker, invited him to tell their guests how successful he had been.

"I think many of our friends would be quite surprised to learn that you appear to have had very little difficulty finding people prepared to sell up and move, is that not so, Mr Croker?" he asked, and Mr Croker smiled broadly and nodded.

"Oh, certainly, Sir William, I have been myself astonished at how ready people are to sell, when it is pointed out to them how they can advantage themselves and their families by selling out at the right time. I had expected a good deal more resistance in the country, but this has not been the case. My accountant, Mr Pipes, has been able to demonstrate to many landholders the enormous advantages of selling while the market is up," he replied, inclining his head in the direction of Mr Pipes, who with the merest bow acknowledged the compliment in his employer's statement.

"And do you hope to buy up land in this part of Derbyshire, too?" asked a woman at the end of the table.

"We hope to; that is certainly our intention, but we have not made any purchases yet. There are some good prospects, though, and I intend to pursue them assiduously," Mr Croker declared, adding, "I was up looking at two of the places Mr Gardiner suggested might be worthwhile, in particular, a property in the Lambton area, Oakleigh Manor."

Robert and Rose exchanged knowing glances, but Miranda could not hide her astonishment. Clearly, she had no knowledge of their schemes.

"And what was your opinion of the property, Mr Croker?" asked Rose.

"Well, I haven't reached a judgment on either place, Mrs Gardiner, perhaps because in both cases I have not spoken with the owners yet, but I will say that Oakleigh Manor is a fair prospect," Croker replied. "The land available is small, admittedly, but it is very happily situated and conveniently accessible by an excellent road. I should certainly have liked to have met the owners, but they must have been away at the time I was in the area. I saw only a rather dark young woman gathering plums in the orchard, probably one of the maids; she was eating as many as she was collecting, taking advantage of the absence of her mistress, no doubt," he quipped.

At this, Rose Gardiner laughed and said in a penetrating voice, "Oh no, she was not, Mr Croker, you are indeed mistaken; that was no maid, it was the lady of the manor. Teresa Courtney is the daughter of an Italian flower farmer and is exactly the sort of person who *would* be seen standing out in the garden eating plums! It is so like her; she has no understanding of her position at all."

The silence around the table and Robert Gardiner's red face was sufficient to demonstrate the general embarrassment of the company, and soon afterwards, Lady Bilson rose and withdrew, followed by the rest of the women, leaving the men to continue their conversation over the port. This, however, did not appear to convince Rose that she had gone too far. As the ladies gathered in the drawing room, she continued to ridicule Mrs Courtney's "quaint taste in clothes and rustic manners," which she attributed to her "foreign antecedents." Resplendent in her fashionable gown of silk and lace, she proceeded to describe the embroidered wedding gown that Teresa had worn and recalled for the benefit of anyone who cared to listen the fact that the church was overflowing with scented flowers—leaving the congregation in no doubt that the bride's family were flower farmers.

Plainly upset by her mother's unpardonable rudeness, Miranda left the room to walk out onto the terrace. By the time the gentlemen joined them, the ladies had turned their attention to someone other than Teresa. Later, Miranda, who had been in conversation with Mr Croker on the terrace, returned to the drawing room, although she was not inclined to join the rest of the ladies.

On the journey home, she took her mother to task. "Mama, I really do believe you went too far tonight; all that talk about Teresa being a flower farmer's daughter and her wedding arrangements—I think you were being very unfair," she said in a quiet but determined voice.

"Unfair?" Rose was outraged. "Whatever do you mean, Miranda? I said nothing that was untrue; I am sure she has no objection to being known as a flower farmer's daughter; it is what her family does. They certainly do not conceal it, and I am quite prepared to wager that she is very proud of it."

"She may well be; they are her family, but I am not," said Robert, interrupting his wife, "and I would ask, Rose, that you try to remember that Jude Courtney is my nephew before you ridicule his wife at the next dinner party we attend. I cannot comprehend it; can you think of nothing more useful than sniping at them? It does us no good at all; everyone will assume that your remarks are prompted by envy, because Jude has inherited Oakleigh."

Rose was unaccustomed to being reprimanded by her husband and was clearly put out by his reproof. She snapped back quickly, "Ah well, perhaps we should have let Miranda marry him; that would have pleased you, I am sure, because that way you would have finally got your hands on Oakleigh Manor. You have been obsessed with it for years."

This time Robert was furious. "Don't be ridiculous, Rose," he said angrily, "it is you who are obsessed with it. You have never ceased to complain about my mother's will and now you have taken to abusing my late sister Emily and her son and daughter-in-law. I have said nothing to denigrate them, even though I will confess I have been hurt by the fact that I was not considered by either Mama or Emily. Yet you have been unceasing in your disparaging comments addressed to anyone and everyone we meet. I am mortified by your conduct and must ask you to cease this futile campaign."

Even Miranda looked shocked; she had hardly ever heard her father speak to her mother in such censorious terms. But it seemed that this time, Robert was not to be gainsaid. When Rose attempted to make light of it, claiming that it was only a joke, he would have none of it.

"Perhaps that was your intention, but as I am sure you would have noticed, the effect of your words was quite the opposite. Even the Bilsons, who are not the most cultivated of people, were embarrassed by your remarks, and I suppose you were not aware that the mayor's wife is herself of Italian descent. We have no knowledge what trade or industry her family was engaged in, and your insensitive remarks may well have offended a very important personage in this town. I know that he never spoke a single word to me after the ladies had left the room."

Following that revelation, nobody spoke a single word during the rest of the journey, and when they reached the house, they went their separate ways to their rooms. For the first time in her life, young Miranda Gardiner felt some modicum of admiration for her father. She had long felt heartily ashamed of her mother's unworthy behaviour, but with little hope of seeing her suitably put down. Despite the inevitable discomposure she had felt at witnessing the conflict between her parents, her feelings were of relief.

At breakfast on the morrow, Miranda found herself alone. Her father had already eaten and left the house, and Mrs Gardiner had elected to take hers in her private sitting room. Her maid had been seen taking a tray upstairs, and Miranda, who was familiar with her mother's methods of domestic warfare, decided to ignore her family and please herself. It was a fine morning, with a light breeze blowing across the vale, and Miranda could think of nothing better to do than take her horse out for a ride. Since there was no one of whom to ask permission, she went down to the stables and asked for her horse to be saddled up, while she went upstairs to change into riding clothes.

Chapter Seven

WHEN ROBERT GARDINER LEFT the house that morning, his mind was in a state of confusion. He was certain only of one thing: After the mortification he had endured on the previous evening, he needed to get away from the house, from Rose and his in-laws, and he needed to think.

He had never been much of a thinker. Unlike his brother and sisters, Robert had never spent much time in contemplating either the purpose or the value of any of his actions; rather, he had been frequently faced with situations in which the consequences of something he had done had caught up with him, and in the ensuing days and weeks, he had needed the assistance of his family or friends to deal with them.

Since the death of his mother, he had found himself isolated; unable to turn to any of his siblings for advice, he had left most of the significant decisions affecting their family to his wife and his father-in-law. Quite obviously, this strategy had failed and he needed to find another. It was a realisation that he was loathe to admit to anyone, particularly not to his elder brother Richard, whose reputation and standing in the community made it impossible for Robert to approach him without suffering the most extreme embarrassment. His sister Caroline on the other hand was, he thought, likely to be less judgmental.

When Caroline Fitzwilliam saw her brother alighting from his horse and approaching the house, she was at once amazed and afraid—amazed that he had come, for it had been many months since Robert had visited them, and afraid that this visit must therefore mean bad news! Could something have happened to Rose or, God forbid, Miranda? Caroline was filled with trepidation as she went out to greet him.

For his part, Robert could not help but recall his visit to his sister Emily over twenty years ago, when he had first thought himself irrevocably in love with Rose Fitzwilliam. He had been afraid that his humbler origins, being the younger son of a man who had made his fortune through trade, with no pretensions to a professional qualification, unlike his brother Richard, would cause either Rose or her parents to reject his suit.

When he had admitted as much to Emily, she had scoffed at his fears and given him the encouragement he needed to proceed with his proposal. Then Rose had accepted him, and Robert's reaction had been more one of relief than romantic euphoria, like a man waking from a nightmare.

Now, with Emily gone and his marriage in what could only be termed a parlous state, Robert could not fail to see the irony of his present visit to Caroline. He had come to ask for her advice, and the reason for his concern was the very opposite of what it had been twenty years ago.

Caroline, seeing his grave face as he stood at the front door, feared the worst. Someone was dead. She was aware that Rose's father had been ill but did not believe he could have died so suddenly.

"Robert, my dear brother, you look so dejected. What is it?" Taking his hand, she drew him into the hall, and as they went in to the sitting room, Caroline called to the maid to order some tea. When her brother said nothing, she was surprised, for she had expected some dire announcement. Yet, as he remained silent, she persisted, "Robert, has something happened? Is it Sir James? I had heard from Lizzie that he was ill, but I did not think it was that serious…"

He interrupted her gently, placing a hand upon her arm, "No, no, Caroline, it is not Sir James, and no one is ill—unless it is I, myself."

"You?" She was shocked. "How are you ill? Have you seen a doctor?" she asked, well aware that her younger brother was not renowned for his sense of responsibility.

"No, I have not," he replied, provoking a warning about the foolishness of ignoring the early symptoms of disease.

"Why haven't you, Robert? You should at the very least talk to Richard…"

But this time Robert waited until she had finished and then decided that it would be simpler to start over again. "Caroline, I am not ill, that is, not in any physical sense, and before you think I have lost my mind, let me say it—no, it is not that either. I do not believe I need a doctor, but I do need your help with a problem."

"A problem? Is it money?" she asked, for she knew that in the past, many of Robert's problems had to do with money or the lack of it.

But he shook his head vigorously and said, "No, it is not money. If only it were, it would be much easier to resolve."

"What then?" His sister looked quite bewildered.

Robert appeared tongue-tied, and as the maid brought in tea and cake, Caroline thought he looked like the confused young brother they had had to rescue from a variety of scrapes and wondered what could possibly have happened to make him look so miserable. Waiting until the maid had left the room, haltingly at first and then in a torrent of sometimes incoherent words, Robert told her everything. By the time he had finished, so bleak was his tale, Caroline was unsure whether she should be relieved that his affliction was not a disease or should wish with all her heart that it was.

"At least with a disease, one can offer some comfort, there may have been some hope of a cure," she said when relating the circumstances of her brother's visit to her husband that night. "Oh Fitzy, it is a terrible tale. The way he tells it, he has had very little contentment and scarcely any happiness in his marriage over many years. It would seem that Rose takes notice of no one but her father, and even Miranda appears to have little affection for either of her parents. Poor Robert, I know he is not the most sensible of men, and he is as much to blame for his predicament as anyone, for there is no doubt that he has been weak and indecisive, but even he does not deserve this."

Colonel Fitzwilliam was sympathetic but cautious about becoming involved in the coils of his brother-in-law's tortuous problems. He had never been comfortable with the arrangements of Robert's life with his in-laws, and being at a time of life when ease and comfort meant everything to him, Fitzwilliam had no inclination to confront them. He spoke with a degree of caution, hoping to warn his wife of the possible pitfalls of the situation.

"I have been aware that Robert was not as happy in his marriage as one might have wished him to be, but I did not know that things had reached such a pass as this. He has not helped his cause by his past behaviour towards Mrs Gardiner and Emily. I know that neither Darcy nor Lizzie would wish to be involved in helping him. He has lost their respect a long time ago," he said.

"But he is my brother, Fitzy. I can hardly turn him away when he comes to me for advice," Caroline protested.

Fitzwilliam nodded; he knew well that, with her generous heart, Caroline could not refuse any appeal for help. "What advice did you give him, my dear?" he asked, genuinely interested to know how she might have counselled her brother. Her answer surprised him.

"I did not know what to say. His circumstances were so dismal and his mood so despondent, I could not think of anything worthwhile which might bring some prospect of improvement to his situation. Oh Fitzy, I felt so helpless; never having suffered such misery myself, I had no suggestion to make that might have given him hope. All I could do was to offer words of comfort, yet he needed something more. If only Emily were here, she would have known what to say. He told me how he had gone to her when things had first started to go wrong and she had advised him to take Rose away, perhaps to London, where they would have a better chance of a life together away from the influence of her parents."

"Sage counsel indeed, but I doubt if Robert followed her advice," her husband responded, and Caroline had to agree.

"Indeed it was, but of course, Rose would not hear of it, and Robert, being unwilling to argue, had never mentioned it again. He understands now that it was his initial lack of will that has made things much worse than they need have been, but I fear it may be too late."

Fitzwilliam was thoughtful. "Did he tell you what particular circumstance led to this present rift? Why, when he has not spoken of this matter in all these years, has he done so today? Something must have happened to cause him to come to you?"

Caroline was circumspect in her answer. "There was something that drove him to come; it has to do with Rose, but I do believe it concerns someone else as well. He would not say it outright, but there is another person involved, I am sure of it, and I think it may be a man."

Her husband seemed quite shocked. "Caroline, you do not mean to say that Rose is engaged in some clandestine affair?"

"Oh no, if that were the case, I believe Robert would have told me. Rose is pretentious and vain, but I do not believe she would be so stupid as to risk her reputation by becoming involved in an affair. But I am convinced that the present problem concerns someone who has influence over her."

"And did he not say anything to you to suggest who this person might be?"

"No, he did not, but there were hints of it in everything he said. Oh Fitzy, if only there was some way to discover the root of this trouble, something might be done to remedy it."

Caroline was desperate to help her brother, even though she had little respect for him. As the eldest in her family, she had always taken her responsibilities towards her siblings seriously, but while she had known the agony of loss through the untimely death of her son Edward and had helped her sister Emily cope with the death of two husbands, Caroline had little experience of the trauma of marital misery. A long and happy marriage to a man who loved her deeply, whose word she had never doubted, ill-qualified her to assist her unhappy brother.

While her experience in practical matters and sound common sense would certainly have enabled her to advise him on restoring the health of an ailing enterprise, she had little to offer him on the much more painful business of repairing a shattered marriage.

Bidding goodbye to his sister, still in a deeply dejected state, Robert had ridden to the inn at Matlock and taken some alcoholic refreshment before returning home, leaving the main road for a route that traversed the woods. As he emerged from the trees and approached the outskirts of the village, he was pleasantly surprised to see his daughter Miranda ride out of the copse and into the lane ahead of him. Even at that distance, he recognised her riding dress and hat. Calling out to her, he urged his horse forward, and as he caught up with her, she turned and, seeing him, smiled.

When he had last seen his daughter the night before, her mood of anger and shame had been so deeply etched upon her face that Robert could scarcely recognise the young girl who smiled at him now. There was no trace of the discomposure she had felt so keenly at the Bilsons' dinner party and afterwards; indeed it might almost be said that she looked quite pleased with herself.

So deeply sunk was Robert in his own melancholy that apart from being relieved to see Miranda in such good spirits, he made no attempt to discover what had wrought the change in her.

They rode home together in a companionable silence and found on their arrival at the house that Rose had already left to attend a meeting of her "ladies' group," for which relief both father and daughter appeared very grateful. While Miranda had her own reasons for defying her parents, she was also acutely aware of the humiliation that her father often suffered at the hands of her mother and grandparents, and it had made her very angry.

It was late evening when Robert, hearing the sounds of a carriage coming up the drive, looked out of the window of his bedroom, where he had spent most of the afternoon, and saw his wife alighting at the front entrance.

As the carriage moved away, he saw also a man dismount and hand the reins of his horse to a groom before following her indoors. While he could not be sure in the fading light, Robert felt certain he knew him and went downstairs to ascertain who the visitor might be.

On entering the saloon, he was not altogether surprised to discover that it was Wilson Croker. With a glass of sherry in his hand, he stood up and bowed. Rose greeted her husband as if everything was as it should be and informed him that she had met Mr Croker in the village as she was leaving the meeting of her ladies' group and he had insisted upon escorting her home.

"Even though I assured him I would be perfectly safe," she said, and Mr Croker then muttered something about being uneasy with the idea of ladies travelling alone at this hour.

Robert's mild surprise increased when Croker informed him that he was intending to call on Mr and Mrs Courtney at Oakleigh Manor on the morrow.

"Mrs Gardiner has very kindly offered to introduce me, which will be a considerable advantage, and I appreciate it very much indeed," he said, causing Robert to look askance at his wife, who immediately excused herself and went upstairs, leaving the two men sitting awkwardly alone.

Robert had no wish to bring up the extraordinary matter of his wife's offer to introduce Mr Croker to Jude Courtney and his wife, who were after all his relations. He thought there had to be some explanation, but, as usual, was unwilling to risk embarrassment or conflict by asking outright what might be disconcerting questions.

He offered Croker another drink, took one himself, and relapsed into an uncomfortable silence until Miranda came downstairs, dressed for dinner. On seeing Mr Croker with her father, she seemed somewhat shaken.

Croker, apparently unperturbed, rose, bowed, kissed her hand, and asked the usual meaningless questions to which Miranda gave some equally inconsequential answers, which puzzled Robert exceedingly. He did not know they knew one another so well. He could not help feeling that there were things happening around him over which he had no control at all. By the time Rose returned, having changed for dinner, Mr Croker was ready to leave, but it took very little persuasion from her to change his mind.

Robert, who had had a long and arduous day, was more than a little irritated at the prospect of having to endure the company of Croker for a few more hours. But neither his wife nor strangely his daughter appeared at all concerned, and Croker proceeded to entertain them with unlikely stories of his sojourn in the United States, where he had lived as a boy, and in Europe, whither he claimed he fled each year to escape the dreadful English Winter.

Robert, who had at first found much to admire in Croker, who in looks and demeanour was all that he was not, was beginning to feel increasingly aggravated by his manner, which he found to be disdainful and high-handed. This was not improved by the way in which both Rose and Miranda seemed to hang upon his every word. The more he heard of the improbable adventures of Wilson Croker, the less he liked him, and when after dinner they moved to the drawing room, Robert, claiming to have developed a headache, retired to his room, leaving the ladies to be further diverted by their guest. Judging by their laughter and the lateness of the hour when they finally came upstairs, Mr Croker had had no difficulty entertaining them.

Before he fell asleep that night, Robert had decided that he would speak with his wife and ask her about her offer to introduce Mr Croker to Jude Courtney and his wife. He would ask for an explanation. What was Croker intending to talk to them about? Did he intend to make them an offer for a part of their property? These were questions to which he needed answers, and he told himself that he was determined to get them.

Unhappily, however, when he went down to breakfast on the morrow, he found himself alone. Mrs Gardiner, the servants told him, had risen very early, breakfasted, and taken the carriage to drive into town. Miss Gardiner had foregone breakfast and ridden out, accompanied by one of the grooms. There being nothing very unusual in any of this—both his wife and his daughter frequently went out without him—Robert shrugged his shoulders and sat down to his meal. When Rose returned around midday, Robert was waiting for her. He was keen to discover what had transpired, but she had very little information for him.

"All I did was to introduce Mr Croker to Jude Courtney and his wife. They seemed happy enough to meet him, though I must say I thought they could have offered him something more than tea! They went out to look at the property, and when they sat down to talk business, I left," she said with a degree of nonchalance that shocked him.

"What business were they going to talk about? Did they say anything about selling any of the land?" Robert asked.

Rose appeared neither informed nor interested. "I couldn't say; I didn't ask. I have no interest in their business or their land. If Mr Croker makes them an offer and they decide to sell a part of their property, surely that is their choice. It is well known that Jude would like to have more cash to improve the farm; perhaps Mr Croker may offer to lend them some money, and they may negotiate a loan," she suggested, in a voice that made it clear she did not care what arrangements they agreed to.

Robert was by now deeply disturbed. He knew well that his nephew, Jude, would not be a match for the cunning Croker, whose life's work consisted of buying and selling at a profit with little regard for the consequences to others. They had heard his tales of deals done, loans given, and foreclosures made, all of which appeared to advantage Croker at the expense of someone else with less wit, money, and influence to pit against him.

Robert could not help feeling deeply suspicious, not only of Croker's intentions but also of his own wife's motives in this matter. Rose had never made any secret of the fact that she had no respect for Jude Courtney and had been seriously affronted by his marriage to Teresa Mancini. While expressing relief at having successfully thwarted a possible misalliance between Jude and Miranda, she had ridiculed mercilessly his subsequent choice of an Italian flower farmer's daughter to be his wife. Her involvement in this matter could not be a benign one, he thought. Robert needed to know what was afoot and tried again.

"Did Croker not say anything to you about the sort of proposition he might put to them?" he asked, adding, "Neither of them are very experienced in matters of business. I should feel responsible if they were to be gulled into anything against their interests."

This time, she laughed before saying, "This concern of yours is new, Robert. I recall you were quite ready to advise them to sell a portion of their land to Mr Croker, when the matter was first talked of. You had no reservations then; what has brought this on? Could it be you were hoping to obtain some form of benefit for yourself, a commission, perhaps?"

Robert was outraged as he denied having any such motive. "Certainly not. I was aware that Jude did need money to develop the farm—he told me so himself; my suggestion that Croker may wish to look at their property and make them an offer for some part of the land that lies unused, outside the home farm, was made in the hope that it might suit both parties. Croker seemed genuinely interested, and I thought there was no harm in it. Jude could always refuse to sell. I had no thought of making any money from the deal if it went through. In any event, I did not believe that Croker had made up his mind about the land; when he spoke of it at the Bilsons' dinner party, he seemed undecided."

Rose had a supercilious little smile on her lips as she answered, "Well, he seems to have made his mind up very smartly since then, because he told me last afternoon that he was exceedingly keen to close a deal if possible. He was concerned only that he had not been able to meet the owners socially before making a business proposition. Which is why I offered to introduce him to them. I must confess he was excessively grateful."

Robert's unease increased as she spoke. "My dear, I do hope you will not be held responsible should they be imposed upon in any way. After all, we have only met Croker recently and know very little about him except what he has told us. I should be very cautious about introducing such a person to friends or relations who have not a great deal of knowledge or experience in business matters."

Rose was quite indignant. "You are not suggesting, I hope, Robert, that Mr Croker is a person of questionable character? After all, it was you who introduced him to my father as a successful businessman." There was no doubting her tone, and Robert knew that if anything at all were to go wrong, then *he* would carry the blame.

"Of course not, but your father is himself an experienced businessman. I wish you had alerted me to this before you took him to meet Jude Courtney and his wife. They are both quite young and unaccustomed to dealing with men like Croker. I cannot help feeling responsible."

Rose was clearly irritated. "Oh, do stop fussing, Robert. I do believe you take far too much upon yourself. Jude and Teresa must surely be able to understand if a proposition is in their own interest. Even if *he* isn't very bright, *she* looks shrewd enough to be able to tell if a deal is sound," she said and, rising from her chair, swept out of the room. It was her way of declaring a subject closed.

Robert spent some hours alone, unable to quiet his troubled conscience. No matter how he regarded it, the haste with which Croker had appeared to decide on the business of Oakleigh Manor made him very uneasy indeed. He did not strike one as the kind of man who would enter into a deal in haste. Not unless he was certain that he was going to make a considerable profit, and that was causing Robert some concern.

Late that afternoon, he left the house and went directly to find Croker, hoping to persuade him to reveal what sort of proposition he had made to the Courtneys and how they had responded to it. He knew the man had rooms at a hotel in Derby, but was also known to stay, when he was in the district, at the Matlock Arms. It was raining when he reached the inn, but on enquiring, Robert discovered that Croker had not been in at all that day.

Disappointed, he was about to proceed to Derby, when he saw Darcy Gardiner crossing the street to take shelter from the rain and, on an impulse, called out to him. Unlike his elder brother, Edward, whose wife Angela was a confidante of Rose Gardiner, Darcy had had very little contact with his uncle's family. Because of his special concern for his aunt, Emily, and her son, Jude, and his intimate knowledge of their financial affairs, Darcy had long held Robert and his wife in very low esteem, chiefly on account of what he had deemed to be their greed. Their apparent impatience to get their hands on Oakleigh Manor even before Emily Courtney's death and the undignified show of annoyance at the reading of her will had all worked against them in Darcy's eyes. Which is probably why he appeared surprised and not entirely pleased to be hailed by his uncle, who was standing in the rain outside the Matlock Arms.

However, his natural politeness overcame his aversion and he joined him inside. They sat down to a drink, and Darcy could not help but notice that his uncle appeared so discomposed he could scarcely sit still.

It took Robert quite some time to bring up the matter of Oakleigh and Mr Croker. Having been told there was important information which Robert wished most urgently to impart to him, Darcy sat waiting impatiently for his uncle to begin.

Robert fidgeted and sipped his drink and looked nervously around as though he expected someone to walk in and accost him. Darcy began to wonder if his uncle was not quite right in the head, when Robert finally spoke in a hushed voice.

"Darcy," he said awkwardly, "I know we haven't always agreed on everything; indeed, I understand why your parents and the Darcys have behaved rather coldly towards me, and I do not blame you for this. There have been things said and done of which I am not very proud. But this is no time to be trawling over past mistakes. Something has come to my notice that must be stopped, and I need your help to stop it."

Darcy was so bewildered he could not believe he was hearing right. He looked closely at his uncle, wondering if he had perhaps been drinking, but there was no sign of it, and the intensity of his voice suggested that he meant what he said, even if Darcy could not make much sense of it.

"Sir, I am at a loss to understand you, I have not the slightest knowledge of what you speak. What is it you wish to stop and how can I help?" he asked.

Robert's reply was even less comprehensible. "It is a matter of the greatest concern, at least it will be quite disastrous, if it cannot be stopped. Let me put it another way: Your cousin Jude Courtney is at risk of making a very serious error of judgment, and unless we can stop him, he will be ruined and quite likely Oakleigh Manor will be lost to the family forever."

The reference to Oakleigh Manor immediately alerted Darcy, arousing his suspicions. He was convinced it was another ploy: His uncle Robert and his scheming wife were once again attempting by some ruse to get their hands on Oakleigh Manor! So sceptical did he look that Robert realised Darcy did not believe him. Indeed, unless he told him everything, it was very unlikely that his nephew would agree to help him avert the disaster that Robert was certain was about to overtake young Jude Courtney. It wasn't easy, because not only was Robert's credibility uncertain, he was also an extraordinarily inarticulate man, particularly in a crisis. When misfortune loomed, his first instinct had always been to run away, get out of the line of fire, and avoid, as far as possible, any confrontation. It was a philosophy that had never got him out of trouble, yet he had pursued it pertinaciously for most of his life. It had earned him a reputation for weakness and moral cowardice that had saddened his father and almost broken his mother's heart.

And his marriage to Rose Fitzwilliam, whose first and last concern was almost always the promotion of her own advantage, had added a degree of self-ishness to Robert's character that had taken him further away from his family, particularly his mother and sisters. As for Darcy Gardiner, he had grown up despising his uncle.

This time, however, it did seem that the scales had fallen from his eyes, and Robert had determined that he had to face up to the consequences of something he had begun, without considering the inordinate amount of damage it could do to innocent persons like his nephew Jude and his wife. Keen to make a favourable impression upon his business acquaintances and to associate himself with the successful and personable Mr Croker, he had suggested that Jude Courtney might be willing to consider selling some part of his land and had offered to help Croker negotiate with him. That Rose would become involved and pursue the matter had never occurred to him. Now, he was desperate to undo the damage, but had no idea how to go about it.

As Darcy listened, incredulous, he related his story.

"And what makes you think this Mr Croker intends to do more than make Jude an offer for some of his land, an offer which he may well refuse?" Darcy asked.

"I had thought that was all he would do, until this afternoon, when Rose informed me the man was so keen he may offer Jude a substantial loan to develop the home farm," Robert replied.

"A loan? But how would Jude repay him? The farm doesn't make a lot of money; I have seen the accounts," said Darcy.

"Precisely, and that is why I fear for him. Croker may offer him a loan on reasonable terms, but with a mortgage on the farm as surety."

Darcy leapt up. "Good God! That would certainly be the ruin of him," he exclaimed. "My grandfather Mr Darcy persuaded my aunt Emily to put a codicil in her will that no part of the estate could be sold without the consent of at least two members of the family, but even he did not anticipate a situation such as this. Jude may not sell any part of it, but he can be tricked into a mortgage that will cost him everything. I can see now why you say it has to be stopped," he said, and Robert's relief was palpable.

"And will you help me?"

Darcy thought for a moment and nodded. "Yes, but I have to send a message to my wife, else she will worry that I am late. We are due to leave for London tomorrow afternoon."

"Is your carriage here?" asked Robert.

"No, I rode into Matlock," Darcy replied.

Robert had a suggestion. "Well, let us go there first and allay your wife's fears. We can go in my carriage. The landlord will surely let you stable your horse here overnight. One of my men will bring it over to you tomorrow morning." Darcy agreed, and they left soon afterwards.

When Darcy had given his wife a brief explanation of their mission, she was anxious and yet did not doubt that they were right; something had to be done. She was, however, much more hopeful that Jude was unlikely to sign any document without consulting his family.

"He is a naïve and trusting young man, but he is no fool, and furthermore his wife is a good deal more practical than he is. I cannot believe she will let him do it," she said confidently.

Darcy and Robert travelled to Oakleigh Manor through darkness and driving rain. Neither man said very much, but both hoped they were not going to be too late. When they reached the farm, they found not only Jude and Teresa, but Mr Mancini and another man with them enjoying a bottle of wine. To say they were surprised to see their visitors would be an understatement, but they overcame their astonishment and invited Darcy and Robert to join them.

The stranger was introduced as Teresa's uncle Pasquale, recently arrived from Italy. He was a partner in Mr Mancini's enterprise, Jude explained, adding that Signor Pasquale was interested in leasing some of their uncropped land to start an herb farm. This was all very well, but Darcy and Robert were impatient to discover what proposals they had received from Mr Croker that morning.

It was Robert who asked, a little awkwardly, if they had had a visit from a Mr Wilson Croker. Jude and Teresa answered almost together. Yes, they said, he had been there, and indeed, Mrs Rose Gardiner had been with him, too, but she had not stayed long and Mr Croker had left soon afterwards. When the gentlemen seemed not to comprehend, Jude explained, "He wished only to have a look around the property and asked if I would consider selling some of the unused land for development. He admired the prospect from the top of the hill and talked of building houses for families who wished to move to the country. But when we explained that Teresa's grandfather and uncle intended to expand their farming activities on our land and Teresa told him she was planning for us to start a pig farm, he appeared to lose interest in the idea, I think."

Darcy agreed that the prospect of building houses for the newly rich in close proximity to a pig farm might not have seemed as attractive as he had first thought. By this time Robert was beginning to look confused.

"Do you mean to say Croker made no attempt to offer you a loan to help improve the home farm? You did tell me some time ago that you needed some capital to do just that..."

"Ah yes, but that was before Teresa's uncle Pasquale wrote to us and offered to lease some land for an herb farm. We agreed, of course. He will pay us in advance, and we intend to use that money to set up the piggery. That is all we need. Mr Croker made no mention of a loan, and we would not have been interested if he had. So it has worked out rather well."

"So it seems," said Robert, nodding but still looking puzzled. After some convivial conversation and a glass or two of Mr Mancini's wine to toast the success of the herb farm and the prospective piggery, Darcy suggested it was time to leave, reminding Robert that Kate and he were catching the train to London on the morrow.

On the way back, Darcy's mood was considerably lighter than Robert's. He was relieved that there had after all been no real crisis to avert, no need to warn Jude about Croker or prevent him from signing a mortgage. In fact, it had all been a rather vexing waste of time and effort, and he wished with all his heart that he was back at home, out of this appalling weather. But he was sufficiently good-natured not to say so to his uncle Robert, who in view of the circumstances, was looking much less distressed than he might have done, had things turned out differently. Perhaps, thought young Darcy Gardiner, he had misjudged Robert; maybe he was weak and ineffectual, but he did have a conscience after all.

Chapter Eight

THE WEATHER WORSENED THROUGH the night, and Robert, reaching home rather late, found everyone except two footmen had gone to bed. After a cursory attempt at dinner, which consisted of more wine than meat, he went up to his room where he fell into bed and a deep sleep.

Meanwhile, over a late dinner at home, Darcy Gardiner entertained his wife with the extraordinary story of his uncle's attack of guilt and the farcical and wholly unnecessary attempt to save his cousin Jude from the clutches of Mr Croker.

"For a while, he did convince me that there was a risk of Jude being gulled by Croker into accepting a loan, which of course, he could never repay, with all the evil consequences that would follow. My uncle was in a state of desperation like I have never seen before. I believe he felt he would be held responsible if things had gone awry and the property was mortgaged and lost. But we need not have been concerned; Jude is in excellent hands, his sensible wife and her Italian family would never let him take such a foolish step, and besides, he claims they had no need of such a large sum of money anyway. Mr Mancini and Uncle Pasquale have come to the rescue. You should have seen Robert's face when they said that all they wanted was sufficient money to start up a piggery!"

Kate laughed merrily. "Not the most salubrious site for modern mansions to accommodate Croker's wealthy clients, then?"

"No indeed," said her husband. "I could almost see him reeling back from the prospect…"

"And the smell!" added Kate as she enjoyed the likely embarrassment of the handsome man with the stylish hat she had seen in the company of Robert Gardiner not very long ago. "What is most difficult to believe is that your uncle Robert seems to have developed this conscience very late in the piece. There was no sign of it earlier. Did he admit to you that he had had any reservations about Mr Croker?" she asked.

"He did not at any time," Darcy replied. "It would appear his suspicions about the man deepened upon discovering that his wife was showing some interest in the deal. My uncle knows that Mrs Rose Gardiner has no great love for the Courtneys and feared that she may well have egged Croker on; the two are good friends apparently," he offered as he drained his glass.

His wife giggled. "Poor Mr Gardiner, that is not a happy situation, surely?"

"I would not have thought so, but, my love, at least it is not a situation with which we need concern ourselves. Now that Jude and Oakleigh are safe, we can leave for London without any further anxiety on that subject." So saying, her husband indicated that he was for bed.

On the following morning, the debris of the storm lay everywhere, delaying everyone and everything, including the trains. Darcy and Kate were advised that a tree fallen across the tracks farther up the line had to be cleared before their train could leave. While they waited, their luggage all ready and loaded up into their carriage, Darcy remembered that his horse had been left overnight tethered in the stables at the Matlock Arms.

"My uncle Robert did promise to send a man over to collect him for me; he must have forgotten all about it," he said and was about to ask the steward to attend to it, when the horse, ridden by a young man from the Fitzwilliams' stables, came into view, on the river road below them.

He was riding hard and looked quite troubled when he came up to the house and dismounted, handing the horse over to a stable hand. Darcy moved to give him a couple of coins for his trouble, which the lad accepted gratefully, but not before he had apologised for being late.

"I am sorry, sir. I was supposed to have got him early this morning, the master told me last night, but things have happened up at the house, and I could not get away," he began to explain.

Darcy interrupted him, "Oh I understand, the storm has done a lot of damage all across the district... I daresay there was much to be done clearing it away..."

The lad nodded but said in a strained voice, "Yes, sir, there was that, sir, but I meant it was because of Miss Miranda... she has gone missing, sir."

"What? Miranda missing? What do you mean?"

The lad looked as if he doubted whether he should say much, more and Darcy urged him on, "For heaven's sake, Miranda is my cousin; you can tell me."

"Well, sir, I don't know very much more, only that her maid went to her room this morning to take her tea and found her bed had not been slept in. She was nowhere to be found; they told Mr and Mrs Gardiner, and the place has been in uproar since then, sir."

Darcy was speechless, appalled by the prospect that while Robert and he had been off on some fruitless errand on the previous afternoon, Miranda might have been in grave danger, lost, hurt in an accident, kidnapped even.

After the lad had left, Darcy went indoors and, finding Kate waiting in the sitting room, gave her the bad news. Her astonishment was not as great as he might have expected, but she did agree that it was indeed a serious matter. Miranda Gardiner's escapades had not gone unnoticed within the family, and while Kate respected her husband's concern for his young cousin, she was not as anxious as he was for her safety. However, she was too sensible of his feelings to say anything contrary.

"Did you wish to postpone our journey and perhaps offer to help Robert look for her?" she asked gently.

But Darcy wasn't sure. "No, it is very unlikely that my help, if I were to offer it, would be welcome. Robert's wife and her parents are all exceedingly clannish, unwilling to take anyone into their confidence. They may wish to keep this whole business quiet until Miranda is found. If my uncle had thought to ask for my help, I would certainly have gone, but I do not feel I ought to interfere. I should feel awkward... we do not know yet what has happened. It is possible she may have already been found safe and well."

Although Kate felt somewhat uneasy about travelling to London in the circumstances, Darcy did point out that he had important appointments at Westminster and it was best that they continue with their plans.

"I have made promises to Colin Elliott and others, which I must keep. But I should like to call on my parents before we leave and inform them of what has happened," he said, and Kate agreed at once.

When they arrived at Camden House, Darcy's mother came out to greet them. In her hand was a note that had been delivered earlier that morning. It was from Robert to his brother Dr Richard Gardiner, asking that he come immediately, because his father-in-law, Sir James Fitzwilliam, had suffered what seemed like a heart attack. The note had been hastily penned, and there was no mention of Miranda.

"Your father went at once, of course," Cassandra said, and it was clear to them that she knew nothing of Miranda's disappearance. "I cannot think what could have brought this on…"

Darcy put an arm around his mother and, as they moved indoors, told her the news they had heard just a short while ago. Cassy stood still, as if petrified, a hand to her mouth. When she spoke, she sounded strained and shocked.

"Good God, this is dreadful news. Sir James and his wife adore Miranda. I am no longer surprised that he has suffered a heart attack. Poor Robert, how must he feel?"

Darcy and Kate told her all they knew; they could not stay long, not even to take tea, but left promising to write and begged her to send them any news by electric telegraph, which Cassy promised to do every day. As they drove away, Kate turned and saw Cassandra standing at the entrance, shaking her head, still unable to believe what she had heard.

It was raining when they arrived in London, hours later than expected. They took a hansom cab to the house in Portman Square. Darcy had looked forward to this time as the culmination of a long-fought campaign for a Public Education Bill, which Mr Gladstone had promised them at the election. It was to be presented to the Parliament at last. Kate disliked London, especially in the rain. She hated the puddles, the dirty roads, and the smells, and longed to be indoors. She was tired too and, on reaching the house, went directly upstairs to rest and change.

There were two messages for them on the table in the hall. One was from Colin Elliot MP, confirming Darcy's appointment for the following day at Westminster; the other was a note from Becky, informing them that she and Mr Contini were in London staying with his uncle and aunt at Grosvenor Street. They looked forward to meeting Darcy and Kate, she said, promising to call on them very soon.

Darcy took them up to his wife, recalling for her benefit that his own involvement in Mr Gladstone's political campaign had been supported by Becky and her late husband, Mr Tate.

"Anthony Tate was a dedicated campaigner for public education, using every opportunity to promote the cause through his newspapers and journals. Becky was his secret weapon; she was eloquent and charming and very persuasive," he explained. "She must be very proud of their achievement."

"It seems a great pity that Mr Tate did not live to see the bill presented to Parliament," said Kate, and Darcy agreed that it was, but added, "Though if you look at it through Becky's eyes, he did treat her pretty badly after all the years she had spent working for his causes. My grandmother Mrs Darcy told me last Christmas that Mr Tate had been quite unfair to Becky. He did leave her plenty of money in his will, but she must have Jonathan Bingley's approval to use any of it!"

Kate seemed shocked. "Poor Becky, what an uncomfortable situation! Are they good friends?"

"I believe they are. I understand Jonathan and Mr Contini were at school together. That should help," said Darcy, adding, "Which is why I doubt that she has too many regrets about Mr Tate's demise, and of course, they had lived apart for some time before his death."

They were resting before dressing for dinner; Kate was so weary she kept falling asleep, but sat up suddenly when a maid knocked on the door with a message addressed to Darcy. It had been sent by electric telegraph from Derbyshire. Darcy tore it open. It was from his mother, and it was brief.

This is to allay your fears about your cousin Miranda. There has been some good news; she is alive, and we hope she is well. However, there is bad news too. Sir James has not recovered consciousness, and your papa fears he may be past recovery. I shall write express tomorrow if more information comes to hand.

Darcy handed the message to his wife. "It does not tell us very much, but at least it is good to know that Miranda is safe," she remarked.

"Mama says nothing about her being safe, simply that she is alive," Darcy warned, and Kate was aghast.

"Oh no, Darcy," she protested. "You cannot believe that."

"Well, my love, I certainly hope Miranda is safe; we shall have to wait a day or two to find out," he said, "but with that family, I do believe anything is possible. Mrs Darcy says that Miranda has been so thoroughly spoilt, indulged by her grandparents and her parents, that her judgment is quite confounded."

When his wife appeared sceptical, Darcy went further. "This is not generally known, dearest, except to a few members of the family, but Rose Fitzwilliam, when she was very young and beautiful, fell in love with and became engaged to a man—a physician, I believe—who subsequently died while working somewhere in Africa. I am not aware of all the details, but it is said that Rose almost died of shock and sorrow, and for many years lived like a recluse, meeting no one, riding in the woods alone for hours each day. During this time, her parents were so afraid that she would die or even take her own life, they denied her nothing, let her do whatever she pleased. Well, one day, she met my uncle Robert and decided, quite suddenly, that she wanted to marry him. Presumably, they agreed, and of course, he, stunned by the fact that she had accepted him, did exactly the same as her parents had done—indulged her every whim."

"Which was probably the very worst thing for Rose," said Kate.

"Indeed, so with no one to guide her and no one to say nay, she did whatever she pleased. And when young Miranda came along…"

"It was the same all over again?" Kate suggested.

Darcy sighed and said, "You are absolutely right, my love, and the result?"

"Like mother like daughter."

"Precisely. What is worse, they dislike each other intensely and will do anything to get away from one another."

"Oh dear, now I see what you mean about Miranda's judgment. It cannot have been improved in such circumstances."

"Improved? I would say it is practically nonexistent," said Darcy, adding ominously, "As for the consequences of all this, we shall have to wait awhile to discover the truth. I should not be at all surprised to hear that young Miranda has become involved in some silly escapade."

On the day following, Darcy left early for his appointment with Colin Elliott at Westminster. He arrived in an optimistic mood, looking forward to seeing the fulfilment of a long-held hope.

Growing up in and around Pemberley, he had been aware of the need for public education. He knew intimately many of those families who had neither the means nor the influence to have their children taught by good teachers in proper schools. Darcy had played cricket with young men, and his mother and grandmother had in their employ young women, who but for their lack of schooling could have aspired to much better situations.

His grandparents, aunts, and cousins, like Kitty Bennet and Becky Tate, had been involved in setting up and running the small parish schools at Kympton and Pemberley, providing schooling, particularly for girls from the villages within the estate. Yet all these schools depended upon the uncertain benevolence of individual landlords and the dedicated work of women like Kate and Jessica. The government spent little or nothing on public education.

Now, he thought, with the new Public Education Bill, all that was about to change, and Darcy knew that Becky too would be feeling a similar sense of excitement and satisfaction. Becky and her late husband, Anthony Tate, had been assiduous in their pursuit of local councillors and members of Parliament in order to press upon them the importance of their belief that a better educated populace would make better citizens for Britain in a world where knowledge was fast becoming the essential currency in a growing marketplace of ideas and inventions.

On his arrival at Westminster, Colin Elliott greeted him cheerfully enough, but Darcy was surprised that he did not appear as triumphant as he had expected him to be. Perhaps, he thought, being a member of the government of Mr Gladstone, Mr Elliott had become more sanguine as he grew accustomed to the success of their campaign. The truth, however, as Darcy was soon to discover, was somewhat different. Compromise, that vital ingredient of political negotiation, had produced a contentious result.

Returning to Portman Place later that day, he could not hide his bitter disappointment. Kate, sensing immediately that something was wrong, asked, "Darcy? You don't look at all happy. I expected you to come through the door singing. Dearest, what is it? Did you not meet Mr Elliott?"

"Oh, I met Mr Elliott all right," he said, and she was confused.

"Well then? Did you get to see the bill?"

"Oh no, I shan't get to see it until after it is presented to the Parliament, but there is no need, I already know what is in it," he replied.

"And…?"

"And, my love, it is nothing like the Public Education Bill we campaigned for and were promised by Mr Gladstone. It does not provide for free public education funded by the government at all. Instead it is a collection of ideas drawn from several sources—principally from the National Education Union, which demands that more public money be given to the church schools, so they can continue to provide instruction as they do now with little or no direction. It will do very little to improve the chances of the poor. It is so disappointing, Kate, I cannot believe that we have been so badly betrayed."

Kate tried to comfort him. "It cannot be that bad, Darcy, surely?"

"It can and it is. Wait until Becky hears about this; she will be very angry."

Mention of Becky reminded Kate, "Becky and Mr Contini called while you were out. I have asked them to join us for dinner this evening. I had hoped there would be something to celebrate. I am sorry the political news is not so good, but in truth, there is some other news that might perhaps please you a little more."

Darcy looked interested. "Has there been more news from Mama about Miranda?" he asked.

Kate shook her head. "No, but I have some news for you," she said, and as he listened, his face lighting up with joy, she told him she was going to have a child.

She had not imagined that he could change so completely in a matter of seconds and was astonished as he gathered her into his arms in a warm embrace and held her close.

"Dearest Kate, are you sure?" he asked.

"Yes, I am now. I had confided in your mother, and she advised that I see Doctor Tilney when in London. Well, he called today and has confirmed it," she said, and it was quite apparent that Darcy's disappointment with the Public Education Bill would soon be eclipsed by the intensity of their shared delight in this good news.

When Mr and Mrs Contini arrived for dinner that evening, Darcy gave them the disagreeable news first, allowing Becky sufficient time to express her aggravation and disappointment, even a sense of betrayal, before Kate drew her aside and gave her the news, which considerably improved Becky's mood.

For all her aspirations, Becky was a realist and had learned to value personal happiness above public achievement. No amount of satisfaction at the gains they had made together in public life would ever make up for the coldness that had destroyed her intimate relationship with Mr Tate after the death of their daughter, Josie. Hearing Kate's happy news, she embraced and congratulated her with genuine warmth and urged her not to let Darcy waste any time on regret and disappointment over the Education Bill.

"He, more than anyone else I know, has worked hard for this cause. He can have the satisfaction of knowing, as I do, that without that effort, there would have been no bill, no money for public education at all, and no chance of any schooling for the children of England's poor. Much has been achieved. Dear Kate, do not let him waste the next few weeks and months on fruitless argument and recriminations. You must draw him into enjoying what is to come for both of you in the future, rather than hankering after some political goal, which lies outside his control."

Kate agreed, but pointed out that from her own knowledge of her husband, she knew he would be deeply disappointed by the Education Bill. "Of course he will—so am I and so will all thinking people be, who supported Mr Gladstone, believing his promise," said Becky, "but, my dear Kate, it is as nothing when compared to the great joy that your child will bring into your lives, and it is upon that you must concentrate his mind."

They went into dinner, and despite the initial disappointment, the excellent food, wine, and good company raised their spirits. Both couples found plenty of matters to discuss and, in doing so, discovered that they were agreed upon many of them. Consequently, they were in a far more buoyant mood when they withdrew to the drawing room. Sweets, tea, and coffee were being served and enjoyed, when the doorbell rang and a servant brought in an express letter for Darcy. It was from his mother. Cassandra had been as good as her word and was writing to apprise them of the most recent news received regarding young Miranda Gardiner. Darcy excused himself and withdrew to read his letter in private. She wrote:

My dearest Darcy and Kate,

Since my last message, circumstances have changed. Let me hasten to assure you, lest you are alarmed at my words, that Miranda Gardiner is, as I told you then, alive and unhurt. There has been no accident, as we had feared. That is the good news and indeed the only good news we have received.

Your father has been at his brother's side all day, helping to discover the truth or otherwise of a variety of rumours and attempting in the midst of all this chaos to do something for Sir James, who sadly has sunk deeper into a coma and is unlikely to survive this night.

While that is bad news, it is not yet the worst, for that was still to come. When your father returned last night, he brought us the news that had arrived at the Fitzwilliams' place a couple of hours earlier. I am writing at once with the hope that this letter will reach you by nightfall tomorrow.

I am so shocked I can scarcely believe it as I write, but Miranda Gardiner has eloped with Mr Wilson Croker. They are gone to Scotland, and if Miranda's letter to her parents is to be believed, they are to be married on the morrow.

Your father says he felt only a sense of relief. He was more shocked by the unfeeling arrogance of Miranda's letter than by her actions. However, he says, Robert and, even more particularly, Rose are in utter turmoil. Robert's wish was apparently to send someone after them, but to what end? Your father had advised against it. Rose had been in hysterics, and her mother, Lady Fitzwilliam, had followed suit. Richard says they have both withdrawn to their rooms to bemoan the marriage, for which they blame poor Robert, who introduced Mr Croker to the family! They hold him responsible and claim that if Robert had not befriended Mr Croker, nothing would have occurred. Richard believes differently.

There is, at this stage, not a great deal more to tell, so I shall close and despatch this letter by express. Should anything further occur, I shall write again.

Cassy concluded with her love and did not forget to ask particularly after Kate's health, without specifically mentioning the reason for her enquiry. With the knowledge he had now, Darcy understood the purpose of her question.

Returning to the drawing room, Darcy handed Kate the letter and said, "I think while you read it, Kate, I will inform Becky and Mr Contini of the substance of Mama's letter and the circumstances in which it has been written. It is unlikely that anything can be done to reverse the events that have occurred, so there is no point in trying to conceal them. Besides, I am quite sure Becky will find the information quite interesting, in the light of certain events that have taken place previously."

Both Becky and her husband looked understandably puzzled, but as Kate moved to sit beside the light in order to make out the writing better, Darcy related some of what had taken place over the last few days in Derbyshire. There was no doubting his sense of shock as he told the tale, not by condemning any of the participants, but without attempting in any way to conceal the responsibility of each one of them.

When Kate, having read the letter, rejoined the company, she looked a little pale as she handed the letter to Becky so she might read it herself. There was no doubt Kate was appalled at what had happened.

"I cannot believe that Miranda, who is not by any means an unintelligent girl, could have become involved in such an escapade. She cannot have had a very long acquaintance with this man, yet she has taken such a step; surely, she must know that whatever the final outcome of this, she must live with the consequences for the rest of her life," she said gravely.

Becky, having perused Cassandra's letter quickly, handed it back to Darcy. "Indeed she must, and so must her mother, her father, and her grandparents, who have indulged her all her life. There is yet another consequence that will follow from this. Just think, whatever good or bad comes of this for young Miranda, neither Rose Gardiner nor her parents will ever be able to speak disparagingly of any other family in the county, nor will they be able to use their position and influence to belittle other people's children, as they have done before, and that is not such a bad result. Do you not agree?" she said quietly. They did agree; indeed, as Darcy pointed out, it was a statement with which it was quite impossible to disagree.

Chapter Nine

ON THE DAY FOLLOWING, Darcy Gardiner, using the information on the card William Courtney had given him when they had met at Pemberley, went round to call on his distinguished cousin. The apartment, in a fashionable part of the city renowned for accommodating celebrated artists and musicians, was not difficult to find, and on being admitted, Darcy was shown into a sunny morning room, where stood a very grand pianoforte. Beside a window was a table, set for breakfast at one end and laden with printed scores and handwritten sheets of music at the other. Clearly, it was the room where William worked, thought Darcy, as he waited for him.

When the door opened and William walked in, Darcy was surprised at how much brighter and more youthful he appeared than when they had last met, but surmised that it must have been because it was not long after Mrs Courtney's funeral. Darcy's mother had remarked at how sombre, almost melancholy, William had seemed at the reading of the will, in anticipation, she thought, of criticism from the rest of the family.

Yet today he appeared most genial as he greeted Darcy and asked after the health of his wife and his parents. Having offered him coffee or tea, according to his preference, William explained that having already received Darcy's letter, he had made arrangements to obtain for them tickets to a concert on the Saturday following.

"I do hope you will enjoy the programme. It is mostly French and German music, but there are a couple of English compositions, too, which I try to include to keep our patriotic audiences happy," he said, as he handed Darcy the tickets, adding, "They are quite good seats, I am told."

Darcy was exceedingly grateful; he had not expected William to go to the trouble of getting the tickets and asked if he could pay for them, but his cousin waved away his offer.

"Certainly not, Darcy, the pleasure is mine; it isn't often that members of my family travel to London to attend one of my concerts. Oh, I know you are also here on parliamentary business, but I shall be delighted to have you and Mrs Gardiner in the audience on Saturday. I hope your wife will like the music I have chosen and the performances, of course."

"Of course," said Darcy quickly, explaining that he was very sure Kate would, being an accomplished pianist herself and knowing a great deal more about music than he did. "And I shall have to rely on her excellent taste and knowledge to guide me through the programme," he added.

William laughed and reassured his cousin that the Saturday afternoon concert was a popular event and the programme was not meant to overawe the audience. "Indeed, it is meant particularly to please and entertain," he said, and Darcy was comprehensively charmed; he could scarcely believe this was the same man his family disapproved of so thoroughly. On his return to Portman Square, he found a note waiting for him from Colin Elliott, inviting him to attend the sittings of Parliament during the presentation of the Education Bill. He wrote:

> I have had a seat reserved for you, and if Mrs Gardiner also wishes to attend, I could arrange for Anne-Marie to take her into the Ladies' Gallery. I expect Mrs Contini may be there also. Darcy, I wish to place on record my own and the government's appreciation of the exceedingly valuable work you have done to further this great cause over several years.

Darcy, though pleased to be so highly commended, was not entirely mollified and did not send an immediate response, wishing to consult his wife before doing so. He could not help a feeling of resentment, not against Colin Elliott, whom he generally held in high esteem, but at the cavalier fashion in which the government of Mr Gladstone had reneged on one of its most significant promises. Darcy Gardiner, who had grown up under the tutelage of his distinguished grandfather, Fitzwilliam Darcy, had been taught to value integrity and the worth of a gentleman's word. He found it difficult to accept that politicians, who aspired to the highest public office in the land, could so easily slide out of promises given to the people.

Consequently, he did not wish to attend the Parliament, but neither did he want to offend Mr Elliott and Anne-Marie by turning down the invitation. His father, Doctor Richard Gardiner, had instilled in him the importance of not causing offence to men of influence.

"They often control the purse strings of government and business organisations that we may need to use in order to help the poor. If you offend them, they are more likely to remember you, and when you seek their help for some worthwhile project, they will turn you down. There is no sense in it, is there?" he had said, and Darcy understood exactly what he meant. Doctor Gardiner had had many unhappy encounters with local councillors himself.

When Kate returned from the shops, Darcy showed her Colin Elliott's note, and her response, because it solved all his problems, absolutely delighted him. Handing back the note, she said, "Oh dear, how very unfortunate; it is the very same day on which Becky and Mr Contini are going down to Richmond, and we have been invited to join them. We are all asked to dine with Signor and Signora Contini at their villa above the river. The Continis, Becky informs me, have long been patrons of the arts, and can you guess who is to be the chief guest on the evening?"

Darcy could not think who it could be, he said. Kate's eyes danced as she prolonged the moment and then said, "It's the distinguished conductor William Courtney, who is just finishing a series of concerts in London and leaves for Vienna at the end of the month. Now, what do you say to that?"

Darcy was amazed. It was such a happy coincidence. "And have you accepted for both of us?" he asked eagerly.

"Indeed I have. I knew we had no other engagements on that day, and I was sure you would not wish to miss the opportunity."

Darcy put his arms around his wife. "My dearest Kate, you have saved me from a most uncomfortable situation," he said and explained his own reluctance to attend the Parliament on the day.

"I should hate to have to refuse Mr Elliott's invitation for fear of offending him, but this way, if we have a prior engagement…"

"And such an engagement as this?" she added.

"Indeed, there can surely be no offence taken?"

"None at all, I can guarantee it," she concluded, and they embraced with relief.

Darcy then proceeded to give her his good news concerning the tickets for Saturday's concert, which only increased her pleasure.

"I can hardly wait to write to my mother," said Darcy. "William has been *persona non grata* for years; most members of the family have scarcely seen him except at the occasional wedding or funeral, and here we are, meeting him, attending his concert after which he has invited us to call on him in his dressing room. Then, a few days later, we shall be dining with him at the Continis'. I cannot believe it is happening, and, Kate, this morning, I was afraid he might be annoyed at my calling so early, but he was utterly amiable and welcoming. I believe if I had stayed any longer, he would have insisted that I had breakfast with him!"

Kate could see that her husband, himself an engaging and sociable young man, with the desire to see the best in every person, was seriously at odds with many members of his own family who had accused William Courtney of self-indulgence and inordinate ambition, which had interfered with his duty to his parents. Darcy, while he was aware of William's apparent indifference to their plight, was yet to be convinced that his cousin was guilty of deliberate callousness.

"Darcy, do you suppose William is unaware of the animosity his conduct has caused, or is he indifferent to it?" Kate asked.

Darcy's reply was unambiguous. "I cannot believe that he does not care. He does not strike me as a cold, arrogant, or unfeeling sort of person. There must have been some reason, apart from his desire to pursue his musical ambition, that caused him to act as he has done."

"But what could it be? Do you suppose we will ever know?" Kate asked.

"Only if he chose to reveal it to us; for my part, I no longer believe it is my business to discover the reason for his conduct, especially since my aunt Emily Courtney's death. I wonder what Becky thinks," he said.

Kate shrugged her shoulders. "Becky was so close to your aunt Emily, she cannot forgive William and Elizabeth for their neglect of her. I fear she believes they are both selfish and cold-hearted," she said sadly.

Darcy could not agree. "I must confess, I know nothing of Elizabeth Harwood and her husband, except they are not generally liked by my grand-mother or my mother. My grandfather is suspicious of Mr Harwood's business dealings, and there is some reason to believe that they are both rather selfish and, at the very least, insensitive. But William, I think, is quite different. I would not wish to make such a judgment about him until I knew more about his circumstances and was better acquainted with him."

This time Kate, determined to lighten the mood, quipped, "Well, perhaps you will have an opportunity to do just that when we meet at the Continis next week. There is no better occasion than a good dinner party to bring people together."

The concert on Saturday afternoon was a triumph. The great hall was packed to capacity; Darcy and Kate felt truly privileged to have such excellent seats with a clear view of the stage. Nor were they too close for comfort. Kate told a hilarious tale of sitting in the front row of the bandstand in a park in Dublin when they were children, and the conductor's baton flew out of his hand into her lap.

They were delighted to find that the programme listed a couple of their favourite compositions, including a beloved Mozart serenade, some operatic arias, and a few popular English compositions by Handel and Boyce. They could look forward with confidence to enjoying this performance.

William Courtney, when he appeared, received such an ovation that it left Darcy confounded that few members of the family, except Georgiana Grantley and her husband, had attended his concerts with any regularity. His grandparents disliked travelling to London, and his parents were always so busy, they never seemed to have the time. He wished he could have had them there with him to experience William's work and the prodigious public appreciation he so obviously enjoyed.

They had sat entranced by the music, stunned each time the applause thundered around them, wondering how it was that this man had become so distant from his family that so few of them knew the depth of his talent and the extent of his reputation.

They were almost halfway through the programme when William Courtney addressed the audience. Hitherto he had simply bowed low to acknowledge their applause before leaving the stage, returning later to begin the next item on the programme.

But now, something different was happening on the stage. Some members of the orchestra were moving aside to make a space just a few feet from the conductor's podium, and William introduced the next performer, a young soprano, Fraulein Clara, who, when she appeared, received tumultuous applause and cries of delight from an audience that clearly knew and appreciated her talent. And her talent was considerable. When she sang songs by Schubert and Mozart, no one could have been left in any doubt of her gift. Prolonged applause and cries for more brought two encores, after which she curtseyed deeply and held out her hand to the conductor, who kissed it gallantly, before she departed the stage. Although Darcy and Kate, like many in the audience, hoped she would return and sing again, she did not.

Afterwards, they were cordially received by William in his dressing room, where they assured him of their enjoyment and thanked him sincerely for the privilege, mentioning particularly the singing of Fraulein Clara. He acknowledged their praise with obvious pleasure and commendable modesty. Returning home, they could speak of little else.

On the morning after, Darcy took a note thanking William together with a basket of fruit round to his apartment, but sadly, William was not in, and his servant accepted them and promised most faithfully that his master would have them as soon as he returned.

"It was the very least I could do," said Darcy when, two days later, they were on their way to Richmond with Becky and Mr Contini asked if they had enjoyed the concert. Both Kate and Darcy had enthusiastically agreed that they had rarely heard such music so well performed.

"I must confess I was not very knowledgeable about such matters before I met Kate, but since our marriage, she has educated my taste and sharpened my appreciation of music," Darcy admitted, "and I could find no flaw in any of it."

Kate intervened to say how very wonderful had been the singing of the young soprano, Fraulein Clara. "I can honestly say I have never before heard such a perfect rendition of the Mozart aria from *The Marriage of Figaro*, and her Schubert was divine."

Becky Tate, who had exchanged glances with Mr Contini at the mention of Fraulein Clara's name, smiled. "Yes, I understand she has a remarkable voice, as well as being quite astonishingly pretty," she said.

"She is indeed," said Kate, and keen to know more about the singer, she turned to Becky and asked, "Do you know Fraulein Clara?"

Becky shook her head. "No, I have never met her, nor heard her sing. But my husband's aunt, Signora Contini, is a very great admirer of Fraulein Clara. Of course she is an even greater devotee of William Courtney. She considers him an outstanding musician, as good as any conductor in Europe today," she said.

Darcy agreed with great enthusiasm. "I can well believe it," he said, adding, "I confess I am astonished that our family is not keener to associate itself with someone as talented and distinguished as William Courtney. He has made some mistakes, it is true, but for my part, I think there must be good reason for it. I am proud to be his cousin, and when we return home to Derbyshire, I have every intention of letting my parents and my grandparents know what I think."

Kate did notice that, at this point, both Becky and Mr Contini looked at one another and neither appeared to want to say anything to endorse Darcy's words nor, apparently, were they going to contradict him. The sudden strange silence that ensued seemed to unnerve Kate, who tried to steer the conversation towards a more mundane subject.

She was unfamiliar with these parts of the country, where the reaches of the river Thames had managed, by virtue of the wealth of those persons who lived upon its higher banks, to escape some of the worst depredations of Victorian industry that were choking the life out of it downstream.

In what seemed a genuine desire for information, she asked, "Have these fine houses been here very long, Mr Contini? Some of them appear to have very settled gardens."

Becky's husband answered her, "Quite long, I think, Mrs Gardiner. When I was a little boy and went to boarding school, one of my friends had a house here and I would be invited every year at Michaelmas to spend the holidays with him. I recall it was a most magnificent place, like I had never seen. Then, many years later, I was delighted when my aunt and uncle purchased a much more modest dwelling in the same part of Richmond and I could visit them here. For me, it was like a childhood dream come true!" he said and proceeded to tell her more about it.

Kate was fascinated; having spent most of her life in Ireland, she knew little of the history of southern England and least of all the story of London and its environs. Mr Contini knew a good deal more, having grown up in these parts.

Their companions listened, enjoying his lively narrative until they were almost at their destination.

For all his descriptive skill, Mr Contini's account had not adequately prepared Darcy and Kate for the picture that met their eyes when they alighted from their vehicle. Standing upon a natural eminence and set in a small but exquisitely landscaped park, the Continis' villa was a triumph of simplicity and fine architectural design.

Though quite modest in size, its classical lines combined with discreet inno-vation and skilled craftsmanship to set it apart from some of the more opulent examples they had passed on their journey from London. With its views of the river and its proximity to Richmond Park, it was indeed a most handsome residence.

Becky's husband had alighted and helped the ladies out before the servants appeared to attend to their luggage. Once within, they were immediately impressed by the elegance and good taste of the interiors from the furniture and drapes to the artworks and accessories, many but not all of which were clearly Italian in origin.

Their hostess, Signora Contini, arrived to welcome them, ask after their comfort, and invite them into a reception room with wide-open French windows that gave access to the lawn. She apologised for the absence of her husband, who would join them later, and urged the travellers to partake of an array of delectable pastries and cakes, while the Signora dispensed tea and coffee. Her warm hospitality and open affection for both her nephew, Aldo, and Becky reminded Darcy and Kate of snippets of information they had gathered about the Continis from conversations at Pemberley and Camden House; they had long been close friends of the Darcys.

As they enjoyed the refreshments, Signora Contini informed them that Mr William Courtney and his party were arriving a little later, but were not staying overnight at the villa.

"Sadly, we have not sufficient rooms to accommodate them all, and though I should have been happy to have Mr Courtney to stay, he was not keen to split up his party. So they are to spend the night with a friend at the White Lodge, while you will stay with us," she said, reminding them that the soiree was not a formal one and they need not stand on ceremony.

"There will only be a few other guests, whom I think you will enjoy meeting, so please do not feel you have to be formal at all. We expect to be no more than fourteen at dinner, and once you have been introduced, you may sit as you please, except Mr William Courtney may choose first where he would wish to sit, since he is our honoured guest tonight," she explained.

"Will we have the pleasure of hearing Mr Courtney play?" Kate asked, adding quickly, "I understand he is, in addition to being a distinguished conductor, an excellent performer on the pianoforte, too."

Signora Contini beamed. "Of course, yes, he is a very superior pianist, and I think if we ask him he will not refuse us. But, tonight, I am hoping we have something even better—but I cannot say any more, I must not spoil the surprise… yes?"

Everyone turned to her, but she was very firm and would say no more. They must all wait a few hours more to find out, she said, seeming to promise without saying it that it would be worth the wait. Shortly afterwards, two maids arrived and escorted the guests upstairs to their exceedingly comfortable rooms, while other servants scurried around clearing away the tea and preparing the rooms downstairs for the evening with fragrant flowers in long Venetian glass vases, fine porcelain, crystal, and silver tableware.

Despite their close acquaintance with Pemberley, with whose gracious ambience and elegantly appointed rooms they were quite familiar, Darcy and Kate could not but admire the tasteful luxury of the Continis' villa.

When they came downstairs some hours later, they found the place transformed, with the folding glass doors between the reception hall and the drawing room having been fully opened up to create a splendid space, beneath a glittering chandelier, while in the corner of the room, upon a small, low stage, stood an elegant instrument, an Italian grand piano.

Kate, who could well appreciate its particular beauty, had to suppress a little gasp of pleasure as they were joined by Becky, her husband, Georgiana Grantley. She was a particular favourite of the Continis, who had known and loved her since she was a little girl. Her brother, Mr Darcy, had entrusted her into their care without reservation, and a warm relationship had developed between them, which had greatly enhanced Georgiana's own understanding and appreciation of art and music.

Georgiana was pleased indeed to see Darcy and Kate again, and greeted them warmly. "I did not know you were going to be here. When Signora Contini told me you were already here, I was so very happy I had agreed to come, even though I do feel guilty about leaving Dr Grantley on his own. He has not been well ever since that bout of influenza last Winter. He has not shaken off the cough that came with it, and now he will see no more doctors; he says he is tired of them all and wishes to concentrate upon his paper for the Bishop's conference," she explained.

Both Kate and Darcy understood that it must have been for her a difficult decision; Georgiana's devotion to her distinguished husband was well known. With her was her youngest daughter, Virginia, a rather reserved young woman who had, sadly for her, inherited none of her mother's good looks, save for a fine, healthy complexion.

But she could play the pianoforte, and Signora Contini soon persuaded her to leave her mother's side, sit down to the instrument, and entertain her guests while they waited on the arrival of Mr William Courtney and his party from Richmond Park.

They were a little late arriving, their vehicle having had a problem with a horse throwing a shoe, but when they did enter the room, no one in the company could have been disappointed. Mr William Courtney himself stood out, being very tall with dark hair and most elegantly attired as befits a renowned musician.

All of the ladies, including those who had known him since childhood and others who were meeting him for the first time, declared him to be one of the handsomest men they had ever met. As the evening progressed and some of them came to know him a little better, their admiration would surely increase, for to his good looks they could add his gracious manners and complete lack of pretentiousness.

With him came a party of five, three men and two women of whom four were fairly unremarkable except they were all very well dressed and played various musical instruments; the fifth, a veritable vision of loveliness, beautiful, elegantly gowned and coiffured, was none other than Fraulein Clara. Darcy and Kate looked at one another and then across at Becky and Mr Contini, who did not appear to be at all surprised. Perhaps they had been forewarned by Signora Contini, thought Darcy, who for the first time began to think there was more to this soirée than met the eye.

William and his party were introduced to the rest of the guests, whom he was seen to greet and converse with in an easy manner, remarkable for its lack of affectation. When he came around to Darcy and Kate, he was so openly and sincerely pleased to see them and drew them into his circle so naturally as they went in to dinner that they were quite charmed.

Signora Contini was as good as her word; having taken her place to the left of her husband, she waited until William Courtney was seated to his right and then let her guests sit as they pleased until all the places were taken. As they were almost all couples or at least pairs, they arranged themselves quite comfortably around the large table. Fraulein Clara was seated next to William, while Darcy and Kate found themselves opposite the celebrated couple. It was from this vantage point that they were able to observe during the meal small signs and indications of intimacy that led to the birth of a completely new idea.

When afterwards the ladies withdrew to the drawing room to be joined later by the gentlemen, Signora Contini proceeded to do what all her guests had been waiting for: request Mr Courtney to take his place at the grand piano. He obliged without fuss, delighting his audience with a couple of poetic Chopin nocturnes, and then surprised them when, by way of a *pièce de resistance*, he held out a hand to Fraulein Clara, whom he guided into place beside the instrument before seating himself down to accompany her. When she sang, the company was left in no doubt of her talent, but also of the remarkable affinity between singer and accompanist.

Having sung two songs and charmingly agreed to an encore, the lady stepped down; William rose and kissed her hand, leaving Kate convinced that the couple must be more than a perfect musical match.

Later that night, when the rest of the guests had departed and they had retired to their room, Kate confided in her husband.

"Darcy, I am beginning to think that William and Clara are lovers. You could not fail to notice the closeness and the perfect understanding between them. Do you not agree?" she asked as they got into bed. Darcy, who had been reaching the identical conclusion, though with somewhat less insouciance than his wife, nodded and said, "I do, and I am beginning to believe that it probably has something to do with the fact that William has been less than candid with his family, specifically with his late mother, my aunt Emily."

"Do you think he stayed away because he wished to avoid telling her, fearing her disapproval?" Kate asked.

"I do, and that of Mr and Mrs Darcy, no doubt, and my parents. I cannot believe they would have welcomed an opera singer with open arms, can you? It would seem that Signor and Signora Contini certainly knew all about it, though."

"And Becky," she prompted.

"Indeed, although I would venture to suggest that her knowledge is more recent than theirs. Remember that William has been a close friend of the Continis; they have probably been in his confidence for some time. No, Kate my love, it would seem that we were the only ones who were completely ignorant of the situation until tonight," he said and mumbled as he climbed into bed beside her, "Now, I wonder what Mama would say when she hears about this."

Kate was wide awake. "Do you mean to tell her?" she asked in some astonishment.

"Hmmm... I do, I think I must," he said, rather drowsily, "or she will never understand and she will never forgive William, which would not be fair to either of them."

Kate wasn't sure she knew how this was to be accomplished, but said no more. They had learned a good deal in one evening; they were to learn even more the following day. When Darcy and Kate came down to breakfast on the morrow, they found only Becky and her husband at the table. Clearly, Signor and Signora Contini had decided to take theirs upstairs. It had been quite a late night; some of the guests had seemed loathe to leave until William Courtney and his party had departed.

Trying to make conversation, Kate remarked that Fraulein Clara had been in fine voice last night, with which Aldo Contini agreed enthusiastically.

"She certainly was. I have rarely heard such a sweet tone in such a young soprano. It is quite remarkable."

"And a most excellent choice of songs, too, perfect for her voice and the occasion," Kate added, and Darcy was equally full of praise.

"Indeed, I grow very tired of young ladies who sing endless difficult compositions, meant chiefly to show off the range of their voices rather than entertain their audience."

Becky said casually, her eyes still on her plate, "I would suggest Mr Courtney, with his wide knowledge of concert repertoire, may well have been responsible for that happy choice. I understand that William has had a great influence upon Fraulein Clara's musical development. When they met, she was just an incidental singer in a dance hall; apparently, yet as you can see, she is now a diva!"

"Has William Courtney known Fraulein Clara long, then?" Kate asked.

"Oh yes," Becky replied, having first looked around to ensure that the servants had left the room. "He first found her singing in some little place in Vienna while he was on a concert tour of Europe. He was so impressed with her voice, he invited her to sing at one of his concerts and, I understand, she has been with him ever since."

Kate and Darcy looked at one another and then at Becky. "Do you mean she has joined his concert party?" Kate asked.

Becky smiled. "Well, yes, in a manner of speaking," she said and then dropping her voice, added, "In truth, I am told they are lovers and have been for over two years. It is well known in musical circles, especially in Europe, though it is not spoken of here in England and is certainly not known to his family in Derbyshire, of course."

Aldo Contini, who had kept well out of the conversation, intervened to say that he understood from his aunt Signora Contini that Mr Courtney wished to marry the lady, but feared his family would not accept her.

"He is very devoted to her, I believe," he added.

Darcy's face revealed exactly his disappointment and confusion. "I cannot comprehend it. Why should William have been so afraid of his family's disapproval? He is quite independent of them, surely if he loves her and wishes to marry her…"

Becky interrupted him gently. "My dear Darcy, William is a celebrated conductor from a respectable family. His father was a clergyman and his mother a veritable saint. Fraulein Clara is a nobody, with a pretty face and a good voice, whom he discovered in a dance hall in Vienna! How do you suppose his family would have responded? Do you think his sister, Eliza Harwood, would have accepted it? Or Mr and Mrs Darcy? I doubt that even Cassy would be comfortable with the situation. Is it likely that they would have accepted Fraulein Clara? I think not."

Darcy was not prepared to agree. "You may be right about the others, Becky, but I do not believe for one moment that his mother, my dear aunt Emily, would have been set against it. Look how well she accepted Jude's choice of Teresa."

"Indeed, but there is no comparison between young Jude, who wanted to be nothing more than a farmer, and William, for whose musical career his mother sacrificed almost everything. And Darcy, I do believe William knew this and did not wish to disappoint her."

"And is it possible he will marry her now?" Kate asked.

"It is possible, but unlikely," replied Becky.

"But why not? Now Mr and Mrs Courtney are no longer alive, surely William is free to marry without any inhibition," Kate persisted.

Aldo Contini intervened again, explaining patiently, "In musical circles, there is no prohibition against a musician having a mistress; many do. Some have both a wife and family as well as a mistress. It is accepted in the same way it is accepted here that the Prince of Wales may have a mistress or two, and people turn a blind eye, as you say. But were Mr Courtney to marry the lady, he may offend some people in high places, especially here in London, persons like Her Majesty the Queen, and certain doors will be closed to him forever."

"But she may continue to live as his mistress without any consequences?" Kate seemed bewildered.

"Indeed, except perhaps for herself. But she is devoted to him, she owes everything that she is today to Mr Courtney and his encouragement of her talent." Mr Contini shrugged his shoulders and said, "Sadly, it is unfair, I agree, but it is the way of the world, Mrs Gardiner."

There were tears in Kate's eyes, and the sigh that escaped him made it clear how very disappointed Darcy was, and yet, there was nothing he could do about it. In his heart, he felt a deep sadness for his cousin.

The journey back to London was not as pleasurable as the one out to Richmond had been, despite the fact that their companions were the same. What they had learned at Richmond weighed heavily upon their minds, and while it seemed everyone had an opinion on it, no one was comfortable with the subject, so it went unmentioned, making for a most unusual reserve between the two couples.

Kate was tired, and Darcy, concerned for her condition, wished only for the journey to end. That it rained intermittently along the way served only to make the road seem longer.

It was late when they reached Portman Square; they thanked the Continis sincerely and went indoors. There were a few cards and a sealed note on the table in the hall, which Darcy picked up as he went upstairs.

Dragging off his boots, he lay on a couch in his dressing room and opened up the note. He was surprised to find that it was from William, inviting him to call at his apartment on the morrow at any time after 10 a.m.

When Kate appeared, bathed and ready for bed, Darcy accompanied her to their bedroom and showed her the note.

Kate was amazed. "Clearly he wishes to speak with you about some important matter. Do you suppose he intends to take you into his confidence about Clara?" she asked eagerly, but Darcy was not prepared to speculate. "I cannot be sure; I hope so. If he did, I know what I would say. At the very least, it may mean that he is prepared to be frank with me, and I would appreciate that very much," said her husband.

~❧~

After a late breakfast, Darcy called for a hansom cab and set off for his appointment with his cousin. He was unsure what he could expect, but hoped that it would provide an opportunity for openness between them.

Arriving at the apartment, he was shown into a pleasant morning room, where he waited but a few minutes before William Courtney walked in. Darcy rose and they shook hands. As William urged him to be seated and offered him a glass of sherry, which Darcy politely refused, he noted that his cousin, though still very elegantly dressed, appeared rather more strained than he had been the previous night, where he had clearly felt he was among friends. He seemed restless and uneasy, and Darcy was sure William had something of consequence to say to him. As they faced one another, Darcy seated and William standing in front of him or walking around the room, the two men seemed to realise that this had to be a moment of truth between them. Further concealment was impossible.

After some hesitation and walking around the room in an increasingly distracted manner, William stopped in front of his cousin and said, "Darcy, I owe you an apology. What I am about to do is unfair to you, and I am indeed sorry to have to involve you in a matter that I should have had the fortitude to deal with myself. I should have been open and frank with my family and especially with my dear mother. She deserved better from me. Indeed, when I came to Derbyshire for her funeral, I did contemplate quite seriously telling either your father or my aunt Caroline the facts, but I could not bring myself to do it. I guess I was not willing to risk even greater censure. So I'm afraid I squibbed it," he said, looking somewhat ashamed. "And now, I am truly sorry for using you as I am about to do, to explain to my family and such friends as I might still have in Derbyshire my present situation and future intentions."

Darcy listened and watched, transfixed, as William continued, "The matter, as you may have guessed already, concerns Fraulein Clara, whom I have known for some years now. She has been my protégée and loyal companion, and I love her very dearly."

Darcy made some attempt to convey his appreciation of the young lady's talent and beauty, but his cousin held up a hand. "I know, she is beautiful and very gifted, but, Darcy, above all that, she is an absolute angel. She not only loves me, she understands and appreciates what my music means to me; it is my life. I love her and I have asked her to marry me, Darcy. I know several members of my family, especially my sister, Mrs Harwood, and even my brother-in-law, Julian, will be shocked. Their disapproval, based for the most part on their ignorance of her nature and character, is guaranteed, and I do not intend to subject Clara to their prejudices and criticism." He continued in a determined voice, "For these and other reasons, I do not believe it will be possible for us to marry and live here in England, which is why I have decided to return to Vienna, which is Clara's home and the city in which we first met so fortuitously."

Darcy listened as William went on, "We will be married and make our home there. I shall visit England, of course; I have engagements already confirmed for concerts here in London and in America, but my home will be with my wife in Vienna."

At first Darcy did not know what to say; he had been both shocked and saddened by William's words. Yet, for the first time he had also been able to reach some understanding of his cousin's situation. He tried to convey this but had great difficulty getting out the words.

"William, you have no need to apologise to me. I thank you for taking me into your confidence, and let me assure you that whatever any other member of your family may think, I am very happy for you. Fraulein Clara is a beautiful and gifted young lady, and you are indeed fortunate that she loves you so well. That is a great blessing. Yet, I am sorry that you feel you must leave England, which is your home. Are you completely certain that if you spoke directly to your family, they would not understand and come to accept that you love Fraulein Clara and wish to marry her?"

He seemed to be pleading with William, who smiled kindly and said, "My dear Darcy, your kindness and generosity does you great credit, but I am not very confident that too many members of my family will feel as you do. Some may—my aunt Caroline will probably understand, Mama used to say she has a romantic heart, and of course she had a great romance herself with her Colonel. But if I am to be quite honest with you, Darcy, I have to say that I have neither the time nor the inclination to submit myself and my dear Clara to their judgment. I intend to be a bit of a coward and let you explain the situation to them. It may not be easy, and I certainly have no right to ask it of you, but will you do me this great favour, Darcy?"

Darcy looked directly into his cousin's eyes and said, "Of course, if that is what you wish. But will you in return answer me one question? It is something that has troubled me."

"Certainly, ask away," William replied.

Darcy steeled himself to ask, "Why, over all these years, did you not keep in closer contact with your mother? She, all of us, felt deeply hurt that you did not visit her. That, more than anything else, has hardened the hearts of your family and friends against you, especially my grandparents, who loved Aunt Emily dearly and will make it more difficult for them to accept uncritically your decisions." He was eager not to be misunderstood. "While Kate and I will gladly explain your present circumstances, the rest of your family may not accept that you could not find time enough to visit or write more often than you did, even when your mother was very ill."

William answered directly and without any attempt at subterfuge. "Darcy, Mama knew I could not visit as frequently as I should have liked to. I was often away on tour, and I always kept her informed of my plans. But I did write to her, and Mama always replied *poste restante*," he said.

"Darcy, I was very conscious of everything she had done for me to enable me to make a successful musical career. She told me she intended to leave the farm to Jude, and I agreed. I certainly had no need of it. When I saw her after my father's funeral, I tried to help her, but she specifically forbade me to send her any money. We may not have met often, but my mother knew a good deal about my life; she even knew that there was someone I cared for. I did not tell her who it was, because I feared she might confide in Jessica or Elizabeth, and it would not have been fair to Clara to let her name be tossed around and her reputation traduced. Besides, I was aware that Mama was ill and had no desire to cause her more anxiety, so I concealed Clara's identity from her, but she knew there was someone, and in one of her last letters to me, which I have here, she wished me success in my concert tour and in my pursuit of personal happiness. So in truth, she did give me her blessing."

William had taken out a packet of letters from his bureau and laid them open on the coffee table before Darcy, who could see quite clearly that they were in Emily's hand. He did not wish to pry or to read them, but the direction and dates were sufficient evidence that William had spoken the truth. Clearly, mother and son had corresponded quite regularly, even though Emily had not chosen to reveal this to the rest of her family. Perhaps, Darcy thought, it was her way of protecting William's secret. He knew how very dearly Emily loved her son.

"But, William, had you told her, she would not have hurt your feelings; she loved you very much. She would have been most unhappy to know that you intend to leave England for good," said Darcy, still struggling with his feelings. He had grown very close to Emily over the years when he had helped with the management of her household and farm.

"I know," said William, "but, Darcy, with Mama gone, there are very few reasons for me to regret leaving England. Sadly, I am not very close to many members of my family. I shall miss you, of course, though I have only recently come to know you well, and I hope that you and Kate will visit us in Vienna one day. It is a wonderful city, and you will be very welcome in our home. Meanwhile, I have only happiness to look forward to in marrying the lady whom I have loved for so long and whose affections I have enjoyed and cannot live without. I shall count on you to hand these letters to Mr and Mrs Darcy, Jessica and Julian, and your parents, and satisfy the curiosity of my family. Will you wish me happiness, Darcy?" he said, handing Darcy a few sealed letters.

Darcy bit his lip; he felt deeply the emotions that this encounter had aroused in him and, rising, grasped his cousin's hand. "Of course I will, William; how could I not? I, who know what it is to enjoy that special bliss of loving and being loved in return, wish you both every happiness and will gladly be the bearer of your good news to the family, for it is indeed good news. Have no doubt of it."

Clearly moved, William impulsively embraced his cousin and said, "Thank you, Darcy, and God bless you. You will write to me? The *poste restante* address on my card will always find me. I shall look forward to hearing from you. You must send me all the news from Derbyshire."

Darcy promised he would write and could not help the stinging tears that he fought back as he put William's letters in his pocket and left the apartment. He did not know when he would see his cousin again. At least, he thought, there was one piece of great news, which everybody would be glad to receive. Contrary to all their suspicions, William Courtney had not coldly neglected his mother in selfish pursuit of his career. Mother and son had confided in each other intimately, almost to the end. It was a discovery that had changed Darcy's own estimation of his cousin, and he hoped it would do the same for others in the family, especially Jessica and his grandparents. He knew they would not all be of one mind; some, being predisposed to dislike William, would be more difficult to persuade than others. His own parents would probably be fair; so perhaps would his grandfather, Mr Darcy, when he knew the whole truth. He could not vouch for Mrs Darcy, though, or Julian—they seemed to have their minds set against William already.

As for Robert and Rose, their opinion of anyone seemed dependent only on their own perceived self-interest, and he could not imagine that they would have any reason to think better of their nephew and would probably delight in thinking the worse of him.

Be that as it may, Darcy was determined to work untiringly to restore his cousin's reputation amongst his friends and family. For the first time since he had become seriously concerned about the matter of William Courtney, Darcy had reason for hope. He was now convinced that this least understood and most distinguished of Emily's children had not betrayed his mother's ideals at all. Not only had he continued to write to her, but in putting his love for Clara before all else, William was closer to his mother than anyone could have known. Had not love been the guiding principle in all of Emily's life? When regarded in such a light, William Courtney's story was one Darcy felt he would be quite proud to tell.

When Darcy revealed these matters to Kate, she was as astonished as he had been and wondered how he would break the news to the rest of his family.

"Are you sure they will not be very angry at being kept in the dark?" Kate asked, anxious that her husband should not bear some of the opprobrium for William's perceived misdemeanours. But Darcy reassured her, "I have no doubt that some of them may well be angry. My grandmother is not very forgiving, and Julian may not be very sympathetic, although in his case, I am hopeful that Jessica, being more tender-hearted, may in time persuade her husband to see her brother in a kinder light. As for the rest, I feel sure that when I have disclosed everything I know, all that William has told me, they will understand… They will at least see that William has not behaved so badly after all."

Darcy's youthful optimism was not entirely shared by his wife, who knew that in such disputes family members could not always be counted on to act with a degree of rationality, and she hoped, for his sake, that Darcy would not be disappointed and hurt by the experience.

On returning to Derbyshire, both Darcy and Kate found plenty to employ their time. She at the school, which was soon to open for the new term, and he at Pemberley, where many of the new ideas he had introduced were being applied for the first time and he was anxious to see that everything was done right. He knew Mr Darcy counted on him and was keen not to disappoint his grandfather.

He had ensured that the letters from William Courtney had been delivered, but was uncertain how each of the recipients had responded to the information they contained, except in the case of his parents, who had received the news with remarkable equanimity. His mother had read William's letter with interest, and on reaching the paragraph about William's intention to marry Fraulein Clara, Cassy had announced, "Oh, William is getting married and in Vienna! Did he tell you all about it, Darcy?" and when Darcy had acknowledged that he had, she'd continued reading as though there was nothing extraordinary at all about the news. By the time his mother had reached the end of the letter, Darcy had decided that William need not have feared Cassy's reaction at all. He did, nevertheless, take the time to sing his cousin's praises and reveal the facts about his correspondence with his mother, and Kate added her admiration for the talent and beauty of the young lady who was to be his bride. Cassy had smiled and accepted the information without comment, while Dr Gardiner had taken the news with barely a raised eyebrow, reminding his wife that they had spent a very pleasant holiday in Vienna some years ago. "It's a very beautiful city and renowned for its music; it should suit William very well," he remarked before returning to his reading.

It was quite clear to Darcy that his parents, no matter what opinion they held of William's previous conduct, were not going to express any criticism of his planned marriage to the young opera singer.

Visiting Pemberley one afternoon, Darcy wondered whether his grandparents would be as restrained in their response to William's news. He got no indication at all when both Mr and Mrs Darcy made no mention of William's letter throughout the entire afternoon. It seemed as though they were determined to ignore him and the news of his marriage altogether. Taking their cue from them, Darcy and Kate said little, except to relate how well they had enjoyed the concert and the ensuing visit to the Continis' luxurious villa in Richmond. This information was received with expressions of pleasure, but nothing more.

Not until Mrs Darcy had retired upstairs to rest before dinner and his grandfather had walked out with them to their carriage, did Darcy get any satisfaction. Waiting until Kate was settled in the vehicle, Mr Darcy had drawn his grandson aside, out of earshot of the servants, before saying, "I would not be too disappointed, Darcy, I know you are wondering how we have received William's letter; remember that your grandmother loved Emily very dearly and was exceedingly hurt by what she supposed to be William's neglect of his mother. Cassy was here yesterday, and she has told us all the news you brought back from London; both your grandmother and I were relieved to learn of the letters that had been exchanged between William and his mother; at the very least it means that Emily did not feel abandoned by her son at the end. I am glad that William has explained his behaviour, but it will take some time for us to come to terms with it."

Then, as though he sensed Darcy's growing disappointment, he added in a gentler tone, "However, I do want you to know that I am very happy that you have met with your cousin and intend to remain in contact with him. Emily would have been pleased, too; she would not have wanted William to be estranged from all his family on account of a misunderstanding. As for his marriage to this young lady, Fraulein Clara Kunz, it is a matter entirely for William; we wish him well, and I shall write to him acknowledging his letter and conveying our best wishes for his happiness. Perhaps, when you are next in touch, you may wish to add my own congratulations for his remarkable success in his musical career. I am delighted for him."

There was no doubting his sincerity, and Darcy, elated and happy, was eager to respond, "Thank you indeed, sir; I am very glad that you approve; I had feared that some members of the family may have been distressed at my praise of William, but I assure you—"

Mr Darcy interrupted him gently, "Some may, but, Darcy, you have acted with the very best intentions, and I believe you have done the right thing. If others disagree, it does not in any way reduce the value of what you have done. I think you did well."

"Thank you, sir," Darcy said again, and this time, noting that Kate was leaning out of the carriage, wondering what had become of her husband, Mr Darcy moved him towards the vehicle, waited until the door was shut, and waved them on.

As they drove away, Kate turned to Darcy. "What did he say? Was he very angry with William?" she asked, eager to discover what had passed between them.

Darcy smiled. "Not at all," he said, "knowing all the facts as we do now, that would be most unfair to William, and as you know, Mr Darcy is never unfair."

End of Part One

THE LEGACY OF PEMBERLEY

Part Two

Solitary Lives

Chapter One

GEORGIANA WAS RETURNING TO Pemberley. Her son Frank Grantley, the rector of Kympton, and his wife, Amy, had travelled to Oxford to fetch her home. Since the death of Dr Grantley a month ago, Mrs Grantley, though much loved by her friends in Oxford, no longer had a home there, nor a significant role to fill in the academic community of which her husband had been such a distinguished member.

Georgiana was well provided for, having both her own income and a substantial benefit left to her by Dr Grantley. She had, therefore, the capacity to purchase for herself a property anywhere she chose to live, but had decided to accept the invitation from her brother and sister-in-law to spend some time at Pemberley first before deciding upon what to do with the rest of her life. Her letter to Elizabeth made it clear she was very appreciative of their offer. She had written:

Dearest Lizzie,

I really do not know how to thank you and my dear brother for your kindness and understanding. While Virginia and I could have gone to Hampshire for a while, it would not have been very convenient for my dear daughter, and I should have felt in the way, for their arrangements at the parsonage are not commodious nor so well suited to accommodating visitors for longer than a few days. There are also the grandchildren to consider.

I had given some thought to taking a town house in London for a few months, though I have no liking for the hustle and bustle of life in town, but when your letter arrived, I had no difficulty in deciding to come first to Pemberley…

There had never been any question in the minds of Mr and Mrs Darcy of the rightness of their decision, for they both loved Georgiana dearly and had wished to help her endure the loss of a loving husband to whom she had been devoted for many years. Nevertheless, they awaited her arrival with some trepidation, because neither knew quite how to deal with the grieving Georgiana and Virginia, of whom they knew little, save she was inclined to be rather reserved.

Richard and Cassandra Gardiner, Julian Darcy and his wife Jessica, and even Jane and Mr Bingley, although the latter was still unwell, were all gathered at Pemberley to welcome them.

Pemberley had been in mourning already when the news arrived from Oxford that Dr Grantley had succumbed to pneumonia, following an attack of bronchitis that had left him debilitated last Spring.

The blow had been doubly hard on Mr Darcy, who had but recently lost his cousin Colonel Fitzwilliam. After a year of unrelenting heart disease, the colonel had died, leaving his wife, Caroline, bereft. Elizabeth knew the depth of his grief at losing two of his dearest and most intimate friends.

Yet, despite this, his first thought had been for their wives and families, for Lizzie's cousin Caroline and his sister, Georgiana. Darcy's concern had been to secure their present comfort and future well-being.

With Caroline there had been no immediate problem, since their farm at Matlock was secure, and despite her deep affection for the colonel, Caroline's many interests and activities in the community would help her cope better with her sorrow than Georgiana, whose happiness had depended almost entirely upon the encouragement and approval of her husband. Both women had the company of an unmarried daughter; yet while Rachel Fitzwilliam was generally known to be an amiable and sensitive young woman, Virginia Grantley could be awkward and, since the death of her father, even more submerged in her grief than her mother.

Lizzie was particularly concerned. "Each time I see Caroline, I am desolated by her loss, for they loved each other well and I can see how much she misses the colonel, but at least I am encouraged to hope by Caroline's great strength and good sense, which pervades everything she does. I confess I am not so confident about Georgiana," she told her sister Jane and Cassy as they were taking tea together. "Dr Grantley was a good deal older than Georgiana, and I believe he replaced the father she had hardly known and the brother who had taken his place for many years of her childhood and early youth."

"Do you believe, Mama, that Aunt Georgiana will find it more difficult to face life alone than Cousin Caroline?" Cassy asked.

Before Elizabeth could answer, Jane spoke softly, "Cassy, my dear, it is not something any of us can contemplate with equanimity. I am so afraid for Mr Bingley because he, despite having been so fit and well, seems unable to shake off this last affliction, and not even Richard can explain it. Oh Lizzie, I am so worried." She cried and bit her lip to keep from weeping.

Elizabeth turned to her sister and took her hand. "Dearest Jane, how thoughtless of me to be rattling on about Caroline and Georgiana with no concern for how you must feel about Bingley, but mark my words, he will improve, now he has given up riding out every morning in all weather. I believe Richard has ordered him to rest, and that is very good, too. Indeed, I thought he looked so much better today, do you not agree, Cassy?"

Cassandra nodded but forbore to say very much more, for she knew from her husband Dr Gardiner that Mr Bingley was much weaker than he had been a year ago. His chest had been badly affected by a severe bout of influenza, and the cold English Winters had done little to help his recovery. Cassy recalled that her husband had looked very grave when he last returned from a visit to the Bingleys at Ashford Park.

When she spoke, it was to suggest something practical. "I think, Aunt Jane, if you could travel south this year to a warmer climate for the Winter, Mr Bingley will certainly benefit greatly. I agree with Mama that he looks much better, and I am sure that more rest will help his recovery, but many of these respiratory ailments are exacerbated by the damp and cold of our northern climate. Will not Mr Bingley agree to travel to Spain or Italy...?" but before she could get much further, a vehicle was heard coming up the drive and they went out to greet their visitors.

Georgiana Grantley stepped out of the carriage, followed by her daughter, Virginia, and her daughter-in-law, Amy. Frank Grantley was already busy helping the servants unload their luggage, which was considerable.

"And there is more, following by train," he said, "including Mama's harp and pianoforte and of course hundreds of Papa's books…" At these words, Virginia, whose red eyes and sodden handkerchief were sufficient evidence that the journey had been a somewhat distressing one for all concerned, burst into tears and ran indoors, leaving Georgiana to explain apologetically that while much of her husband's library had been donated to his college, there were many personal items that she could not bring herself to discard.

"I could not decide which should or should not be saved," she said tearfully, "and Virginia had not the heart for the task; it always ended in tears."

Mr Darcy, who had by now taken charge of the situation, put an arm around his sister and took her indoors, reassuring her as he did so, "Georgiana, my dear, you have no need to explain; of course you could not discard his books and papers. Had I been asked, I should have insisted that anything which Francis did not wish to be gifted to his college must surely be lodged here at Pemberley. It belongs in our library, and there is ample room to accommodate all of it. As for your harp and pianoforte, they are simply returning to their original home in the music room, where you can play them if and when you choose."

Georgiana thanked her brother and turned to embrace Elizabeth, Jane, and Cassandra before moving to greet Jessica and her baby, Marianne, who were seated by the window.

"She is beautiful, Jessica, and has certainly grown since we last saw her, has she not, Virginia?" she said, and then of course recalling that, on that occasion, Dr Grantley had been with them, both mother and daughter dissolved into tears again. It was the same again when Richard asked if they'd had a comfortable journey, and later when Frank and Amy left to return to their children at the rectory in Kympton. Fortunately, Cassandra had ordered tea and plenty of refreshments, and when they were brought in, there was something to do, for they could all eat and drink, instead of indulging in their mood of deep melancholy.

While no one wished to deny that Georgiana and her daughter had suffered a great loss, both Cassy and Elizabeth wondered at their inability to contain their feelings. Every attempt at conversation, no matter how mundane, would result in tears, and soon the room relapsed into silence as persons ate and drank, but hardly spoke except with caution, lest the floodgates be opened again.

Jessica's child became fretful, affording her a reason to excuse herself and take her daughter upstairs, while Jane, always tender-hearted, became tearful herself as she pondered the sad fate that had befallen Mrs Grantley. Since her own husband had been taken ill a year or two ago, Jane had begun to brood about the dreadful prospect of widowhood. The deep love and long, happy marriage they had shared had not in any way prepared her for the day when she might have to face life without Mr Bingley. She had simply refused to contemplate the possibility that she might outlive him, because unlike Georgiana and Dr Grantley or Caroline and Fitzwilliam, there was no great difference in their ages. Like her brother-in-law Mr Darcy, Bingley had always been fit and healthy, and since they both led temperate and sensible lives, she had assumed that he would remain so into the future.

While it was not a proposition she would ever put to her sister Lizzie, it did seem to Jane to be rather unfair that while Mr Darcy showed few signs of indisposition, her own dear husband had fallen victim to a malady that he appeared unable to shake off. It was a feeling Jane tried persistently to push into the back of her mind, chiefly because she could not share it with anyone. Yet, she, with her affectionate heart, was least equipped to endure her anguish alone. Seeing Georgiana and Virginia in full formal mourning, tearful and bereft, had brought it all back again, and when everyone else had settled down to their tea, Jane, who had hardly left Mr Bingley's side, went to get her own. Elizabeth, sensitive to her sister's feelings, joined her at the table, and as they filled their cups, the sisters touched each other's hands and looked at one another, acknowledging silently their mutual apprehension.

Later, when the visitors had retired to their rooms, where Georgiana was moved to tears once more when shown to the suite that had always been hers, Elizabeth and Jane would spend time together, as they had always done. The sisters shared their hopes and qualms, but just as there were some things, a very few perhaps, that Lizzie would never speak of for fear of hurting Jane, so her sister remained silent on this, her deepest anxiety.

Eager not to betray herself, Jane expressed her concern for Virginia, who had appeared totally unable to restrain her grief at the loss of her father. Throughout the time they had spent in the sitting room, she had sobbed or sat in a state of deep dejection, unable or unwilling to converse with or be comforted by anyone. "Lizzie, I do worry about Virginia," Jane said. "Amy tells me that she did nothing at all to help her mother prepare for their journey. Amy had to pack her trunk, persuade her to rise, and put on her travelling clothes. Clearly, she has been deeply stricken by Dr Grantley's death."

Elizabeth was not quite so tolerant of her niece.

"No more than any of the others or Georgiana herself, surely," she said. "Yet while Georgiana's grief is clearly great and understandably so, she must be given credit for managing to organise most of what needed to be done with only some advice from Darcy and some practical help from Frank and Amy. She has spent almost a month completing a number of tasks, many of which would have been painful to her, carrying out Dr Grantley's wishes in relation to his work and effects, all with little or no help from Virginia, who has been prostrate with grief for most of that time. Now Jane, perhaps I am being a little severe, but I would call such conduct somewhat self-indulgent, wouldn't you?"

Jane, usually unwilling to criticise anyone too harshly, had on this occasion no alternative but to agree with her sister. It had become clear to both of them and perhaps to others gathered to welcome the Grantleys to Pemberley, that Georgiana's grief was greatly exacerbated by her daughter's unremitting mourning. "I suppose, Lizzie, it is not unusual in the youngest child in a family, who has been very close to her parents," she said, trying to soften her sister's judgment a little.

Elizabeth agreed. "Oh indeed, I do not deny that. I understand from Darcy that Virginia helped her father a great deal, reading to him when his eyesight grew weak, finding the passages he needed to quote in his writings, even transcribing some of his papers in her own hand. No one will deny the depth of her affection nor her right to grieve for her father, but, Jane, as we all know to our cost, grief, if indulged to excess, becomes a cruel master, and it is surely not too much to ask that Virginia should also try to assuage her mother's sorrow, as well as her own."

Jane nodded and said sadly, "Indeed you are right, Lizzie, and it is a lesson we, all of us, have to learn well. I hope with all my heart that now that they are at Pemberley, both Georgiana and her daughter will find the strength to master it."

Chapter Two

IT WAS ENTIRELY UNDERSTANDABLE that Georgiana Grantley should experience a heightened degree of nostalgic grief upon entering the suite of rooms that had been hers before she married and where most of her youthful dreams had been spun.

She did try, however, to explain to her daughter that these rooms had been hers during a time of great happiness, when first under the guardianship of her brother and later as a companion to her sister-in-law, she had developed from a shy, awkward girl into a graceful and amiable young woman. It was then she had learned from her new sister-in-law that life did not always have to be serious and there was plenty of good fun to be had by observing and occasionally putting down certain pompous people. It had been the time also when her awareness of art and music had been lifted from simple enjoyment to genuine appreciation under the loving tutelage of the Continis, making it conceivable that a man of such distinction and learning as Dr Francis Grantley could see in her a future wife. Her response, then, to returning to these maidenly rooms was not surprising. Much more astonishing was the manner in which her daughter Virginia, ignoring everything her mother had said, burst into tears, threw herself on the bed, and sobbed into the pillows, as though she and not Georgiana had been the former occupant of these rooms.

Too tender-hearted to remonstrate with her daughter and unwilling to appear insensitive to her grief, Georgiana attempted to comfort her, then sank into a chair by the window and, gazing out at the familiar aspect, across the beloved grounds of her childhood home, lapsed into a silence from which she was roused only when her maid arrived to ask if the ladies would bathe before dressing for dinner. Georgiana said yes, but Virginia declined the offer, declaring that she wanted neither a bath nor any dinner.

"I cannot understand how anyone can even think of dinner!" she cried. "Why, each time I sit down to a meal, I see dear Papa at the head of the table and I know he is no longer there."

Her mother suggested gently that at Pemberley it might not be so painful because Mr Darcy would be at the head of the table and there would be other guests, too, like Cassy and Jessica and their husbands. "Besides," she said gently, "you had hardly any breakfast and nothing to eat on the journey. Do you not think you should at least try to eat something? It may do you some good, my dear."

Virginia was adamant. "I cannot," she declared. "I think always of Papa and should only embarrass Mrs Darcy and her guests if I were to weep at the dinner table. Let me stay here, Mama; you go down and tell them I am too tired from the journey." Then as an afterthought she added, "Unless Annie could maybe bring me up something on a tray?"

Georgiana had no alternative but to agree and indicated as much to her maid. She knew Virginia had a partiality for meals served in her room. Soon it would become the topic of conversation among the servants, many of whom had fond memories of her mother but hardly knew Miss Virginia at all. Her present behaviour was unlikely to endear her to them.

None of the diners seated around the table that evening seemed at all surprised by the non-appearance of Virginia; indeed, they were more interested in her mother's well-being. Not a very talkative person herself, Georgiana could not completely satisfy either Elizabeth's or Mr Darcy's concerns, as she restricted her remarks to brief accounts of their journey from Oxford, including a paean of praise for the kindness of her son Frank and his wife Amy, without whose help she could not have made the journey. She varied these comments with quiet but sincere expressions of gratitude to both her brother and sister-in-law for their advice and generous hospitality.

"I was, for a while, very confused as to what course of action I should follow. There were all those papers to organise and matters regarding the college to settle; I had little hope of getting it all done before the month was out, when we would have had to vacate the house for the next incumbent. But for your wise counsel and my dear Frank's excellent planning, I doubt we should have been here tonight. It was very generous of Frank and Amy to leave their children for so many days and come to Oxford to help us move. I wondered at Amy's being prepared to do so, but she assured me they were well looked after," she said, to which Elizabeth added gently, "Indeed they were, because Caroline had them and their nurse over at her house in Matlock, where I am quite certain they would have lacked nothing."

Georgiana looked somewhat surprised. "Did she? Ah yes," she said quietly, as though realisation had just dawned upon her. "Caroline, of course, now I come to think of it, I do believe Amy did mention it. That was very kind of Caroline."

Cassy, who was at the farther end of the table, safely out of earshot, could not resist remarking to her husband, "I cannot imagine why she is so surprised; they are Caroline's grandchildren too, after all."

Richard nodded but said nothing. An experienced physician, he was more circumspect than his wife; later, when they were back at home in the privacy of their bedroom at Camden House, he was more explicit.

Cassy could not comprehend how her gentle aunt had seemingly lost touch with the realities of ordinary life. "How is it possible that she could be suddenly so remote, so detached from every other person that she is no longer sensible of their feelings, except where they impinge upon her own?"

Her husband had an explanation. "Do not be so harsh on her, dearest, it is not unusual after such a loss as Mrs Grantley has suffered to become a little unbalanced," he said, adding, "Even the most rational amongst us may, in response to the death of a much loved child or spouse, come to regard the rest of the world with a degree of detachment, suspicion even, because they cannot share our pain."

Cassy understood, but had her reservations. "But to the extent that it can alter one's character?"

"It can indeed, in certain circumstances. Your aunt Mrs Grantley, having lost her father at a very early age, depended wholly upon her brother's judgment and approval. When she married Dr Grantley, a man much older than herself, being still very young, she clearly transferred that trust and dependence to her husband, whom she loved dearly. Everything she learned thereafter flowed from him, and all her activities in music and her work in the church lay within the framework of their marriage," he explained.

"By that do you mean that she had no interests of her own and looked to no other person other than Dr Grantley for her values, seeking only his appreciation?"

"I do. It is not unreasonable to suppose that, having sought and received his opinion on almost every matter of any consequence and having followed his advice conscientiously for many years, she has lost the capacity to think or feel as others do. It is not that she is selfish or self-centred, but that she is suddenly bereft of the source of all her beliefs and is somewhat confused."

Cassy was confused, too, yet Richard had given her a few clues to understanding Georgiana's situation. "I am not certain Mama will understand; Papa will try because he loves her dearly, but I fear my mother will become impatient with them, particularly if Virginia keeps on with this excessive grieving. She appears to have resolved never to be consoled, and Mama, who is no stranger to such sorrow, will soon find her behaviour tedious, I fear."

At that, Richard shook his head. "Now there you have me at a disadvantage, my love, for I know nothing of Miss Grantley. I believe I have met her on but two occasions before today and cannot give you any logical explanation for her behaviour, which even for a very young girl would be unusual. In a young woman of her age, it is quite extraordinary. In most of the cases I am acquainted with, the younger women, usually daughters, support and comfort their mothers, not aggravate their woes. I must admit, my love, I am unable to account for Miss Grantley's behaviour."

It was late, and Cassy, knowing he had an important meeting with the hospital board on the following day, pressed him no further on the subject, allowing Richard to think that she was reasonably satisfied with his explanation. She did, however, have grave misgivings about Mrs Grantley, her daughter's extended stay at Pemberley, and the strains it could place upon her mother.

As her husband slept, Cassandra was reminded that her brother Julian was not the most patient of men, and she pondered whether the household at Pemberley could possibly accommodate them all without aggravation. She felt for her parents, who had out of generosity invited Mrs Grantley and her daughter to Pemberley, and searched her mind for some way to alleviate the situation. Her own children, except for young James and Laura Ann, were married, and James was presently at boarding school. Cassy wondered whether she should invite the Grantley·ladies to stay at Camden House for a while, allowing her parents some respite from their relentless grieving. It was not something she could initiate without her husband's consent, but even to put the proposal to him, she felt the need to discover a little more about the situation that obtained at Pemberley.

It was with this proposition in mind that, two days later, Cassandra sent a note to her young sister-in-law Jessica, inviting her to tea the following afternoon. The servant returned with a note accepting the invitation; Cassy was pleased. However, when on the morrow, Jessica arrived at Camden House, it was with news that brought no pleasure at all.

Even as she alighted from the vehicle that had conveyed her, baby Marianne, and her nurse, Cassandra could see that all was not well. Jessica's countenance was strained and pale. Cassy went to her at once.

"Jessie dear, you look so distressed. What has happened?" she asked.

Clearly Jessica did not wish to say anything in front of Nurse Matthews and the servants, but indicated she would do so later. Cassy took them indoors and arranged straight away for the nurse and her young charge to be shown into the playroom, a light, airy room opening onto a small walled garden, where Cassy's own children had played.

"I hope you will be comfortable here, Nurse Matthews, I shall have some refreshments sent in to you," she said, and having given the necessary instructions, she then urged Jessica to take tea with her in the intimate private sitting room upstairs, where they would be able to speak freely. Cassy could not imagine what had happened in so short a time to so upset Jessica. At first, she seemed unwilling to talk about it. She took some tea and cake and partook of it slowly, while Cassy restrained her avid curiosity, unwilling to place any further strain upon her young sister-in-law, who looked almost unwell. When after several minutes, silence, Jessica finally put down her cup and saucer, she looked directly at Cassandra and said, "Oh Cassy, I haven't even thanked you for asking me; I was so pleased to come away from Pemberley today. Julian is gone to Derby for the day, and Mrs Darcy is so anxious, she has not come downstairs at all. Mrs Grantley keeps to her room, and the household is in complete confusion."

Cassandra could not believe her ears. She had been prepared for reports of some aggravation resulting from the strain of having Georgiana and her daughter to stay, but that the usually well-run household at Pemberley had been confounded? She could not credit it.

"But why, Jessica? What has happened to bring about this disruption? Surely you are not going to tell me that Mrs Grantley and Virginia are the cause of this situation?"

Jessica looked distinctly uncomfortable as she shook her head. "Not Mrs Grantley, no, she has been quiet and amenable, and everyone feels for her. She is still grieving for Dr Grantley, and we understand that, but Virginia is impossible," she said, and her voice broke under the strain of her feelings, and her eyes filled with tears.

"In what way, Jessie? I know she was being tiresome and demanding the other day, but since then, has her behaviour not improved at all?"

"Indeed it has not," cried Jessica, who then blurted out a tale that left Cassandra incredulous.

The day after their arrival at Pemberley, both ladies had been expected to sleep later than usual, being tired from their journey. The housekeeper, on Mrs Darcy's instructions, had arranged for their breakfast to be taken up to their suite. The maids had reported that Mrs Grantley had been awake and dressed when they took it in, while Miss Virginia had been asleep and had expressed her annoyance at being disturbed in no uncertain terms. Later, Georgiana had come downstairs, and Jessica had seen her in conversation with Mr and Mrs Darcy on the terrace and walking about the west lawn with them.

"It appeared to be an animated conversation, and I assumed they were all talking about the new work that Mr Darcy had had done in the lower meadow and beside the lake. I could not hear what they were saying, being on the floor above, but it seemed as though her brother was explaining something to her, and she appeared to be listening quite intently. At least I could see that there was some progress from her state of the previous night."

"And Virginia? Where was she?" asked Cassy.

"She never left her room. Indeed, I think the maids claim that she hardly left her bed, all day long—the chamber maid had complained that she had been given no opportunity to make up the bed, and Virginia had protested when she drew back the curtains," replied Jessica.

Cassandra was exasperated. "What is wrong with her, Jessica? Does she not understand that her behaviour must cause aggravation and hurt to the rest of the family, including her own mother?"

Jessica shrugged her shoulders. "I honestly do not believe that Virginia cares at all whom she hurts and what trouble she causes. She is, I think, a wholly selfish person, and says and does just whatever she pleases at the time, regardless of the consequences," she replied.

"And today? How has she been this morning? Has there been no change in her conduct and disposition?" asked Cassy.

Jessica laughed a rather false laugh, which did not convince Cassandra that what she was about to hear was going to amuse her. "Her behaviour has certainly changed today; when the maid took her tea up to her room, her bed was empty and Virginia was gone!"

Cassy gasped, "Gone where?"

"Well, for a couple of hours, nobody knew," replied Jessica. "You can well imagine what alarm this caused. Mrs Grantley was distraught, and poor Mr Darcy, he looked as if all the cares of the world had descended upon him."

Recalling the strange circumstances of Miranda Gardiner's disappearance and elopement, Cassy asked, "Where was she found?"

"She was not found," Jessica replied. "She just walked in some two or three hours later, as though nothing had happened, and when Julian, who saw her arrive, asked where she had been, Virginia asked him to mind his own business. She said she had been walking out in the woods and apparently did not think to tell anyone where she was going. She had risen early before the rest of the household was about and slipped out down the side stairs leading to the rose garden," Jessica explained.

"Did none of the servants see her go?" asked Cassy.

"It turns out that two of the men working in the grounds did see a lady out walking quite early in the morning, but not knowing who she was, they said nothing about it to anyone," said Jessica, adding, "But, Cassy, after all this, when Julian and later Mrs Darcy pointed out the dangers of wandering around the woods, which are unfamiliar to her, she argued with them both and told Julian that since he was never to be the Master of Pemberley, he had no right to question her actions. Julian is furious!" said Jessica.

"I am not surprised. I should be as well. Did not Mama say anything to her?" Cassy asked.

"Oh yes, she did, and Mr Darcy, coming in, overheard the argument and stepped in to explain that it was a house rule at Pemberley that no one—whether they were a guest or a member of the household—was to wander away from the house without leaving word with a member of the staff, in case there was an accident. He warned her that the woods were not safe, times were hard, there could be poachers and other unsavoury characters about, and an unwary person with no knowledge of the district could be in grave danger if he or she was alone. He sounded very stern," said Jessica.

"And did Virginia appear chastened?" asked Cassy, with a smile.

"Not at all," replied Jessica. "Indeed, when her mother protested that she had been worried, she shrugged it all off as an unnecessary fuss and declared that she would prefer to go to her sister Anne in Hampshire or her brother Frank at the rectory in Kympton rather than live under such unreasonable rules at Pemberley."

Cassandra's smile disappeared; her concern was for young Amy Grantley.

"God forbid, poor Amy, what on earth will she do with Virginia at the rectory? The house is scarcely large enough for their little family, and they have few servants. Virginia will set the place at sixes and sevens."

"I think Mrs Darcy has already made that plain and her mother has advised against it, but it appears Virginia is quite determined and plans to move this very afternoon to her brother's house. When I left, she had retired to her room to pack her things," said Jessica, and as her sister-in-law put her arm around her, she sighed, "Oh Cassy, I cannot believe that in the space of two days, our happy lives have been so severely disrupted and everyone is heartily tired of Miss Virginia Grantley. I should not be surprised if Mrs Darcy already regrets having invited them to Pemberley."

Chapter Three

CAROLINE AND HER DAUGHTER, Rachel, were in Colonel Fitzwilliam's den, which he had never dignified with the words study or library, although it had served as both of these, sorting through a motley collection of books and documents.

Caroline's grief at the death of her husband was profound, but with her sister Emily gone and her daughter Isabella having moved away from Matlock after her marriage to Mr Bentley, she felt unable to impose her sorrow upon the only one of her children still at home. Her daughter Rachel was now her chief companion, and the two were very close.

There were many things that needed doing, and it was best that they proceeded as expeditiously as possible, which was why Caroline had decided that they would spend most of Sunday on the difficult task of clearing out her husband's room and putting its contents in some order.

Despite the anguish both mother and daughter suffered as they sorted and disposed of the colonel's papers, each seemed determined to spare the other any further pain, taking care not to dwell upon those items that might heighten and prolong their distress. But, try as they might, they could not restrain their sorrow when, in a leather portfolio in the bottom drawer of his desk, they found a collection of letters from his wife and children dating back many years. There were loving letters from Caroline written before they were married, a handwritten piece of music, brief affectionate notes from the children, and scraps of poetry or little sketches done in the schoolroom, all fondly collected and placed safely in a writing case, more securely held than many more important documents.

Both Caroline and Rachel wept, and as their tears fell, they embraced and held one another in an outpouring of grief like they had not experienced since the day of the colonel's death. After some time, Caroline rose and announced that they could do with some tea.

"Cook and Molly are both gone down to the village for the afternoon; I'll make the tea if you prepare the tray, and there is some fruit cake in the pantry," she said. Rachel went at once to do as she asked. They took the tea tray into the sitting room and had settled into their chairs when a vehicle was heard approaching. Rachel went to the window to look.

"It's Aunt Cassy!" she cried, clearly delighted, and went to open the door.

Caroline followed her and greeted Cassandra as she entered, but even as she did so, inviting her to take tea with them, she realised that this was no casual visit. Cassandra appeared distinctly ill at ease and could scarcely contain her disquiet until they were in the sitting room. She apologised for arriving at what must be an inconvenient hour, only to be assured that this was far from being the case. She then proceeded to pour out her concerns about the extraordinary goings-on at Pemberley since the arrival three days ago of Georgiana Grantley and her daughter, Virginia.

As Rachel poured Cassy a cup of tea, Caroline listened, amazed, almost unable to believe the preposterous tale. However, when Cassandra reached the point of Virginia's declaration that she intended to move to live with her brother Frank's family at the Kympton rectory, Caroline cried out, "Oh no, no she must not. It is not fair! Amy could not possibly cope with someone like that. She has her hands full with the children anyway. Besides, they have not the room to accommodate her."

"Which is why I thought I had to come and warn you, Caroline," said Cassy. "Jessica tells me that Virginia was determined to go, indeed she was busy packing her things and demanding to be taken to Kympton directly."

Caroline's distress was palpable. Amy was the gentlest of her children and her husband, Frank, the kindest of men; she could not believe that they were about to be imposed upon in this way.

"Cassy, what on earth shall we do?" she asked helplessly.

"Perhaps we could invite Virginia over here," Rachel suggested. "There's plenty of room; she could have Bella's room, or mine and I could move into Bella's. We'd hardly notice her presence."

Cassandra looked sceptical. "I would not count on it, Rachel. Virginia is hardly the sort of person whose presence would go unnoticed! I am not sure that your mother and you could, in your present state of mind, put up with Virginia."

"But at least she is unlikely to be in the way here; there is room enough for the three of us. At the rectory, she would be under Amy's feet all day and she would upset the children and the servants!" said Rachel.

Caroline was inclined to agree with her daughter.

"Perhaps we should go directly to Kympton; if she is already there, as she may well be, we could pretend we were visiting Amy and Frank and invite Virginia to spend some time with us," she said.

Cassandra was not entirely certain that this was the right course of action, but she had no alternative to offer. Richard had absolutely refused to have Virginia over to Camden House.

"By all means invite Georgiana," he had said to her the previous night, "I should be perfectly happy to have her to stay, but I will not agree to Virginia coming here. She will probably disrupt our household just as she has done at Pemberley."

Caroline hurried upstairs, while Rachel quietly cleared away the tea things. Watching her, Cassandra could not help wondering why Rachel, whose gentle disposition complemented her appealing looks, was as yet not spoken for. Perhaps modern young men were less appreciative of simple, good-natured girls, she thought, which was certainly a pity, for Rachel Fitzwilliam would make some fortunate gentleman a very good wife.

By the time Caroline came downstairs, ready to drive to the rectory, Rachel had everything tidied and was ready to depart.

She was unfamiliar with Virginia Grantley and asked, "Do you think Virginia would think it odd that we would invite her to stay?" To which Cassy replied that she could see no reason at all for that.

"What I meant was," Rachel continued, "since she is not very well acquainted with either Mama or me, is she likely to feel awkward and perhaps refuse the invitation?"

Cassandra shook her head. "I doubt it very much, Rachel. From what I have seen and heard of Miss Grantley, feeling awkward is not an experience familiar to her. My belief is she will accept any invitation if she is convinced it is in her own interest to do so. If she understands that she could be more comfortable and less constrained by rules at Matlock, she will have no hesitation in accepting your mama's invitation."

Caroline, who had just entered the room, heard her remark and said, "Well then, we shall have to make quite certain that she understands how much more comfortable she will be here and what freedom she will have, for we have no rules at all, except no one must go into the farmyard and frighten the animals."

They all laughed at that, and Cassy assured them that she could guarantee that Virginia would not set foot in the farmyard. "She is far too fastidious a lady for that!" she said.

≈

The journey to Kympton rectory did not take long. When they arrived, they were surprised indeed to find Amy and her children in the garden with their nurse and no sign at all of Virginia. Obviously delighted to see them, Amy came at once to greet her visitors, inviting them into the house for tea.

"I am sorry you have just missed Frank; he is gone to church to take Sunday school. But, if you can stay awhile, he will be back straight after evensong. He would be very sorry to have missed you," she explained, but both Caroline and Cassandra did not appear to be listening.

Looking around, they seemed rather puzzled, and Amy asked, "What is it, Mama? You seem preoccupied. Has something happened?"

It was her sister, Rachel, who said, "Amy, has not Frank's sister Virginia been here today?"

Amy looked puzzled. "Virginia? Oh yes, she has been and gone, all in the space of one hour. She arrived this morning, very early indeed, with all her things and a maid in one of the grand carriages from Pemberley, and asked Frank if she could stay for a while. Before he could answer, she went upstairs as if to inspect the accommodation and came down again in a very short time, to say that she did not think the spare room could hold her trunks let alone herself in comfort," she said, and the others gasped.

"Frank was rather upset, but I did point out that the rectory was only a modest dwelling for a clergyman and his family, and had never been designed to accommodate distinguished visitors with lots of luggage. I did apologise for the size of the spare room and told her she was very welcome to stay, but it seems she had already made up her mind. I offered her a cup of tea, which she refused, and very soon afterwards, she left to return to Pemberley. It was fortunate that the man had not unloaded her trunks; it would have been such a waste of time and effort to have done so, since she was hardly here above half an hour," Amy explained cheerfully.

"Oh Amy, my poor child," said Caroline, but Amy did not appear to have suffered at all as a result of Virginia's extraordinarily brief visit.

She laughed, "Oh Mama, there is no need to feel sorry for me; I was so relieved I almost wept. Jessica had warned me about her, and I was apprehensive that she might stay. Poor Frank, he felt so wretched; he was appalled by her rudeness, but I told him to say a special prayer at evensong, thanking God for our very small spare room! I do love that little room and shall never complain about it ever again," she said, her laughter filling the room, and the others could not help laughing with her.

When they had all sat down and partaken of tea, and the nurse had taken the children upstairs for their bath, Frank Grantley arrived home. His pleasure at seeing them there was diluted by his considerable embarrassment at the conduct of his sister, for which he felt the need to apologise to his mother-in-law as well as his wife.

"I am unable to explain it, except to say that she is probably so upset at my father's death, she has become deranged. I have no recollection of seeing her behave in this manner when we were at home. But then I suppose she would not have done so; my father would not have tolerated it, and she had more regard for him than for me."

It was not an explanation that either Cassy or Caroline could accept, but out of consideration for Frank, neither said anything to the contrary.

"Did she say what she intended to do?" asked Caroline. "I understand she has declared that she does not wish to continue at Pemberley."

Frank said he had gone out to the carriage as his sister had prepared to leave and had heard her say that she was sure Anne's house in Hampshire had more suitable accommodation.

"Does that mean she intends to travel to Hampshire?" Caroline asked.

Frank was unsure. "I'm afraid I cannot say for certain; she revealed nothing of her intentions, and I was so dismayed by her remarks that I was pleased to see her depart and asked no further questions. I have to confess that my sister Virginia and I have never been very close, which is probably my fault, because I was never at home long enough to be much of a brother to her," he said, by way of explanation. It was an explanation that was not very fair to him, Caroline thought.

Cassandra and Caroline decided on leaving Kympton rectory to proceed to Pemberley, which was but twenty minutes' drive from Kympton. There was still plenty of light in the sky, and Caroline thought they could gain some advantage by meeting Georgiana, and if Virginia was not to be seen, she could leave the invitation with her mother.

"Georgiana may well be able to persuade her that it would be simpler to move to Matlock than to travel alone across the country to Hampshire."

"It would mean travelling on the trains, too, unless Mr Darcy can be coaxed to let her have a carriage for the journey," said Rachel.

"I cannot believe Papa is in any mood to be coaxed to offer Virginia the use of a carriage. To transport her to the railway station, yes, but not to Hampshire, I don't think," said Cassy with some confidence. She knew her father well and was certain he had no time at all for spoilt and selfish young women like Miss Grantley.

When they reached Pemberley, the slanting rays of the setting sun were striking the windows, which glowed in the evening light. Rachel gasped at the beauty of the place, and even Cassy, who was so familiar with the view, caught her breath as they drove towards the entrance. Mr and Mrs Darcy were sitting on the terrace with Georgiana, and they came across to welcome them as they alighted from their vehicle. Inviting them in, Elizabeth asked the servants to bring out more refreshments for their visitors.

Having done so, she turned to Caroline and whispered, "You are come at a most auspicious moment indeed. Virginia has a headache and has withdrawn to her room. We are not likely to have the pleasure of her company for the rest of the evening."

Caroline was well pleased. This circumstance suited her plan very well. Seating herself beside Georgiana Grantley, she waited a few minutes before asking after her family in general and Virginia in particular. It was an entirely natural question; both women had been recently widowed and both had unmarried daughters of almost the same age. While the two young women hardly knew one another, their mothers were friends, and when Caroline asked if Virginia would like to spend some time with them at Matlock, there was nothing but sincerity in her voice.

"We have plenty of room and with just Rachel and I; Virginia would almost have the place to herself," she said.

Georgiana, clearly surprised, turned to look at her face and after a moment of bewilderment said, "Oh Caroline, that is so very kind of you. I am sure Virginia would love to come to you at Matlock. Indeed I shall tell her about it tonight," she said with such an excess of enthusiasm that Caroline was convinced it was a sign of immense relief.

Sitting next to her mother, Rachel sighed; there was no escape now.

Back at Matlock, Caroline and Rachel determined that they were going to make the very best of this visit, however difficult it was going to be.

"If she does accept, we have to ensure that she is pleased and happy, else she will leave and impose herself upon poor Amy and Frank, and we cannot have that. Rachel, my love, I am counting on you to do your very best," Caroline warned.

Rachel laughed. "Have no fears, Mama; her every wish shall be my command."

"Oh my dear child, even I shall not hold you to that promise," said her mother, and they went upstairs together, content with their achievement.

Now, everything would depend upon Georgiana's powers of persuasion.

Chapter Four

MEANWHILE AT PEMBERLEY, MRS Darcy was not entirely satisfied that Caroline's invitation to Virginia had been the right thing to do. "What if she should create dissension and unhappiness there, too?" she asked as she and Mr Darcy sat taking tea in their private sitting room. "It seems she has a talent for it, and poor Caroline and Rachel, having only recently lost the dear Colonel, how would they cope with such a situation?"

Her husband's countenance was grave, but there was also a twinkle in his eye as he tried to reassure her. "Dearest, I believe you need have no fears on that score. If anyone in this family can set Virginia down, it will be Caroline. She is both forthright and sensible, with a determination that enables her to deal with the most vexing situations."

"She will certainly have her fair share of those with Virginia making a variety of demands upon her. I worry that with only Rachel and a couple of servants to help her, Caroline may well be driven to distraction. Perhaps I should suggest that Virginia take their maid with her. I am sure Georgiana will not mind sharing my Susan," Elizabeth said.

Mr Darcy felt able to endorse that idea, and Elizabeth decided she would look in on her sister-in-law before going to bed. It would give her an opportunity to discover whether Georgiana had succeeded in persuading her daughter to accept Caroline's generous invitation to Matlock.

To her amazement, when Elizabeth entered her room, Georgiana was smiling. It was not something she had done much of recently.

"It is such a pleasure to see you like this, Georgiana," said Elizabeth as they embraced. "May I assume from your happy mood that Virginia has agreed to go to Matlock?"

"Indeed you may, Lizzie. I was quite surprised myself; she welcomed the offer and asked that a message be sent to Caroline thanking her for the invitation. I am sure Virginia realises it is far preferable to travelling to Hampshire. Perhaps we can arrange to send one of the men over tomorrow morning with a note for Caroline?" she asked tentatively, and Elizabeth was in no doubt that it could be arranged.

"Of course, my dear, that would not present a problem at all, and when Virginia wishes to go herself, Mr Darcy will let her have one of the carriages so she can transport her things and your maid conveniently. If you do not mind sharing Susan with me, it will be best for Virginia and Caroline if Annie went, too."

Georgiana did not wish to trouble anyone, she said, but Elizabeth insisted, "It will be no trouble to anyone, and if Virginia is content to stay awhile at Matlock, just think, it will give you a chance to spend some time with your brother and me. We have longed to have you here at Pemberley."

"And, Lizzie dear, I have long wished to come back. I have missed the happy times we used to spend together and look forward to recalling some of those days with both of you as well as Julian and Jessica," she said.

Recalling the events of their first evening at Pemberley, she continued, "Lizzie, I must apologise for Virginia; she has always been rather headstrong, and it hasn't been easy for me to control her, but with Dr Grantley it was different…" And here she could not help the tears that flowed down her cheeks as she sobbed. "He always counselled her, and she would take more notice of him than of me. Oh Lizzie, I do miss him so."

Elizabeth felt for her sister-in-law; married young, to a man she loved and esteemed, Georgiana had never sought the independence of mind and spirit that Elizabeth, Caroline, and Cassandra prized so highly. Suddenly, it was as though the years had rolled back and she was facing the same diffident young girl she had first met at Pemberley. Elizabeth's generous heart was moved, and she held Georgiana close until her sobs ceased.

By the time she went back to her bedroom, Mr Darcy had concluded that Virginia must have accepted Caroline's invitation, which was why Lizzie was taking so long with Georgiana. They were probably making plans, he thought, and when he saw her smiling face, he knew he was right.

At first, she was bewildered and demanded to be told how he knew, but she soon abandoned that question in favour of telling him all the good news.

"You will let her have the small carriage for the journey, will you not, my dear?" she asked, and he laughed.

"Lizzie my love, she can have two carriages if you wish it: one for herself, to ride in state, and one to transport her maid and luggage. If Georgiana and you can assure me that Virginia is going to stay at Matlock and not return within twenty-four hours, I may send a couple of grooms on horseback to escort her on the journey! How do you think she will like that, Lizzie?"

Elizabeth laughed; he was teasing her, and she knew it, but it was such a welcome change from the grave, almost dour mood into which Mr Darcy had fallen since Georgiana and her ill-tempered daughter had arrived at Pemberley, that she was delighted.

At least, she thought, she would have her husband and family to herself in an atmosphere of pleasant and convivial hospitality for which Pemberley, certainly since her marriage to Mr Darcy, was renowned.

Elizabeth was delighted with the achievements of the day and gave thanks for the generosity of Caroline and Rachel.

❧

At Matlock, arrangements were afoot to accommodate Miss Grantley. What had been undertaken as a duty, a mission to rescue poor Amy and Frank, was taking on the proportions and gravity of a military operation.

Caroline and Rachel had commandeered all the servants except the cook, who was under strict orders to provide the best possible dinner, to clean, air, and make up not one but two bedrooms for Virginia's use. The finest linen, the softest pillows, and the warmest eiderdown were all pressed into service to induce Virginia Grantley to enjoy her stay.

When, on the day following, she arrived, complete with her maid and a manservant from Pemberley to carry her many trunks and boxes up to her rooms, Caroline and Rachel greeted her warmly.

They hoped she was going to enjoy her time with them, Caroline said, to which Virginia replied she was quite sure she would, because Mama had said they didn't have all those insufferable house rules like Mr and Mrs Darcy imposed upon their visitors at Pemberley.

Caroline raised her eyebrows, but Rachel intervened very quickly, before her mother could say a single word.

"We do have one rule, but it's really for the sake of the farm animals. No one is allowed to go through the gate, down to the lower meadow, because the sheep can get quite angry and it would not be safe for any of us to be in there among an irate mob of sheep," she explained reasonably, and Virginia replied that she had no desire whatsoever to go in among some silly sheep, angry or not, so that particular rule would not bother her at all.

Entering the house and proceeding upstairs to the rooms that had been prepared for her, it was clear that Virginia was somewhat bemused. Unaccustomed to being treated with gentle courtesy, mainly on account of her own unfriendly disposition, a fact that she did not care to admit, Virginia was finding it difficult to comprehend her new situation, but on seeing her tastefully appointed rooms, she turned to Rachel, who had accompanied her, and said a remarkably gracious thank you.

Going to the window, she looked out across to the foothills of the peaks and said, "This is so pretty, I know I am going to enjoy my stay here."

Rachel, leaving Virginia and her maid to unpack, flew downstairs to report to her mother that they had passed the first test. The accommodation and the view were acceptable!

Later, having taken tea in her room and rested for a couple of hours, Virginia came downstairs suitably attired for the evening, and Caroline was very glad that cook had produced a delicious meal.

Perhaps it was the fact that neither she nor Caroline had any intimate knowledge of one another, which made it simpler to be pleasant, or it might have been the softness of Rachel's nature that smoothed the rough patches and sharp edges of each situation. Whatever it was, the day passed without any unpleasantness and much hope that their carefully laid plans had worked. It did seem that Miss Virginia Grantley would stay.

Caroline had been determined that she would do everything possible to ensure that Virginia would feel welcome, and she had succeeded.

It was with immense relief that she retired to her room that night, the room she had shared with the husband whom she had loved as a girl, even before she knew what it was to be in love. Only in the privacy of her room would she give in to the feelings of utter loneliness that assailed her.

Rachel heard her mother sobbing in the night.

Surrendering her own bedroom to their visitor, she had moved into the small dressing room next to Caroline's room, and as soon as she heard the sounds of her grief, she leapt out of bed and came quickly to her mother's bedside.

It was not the first time and it would not be the last that she would come to her and they would weep together and comfort each other. Only Rachel, of all Caroline's family, knew how deeply she suffered the loss of her husband.

On the morrow, Virginia slept late and took her breakfast in her room, but when she was ready to come downstairs, she found Rachel waiting for her.

"What would you like to do today?" she asked brightly, and Virginia, surprised again, responded that she would like to look around the farm.

"I promise not to invade the lower meadow and upset the sheep," she said, and Rachel could have sworn there was a hint of humour in her voice.

"In which case, you will need to borrow a pair of my boots; those pretty shoes will soon be ruined if you were to walk around the farm in them," she warned, and having provided Virginia with the requisite footwear, she pulled on her own well-worn boots and they set off along the path leading to the river, which formed the boundary of the property.

Seeing them go, Caroline smiled and wished she had the skill to sketch the two contrasting figures walking briskly down the path.

Although both young women were almost the same age, Virginia, being taller and more amply endowed, appeared the older of the two. Rachel, smaller and more delicately built, was in her mother's biased eyes the prettier. As to their dispositions, well, there was no comparison; yet they seemed to get on well enough, for by the time they returned from their tour of the property, clearly tired and hungry, they were talking like old acquaintances.

Caroline would have liked to visit Elizabeth and tell her everything, but unwilling to leave Rachel to look after their guest alone, she had to be content with writing a letter, which was carried by a servant to Pemberley later that week.

Dearest Lizzie,

It is now three whole days since Virginia Grantley came to stay with us, and I am writing to tell you of the extraordinary circumstances in which we find ourselves.

First, let me say that to our considerable relief, Miss Grantley was delighted with the accommodation prepared for her. She has both Isabella's room and the one adjoining, which my dear Rachel gave up heroically so that Virginia and her maid may be comfortably accommodated.

The two of them have struck up what I am not yet willing to call a friendship, but it has all the signs of becoming a connection that may well benefit Virginia, who appears to me to be a singularly friendless young woman.

It is not immediately apparent if there is a genuine change in Virginia or if she is playacting to suit her present circumstances. Whichever it is, though she continues to be demanding, she is never rude, and whilst she speaks her mind very decidedly, I have noticed that she also listens whenever Rachel answers one of her innumerable questions. Contrary to my first impression, she is not lazy, and while she undertakes no real work, she seems quite ready to join Rachel in many of her activities. This afternoon, they are off to sketch the strange rocks on the far side of High Tor.

Dear Lizzie, whether this is the result of our simple hospitality or my daughter's disarming openness, I cannot tell, and indeed, I believe it would not matter, because at least it has given both Amy and Georgiana some respite from the strains they suffered before. More importantly, it has allowed Virginia to be something other than the hurtful, obnoxious creature she had become with her own family.

Elizabeth lost no time at all in finding her husband and showing him Caroline's letter, and his astonishment was no less than hers had been.

He read the note through twice and sat down before saying with a sigh, "So it seems I was wrong, Lizzie. There was no need for Caroline to set her down. Virginia has been able to recognise Caroline's generosity and Rachel's genuine goodness and has decided quite deliberately that she has nothing to gain and everything to lose by disrupting this idyllic situation.

"No doubt she is enjoying the attention and their hospitality; it is still possible that boredom could set in and she may not be as amenable or as easy to please, but at least for now, Caroline's plan has been a complete triumph!"

Elizabeth agreed and expressed her sadness that she could not show the letter to Georgiana; she feared her sister-in-law may be offended by Caroline's frankness.

However, when they met later that evening before dinner, Georgiana revealed that she had received a note from Virginia, which she was happy to pass around for her brother and sister-in-law to read.

While it had none of the interesting detail that Caroline's had contained, the fact that Virginia had put pen to paper to tell her mother that she was enjoying her stay at Matlock was remarkable in itself. She wrote:

Mrs Fitzwilliam is most hospitable, and Rachel is the most artless person I have ever met. She lacks any pretence and speaks only the truth, which makes her a very easy person to get on with.

We have talked of books and music (Mrs Fitzwilliam has a wonderful old piano with the sweetest tone), sheep, geese, and rabbits and have spent two afternoons sketching the peaks, which may be viewed quite easily from here.

If the weather is suitable, we may attempt to go farther afield to a place called Dovedale, which I am assured is not to be missed, but we may only go if Mrs Fitzwilliam is free to accompany us, for she will not permit two young women to travel there unaccompanied.

Mama, I think I should like to continue here for a further week at least, if Mrs Fitzwilliam has no objection...

Both Mr Darcy and Elizabeth expressed their delight at the tone and content of the letter, and Georgiana could not hide her relief.

Afterwards, when they had finished dinner and withdrawn to the drawing room, she moved, without any prompting, to the grand piano and began to play. It was the first time she had done so willingly since Dr Grantley had been taken ill several months ago.

Chapter Five

THE ARRIVAL OF MR Daniel Faulkner in Derbyshire was announced
in a letter containing an invitation to a dinner party and ball at
Ashford Park.

Daniel, the son of Dr Faulkner and Maria Lucas and brother of Jonathan
Bingley's wife, Anna, had returned to England after almost twenty years in
the distant antipodean colonies of New South Wales and Victoria. It was an
appropriate occasion for one of Mr and Mrs Bingley's social assemblies, for
which Ashford Park was quite well known.

Daniel's family, and in particular his mother, had almost given up hope
of ever seeing him again, believing that Daniel had set his roots so deeply
in the alien soil of the Great South Land that he would have no desire to
live in England again. When a letter had arrived disclosing his intention
to visit his family and spend some months in England, they had all been
quite incredulous.

Mrs Faulkner had sent a servant with a note summoning her daughter
Anna to Haye Park, so she might see her brother's letter to his parents. Her
mother's excitement was so great that Anna had had to beg her not to become
too agitated, lest she should suffer palpitations and fall ill. But Maria Faulkner,
by now in tears from having read her son's letter out loud for about the fifth
time, was not capable of moderate emotion on this day. After some twenty

years, her only son was returning home, and no one could reasonably expect her to be restrained in her joy.

"Just think, my dear child, your brother left these shores when he was not yet twenty-five, and now he is returning twenty years later. He will be almost forty-five years old. Can you believe it?"

Anna could and did believe it; it was a simple calculation which she had already made on reading his letter. Her mother expressed amazement that Daniel, who had sailed for New South Wales as a very young man with no prospects and hardly any money, was returning to England by all reports a mature and wealthy gentleman.

"But I do wonder at his not being married again; perhaps he is coming to England to find himself another wife," she said hopefully, and once again, Anna had to persuade her not to become too enthusiastic about the prospect.

"We cannot know that, Mama; perhaps he is engaged already or maybe he has decided against marrying again. Life out there in the distant colonies can be very difficult, especially for a young woman," she argued.

They knew very little of Daniel Faulkner's life in the antipodes, except by hearsay. While his own infrequent letters had been modest about his achievements, they had heard from others who had returned to England reports of his success; it was said he had made a fortune first in the gold rush and later by investing his money successfully in the wool trade.

There was also the sad circumstance of his wife's untimely death.

He had married a young woman, of whom he had written that she was the "loveliest looking girl in the colony of Victoria," but then, a few years later, she had died in childbirth, and their child, a boy, was being cared for and educated by his late wife's parents in a place called Ballarat, of which the Faulkners knew nothing at all, except it was on the other side of the globe and gold had been found there!

"He says nothing of the boy; do you suppose he will be with him?" Mrs Faulkner asked.

Anna tried once more to calm her mother's expectations.

"That is very unlikely, Mama; the boy must be at school, surely, and his grandparents will not take kindly to the idea of him being dragged away on a long and hazardous voyage to England."

After much discussion, a conclusion was reached that Jonathan Bingley would send a carriage to meet Daniel Faulkner and convey him to Netherfield

Park. It had been Jonathan's idea for Daniel to arrive first at Netherfield and proceed to visit his parents at Haye Park, outside Meryton, on the following morning. Dr Faulkner had been recently unwell, and Jonathan, knowing how excited Mrs Faulkner could become, feared it would be too much of a strain for her husband. Anna, knowing her mother's state of mind, had agreed and was glad to have the time to get acquainted with Daniel before they went on to Haye Park.

She was especially eager to meet her brother, of whom she remembered little and had heard even less. When finally he arrived at Netherfield in the late afternoon, after a seemingly interminable voyage and half a day's journey by road, Anna could not bring herself to go out to greet him. She watched from a window as he alighted from the carriage and Jonathan went to welcome him. She caught her breath as she saw a tall, slim, distinguished-looking man come swiftly up the steps to shake her husband's hand; then when she ran downstairs to meet him, there was no need for introductions, and he enfolded her in his arms as she wept.

Later, he was grudgingly allowed an hour or so to bathe, rest, and change before he was in their midst again, meeting Jonathan and Anna's children and enjoying a meal of fresh food and garden produce for the first time in many months. Everyone was eager to ply him with food and wine and ask him questions about his journey, especially his two lively young nephews Nicholas and Simon, who, though young, were very curious about their new uncle of whom they had heard so much in the last few weeks; and though he was clearly tired, he was not averse to satisfying their curiosity.

The following afternoon, to the absolute delight of his parents, Daniel drove over to Haye Park alone for a private reunion, giving them time to indulge in every emotion and satisfy most of their curiosity about their son, before the rest of the family joined them for dinner.

Daniel Faulkner, if he was, as rumour had it, a wealthy man, did not seem to fit the role at all. He was too open and unwary, too happy to answer questions about himself and the life he had led in Australia, not sufficiently suave or vain. He had been handsome in his youth, and his features remained strikingly good, although the harsh Australian climate had taken its toll upon his skin, which was tanned and lined, and while his fingernails were clean and trimmed, his hands were hard and rough. One could travel far in England to find a businessman bearing such clear physical evidence of hard work.

His manner, too, lacked pretentiousness and self-importance, which characterised most of the newly rich captains of industry. He spoke softly and, whenever he was asked a question, which was often, answered it with a degree of frankness and clarity that surprised them all.

Most remarkable, for Anna, was his willingness to spend time with their aging parents. He would talk for hours with Dr Faulkner, who, though he was a great reader of books, had never travelled outside of Europe and so had a myriad of questions for his son about the strange places and people he had seen. When he had satisfied his father's curiosity, he would seek out his mother or his sister and yield without complaint to their desire to lavish upon him the affection and care they had not been able to provide for twenty years, never complaining of his mother's fussing or his sister's interest in his well-being.

"He is so patient and kind with both Mama and my father, I am amazed," Anna said to her husband when they were back at Netherfield one night. "He is uncomplaining and gentle with the children, like a man who has had a large family, yet he has had but one son. Oh Jonathan, I am so very glad he is my brother and has come back so my dear parents and you and I and the children can know him as he is, rather than hear of some person of whom we know nothing, but that he is successful and wealthy."

Her husband understood how she felt—he knew that Anna had worried that they would never see her brother again—but he was amused at the intensity of her pleasure that Daniel was not as she had feared he would be, a conceited swaggerer filled with his own importance as many men were who had recently returned from the colonies. Jonathan was relieved, too, that the brother-in-law he had never known had turned out as amiable as Daniel had.

"I am glad too, my dear, that he is your brother. I think he is an admirable man of whom you and your parents can be very proud," he had said.

After a fortnight in which the family had had their fill of asking questions and he had been proudly introduced to all their friends and relations in the neighbourhood, Jonathan and Anna persuaded Daniel to travel with them to Derbyshire to meet the Bingleys and the Darcys, whose curiosity about Anna's brother had been by now well aroused by their letters.

Daniel was keen to go. He had few memories of Derbyshire, but was well informed about the industrial towns of the English Midlands to which wool was imported. When he had left England, he'd had little knowledge of the fledgling textile industry; indeed, he'd had no interest whatsoever in any part of the industrial revolution that had swept across the countryside. He had set off for a new country, with a completely different goal. He had not been looking to make his fortune by exploration and enterprise, but a series of fortuitous circumstances and a certain coincidence of interests had altered the course he had set for himself.

Mr and Mrs Bingley had invited a number of friends and relations to meet Mr Daniel Faulkner, but well before the day of the function, he was introduced to the Darcys. Spending a quiet day at Pemberley, Daniel became better acquainted with Mr Darcy and Elizabeth, who had not seen him since he was a little boy, together with Cassandra and Julian and their families. He learnt through their conversations that these diverse people appeared to share many ideas and principles that had been close to his own heart.

Anna and Jonathan had told him of the work that had been done in and around the Pemberley estate to house the poor, educate their children, and support efforts to improve their lives. Daniel had been impressed and said he wished the same could be said for the Australian colonies.

"No one cares enough to do anything for the poor, save for the missionaries, whose hands are full though their pockets are empty. The squatters, who obtain vast tracts of land, unimaginable in this country, often by influence and sometimes corruptly, care nothing for those they displace or exploit in order to make money. The poor and indigent are truly wretched because there are no benevolent landlords like your Mr Darcy and no Mr Gladstones in government, either, to make laws to help them."

Anna was delighted to hear him speak in such compassionate terms and wondered at how he had acquired such ideas while working in a land with a reputation for harshness in both climate and culture.

Both Elizabeth and Mr Darcy had judged Daniel Faulkner to be a genuinely good man with strong principles. They were unable, however, to comprehend why he had left England and gone out to the antipodes.

"He does not appear to be the typical adventurer or explorer, does he?" asked Elizabeth, after the Bingleys and their guest had left to return to Ashford Park, to which Mr Darcy replied, "He does not; you are quite right, Lizzie. It is a question that has been puzzling me all afternoon. Mr Faulkner seems to be a man of principle; I have no doubt of it, which is why the reason for his departure from England and his apparent success in the colonies are far from clear. He does not strike me as the sort of man who is likely to make good in the colonies."

"But surely the fact that he has been successful in business should not count against him?" asked his wife, and Mr Darcy was quick to agree. "Of course not, my dear, it may well be he is one of that rare breed like your uncle Mr Gardiner, an ethical and successful businessman. But I should still like to know what it was that caused him to leave England twenty years ago. It could not have been the inducement of doing business in the colonies; he does not seem the type who would be attracted to such an occupation."

Elizabeth concurred. "I believe you are right. I understand from Anna that Daniel had left England without giving his family any explanation, except to say an opportunity had come up and he was inclined to take advantage of it. I wonder if we will ever know the answer."

It was a question that would not be answered for a considerable time.

On the day of the party at Ashford Park, all was excitement at Caroline's house. They had all been invited, of course, including Miss Grantley, who had surprised them by laying out not one but three gowns on her bed and asking Caroline and Rachel which one would be most suitable for the occasion. "I am not familiar with the arrangements at Ashford Park. I wondered if you would guide me in what I should wear. Mama made me bring several gowns to wear at Pemberley; I do not know if they will suit," she had said.

Neither Rachel nor her mother had paid that much attention to the matter of choosing their own gowns, so it was with some surprise that they went to assist Virginia on her choice. It wasn't easy, for the gowns were all very different and very fashionable, but none seemed quite right for Virginia. She had a very pale complexion, fair hair, and clear blue eyes, and the gowns were all rather more suitable for a darker, younger woman. A black silk was discarded as being too much like formal mourning, a pale cream with silk embroidery was much admired by both Caroline and Rachel, but Virginia wondered if her mother mightn't be offended because it "didn't look sufficiently mournful," which left a dark grey gown with lavender ruffles down the skirt.

"Will it suit?" she asked, looking at them anxiously, and though they both felt the colours did very little for Virginia's complexion, it had a sort of fashionable elegance that would be appropriate for the occasion.

Pleased with their advice, Virginia declared that she would like to retire to her room for the rest of the afternoon and would they inform her maid that she should prepare a bath for her mistress at four o'clock. Caroline and Rachel, lost for words, nodded in agreement and went downstairs. Neither said a word until they were safely out in the kitchen garden, where mother and daughter broke into peals of laughter.

As night fell at Ashford Park, everything was in readiness, and the Bingleys came downstairs to see that all the arrangements were as they should be.

They were both excited by the occasion; it had been a long while since they had given a ball, owing mainly to the uncertain state of Mr Bingley's health. This evening, however, he appeared in far better spirits and claimed that he had not felt so well in years. It was all Jane wished to hear.

Their guests would soon be arriving, and Mr Bingley, who always loved a party, was determined to enjoy this one.

"I could wager any amount you care to name, dearest, that our guest of honour will be in great demand tonight. He is bound to be a popular man," he said, and Jane, knowing her husband's predilection for fun, replied that she was certainly hopeful that he would be well liked, because he was such an amiable gentleman.

"And very eligible, too; Jonathan tells me he made a fortune in gold mining, which he has invested very sensibly. No prospective mother-in-law can afford to ignore such facts," said Mr Bingley.

"He is a good deal older, of course, forty-five or six, I think?" Jane reminded him, at which Bingley merely laughed. "He does look a little weather-beaten, I grant you, but, my dear, what does that matter when a man has both sufficient charm and the means to make a lady happy? I will have to confess that if we had an unmarried daughter in her twenties, which we do not, because all our girls were too beautiful to be unwed for long, I should not have scorned a proposition from Mr Daniel Faulkner. Would you?"

Jane was less enthusiastic. "I cannot say for certain; I have not sufficient knowledge of him to say yea or nay. I know he is Anna's brother and admittedly a very likeable gentleman. Jonathan speaks highly of him, too, so perhaps for a young lady who has not had much success in finding a partner, he could be a good prospect, but I am glad all our girls are happily settled."

Mr Bingley professed astonishment. "My dear Jane, surely you do have not some deep prejudice against Mr Faulkner?" he asked.

Jane shook her head. "No, indeed I have not, but I will admit to having some reservations about his plans to return to New South Wales! It is so far away, any young woman who marries him may well be rich, but she will probably never see England or her family again!"

"There is that, of course," her husband conceded, "but, in the case of some young ladies, that may not be as great a privation as it would have been to our girls. Not everyone desires to settle close to their family."

Jane smiled and reminded him that every mother would grieve if she had no prospect of seeing her daughter or her grandchildren, and that made even Bingley reconsider his enthusiasm for Mr Faulkner.

"That is certainly true," he said, but before their conversation could become too serious, the servants arrived to open the great front doors and announce the first of their guests.

※

Caroline, Rachel, and Virginia were not quite the last to arrive at Ashford House, but the distance they had had to travel from Matlock and the modest vehicle that conveyed them thither had caused some inevitable delays.

This meant that most of the guests, and especially the ladies, had already been introduced to Daniel Faulkner, and while he had not shown any particular interest in any of them, there were a fair few who had expressed an interest in him. Nor were they all young ladies; a few mothers and at least two fathers of eligible young women had enquired about Daniel Faulkner's prospects and asked to meet him.

When Caroline Fitzwilliam arrived with her two young ladies, some of the guests, those who were not dancing or were hungrier than most, were already moving into the dining room, which was why it took awhile for Mr and Mrs Bingley to extricate themselves and go out to greet the three late arrivals.

Coming upon them, waiting rather awkwardly in the hall, Jonathan and Anna set out immediately to put them at ease. Jonathan went to fetch two young gentlemen to escort the young ladies in to dinner, while Anna, seeing her brother in the doorway, called him over and introduced him to them. As

Jonathan returned with two members of the Bingley clan to take Rachel and Virginia in to dinner, Daniel offered Caroline his arm.

"Mrs Fitzwilliam, I am delighted, because among all these people, many of whom I do not know at all, you, I do remember well," he said quietly.

Caroline expressed surprise. "Do you?"

"Indeed I do," he said, "we have met before, on more than one occasion, although, I grant you, it was rather a long time ago and you may well have forgotten all about it."

He revealed that as a young boy of some sixteen years, he, with his parents, had attended the wedding of Cassy Darcy at Pemberley.

"And of course she married my brother Richard," said Caroline, smiling.

"She did, and then the following year, my cousin Amelia-Jane Collins, who was but a couple of years older than I, married Jonathan Bingley, and again I met you and your sister at the wedding."

Caroline was amazed that he could remember, but had to confess she had no recollection of him at all, except that Becky Tate had once told her and Emily that her young cousin Daniel Faulkner had gone off to Australia. "I recall my late husband asking her if you were off to the gold fields and predicting that you would make a fortune. Did you?"

At the mention of the colonel's name, Daniel Faulkner's countenance underwent a change. The smile disappeared and he looked quite distressed as he said, "I have heard from both Jonathan and my sister about the death of Colonel Fitzwilliam. I am so very sorry. Please accept my sincerest sympathy."

Caroline's lip quivered, but she bowed slightly to accept his condolences, thanked him graciously, and then said in a quiet, steady voice, "Colonel Fitzwilliam was a good judge of people and a dedicated Reformist, and we miss him terribly. But you have not answered my questions, Mr Faulkner: was it the gold fields that drew you to Australia, and did you make a fortune?"

He could see that she was determined not to surrender to the sorrow that clearly welled up inside of her as she remembered her husband and decided it was best to indulge her. "Well, since it seems we are to be seated together at dinner, let me tell you all about it then," he said.

Caroline nodded and smiled; as they all went in together, the gathered guests, those who were not too busy eating, may have noticed that Mr Faulkner was escorting one of the most elegant women in the room.

During the dinner, Daniel was as good as his word. He told Caroline of his nightmare journey to New South Wales on board a ship transporting both convicts and sheep. "I don't know which of these were more trouble."

"Sheep?" exclaimed Caroline. "How did they care for the poor creatures on a ship during such a long voyage?"

"Much better than they cared for the convicts, believe me. These were exceedingly valuable sheep, and they had their own sheep doctor to look after them and all the right fodder. The convicts had none of that, and they got flogged into the bargain."

Caroline shivered and said quickly, "Oh, please spare me the details; I am relieved the Parliament has stopped the pernicious practice of transportation; I am so ashamed of what we used to do to people."

"So am I," said Daniel, offering to tell her a more cheerful tale from the goldfields of Victoria, where a small band of miners had rebelled against the authorities and struck a blow for freedom. He had such an easy manner and a most engaging way of telling a story that Caroline found herself so absorbed, she let the food go cold on her plate. His tales reminded her of the stories Fitzwilliam used to tell of life in the colonies of India and Ceylon, and she was fascinated.

Later, when the ladies withdrew to the drawing room, Daniel Faulkner remained behind with the gentlemen, but not for long. He had excused himself, saying he had little taste for port and brandy.

"They are too rich for my palate," he declared as he joined the ladies, who were being entertained by a few of the younger guests, who had persuaded the musicians to provide music suitable for dancing. Invited to participate, he claimed that he had not danced in England for twenty years and was out of practice and unfamiliar with the newer figures and styles.

But later, when he asked first Caroline, then Rachel, and finally Virginia to dance, he proved by his performance that he was in no great danger of losing his skill. Thereafter he entertained them with anecdotes of life in Australia, answering their questions about the distant continent, until the rest of the gentlemen entered the room.

By the time Caroline and her two young ladies were ready to return home, there was general agreement: Mr Daniel Faulkner was a most agreeable and impressive gentleman. There were apparently others of the same opinion, for he had received several invitations to dine with families in the district.

Clearly, the Bingleys' party had been a great success.

The morning after being Sunday, Caroline and Rachel went to church in Matlock. Virginia's maid had indicated that her mistress had been too exhausted after the previous night's function to go to church and was still fast asleep.

Neither Caroline nor Rachel were at all surprised by this news; pausing only to urge the maid to let the lady sleep as long as she wished, they set off on foot. It was midmorning when they returned home to find Virginia still upstairs, having asked for a pot of tea and breakfast to be brought to her room.

"I cannot believe she could be so tired; she danced but twice and spent most of her time sunk among the cushions on the sofa!" Rachel complained, and her mother reminded her to keep her voice down. "We must not upset her, my dear, Lizzie tells me that with Virginia away, Georgiana is a changed woman. She eats and sleeps better and does not weep as often. She must make her mother very unhappy. Poor Georgiana, I wish there was something more I could do to help her," said Caroline.

Rachel was about to assure her mother that she thought they had done quite enough by taking Virginia off her mother's hands, when the doorbell rang and moments later, the maid brought in a note for Caroline.

Cassandra had written to ask them to join a party at the Camden estate for a cricket match and picnic that afternoon. "It would be much appreciated if Rachel would agree to help keep scores. The match starts at midday," wrote Cassy, urging them not to be late.

Looking at the time, Rachel gasped; it was almost eleven o'clock. Rachel loved cricket and was well experienced in keeping scores. "We shall never get there in time. Virginia must be still asleep; I have not heard a sound from her room."

"Go up and tell her about it; I am not so sure she cares for cricket. Ask her if she would like to come," Caroline urged, and Rachel ran upstairs to find that Miss Grantley had indeed returned to bed, leaving her breakfast half eaten.

When Rachel told her of the invitation to Camden Park for a cricket match and picnic lunch, Virginia groaned, her head still hidden from sight.

A muffled voice said she hated cricket and did not wish to go to Camden Park anyway. "Cassy doesn't approve of me; she thinks Mama spoils me. I should prefer to stay here and recover fully from last evening's function. I certainly don't feel strong enough for cricket!" she declared, which response quite delighted Rachel, who went down to her mother with a much happier expression on her face. At least she would not have Virginia to worry about; she could concentrate on enjoying the cricket.

An hour later, they were arriving at Camden Park where some of the would-be cricketers were already practising their skills on the green.

To their surprise, among the eager players was Daniel Faulkner.

"I wonder how he happens to be here? I thought he was staying with the Bingleys at Ashford Park," said Caroline. Her curiosity was satisfied later in the day when, as they sat under the trees keeping scores, Cassy's youngest daughter Laura Ann came to join them. A delicate girl, she was somewhat shy, and while Rachel concentrated upon the scores, Caroline tried to engage her in conversation. "Laura, is Mr Faulkner staying at Camden House?" asked Caroline, explaining that they had met him at Ashford Park the previous evening.

Laura Ann answered quite candidly, "Yes, he is here for a fortnight at least; Mama said Mr Bingley was taken ill late last night, after the ball, and Mr Faulkner felt that he would be in the way and wanted to take a room at the inn at Matlock. But Papa and Mama have invited him to stay with us. He is very nice and friendly, not at all stuffy and pompous."

"Why on earth should he be stuffy and pompous, Laura, simply because he is a little older than the lads?" Caroline asked, trying hard not to laugh, but Laura was unperturbed.

"Well, most of the other such guests have been very pompous and stuffy indeed. But Mama said I must not gossip about him; she will be most annoyed if she knew I had said anything," said Laura, before she slipped away, leaving Caroline more puzzled than ever.

She could not imagine what there was to gossip about Mr Daniel Faulkner. He had been open and frank about his travels and adventures; surely there could be nothing to hide. There was the story of his wife's death, of course, and the child; she wondered if there was some problem with the boy. She recalled that she did not even know the child's name and made a mental note to ask Lizzie or Anna about it.

Darcy Gardiner's team of players had taken the field, which meant that the other team, of which Daniel Faulkner was a member, was going to bat first.

Within half an hour, two of the team were out and back in the pavilion. When a third wicket fell, there was some applause as Daniel Faulkner came to the crease to face the bowling.

"I wonder if he has forgotten his cricket too…" Caroline pondered aloud.

A loud thwack and a cheer heralded the first six of the match, and Rachel turned to her mother and said, "I think you have your answer, Mama."

Caroline smiled to herself, recalling how her Fitzy had loved the game and the fun they'd had every Summer challenging the Pemberley team. "You are right, Rachel; he has certainly not forgotten his cricket," she said and prepared to enjoy the rest of the game.

When they broke for lunch, the "others" had made a respectable total, although Mr Faulkner had got out on the last ball before lunch.

They repaired to the tent for refreshments, when Daniel appeared and said, "Mrs Fitzwilliam, how very nice to see you again. Mrs Gardiner did say you were here, but I have been so anxious about the match, I did not see you. I believe you are keeping scores, Miss Rachel; how did you get on?"

"I am indeed, and I was getting on well enough, until you came out to bat. You were scoring much too fast for me to keep count. I had to get Mama to help," she replied, and he laughed and said he was sorry to have been so much trouble and promised to make fewer runs next time.

"Would that not defeat the purpose?" teased Rachel, and he had to agree it would.

He joined them as they walked out to sit in the shade, and Rachel asked if he had played cricket in Australia. He admitted that he had, but only rarely, for there were not many cricket clubs around, but he had joined a team in the country, he said, composed mainly of farmers' sons and some ex-convicts.

"And is that how you have kept in practice?" asked Rachel.

"I have tried very hard to do so, but it is not always possible. I fear my skills are seriously in need of improvement," he replied.

When Rachel protested that he was being far too modest, because they had all seen how well he could hit the ball, Daniel laughed and, turning to Caroline, said, "I had no idea Miss Rachel was such an enthusiast. I was told she was a good scorer, but it seems she knows a great deal about the game."

Caroline smiled. "My husband used to coach the Matlock team, and Rachel was her father's keenest assistant; he taught her everything," she explained and again, Daniel's countenance grew serious, and he seemed a little distressed at having reminded her again of her late husband. A member of his team came out to look for him, and he excused himself politely and left them.

Caroline could not recall a pleasanter day in several months and said as much when Cassy came to thank her and Rachel for coming in spite of the late invitation. "I must apologise for not having asked you earlier, but we had no idea we would have sufficient men to make up two teams, and when Mr Bingley fell ill last night—not very seriously, thank God—I thought we might even cancel the game. However, Richard assures me he will be much better soon; it was just a very small turn, and no real damage done."

"Jane must be very relieved," Caroline remarked, and Cassy agreed.

"Oh yes, she certainly is that. She worries about him all the time, ever since he suffered that bad bout of influenza a year or so ago. I will confess that I was concerned too last night, he seemed very tired suddenly and had to be helped to his room. Fortunately we had not left, and Richard went to him at once. It could have been quite frightening if there had been no physician present."

Caroline took the opportunity to ask about Daniel Faulkner staying at Camden House and received an answer that convinced her Cassy was being rather circumspect. "Yes, he is come to stay with us for a few weeks; it is a chance for him to get away from Ashford House while Mr Bingley recovers. Daniel felt he would be in the way and was happy to accept our invitation; besides, Richard would like his advice on some restoration work that needs doing in the chapel, so it suits us, too," she explained. Caroline could not help wondering at the diversity of Mr Faulkner's talents. Advising on the restoration of chapels, as well as wool trading and gold mining—it was an impressive list, indeed, she thought.

Later, when Daniel returned to sit with them while the game continued, she asked casually, "I understand you are to advise Dr Gardiner on refurbishments to the chapel at Camden House, Mr Faulkner. The art of restoration must be a fascinating study."

He looked surprised, as though he had not heard her correctly; then he said Dr Gardiner had mentioned it, but he didn't know a great deal about it. He then added that the innings was almost over and he should be getting back to his team. "We shall have to be out in the field very soon, I think," he said. "I hope I see you both again before you leave."

Caroline said she was sure he would, because Cassy had asked them to stay to tea. For the first time since they had met the previous evening, she felt that Daniel had evaded answering a question; she was puzzled as to the reason.

When a sharp shower of rain caused an interruption to the game, everyone went indoors. They met again in the saloon, where Cassy and her helpers were dispensing tea and cake. But, this time, although he was polite and friendly, there was a crowd around them and neither attempted to make conversation. Caroline had a suspicion that Daniel Faulkner was rather grateful. She could not help but wonder why a man, who had been so amiable and open with her on the previous evening, had seemed discomfited by a simple question.

Chapter Six

THE DAY AT CAMDEN Park had afforded Caroline an opportunity
to observe Mr Daniel Faulkner in the company of a great many
people. She had noticed, with approval, that he appeared equally
at ease with the ladies and gentlemen from Pemberley and Camden Park
as he was with the young men of the village, some of whom made up his
cricket team.

It was one of the most agreeable traits she had recognised in him. On the
previous evening, when they had been at Ashford Park, she had thought he
had seemed a little reserved with some of the keener guests, who might have
questioned him too closely or pressed him for information about himself. Quite
clearly, he did not appreciate such intrusive interest.

Indeed, apart from entertaining her during dinner with some amusing
anecdotes from his sojourn in Australia, he had revealed not a very great deal
of himself or his personal circumstances. Which was as it should be, of course;
there was no reason at all why Daniel Faulkner should feel he had to lay his life
open for every curious busybody, Caroline thought.

It was said and generally accepted that he was wealthy, and because he was
friendly and charming, as well being Anna Bingley's brother, he was welcomed
by everyone. Many people knew very little about him and would have liked to
know more, but he seemed in no hurry to satisfy their curiosity.

Caroline wondered why, then swiftly dismissed her concerns; after all, his life was none of her business. It was not as though he was a prospective partner in business or a suitor for her daughter's hand. The thought made her stop and consider again what it was about him that had engrossed her so, but she came to no logical conclusion.

The sound of wheels and hooves on the drive drew her to the window. She was not expecting a visitor and was surprised to see Georgiana Grantley at the door. Concealing her astonishment quite creditably, Caroline welcomed her guest and took her into the morning room, saw her comfortably settled beside the fire, and rang the bell to order tea.

Assuming Georgiana had come to see her daughter, she began to explain that both Virginia and Rachel had gone into Matlock that morning. "I believe it was to do with Rachel's determination to be first at the bookshop to get the latest episode of some new novel by a woman whose name I have forgotten. Rachel is a great reader and is forever buying books. I must confess I no longer have the time to read them, but I am not permitted to escape, because she insists on reading to me every night and claims..."

Even as she talked, Caroline became aware that her visitor was not listening; it was clear that she was distracted by something quite different. It was very unlike Georgiana to be ill-mannered, Caroline thought, so she was obviously troubled. Caroline stopped in mid sentence and asked, "Georgiana, is something wrong? I am sorry; I supposed you were here to see Virginia, and I have been chattering on without taking notice of your concerns. Forgive me; you must think me very rude indeed."

The maid came in with the tea tray, and neither spoke for a while. Then, as the door closed after the maid, Caroline noticed that Mrs Grantley was by now looking quite distressed. Having poured out a cup of tea and handed it to her, Caroline tried again. "I can see now that you are very concerned about something; can you tell me about it? Does it concern Virginia? I do not wish to pry, but if I can help..."

Georgiana put down her cup of tea. "You were half right, Caroline; I did come on account of Virginia, but I was not particularly wishing to see her. It was you I came to see, and yes, I am concerned about my daughter and I was hoping you might advise me."

Caroline was more than a little baffled by this new approach. She was well aware of the problems Georgiana had with her daughter and had thought to help by inviting Virginia to stay. What else she might do, she could not imagine.

When she said nothing, Georgiana took a few sips of tea and continued, "Caroline, have you not been anxious about Rachel?"

Caroline was completely bewildered; what on earth could Georgiana have to do with Rachel, and why did she believe Caroline should be anxious about her? "Rachel?" she said. "Should I be anxious about her?"

"Yes," said Mrs Grantley. "Your lovely Rachel, are you not uneasy that she is as yet unmarried, not even spoken for?"

Caroline looked exactly as she felt, amazed. "No," she replied, "I am not uneasy or anxious at all, because it is Rachel's choice if she wishes to marry or not, and while her late father and I would have been delighted to see her happily married, she has not met a man she can love, for whom she is willing to give up the secure life she has here, and I would certainly not persuade her to marry someone she does not love."

After that little homily, Georgiana looked rather shaken and said somewhat tentatively, "I do understand that, Caroline, but have you not thought what might become of her if, God forbid, you were to die suddenly, leaving her alone? Have you not lain awake at night worrying about it?"

"No, have you?" asked Caroline, quite shocked.

"Indeed I have, ever since Dr Grantley passed away, leaving me to handle all these matters, I have been most anxious about what might happen to Virginia if I were to go also."

Caroline almost laughed out loud but stopped herself in time. "My dear Georgiana, surely there is no reason to suppose such a thing would happen to you? As far as I know, you are healthy and likely to live many more years, and even if such a tragedy should befall you, is not your daughter well provided for under the terms of Dr Grantley's will?" she asked, and Georgiana agreed that she was.

"Yes indeed, but therein lies my other problem; how shall I be sure that any man who asks for her hand in marriage genuinely loves her and is not after her money?"

Caroline had to agree that was indeed a problem for any young woman with a good fortune. She had some recollection of a tale her late husband Colonel Fitzwilliam had told them about Georgiana's large inheritance and the problems that Mr Darcy had faced in protecting her from unscrupulous fortune hunters.

At least, Caroline thought in passing, she had no such problem with Rachel. There was no great fortune for anyone to hunt; she would be comfortable for as long as she lived at home with her mother and would one day inherit her share of the Matlock property, but the colonel had hoped it would be equally divided among their children, unless one of them elected to buy out the others.

Caroline's wandering thoughts were recalled to the present, as it seemed Georgiana was eager to continue. "Sadly, I find I cannot talk to Virginia about it. She is too self-contained; she has no need for my advice. Have you spoken with Rachel?" she asked.

"Do you mean have we spoken of marriage? Yes, we have, and she says she will not marry unless she falls in love, which it seems she has not so far," said Caroline.

"But what of her future?" asked Georgiana, to which Caroline, with a certain amount of irritation, replied, "Her future is for Rachel to decide, Georgiana. Rachel will marry if she meets a respectable man she can love, who can make her happy. If she does not choose to wed, she will, as a result of the generosity of her dear father, have sufficient income to live in reasonable comfort for the rest of her life."

Georgiana persisted, "But do you not feel, as her mother, that you have a duty to see her settled? I fear that if I do not ensure that Virginia is married, I should have failed my daughter."

Caroline smiled. "I do not feel it is my duty to push my daughter into matrimony; I cannot believe it will give me peace of mind to do so, unless I was certain she wished it, too."

Then, turning to her guest, she asked, "Georgiana, may I ask if there has been anything particular that has brought on these concerns now?"

Having first hesitated, Georgiana said softly, "Yes, there is something—or rather someone particular. Caroline, I must beg you to keep this to yourself. I have not said a word to Lizzie or my brother; they would surely laugh at my fears."

Caroline promised her that secrecy was assured.

Georgiana continued with a question. "Caroline, I know there has not been much time, but may I ask if you have formed an opinion about Mr Faulkner?"

Caroline was, for a moment, too surprised to speak. Presently, she asked, "Mr Daniel Faulkner? Anna Bingley's brother?"

Georgiana nodded. "Yes, I did notice that he spent quite some time with you at the Bingleys' party. I wondered if you had come to a conclusion about him; would you say he is an acceptable and trustworthy person?"

Caroline felt as though she was sinking into a quagmire from which she could not escape. She tried to give an honest answer, while seeking some clarity about the question.

"I found him to be a pleasant and amiable man, but then that was just a personal judgment after a very short acquaintance. May I ask, Georgiana, to what end this enquiry goes? Am I right in thinking that Mr Faulkner has indicated an interest in Virginia?"

At this, Georgiana shook her head quite vigorously. "Oh no, not at all. But I understand his situation is very comfortable, and if he were an amiable and respectable gentleman, I should not be averse to such a match," she said.

"Do you mean to put a proposition to him regarding Virginia?" Caroline asked, aghast at the prospect.

"Not directly, no. But I would not discourage it if someone, a mutual friend or relative, were to do it on my behalf. Perhaps you would understand better were I to let you in on a little secret—my own engagement to Dr Grantley came about through the intervention of our very dear friends, the Continis. I had never dreamed he would even consider me, although he was always very kind, but he had confided in Signora Contini and she made me aware of his feelings. Now if it if it were possible that Virginia..."

"And what does Virginia think?" asked Caroline, still unconvinced that there was any real similarity in their situations.

"I have said nothing to her yet of this. Which is why you must not breathe a word... it would alarm her and set her off on one of her silly plans."

"What plans?" asked Caroline.

Georgiana shrugged her shoulders. "Oh, she's always threatening to run away and join the missionaries, but I don't believe she will..."

Caroline heard no more of this unlikely story, because the front door opened, admitting Rachel and Virginia, and all conversation ceased abruptly. Virginia had barely greeted her mother before she threw herself into an armchair and declared she was starving.

"I have never walked so many miles before… my feet are so sore, I do not believe I shall ever walk again!" she complained, rolling her eyes dramatically.

Believing that mother and daughter deserved to spend some time together, Caroline left the room, taking Rachel with her. Looking into the kitchen, she urged the maid to take in more tea and refreshments for Mrs Grantley and Miss Virginia.

As they made their way upstairs, Rachel asked in a whisper, "What has happened, Mama? Why is Mrs Grantley here?"

Caroline answered quickly, "Nothing has happened. Georgiana wished to see Virginia, surely that is not so surprising, considering she did not attend the cricket at Camden Park on Sunday."

At that, Rachel exclaimed, "Speaking of cricket, Mama, can you guess who else was at the bookshop in Matlock?"

"I cannot. Who was it?" asked Caroline.

Rachel smiled an arch sort of smile and said, "Anna Bingley and her brother, Mr Daniel Faulkner!"

Caroline looked a little surprised, as Rachel chattered on, "I think Mrs Bingley was choosing books for Nicholas; she asked me if I had read *Great Expectations*, but, Mama, you will never guess which book Mr Faulkner was buying!"

Caroline looked puzzled, and Rachel laughed and said, "It was the *Book of Common Prayer*! Now what do you say to that?"

Her mother shook her head in exasperation; she'd had quite enough of curious surprises for one day. She could not make it out at all.

By the time Caroline and Rachel came downstairs, Virginia, having partaken of an ample afternoon tea, had fallen fast sleep in the armchair beside the fire and Georgiana was preparing to leave. As she kissed Caroline goodbye, Georgiana whispered in her ear, "Thank you for being so patient and listening to me. I value your advice very much indeed," and then, as she entered the carriage that stood waiting, she said, "And please, not a word to Virginia or Rachel."

"Absolutely not, I promise," said Caroline, and she saw Georgiana smile with relief.

❦

Later, having retired to her room, Caroline confided in her diary:

It is beyond belief that Georgiana intends to prod her daughter into a marriage with a gentleman some fifteen years her senior, of whom she knows very little save that he is Anna Bingley's brother and is said to be wealthy.

That he has lived in the antipodean colonies for some twenty years and may well wish to return there appears not to concern her at all. Nor does she seem to want to discover how he made his money. It is well known that some people who went to the more distant colonies became rich as a consequence of their involvement in some questionable activities. I do not believe this of Mr Faulkner, but I should have thought that Georgiana, if she wishes to consider him as a suitor for her daughter, would be concerned about such matters, especially if she is to accompany him to the other side of the world. If it were my Rachel, I would not be at all sanguine about it. But then, it could never be Rachel, for she will not marry anyone unless she is in love with him, nor would I wish her to do so.

I am troubled too that Georgiana has not consulted either Lizzie or Mr Darcy on this subject. It shows a desire to conceal her intentions from them, which is quite unlike her usual behaviour. Poor Georgiana, poor Virginia, I would not exchange places with them for all the tea in China!

She drew a line under her entry and almost put her diary away, then opening it up again, added a postscript at the bottom of the page:

Poor Daniel Faulkner, I cannot help wondering what he might think, or indeed his sister Anna Bingley, if they knew Georgiana's plans for him. He certainly did not appear to me to be a docile or compliant sort of man; rather he seemed to be the type of person who would very much wish to make up his own mind on such matters, much like my Fitzy was at that age.

That evening, bored and alone because Virginia, claiming to be exhausted and sore, had retired to bed and Rachel was ensconced in a chair by the fire, deep in the latest novel, Caroline set off to walk along the Matlock road with only the late colonel's dog Dasher for company.

It was a pretty, early Autumn evening, with a cool breeze blowing and a red sky presaging, at least for shepherds, a delightful day to follow.

There being still plenty of light in the sky, Caroline decided to walk as far as the crossroads, at which point she would turn around and return home. It had been a regular walk of the colonel's; he would take both dogs, or sometimes just one of his dogs and one of the children with him, when they were young enough to be persuaded.

Sometimes, when Caroline could go with him, they would walk as far as the turn-off to the peaks, from where they could see the towering head of High Tor, against the ever-changing vista of moorland and clouds. It had been their favourite walk, and they had never tired of it.

Today, Caroline was not sure she wanted to go that far; her mood was not sufficiently resilient, and she did not feel confident enough to go alone. She was but halfway to the crossroads when she saw in the distance a tall man approaching, walking briskly on the other side of the road. He carried a short stick, which he swung casually as he walked. The colonel used to carry a short stick, a practice persisting from his days in the army. Suddenly, her memories were too painful, and feeling she could walk no farther, Caroline decided to return home.

But Dasher was clearly not of the same mind. The dog that had trotted along beside her appeared to sniff something interesting in the grass, and in a trice he was away after it. Caroline called out his name, urging him to come back, but the determined hound had raced after its quarry, leaving her standing alone by the side of the road.

She tried in vain to whistle, as the colonel used to do to get the dogs to follow him, but she knew she could not. He had always teased her about it, she remembered, and tears filled her eyes as she stood on the edge of a steep bank, down which she dared not venture. At the bottom was Dasher, standing defiantly, tail in the air, nose to the ground.

Caroline was frantic. "Oh Dasher, you wretched dog… come back here at once!" she called to him, but Dasher appeared not to pay any attention to her at all.

By this time the man Caroline had seen walking towards her had in fact reached her, although she, being so fixed upon the antics of the dog, had not as yet noticed him. He had crossed the road and stood almost at her side. When he spoke, addressing her, she jumped and he apologised at once.

It was Daniel Faulkner.

"I am sorry I startled you, Mrs Fitzwilliam. I saw you and noticed you were in some distress. I was afraid that someone had fallen down the bank. I did not realise it was a dog down there; have no fear, he is quite safe, and they are very surefooted and will not go too far."

"He chased something down, it might have been a rabbit… My husband would whistle to them, and they'd return to him at once… I am afraid I cannot whistle, and he will not come when I call," she said forlornly.

He smiled and said, "Do not distress yourself; I can whistle, and I am sure when he can no longer follow the scent of his quarry, he will come back quite meekly."

Going to the edge of the bank, he whistled and called to the dog, who by now had reached a dead end in a thicket of hawthorn, its Autumn foliage glowing red in the evening light. The rabbit or hare had long gone, and having given up the chase, Dasher sat meekly down and let Daniel Faulkner approach, pick him up, and carry him to where his mistress waited.

"There you are; he's none the worse for his little escapade. They are best kept on a lead, unless you are able to chase them," he advised, and she thanked him from the bottom of her heart.

"I know that now. Thank you very much, Mr Faulkner. I really do not know how I should have persuaded him to return. Rachel would never have forgiven me if I had lost him."

He reassured her that the dog would have come home on its own after tiring of the chase, but admitted that he understood her anxiety and was glad he could be of assistance.

"You appear to know a good deal about dogs," she said. "Do you have many on your property back in Victoria?"

Daniel Faulkner shook his head and laughed. "No, I don't, but I know several sheep farmers who do. But they are mostly working dogs, specially bred and trained to help with the sheep."

This statement led to a conversation about sheep farming and dogs, and life in Victoria, and was followed by an invitation from Caroline. "I am sorry; Dasher and I have probably delayed your journey and upset your plans, but if you can spare the time, I should be very happy if you would take tea with us," she said and was surprised when he smiled and said, "Dasher and you have not upset my plans at all, just delayed them a little perhaps, because I have to confess, I was coming to visit you."

Caroline was delighted. "You were?"

"Yes, you see I was in a bookshop this morning and found this excellent book on the game of cricket, which I thought Miss Rachel might enjoy."

This time, Caroline interrupted to say, "Rachel did say that she had seen you and your sister Mrs Bingley at the bookshop this morning."

"Yes indeed, she was at the counter beside me, but when I turned around, she had already left the shop. I did look for her outside, but she was gone, which is why I thought I would call this evening with the book."

He produced a small package wrapped in brown paper, and Caroline had to say that she thought Rachel would appreciate it very much. She hoped with all her heart that it was not one which was already in the overflowing shelves of her husband's book room. If it was, she prayed that her daughter would be sufficiently tactful and not let Daniel know.

As they walked, he sensed she was tiring and gave her his arm, while at his firm command, Dasher trotted obediently along at their side.

They reached the house while it was still light, and Rachel, who had noticed her mother's absence and had been watching out for her, came rushing out to them. Seeing her mother leaning on Mr Faulkner's arm, she asked anxiously, "Mama, what happened? Are you all right? Mr Faulkner, where did you find Mama?"

He reassured her immediately. "Your mama is quite well, Miss Rachel, just a little tired, I think. She had a little adventure with Dasher. I happened to come along and was happy to help."

Having asked for tea to be served in the parlour, Caroline excused herself and went upstairs to change out of her walking clothes and shoes. When she came downstairs, Rachel and Mr Faulkner were sitting in the parlour before a lively fire, and the tea tray with cake and muffins had been placed upon the low table in front of them. Mr Faulkner was clearly enjoying one while Rachel was turning over the pages of the book.

Caroline, afraid Rachel might say something unfortunate, remarked quickly that it was very kind of Mr Faulkner to have thought of her when he saw the book on cricket, hoping very hard that Rachel would take the hint. Which, thankfully, she did, speaking enthusiastically of having to read it before the next season and learn all those excellent facts, which she was sure she should know, but didn't.

"Good girl," thought Caroline and smiled as she poured out tea for them.

"Where's Virginia?" she asked, not having seen her upstairs.

Rachel looked contrite. "Oh Mama, I'm sorry, I forgot; while you were out with Dasher, a carriage from Pemberley arrived with a message for her from Mrs Grantley, and Virginia insisted on going. She was rather upset, but said she would definitely be back tomorrow."

"Did her maid go too?" asked Caroline.

"Oh yes," said Rachel, "Virginia says she would be lost without her."

"Do the young ladies in Victoria have maids, Mr Faulkner?" Caroline asked casually, but in reality being quite keen to know.

Daniel Faulkner laughed. "Some do, those who are able to afford to bring them out from England and others who may be fortunate enough to find a young person who can be trained to do the work," he explained, adding that there were not many places where you could find a well trained parlour maid or a lady's maid in the colonies.

Caroline wondered what Georgiana would say to that. Perhaps she hoped that Virginia, if she married Mr Faulkner, would take an entire household staff with her to Victoria.

Looking across at Daniel Faulkner and noting his handsome if rather weathered features and hearing the pleasing tones of his voice, she thought how well Colonel Fitzwilliam would have liked him, and again she had to fight the tears that threatened to fill her eyes.

Seeing that it was almost dark, Mr Faulkner rose to leave, but not before he had been invited back to dine with them later in the week, when it had already been arranged that his sister Anna and her husband, Jonathan Bingley, would be joining them too. Mr Faulkner accepted with alacrity and, not long afterwards, bade them good night.

Caroline noticed that Rachel was smiling and said, "He is indeed a most pleasing gentleman, is he not?"

"Indeed he is," Rachel replied, "which is why I had not the heart to tell him that Papa had a first edition of this book, which I have read several times over. It's a very famous book on the game."

"Oh dear," said Caroline, "poor Mr Faulkner, he was so proud of having found it and he walked all this way with it, too. I am glad that you said nothing about Papa's copy. He would have been very disappointed."

"Yes, and then we should not have had such a good conversation about cricket either. He knows a great deal about the game and has played quite a lot of cricket in Victoria," said Rachel cheerfully.

"Did he say when he was returning to Victoria?" asked her mother.

"No, he did not, but he is going to London next week to meet a friend who has recently arrived from New South Wales. Mr Faulkner says he is what they call a grazier—a sort of big sheep farmer. His name is Mr Adam Fraser, and he has been invited by Richard and Cassy to spend a week at Camden Park."

Chapter Seven

AN INVITATION TO A dinner party took Virginia and Rachel to
Camden Park. Caroline had asked to be excused, recalling that the
last time they had dined with Richard and Cassy, Colonel Fitzwilliam
had been at her side, and pleading that she wanted a little more time to grow
accustomed to the fact that henceforth, on such occasions, she would be alone.

Cassandra, sensitive and wholly sympathetic to her sister-in-law's grief,
offered to send a carriage to convey the young ladies to Camden Park and
suggested that they stay overnight, to avoid returning home at a late hour.

"I promise they will be quite safe with me," she said, causing Caroline to
protest that she had had no doubts at all on that score.

"Besides," added Cassy, "my aunt Georgiana will be joining us, so you need
have no concerns for Virginia; she will be doubly secure. Sadly, Mama has not
been feeling well, so she and Papa will not be there, but I am hopeful that Julian
and Jessica will. I shall miss you, Caroline; Daniel Faulkner will be back from
London with his friend Adam Fraser, and I desperately need a few people who
can converse intelligently with two gentlemen from Australia. I know so little
about the place, I shall feel very inadequate, and you know how Richard and
Julian talk shop all the time."

Caroline smiled. Cassy was always the anxious hostess, yet her dinner
parties were invariably successful.

"You need have no concerns about Mr Faulkner, surely; he is a very amiable sort of person and is easily entertained; perhaps his friend will turn out to be of a similar disposition, in which case you will have nothing to worry about," she said, and Cassy looked askance.

"What on earth does a rich sheep farmer talk about, other than sheep and money? And who shall I seat next to him at dinner?" she asked in a plaintive voice.

"Try Virginia," Caroline suggested. "She professes an interest in exotic places. I am sure Australia, with its strange animals and beautiful birds, will divert her sufficiently to sustain a conversation through the meal."

Cassy looked pleased with this intelligence. "Thank you, I shall. That may solve one of my problems. As for Daniel, I suppose..."

"Oh, Rachel will talk cricket with him all night, if you let her," said Caroline, and Cassy looked delighted.

"Will she? Oh well, that is a pleasant surprise. Thank you, Caroline, I am so very glad I came over today, and while I am sorry you will not join us, I do understand," she said as she rose to leave.

They embraced, and Cassy, seeing the tears in Caroline's eyes, put her arms around her, and the two women clung together for a while, for comfort.

Cassandra knew how deeply Caroline was grieving for the husband she had loved so well and recently lost.

❧

It was not from Rachel or Virginia that Caroline learned about Cassandra's successful dinner party, but from her niece Jessica, whom she met in church on Sunday.

The young ladies were still at Camden Park, sleeping off the effects of what Jessica described as "a really marvellous party, like I have rarely attended before. Everyone seemed to have such fun," when Caroline, eyebrows raised, asked, "How good was this party, Jessica, and what made it such fun?"

"I would have to say that it was primarily the presence of the two gentlemen from Australia, Daniel Faulkner and his friend Mr Fraser," Jessica replied and continued to explain, "They brought so much freshness and energy to the evening; there was a lot of interesting talk around the dinner table about fascinating things happening on the other side of the world, not just dreary business and local politics. Julian and Richard had no opportunity to talk about work or the hospital, and afterwards, they devised all manner of amusing word games, and everyone had to take part; no one was allowed to sink into the sofa and sulk or fall asleep, not even Virginia!"

Caroline was more than surprised; she was astounded. "Jessica, you are not going to tell me that Miss Grantley was persuaded to take part in some trivial after-dinner entertainment?" she asked.

"She certainly was and did so with gusto. Even her mother was astonished by her enthusiasm. I have to say that much of the credit must go to Mr Fraser, who, though he was meeting most of the guests for the very first time, was quite undaunted and insisted on getting everybody to participate. It was a most creditable performance."

"And what sort of person is this Mr Adam Fraser?" asked Caroline, genuinely curious.

"Oh a very personable young man, indeed; tall, though not as tall as Daniel Faulkner, quite a bit younger I would think, and very handsome. But what strikes one most about him is how gregarious and cheerful he is. It must be something about the country, about Australia I mean, because both he and Daniel appear to be such optimists, whereas here, we are all set about with critics and loud complainers on every side, are we not?" said Jessica.

Caroline had to agree. She remembered that Colonel Fitzwilliam had often despaired of finding anyone to share his hopes for the nation. When she'd asked him why he was quitting public life, he had said, "I have grown weary of them, my love; they are mostly little men with small minds, with no dreams and no ideals, only an appetite for profit, who have replaced the dreamers and heroes of the past." She recalled that he had shown little interest in local politics thereafter.

Distracted for a moment by her memories, Caroline forgot that Jessica had a carriage waiting for her, and when she offered to drive her home, she was jolted back to the present. "It looks like rain; you should not be walking, Aunt; let me take you home," she said, and Caroline was happy to accept. Before they parted, she thanked Jessica for her kindness and for her most engaging account of the party at Camden House.

"I am so glad we met this morning, Jessica, I would not have missed our little chat for the world," she said. "I doubt if Rachel or Virginia would have half as diverting a tale to tell. They are neither of them as good as you are at recounting such occasions. Rachel has little interest in them, and Virginia appears not to believe in communication at all."

In that matter at least, Caroline was proved right. The two young women returned later that day, claiming to have enjoyed themselves hugely, to the extent that they were utterly exhausted and wanted nothing more than to sleep, which they did until it was almost time for dinner. When they did appear downstairs, Caroline, without mentioning her meeting with Jessica, asked for some report of the previous night's party.

This time it was Virginia who spoke up to say it had been a very good party, while Rachel merely smiled and said she thought everyone had enjoyed themselves.

"Did anyone sing or play? Did you dance?" asked Caroline.

"Oh no," said Virginia, "no one did anything so boring as singing and dancing. We played games instead."

Caroline pretended to be surprised. "Games?"

"Yes indeed, lots of very clever and amusing games with words and phrases and hidden meanings…" said Virginia, before returning to concentrate upon her dinner. Virginia always had a hearty appetite.

"It was Mr Fraser's idea; he got everyone involved in playing games after dinner," Rachel explained, but neither appeared ready to go further and tell her, as Jessica had done, why they had had an extraordinarily enjoyable evening. Perhaps, thought Caroline, they were still weary and would talk more later.

But they did not, leaving her completely baffled. She could not understand why it was that two young women who had so enjoyed themselves at a party would be reluctant to confess it.

Some explanation came a few days later when Georgiana Grantley sent Caroline a note, and a carriage arrived from Pemberley for Virginia. Georgiana explained briefly that she wished to have Virginia back at Pemberley for a few days, mentioning that Mr Faulkner and his friend, Adam Fraser, who had recently arrived from New South Wales, would be dining with the Darcys on Thursday and staying over to shoot on the morrow.

I think you will understand, dear Caroline, why I believe it is a good idea for Virginia to be present, she wrote, and Caroline smiled to herself. Clearly, Georgiana was pursuing her previously expressed goal of finding a husband for her daughter and was hoping that Virginia would find one or other of the gentlemen from Australia acceptable.

As to the two gentlemen concerned, not having the advantage of meeting Mr Fraser, Caroline had no way of knowing how he would respond to Georgiana's plans, but she was more certain than ever that Daniel Faulkner was an unlikely candidate.

That night, as they dined alone for the first time in a fortnight, Caroline and Rachel clearly enjoyed the absence of their house guest. Neither wished to seem ungracious, but both mother and daughter could not hide their relief. Virginia, despite their best efforts, remained unlovable, demanding, often aggravating, and occasionally insufferable. "How much longer will Virginia stay with us, Mama?" Rachel asked, when the servants had left them.

Caroline looked reproachful. "Rachel, I thought you were getting on well with Virginia. She has not been upsetting you, has she?" she asked.

Rachel's expression spoke volumes. "No more than she upsets anyone else, I suppose, but, Mama, I really would like to have some time to myself. I don't mind Virginia staying with us; I don't even mind her occupying two rooms; I just wish she would not always require me to attend to her and follow her lead in everything. I should like some time to read, draw, or practice the piano, but it seems Virginia is bored by all of those things and always wishes to do something else, and she must have me with her. She enjoys having an audience, I think."

Caroline was contrite and very sympathetic. "Rachel my dear, I am sorry. I hadn't realised that Virginia imposed upon you, at least not to that extent. I certainly did not intend for her to do any such thing; you should not have let her, or at least, you ought have told me."

Rachel, whose good nature would not allow her to blame her mother for her troubles, refused to complain further. "It is of no great importance, Mama… I know you invited Virginia to stay to give her mother and Mr and Mrs Darcy some respite; I have no complaint about that at all. Compared to theirs, the inconvenience to me is very little," she said, and Caroline, touched by her generosity, tried to reassure her daughter that perhaps the end of her vexation was in sight. "It seems to me that Virginia may soon be returning to Pemberley for good; her mother wishes it, I think," she said.

Rachel smiled. "But does Virginia wish to return?"

Caroline was thoughtful, weighing her words carefully. "I rather think that would depend on one or other of the two gentlemen from Australia. Georgiana seems keen to have Virginia at Pemberley this week, and I understand Daniel Faulkner and his friend Mr Fraser are to be guests at Pemberley." When Rachel said nothing, her mother asked, "What do you think, Rachel?"

"I don't know what to think, Mama, Virginia has said nothing to me on the subject. I did notice that she seemed to enjoy Mr Fraser's company the other night at Camden House. She was laughing a lot, and so was he, but I cannot say if that meant anything. It was unusual, I will admit, to see Virginia so willing to be entertained and take part in the games, she is usually not so amenable, but I cannot say if that had anything to do with the gentlemen from Australia."

"And Mr Faulkner, was he not as involved with the games as his friend?" asked Caroline, very casually.

Rachel answered without any hesitation. "Yes, he was, but he was on Jessica's team, not Virginia's, and so was I."

"So, it was a contest between two teams? Whose team won?" asked her mother, with a smile.

"Ours did. Mr Fraser was very good; he knew many of the answers, but Virginia and Julian did not," Rachel explained and added, "I think Virginia was rather cross, but Mr Fraser seemed to laugh it all off. He didn't take it very seriously at all."

"Mr Fraser sounds like he must be a pleasant sort of person. Is he?"

"He is, I think, but then I hardly know him, Mama. He is genial and tells a lot of entertaining stories about his life in Australia, which Virginia enjoyed very much. She said, when we went to our room afterwards, that she had not had so much fun in years," said Rachel, and Caroline smiled.

"Well, if Virginia has as much fun at Pemberley on Thursday, she may well decide to move back there permanently. Do you suppose the two gentlemen enjoyed Virginia's company?" she asked.

Rachel laughed, appearing a little embarrassed when she answered, "I don't really know, Mama. Mr Fraser seemed to be having fun, although Mr Faulkner was a little reserved, I thought. We talked a lot during dinner, about cricket and music—he knows a great deal about music, too. Afterwards, I thought he seemed rather uneasy, but I cannot be sure. He does seem very different to his friend Mr Fraser."

The servants came in to remove their plates and Caroline changed the conversation, but made a mental note of Rachel's comments, which she found quite intriguing. Clearly her daughter had been sufficiently interested to take notice of the difference between the two men.

The rest of the meal was spent in trivial talk about the sweetness of the fruit and the excellence of the cheese at Camden House. "They grow and make their own," said Rachel, "the dinner was truly delicious."

They never did find out what exactly happened at the Pemberley House party, but were free to speculate when, a day or two later, the maid whose services Mrs Grantley and her daughter had shared arrived to pack up Virginia's things and take them away.

A brief note from her mistress thanking Caroline for her kind hospitality had been delivered, while Rachel had received a little gift from Virginia with a note that said, *Thank you, and I am sure you must be happy to have your room back.*

Caroline was quite certain that this meant Georgiana's hopes for Virginia were close to being fulfilled. However, that she had no way of knowing which of the two gentlemen was involved, she found exceedingly vexing.

As for Rachel, it appeared that she was unconcerned about the matter. Grateful to have her home restored to its former tranquil state, she went about rearranging the rooms and indulging in all those simple pleasures she had postponed in order that Virginia might be satisfied. She could, whenever she wished, wander at will into the farmyard or walk by the river that formed the boundary of the property to sketch or collect wildflowers, practice her piano in the music room or read, while lying in the hammock her father had slung between two trees in the orchard. It was bliss. Her mother, understanding her feelings, left Rachel to her own devices.

After a week of such singular enjoyment, Rachel had begun to feel guilty that she had not paid sufficient attention to her mother. It was as though she had become intoxicated with the sense of freedom that Virginia's sudden departure had given her, to the exclusion of every other feeling.

On the afternoon in question, Rachel had been sketching by the river when she decided, quite suddenly, that she had been neglecting her mother and needed to get back home to her. Besides, the sky was clouding over and it looked like rain.

As she packed up her satchel and prepared to leave, she caught sight of two people, a man and a woman, walking among the trees on the far side of the river. They were too far away to be easily identified, but Rachel thought the man looked familiar. As the couple moved deeper into the woods, she lost sight of them; then, hearing laughter, she turned around and at that moment recognised the laughing voice of Mr Adam Fraser. She had heard that laugh many times at the dinner party at Camden House and was sure she was not mistaken. Puzzled, she lingered a few more minutes, in order to be sure, but the pair had disappeared from sight, and with rain threatening, she decided to make her way back to the house.

Approaching the house, Rachel saw her mother and a gentleman at the front door. It was unmistakably Mr Faulkner, and he looked as though he was just taking his leave of her.

Stepping out into the drive, he saw Rachel and stopped. "Miss Rachel! How very nice to see you again. I believe you have been out sketching in the woods."

The mention of the woods made her jump. "No, I mean yes, I have been out sketching, but I did not go into the woods, I was down by the river…" she said quickly.

"And did you do much work?" he asked, and again, she was a little awkward as she answered, "No, I fear not, the light wasn't very good and I was distracted…"

"Distracted?" He seemed surprised, and she was relieved when the rain came down in earnest and Caroline called to them, "You will both be soaked through in a minute; you might as well come back in, Mr Faulkner, and Rachel, do go upstairs and change or you will surely catch cold." Rachel obliged at once, glad to evade the questions.

She wanted to be alone to think, and as she delayed getting changed, she hoped that when she came downstairs Daniel Faulkner would be gone.

She was right. As the rain eased, he had borrowed an umbrella and set out for Camden Park. Rachel was surprised to find Caroline standing by the window, gazing out on the darkening garden and looking very anxious indeed. So much so that Rachel, who had intended to tell her mother what she had seen and heard in the woods, became concerned and, wishing not to add to her anxieties, kept silent. Instead, she asked about Mr Faulkner's visit and was even more puzzled when her mother appeared to have very little to say. Her obvious reluctance to speak about it was in complete contrast to her usual openness, and Rachel could not understand it. Quite clearly, Caroline had been disturbed by something, and since she had not appeared to be so before his visit, Rachel felt free to assume that it had to do with some matter concerning Mr Daniel Faulkner.

That night, they dined in an uncomfortable silence to which neither was accustomed. Rachel's concern was expressed in a note she wrote in her diary before she went to bed. She wrote:

> *I cannot make out what it is that worries Mama, and while I am certain that it must be linked to the visit of Mr Faulkner, for as far I could tell, she was quite cheerful before it, I am unable to imagine how he could have said or done anything that could cause Mama to become so perturbed. I am unaware of any circumstance involving Mr Faulkner that could cause her such anxiety.*

As she pondered her problem, her chief concern was her mother's apparent inability to do what they had always done over the years: talk openly about any matter that troubled them.

Indeed, since the last of her siblings had left the nest, Rachel and Caroline had grown closer together, sharing the happiest times and later the difficult, almost unbearably painful days just before and after Colonel Fitzwilliam's death. Those last days and the months following had so bonded their lives together, they had been since then more like sisters than mother and daughter, sharing without reservation both sorrow and joy.

This present disruption to their harmonious and affectionate relationship both baffled and saddened her. Not elegant or demure like her sisters, Isabella and Amy, nor as clever as her brother David, Rachel had been from childhood her mother's pet.

Born not long after her brother Edward's tragic death, she had been at first a disappointment and then, to the soft-hearted colonel and Caroline, an accident-prone little person, who soon became their special child.

Rachel's bond with her parents had proved so secure, she had never felt the restless desire that many children feel to leave their family home and had stated with a remarkable degree of determination that she would not be persuaded to do so, unless she were to fall very deeply in love. The warm relationship she had developed with her mother was a vital part of her sense of security.

Now, she was experiencing the loss of some of that stability, and it troubled her considerably. Having slept rather fitfully, she came downstairs to breakfast and found her mother dressed and ready to go out. The small carriage was waiting at the door.

Caroline had already had breakfast, and as Rachel entered the room, she had risen from the table. Desperate to know what was afoot, Rachel rushed to her side, "Mama, whatever is happening? I have been so worried... Where are you going?"

"Only to Pemberley, my dear; there's nothing for you to worry about." Caroline was surprised at the intensity of Rachel's concern.

"Why must you go to Pemberley? Is there something wrong? Is it me? Is it something I have done? Please, Mama, I must know; can you not tell me?" she pleaded, and Caroline, surprised at her distress, could not help her tears.

"Of course it isn't you, my dearest girl. Whatever gave you that notion? There is a problem, but it has nothing to do with you at all; and while I cannot talk about it now, I promise to tell you all about it when I return," she said, and while Rachel wasn't entirely reassured, at least having spoken out, she felt she was no longer isolated from her mother.

They embraced and Caroline went, leaving Rachel wondering what manner of problem at Pemberley would cause her mother so much distress.

When Caroline reached Pemberley, she was given the bad news that Mrs Darcy had a severe cold and could not come downstairs. It meant that the message she had despatched the previous afternoon asking urgently to see Lizzie and Georgiana had achieved little.

Caroline feared she would now have to see Georgiana alone, and that was not going to be easy. Seated in the more intimate sitting room, rather than the grand saloon, she was nevertheless uneasy about the magnitude of the task she had undertaken. She had fears, too, that her intervention may well be regarded as presumptuous and so do more harm than good.

While waiting alone, she considered for a moment whether she should make some excuse and flee, but it was too late; she heard footsteps in the hall, and the door opened to admit Georgiana and, unexpectedly, Mr Darcy.

Despite the cordiality of their greetings and the genuine warmth of Mr

Darcy's welcome, Caroline detected a certain degree of perplexity in their reception of her, which was bound to render her task more difficult.

While the appearance of Mr Darcy had surprised her at first, she was soon to be grateful for his presence. Caroline assumed, correctly, that Elizabeth, having received her note, had alerted her husband to the urgency of her request and persuaded him to see Caroline in her stead.

The servants brought in refreshments, which they set out on a table, and Mr Darcy, having invited Caroline to help herself, took a chair beside the fireplace, while Georgiana, appearing to be almost as ill at ease as Caroline, could not settle and kept walking restlessly about the room.

To Caroline's question about Virginia, she had replied simply that Virginia had gone to Ashford Park at the invitation of the Bingleys. When she had asked if Jonathan and Anna were still with the Bingleys, Mr Darcy had said they had returned to Netherfield yesterday. "And the gentlemen from Australia?" she had asked casually, to which Georgiana had responded, "Mr Fraser has gone to Scotland on family business; he left last morning and will not be back until Saturday. I understand Daniel Faulkner is still at Camden Park."

Caroline wondered how to begin, how best to move from these trivial pleasantries to the subject that had seemed to her to be so important, she felt duty-bound to reveal it. Again, it was Mr Darcy who came to her rescue.

Setting down his glass, he said, "Caroline, if I have understood Lizzie correctly, you had some information that you wished urgently to impart. Am I right?"

Caroline nodded, and deciding that she must use the opportunity he had provided, she mustered up her courage and said, "I must ask you to bear with me... this is not something I do easily. Indeed, I cannot recall ever having had to do anything like this before. If the need had arisen with any of our children, I am sure Fitzy would have been the one to do it. So, please forgive me if I seem to struggle a little. You may well tell me to mind my own business, Georgiana, but I did think long and hard before I came here."

Her words seemed so unusual to both her listeners, their attention was immediately riveted. Georgiana stopped walking aimlessly about the room, and Mr Darcy had risen from his chair by the fire and walked over to the sofa where she was seated. Standing in front of her, he said quietly, "Caroline, if there is anything we need to know, anything that affects a member of the family, you must feel free to tell us."

She knew she had to speak now. "It's about Mr Adam Fraser," she said slowly and deliberately, watching for Georgiana's response. It came instantly.

"What about Mr Fraser? What has he done?" Her voice was unusually sharp and defensive.

"It is not about what he has done," said Caroline. "It is about who he is."

"What do you mean? We know who he is. He is from a very old and respectable Scottish family," Georgiana declared.

Caroline took a deep breath. "He is not from an old and respectable Scottish family. That is what he claims to be."

"Are you saying his name is not Fraser?" asked Mr Darcy.

"It is, but it has nothing to do with an old and respectable Scottish family. I understand that he is the son of a seaman from California, who made good during the gold rush, and went to Australia, where he made even more money, which he invested in property. Adam Fraser inherited a fortune, but unlike his father, he has not increased it; rather he has squandered quite a lot of it."

"How do you know all this is true?" demanded Georgiana.

"My informant is Daniel Faulkner. He came to see me yesterday, because, he says, he was beginning to worry about some of the things Mr Fraser was doing and saying. He was concerned because they were not entirely honest. I cannot believe that he would lie about his friend."

"His friend?" Georgiana's tone was scathing. "How could he be his friend and yet say such things about him?"

"Georgiana, Daniel is Anna Bingley's brother; he felt that his loyalty was to this family rather than to Adam Fraser, who is a complete stranger to us. He introduced Mr Fraser to us, and when he saw that he was becoming more than an acquaintance and was being accepted by members of this family as a friend and confidante, he thought it was his duty to let the truth about him be known."

"And why should we believe him? Why is it not possible that he is mistaken or has some other motive to make us think ill of Mr Fraser?" Georgiana asked.

Mr Darcy intervened to say, "What possible motive could he have to do such a thing?" and Caroline added, "None that I know of. He did not speak out about Mr Fraser in order to promote himself in my estimation; he was afraid that if we remained in ignorance, believing as you did that Adam Fraser was the son of a respectable Scottish family, he might have insinuated himself into your confidence, and things may happen that you might later regret. I was very reluctant to come to you with this information, but he pleaded with me to do so."

Georgiana was silent, but Mr Darcy asked, "Apart from the matter of his father and the business of his wasted fortune, did Daniel Faulkner tell you anything else about Fraser that reflects upon his character?"

Caroline replied, "He did, not in great detail, because I felt that if you wished to know more, then you should speak to him directly. I agreed only to alert you to the fact that Mr Fraser was not what he claims to be."

"What more did he say?" asked Georgiana, still unconvinced.

"That Mr Fraser, having gambled much of his money away, is in England looking to wed a wealthy young woman; Daniel was afraid that he may have taken you and Virginia in."

Georgiana rose from her chair and said in a bitter voice, "I knew it. It becomes clear to me now. Daniel Faulkner is jealous of Adam Fraser; he must have had hopes of securing Virginia for himself, and seeing that she clearly preferred Mr Fraser, who is younger and better-looking, in his disappointment, he means to defame him by putting out some outrageous slander..."

Even before Caroline could protest, Mr Darcy interrupted his sister, "Georgiana, that is unfair and completely unfounded. Caroline is right; Daniel Faulkner has no reason to slander Fraser. Besides, you have no evidence that he is jealous of him; he has shown no particular interest in Virginia. I believe you ought to take what he has said seriously and think how Virginia might be advised to be cautious in her dealings with Fraser. We know nothing about him except what he has told us."

Despite her implicit trust in her brother's wisdom, Georgiana was unwilling to accept that she had been mistaken in her judgment of Adam Fraser. Her inexperience in the world, brought about chiefly through her total reliance upon the guidance and judgment of first her brother and then her beloved husband, both exemplary men, had not fitted her to make such decisions.

"I cannot believe it," she said. "He has been so open and frank with us; why, only the other day, when he was here, he was telling us about his uncle who has this wonderful deer park in the highlands..."

Caroline smiled. "Indeed, I believe Daniel Faulkner heard him telling that tale, and it was the fact that everyone appeared to believe it without question that concerned him most. There is no uncle with a wonderful deer park in the highlands. Daniel feared that Fraser would draw us all in with his tales of his Scottish heritage and great damage may be done to this family, if he kept silent. Since he had introduced Mr Fraser to us, Daniel feels responsible; he believed it was his duty to alert us to the deception being practised upon us."

Mr Darcy, who had not heard the tale of the deer park himself, said his wife had mentioned it, but since he hated the idea of shooting such magnificent creatures, he had not paid much attention to the story.

"I am more concerned to uncover the truth about his character rather than his fictitious Scottish connections. If he is here on false pretences, it would be bad enough, but if he is also a blackguard and a fortune hunter, then I think some serious action is called for. In the first instance, Virginia must be told."

Georgiana seemed unwilling to accept it. "Virginia will never believe it. In all these years, he is the first gentleman in whom she has shown the slightest interest. She likes him and enjoys his company."

"Georgiana, my dear, there is no certainty that he is a gentleman at all," said her brother quietly, and turning to Caroline, he asked, "Would Daniel Faulkner be prepared to provide me with more detailed information—names, dates, and places—so I can verify some of the facts about this man?"

Caroline agreed to ask him. "He may agree. I think if he felt that you were serious about it, he would be willing to tell you more than he has told me. I was not keen to hear too much, since it did not involve my family directly. What I did learn was sufficient to convince me that I had to warn you. I know Fitzy would have done so. I feel confident that if you were to meet with him, Mr Darcy, he would be willing to reveal much more."

"Well," said Mr Darcy, "we might make use of the time that Fraser is visiting his Scottish uncle, or whoever else he may be, to see what more we can discover about him. Caroline, would you be so kind as to send a message to Daniel Faulkner? Tell him I will meet with him tomorrow afternoon at Camden House. I should prefer that the meeting not be at Pemberley, lest we alert Virginia or Mr Fraser. Georgiana, my dear, I suggest you say nothing of this to anyone until I have met with Daniel Faulkner."

Georgiana appeared to agree with some reluctance, while Caroline under-took to send word to Mr Faulkner, relieved indeed that Mr Darcy was at least willing to pay some attention to the information she had given them, even though his sister preferred to pretend there was no truth in it.

Chapter Eight

RETURNING HOME, CAROLINE FOUND Rachel waiting for her, anxiety etched upon her face. Having promised to tell her daughter everything, Caroline was as good as her word. When they were alone in her room, she related in some detail the matters Daniel Faulkner had told her and the manner in which she had conveyed the information to Mr Darcy and Mrs Grantley.

"Mr Faulkner felt so strongly about it, he came to see me, to ask if I would speak to Georgiana and open her eyes to the truth about Fraser. From his observations over the previous week, he had concluded that both Virginia and her mother were completely taken in by his charm and general *savoir faire*. His account convinced me that it was my duty, however unpleasant, to go to Pemberley. I had hoped to see Lizzie, but she was unwell, and I had the daunting task of trying to convince Mr Darcy and Georgiana."

Rachel listened, eyes wide, hardly saying a word, until her mother said, "Fortuitously, Virginia had been invited to spend a few days with the Bingleys at Ashford Park and the man himself is gone to Scotland, left last morning I was told, to visit his respectable relatives in the highlands!"

At that, Rachel put her hand up to her mouth to suppress a cry of disbelief before saying, "No, Mama, he is not gone to Scotland; I saw him in the woods yesterday, with a young girl. They were on the other side of the river, and I thought I recognised him, but I could not be sure, until I heard him laugh. I knew then that it was definitely Adam Fraser."

Caroline was shocked. "But if it was, then the young woman could not have been anyone we know, because Virginia is with the Bingleys at Ashford Park."

"It was certainly not Virginia," said Rachel. "The girl, though I could not see her face, was much shorter than Virginia and had long, brown hair."

This new information made the whole sorry business much worse than before, and Caroline decided that it had to be conveyed to Mr Faulkner before he met with Mr Darcy on the morrow. Rachel agreed, but begged that her mother should be the one to tell him, and a servant was despatched immediately to Camden House, inviting Daniel to dine with them that evening.

"Since we are compelled to discuss unpleasant matters, the least we can do is enjoy a good meal together," said Caroline as she went to consult the cook about the menu.

Daniel Faulkner arrived at the appointed time to find both ladies waiting for him in the parlour. Caroline had decided that it would be best to get the unpleasant business over and done with first, rather than spoil a perfectly good meal. Besides, it would not do to be talking about Virginia and Adam Fraser with the servants in the room. During her stay, Virginia had not been the most popular of house guests, and the maids, who were heartily sick of her demands and complaints, were unlikely to resist the chance to gossip about her.

Which was why Caroline, having waited until Daniel had sat down with a drink in his hand, said quietly, "Mr Faulkner, I have a message for you from Mr Darcy. Following my visit to Pemberley, he has expressed a wish to meet with you, if you are agreeable, at Camden House tomorrow. I need not tell you that it was not possible to convince his sister Georgiana of the truth of the information I had from you, but Mr Darcy is keen to know the facts. Will you meet him?"

"Of course. If there is anything he wishes to ask me, I should be happy to meet him," he replied, and Caroline was clearly relieved.

"Thank you, I was hoping very much that you would agree," she said.

"How could I not? I have felt in the last week a most uncomfortable sense of guilt as I watched Fraser spin a web of fiction about himself and his activities. At first it seemed he was about his usual tricks; he has made a habit of pretence and conceit when he is in society, but I fear it is becoming more serious and there are those who may be hurt if nothing is said. If anything I can do will help Mr Darcy prevent that from happening, I should be delighted." There was no doubting his sincerity.

Later, Caroline, waiting until Rachel had left the room, told him about the couple she had seen in the woods, and he showed no sign of surprise. "I am sorry to say that I am not surprised; it is exactly the kind of subterfuge Fraser uses. He will pretend he is going away on business, but his business is of the kind he cannot reveal in respectable company. Yet he will return and play the gentleman again with the greatest of ease."

"This girl he was with, Rachel described her as being much shorter than Virginia and with long brown hair. Can you think who she might be?" Caroline asked.

Daniel Faulkner looked pensive. "I cannot say for certain, but he has spoken of a girl he calls Rosie, probably a young person from the village..."

"Rosie! Good God! That could be Rosie Higgins, the innkeeper's daughter," Caroline exclaimed, interrupting him. "She is very pretty and has long brown hair... She helps her father at the inn, serving at table. If it is Rosie and Fraser has compromised her in any way, he will not escape her father's fury."

Daniel Faulkner looked wretched. "I wish I had never brought him into Derbyshire. I feel this is all my fault."

Caroline tried to reassure him. "It is not your fault; Mr Fraser is a grown man and you are not his keeper. Besides, you could not have foreseen the circumstances in which he and Virginia were to meet; so please do not blame yourself. Whilst you meet with Mr Darcy tomorrow, I will send a message to Rosie's mother."

Presently, Rachel returned; dinner was served, and the conversation changed completely.

Cook had produced a simple but delectable feast, with fish, poultry, and home-grown vegetables and fruit, together with a good wine from the late colonel's cellar. It was rarely, since her husband's death, that they had entertained anyone at dinner, and Caroline could not help feeling a little downcast as she recalled with understandable sadness his renowned hospitality and remembered the many pleasurable evenings they had spent in the company of friends and relations over the years of their marriage. Apart from acknowledging Mr Faulkner's appreciation of the meal, she was less inclined to chat, and consequently Rachel, sensible of her mother's feelings and her duty to their guest, decided it was up to her to keep the conversation going.

Not knowing a great deal about the antipodes and even less about the place called Ballarat in Australia, where Daniel Faulkner was said to have made his fortune, Rachel supposed that it was best to start by asking a general geographical question. After they had finished the first course, she asked, "Mr Faulkner, what sort of place is Ballarat? I mean, is it a city like Derby or Birmingham?" she asked and was surprised when Daniel Faulkner laughed, before he answered, "I would not call it a city, Miss Rachel; it would be much more like a small country town now. However, when I was first in Ballarat about twenty years ago, it was just a small settlement on the edge of the diggings."

"The diggings?" she was puzzled by the term.

"Hmm… where the prospectors were living in tents and digging for gold."

This time it was Rachel who laughed before she asked, "And did you dig for gold?"

He nodded and said, "I did, along with hundreds of others, and what's more, I found some, too."

"Lots of it? Enough to make you rich?" asked Rachel, fascinated by these revelations, but her mother, who had heard the conversation, interrupted gently before he could answer.

"Rachel, my dear," she said reprovingly, "you ought not be asking Mr Faulkner such questions."

But he intervened with a smile and said, "I have no objection to her questions at all; please ask whatever you wish to know, Miss Rachel. The answer to your question is no, not lots of it, not enough to make me very wealthy, but enough to enable me to do something more with my life than prospecting for gold."

Rachel was keen to know more about life on the goldfields, but with her mother now alerted, she was a little less direct in her next question. "And did the other people in Ballarat not mind that hundreds of prospectors were digging up their countryside?" she asked, and he laughed gently and said, "It is unlikely, because it is not like England, with little villages and towns that have been settled for centuries. It's an enormous country, much of which has not been explored, and Ballarat was just a settlement on the edge of an area where gold had been discovered in 1851. When it became known, men from many parts of the world rushed there."

"To dig for gold?" she asked.

"Indeed. They had to apply for a licence and stake their claim and dig."

"And did they all find gold, Mr Faulkner?" asked Caroline.

"Many did, in varying quantities; some found very little after much hard work; others were lucky."

"Were you one of the lucky ones?" asked Rachel, causing her mother to protest and Daniel Faulkner to laugh again.

"I suppose I was, in that I spent less than three years in Ballarat, but they were very eventful years. I don't mean just for myself; I was certainly lucky with my prospecting and the partners with whom I worked, but it was also a most interesting period in the history of the town and indeed the colony of Victoria."

Intrigued, Caroline joined Rachel in asking more about the colony, and Mr Faulkner was happy to satisfy their curiosity. "I arrived in Ballarat in the middle of 1852, not long after gold had been discovered just outside the area at a place called Eureka. There were already many hundreds of men there, but hundreds more were arriving every week. I lodged at an inn at first, and having met a couple of men who invited me to join them, I applied for a licence and we set off for the diggings."

"And where did you live on the diggings?" asked Rachel.

"In a tent; everyone lived in tents. There was nowhere else to live."

Caroline found it difficult to imagine the distinguished-looking man seated at her dinner table living in a tent in rough clothes and boots, digging in the alluvial mud of the goldfields, and said so.

"I assure you, Mrs Fitzwilliam, I was a sight to behold. You would not have had me anywhere near your house if you saw me then, but it was twenty years ago and I was young, fit, and looking for adventure and gold. I did not object to a little mud!"

"Was that why you left England and went to Australia?" she asked.

"Not entirely. There was much talk then of war, and I was determined that I was not going to be pushed into the army and sent off to kill my fellow human beings. I had also met a man who had returned from New South Wales who was going back some months later and invited me to join him, and not having anything better to do, I decided to do just that."

"And where is he now?"

"Oh, he is a very successful politician in the colony of Victoria," he replied, and Caroline laughed and said, "Am I right in believing that he was one of your prospecting partners?"

Mr Faulkner confessed that he was and added, "And a brave man he was, too—but I fear I am boring you with all this talk of gold digging, let that be a story for another day, eh?" Then turning to Rachel, he said, "Miss Rachel, your mama tells me you play both the pianoforte and the harp. I am a great admirer of the instrument, but I had not heard a lady play upon the harp for twenty years until I returned to England and heard my sister Anna. Will you not let me hear you play?"

Rachel blushed and protested that she did not play half as well as Anna Bingley, when Caroline said, "Of course she will; Rachel loves her music, and I am sure she will be happy to oblige you after dinner. Will you not, my dear?"

Rachel looked at her mother's face and, turning to their guest, said, "Yes, of course, if you wish."

Daniel Faulkner said nothing would give him greater pleasure, and so it was that the rest of the evening was spent in the pleasantest way and no more was said of the history of the colony of Victoria or the deceitful Mr Fraser.

By the time Daniel Faulkner left them later that evening, both Caroline and her daughter had changed their opinions of him; and it may be assumed that he too had begun to form a different view of the two ladies he had hitherto regarded chiefly as pleasant but casual acquaintances.

With the discovery of Adam Fraser's perfidious conduct and Caroline's determination to expose it, their association had deepened already, yet, as he travelled back to Camden Park, he was thinking not only of the gravity of the meeting he was to have with Mr Darcy on the morrow, but also of Caroline and Rachel. His mind turned to the enjoyable hours he had just spent in their company and the fact that he now considered them to be two of the most interesting and intelligent women he had met in many years.

He had learnt from his sister Anna that Caroline Fitzwilliam was a most remarkable woman, who had worked tirelessly to help her late husband pursue a number of political and social causes, but he had not expected that she would be as independent and personable as he found her to be, nor as handsome.

Her daughter Rachel had a gentle charm that he had found quite engaging. It was difficult to comprehend that a lady with her looks, talent, and intelligence was unwed, indeed had not even been spoken for. During their conversations at dinner and watching her play the harp afterwards, Daniel had caught himself thinking that she was one of the most pleasing young women he had encountered since returning to England.

She was slim and small in stature, with delicate hands. He had noted that the colours and styles of formal mourning did not suit her small figure as well as they did her mother. Yet, when she had sat at her harp, having divested herself of the dark tunic-like over-garment, revealing a soft, white blouse and flowing black silk skirt, she had seemed to look younger—gentle and utterly appealing. It was the image of Rachel he carried with him as he returned to Camden Park.

Caroline could not sleep. She lay awake for almost an hour after retiring to bed, her mind full of disturbing thoughts and images, which troubled her intensely. She was glad to have transferred some of her concerns to Mr Darcy; now he could worry about Georgiana and Virginia. They were his sister and niece after all, and she was confident he could prevail upon them to regard Mr Fraser with more caution.

But she was far more uneasy about young Rosie Higgins. She would have to send for her mother and ask her if Rosie was walking out with a posh young fellow lately returned from the colonies, and if she was, it would be her unpleasant duty to tell Rosie's mother the truth about the blackguard, destroying her hopes and no doubt breaking poor little Rosie's heart. It was not something Caroline, with her romantic disposition, could look forward to with any satisfaction.

On one matter, however, she was feeling considerably happier. Her initial opinion of Daniel Faulkner, as the young man who had gone to Australia to make his fortune on the goldfields, had not been entirely favourable. She had been inclined to think him somewhat feckless and inconsiderate for disappearing to the other side of the earth for twenty years, making only occasional contact with his family. But in the last few days, she had come to know a very different person: a man of sound principles, a most commendable concern for others, and a deep affection for his family. She was happy to admit that she could no longer regard him as she did before.

Meanwhile, Rachel had suffered none of the difficulties that had kept her mother awake. Since she'd had no preconceived notions of Mr Faulkner's character, it had been quite easy for her to decide that he was a very agreeable gentleman indeed, and having decided it, she had fallen into a deep and restful sleep, from which she was awakened only by a persistent bird calling outside her window.

Caroline had risen early and sent a message to Rosie's mother, Mrs Higgins. Unwilling to involve Rachel in this distressing episode, she sent her on an errand of mercy to the house of one of their former tenants. Mrs Binns, whose husband had died a year ago, had moved to live with her son and daughter-in-law in the village.

Recently, Caroline had heard that she had been unwell and had visited her to find the woman very unhappy, mainly because she felt she was becoming a burden upon her son and his wife. Caroline had tried to comfort her, to no avail, but having consulted the parish priest, she had decided to send a hamper of food to the family.

Finding Rachel in a buoyant mood at breakfast, she took the opportunity to send her into the village with the large basket for Mrs Binns. She was sure its contents would make her feel a whole lot better and ensure that her daughter-in-law did not feel at all put upon.

"Tell her I would have come myself, but something very important needed attending to, and I shall drop in and see her through the week," she said and added, "You will spend a little time with her, will you not, my love?"

"I will, Mama," said Rachel, who went quite cheerfully. She enjoyed her little excursions into the village, and the weather that morning was quite perfect for a walk of no more than two miles. The servant, Jack, who accompanied her, carrying the basket, seemed to tire more quickly than she did, and they stopped awhile just outside the inn to let him rest. He sat down on a bench, and Rachel, reminding him to keep a close watch on the basket, crossed the road to the post office to buy some writing paper and stamps.

She was not gone long, and as she was coming out, she saw quite clearly, descending the steps of the inn, none other than Mr Adam Fraser. It appeared to her that he had probably stayed there overnight. Swiftly she stepped back into the shop and waited until he had walked several yards up the street before crossing the road to rejoin Jack and urge him to hurry as they proceeded down the side street where Mrs Binn's son had his house and joinery business.

Rachel was now certain that Mr Fraser had been the man she had seen two days ago in the woods; he was wearing the same jacket that he had been wearing on that day. Quite clearly, he had not gone to Scotland.

Much as she wished to spend more time with poor Mrs Binns, who was so overjoyed by the arrival of the hamper of food that she seemed completely and immediately restored to health, Rachel wanted nothing more than to hurry back home and tell her mother what she had seen. Having despatched the servant, to whom cook had entrusted some other errands, she sat with the Binns family for a few more minutes and partook of a cup of tea, while listening to their words of appreciation, promising to repeat them exactly to her mother; then with their gratitude ringing in her ears, she left to return home.

Unwilling to risk a chance encounter with Mr Fraser, for she had not met him since the dinner party at Camden House and much water had flowed under the bridge since then, Rachel elected to take a more circuitous route home, through the churchyard and across the common.

As she came past the little church that had been closed for several weeks, since the rector had been taken ill, she saw to her surprise that the front door was open and coming out was Mr Daniel Faulkner. At that very moment, he looked across, saw her, and came swiftly down the steps to meet her.

"Miss Rachel, how very nice to see you again, but might one ask what you are doing here in the churchyard all alone? Is your mother here, too?"

Rachel coloured and stammered something about visiting Mrs Binns and wanting to take a shortcut across the common.

"Have you finished your business in the village, then?" he asked and, when she said she had, offered to walk back to the farm with her.

She would have liked to have asked what he was doing at the old church but was afraid it would sound like prying, so she said, "How is the rector? Is he quite recovered, then?" The complete confusion reflected upon his countenance left her in no doubt that he had certainly not been at the church to visit the rector. She explained, "I am sorry, I thought you were at the church to see the rector, Mr Hughes. He has been away for some weeks; Mama said he was very ill. When I saw you, I thought he was back and you were visiting him."

"No, no," he said quickly, "I did not know the rector was ill. I happened to hear from Richard Gardiner that this is a very old church, going back many centuries, and I wanted to take a look inside. The caretaker opened it up for me, which was kind of him, considering I had disturbed him at breakfast," he said lightly, and they laughed together as they walked through the churchyard.

"Are you interested in churches?" she asked, mainly for something to say.

He nodded and responded that the architectural styles were fascinating.

"Are there many churches in Australia?" she asked and he laughed again and said, "No, not many, especially not old buildings like this one, which I must admit is a very well-preserved edifice."

Then changing the direction of the conversation, he asked, "Does your family attend church here?" and she replied that they did not.

"Mama prefers the church on the other side of town closer to the village of Lambton. It was where she and Papa were married," she explained.

His voice was gentle when he said, "You must miss your father a great deal. Richard and Cassy have told me he was a most remarkable man."

"He was," she said softly, "and always full of fun, and yes, we do miss him very much, Mama and I."

The wide brim of her hat hid her face from him, but he could tell from her voice that she was upset and probably tearful. He apologised, "I am sorry; I should not have spoken of him; I have upset you."

"No, indeed, you have not; I do not mind speaking of my father. I miss him, but I am happy to speak of him and tell people about him. Mama does not like to speak of him before strangers; it makes her cry. She was very young when they married, and they were very happy together," she said quietly.

"I completely sympathise with your mama's feelings, and I regret that I did not know Colonel Fitzwilliam. I have heard many excellent reports of him. I know it is a high price to pay for a happy marriage, but then, who would want it otherwise?"

His voice was very low, and she recalled immediately that he had been married too, many years ago, and his young wife had died only a few years later, leaving a son.

Rachel fell silent; she did not feel ready to continue this conversation. She had neither the emotional resilience nor the life experience to comprehend and support his grief, and sought desperately for another subject, but Daniel

Faulkner appeared not to flinch as he went on, "I too have known a similar, grievous loss. It was a long time ago, almost fifteen years, but the years do not make it any less painful."

Rachel said gently, "I know; Mama did tell me, when we first met you; I am very sorry."

"Thank you, Rachel," he said, and as they reached the edge of the common, he gave her his hand and helped her across the muddy ditch that lay in their path, and she noticed that he had called her Rachel, for the first time.

The presence on the common of a small boy with a flock of geese gave Rachel the chance she had looked for to change the mood of their conversation. Calling out to Oliver, the son of one of the tenants on the property, she greeted him and asked after his mother and sisters. The boy came to her and they stood talking for a few minutes more, while Rachel gave him some sweets she carried in her pocket.

Watching her, Daniel was both amused and touched by the ease with which she chatted with the boy, and when she rejoined him to resume their walk, he asked, "How old is Oliver?"

"He would probably be nine or maybe ten years old, I think," she replied.

"And does the boy not go to school?"

"No, he did go to Sunday school for a few years, but there is no school in this village for boys of his age. Many of them are working on farms and in the foundries... but Oliver and his sisters come to me twice a week and learn to read and write a little," she explained.

Daniel looked delighted. "Do they? That is wonderful, and how well do they do?" he asked.

"Quite well, I think. Oliver is not as proficient at writing as his sisters are, but they are all reading very satisfactorily. We are in the middle of *Robinson Crusoe*. Mama is very pleased; she and Becky Tate fought a long battle with the council to get a building for a library, so she is very happy when the children learn to read."

"I can well believe that she would be," said Daniel. "It is a real blessing and you are giving them a great gift by teaching them to read, Miss Rachel. I must congratulate you."

She blushed at his praise, but he could not see her face, as she said, "You do not have to call me Miss Rachel; no one else does; just Rachel would do."

"In which case, perhaps just Daniel should do also," he said, and she protested, "I could not."

"Why not?" he demanded to know.

"It would not be seemly, why, you are…"

"Because I am so much older, eh?"

"No, I did not mean to say that at all," she said firmly.

"Then what did you mean to say?" He was persistent, determined to know.

"I don't know… but it's not because you are older…"

"Well, if it is unseemly that you should call me Daniel, perhaps I should go back to calling you Miss Rachel," he said in a disconsolate sort of voice, which made her say, "Oh, all right then, but only if you agree that when we are in company, it will have to be Mr Faulkner. Agreed?"

He nodded and smiled. "Agreed." They looked at one another and laughed, and it was clear to both that in the compromise they had just reached lay the germ of something new in their relationship, although neither sought to say anything more about it.

They had reached the lane leading to the farm. She stopped to pick some flowers, and he helped her over the stile into the meadow behind the house.

As they made their way to the front porch, Rachel thought she had not spent a pleasanter hour in a long while.

Caroline saw them approaching and came out to invite Daniel in for tea. "I am sure you must be hungry enough after that long walk to take tea with us, Mr Faulkner," she said, and when he thanked her and followed her into the parlour, she added, "Rachel, my dear, before you go upstairs, would you tell Alice to bring us some tea and cake?"

As Rachel left the room, Caroline spoke in a very quiet voice, "I have seen Mrs Higgins, Rosie's mother, this morning."

Daniel Faulkner leaned forward, dreading what he was sure he was about to hear.

"I have quizzed her about Rosie and asked if she has been walking out with a man recently arrived from London. She was quite adamant that she was not. So if Rachel was right and it was indeed Rosie and Mr Fraser she saw the other day in the woods, then the girl is seeing him secretly, unbeknownst to her parents," she explained.

"Which does not augur well at all for Rosie," said Daniel gravely, "because it means Fraser wishes to keep his association with her a secret."

"So he can betray her and get away with it, because no one will know," said Caroline. "Well, I have told Mrs Higgins everything I know about him and warned her to ensure that Rosie knows too." Turning to face him, she added, "The man's a blackguard and ought be exposed."

Daniel, feeling wretched indeed, said, "I knew he was shallow and reckless, but I had no idea he could be as bad as this. If I had, I should never have introduced him to my family and their friends. I think I must owe you all an apology."

"Do not blame yourself, Mr Faulkner; you could not have known that he intended to behave like this in England. He is clearly a man without any scruples, nor any concern for his own reputation. I hope for his own sake he has not made any trouble for young Rosie Higgins, for if he has, her father will surely kill him."

Rachel's return to the room, followed by the maid with the tea tray, put an end to their conversation on the subject. Having conveyed the thanks of Mrs Binns and her daughter-in-law for the hamper, Rachel proceeded to tell her mother about Daniel's interest in the old village church. "Mr Faulkner is interested in the architecture of old churches," she explained, and Caroline seemed delighted.

"Is this true? Because if it is, then you must certainly visit the church at Riversleigh. It is a good deal older than the church in the village, and though it is an odd-looking building with its crooked spire, it has a most interesting carved marble altarpiece, which Mr Darcy claims was saved from destruction in the days of King Henry the Eighth by a devout parish priest who, at great risk to himself, worked all night by candlelight to brick it up. Its real beauty was only revealed centuries later when Mr Darcy's mother, Lady Anne Darcy, found some documents in the Pemberley library and traced them to Riversleigh church. She had the brickwork removed and revealed the altarpiece. If you are interested in old churches, you must see it," she said, and Daniel was immediately fascinated.

"Where is Riversleigh? No one has mentioned it before. Dr Gardiner told me about the old church in the village here, and I agree it is an interesting building, but a carved marble altarpiece dating back to the Middle Ages must be extraordinary. I should very much like to see it."

"Riversleigh is on the northern boundary of the Pemberley estate in the foothills of the mountains. It is beautifully situated, but the living is not worth much, being a very small parish and rather isolated, so it has been vacant for quite a while. If you wish to visit, Cassy will give you the keys; she looks after all that for her father now," said Caroline, pouring out the tea and handing around the cake.

Daniel was very keen. "I must certainly ask her, though I daresay she will be much too busy to accompany me. She appears to have her hands full all day long."

"She does, but Rachel can take you there," said Caroline, adding, "She knows Riversleigh well. My husband used to enjoy fishing there, and he often took Rachel along. I must confess it was one of the few pastimes I did not share with him. I have not the patience to sit still for hours for so little reward," Caroline admitted, and they laughed, as Rachel agreed that if he could get the keys to the church at Riversleigh, she would be quite happy to accompany him.

"It isn't far, if we take the pony cart and travel up the road that runs along the boundary of the Pemberley estate, we should make it within an hour," she said, and when he asked if she would consider making the excursion to Riversleigh on the following Saturday, Caroline was too preoccupied to notice how very easily Rachel was persuaded.

Nor did she observe, after Mr Faulkner had left, that Rachel had the look of someone who had but recently discovered an unexpected source of pleasure. It wasn't often that Rachel was presented with such an opportunity; she had not planned it nor had she foreseen it, but she was quite delighted with the happy way things had turned out that day.

Chapter Nine

AFTER MANY HOURS OF agonising uncertainty, Caroline had decided that she could not in all conscience let Georgiana Grantley and the Darcys remain in ignorance of what she had learned about Mr Fraser. On the following Saturday, with Rachel and Mr Faulkner conveniently out of the way visiting Riversleigh, Caroline went again to Pemberley. This time she saw Elizabeth and found in her a much more amenable and trusting listener than Georgiana had been. Having already heard some part of Caroline's information from Mr Darcy, Elizabeth was ready to believe that Georgiana could be wrong about the man who seemed to have attracted her daughter's attention.

"Is it at all possible that you may be mistaken?" she asked, and Caroline was quite resolute.

"I might be, but what about Daniel Faulkner's account of him and now all these clandestine goings-on with Rosie Higgins? Rachel is absolutely certain that it was Fraser she saw with Rosie in the woods and then again in the village coming out of the inn, while Georgiana believes he is visiting his respectable relations in Scotland! How does one explain such strange behaviour?"

Elizabeth agreed that it would not be easy and added that Mr Darcy did not believe that Fraser was being candid about his circumstances either.

"Following his conversation with Daniel Faulkner, Darcy believes that he has no reason to doubt the sincerity of his account and is increasingly sceptical about Fraser's claims. I believe he plans to speak with Georgiana this evening before dinner; we have no other guests tonight, so he will be able to speak freely."

Caroline was relieved. "Oh Lizzie, I am so pleased to hear that. If anyone can convince Georgiana that Fraser should not be trusted, Mr Darcy can."

Elizabeth agreed. "Indeed, she has always depended upon his judgment, and since the death of Dr Grantley, she does seem to turn more to her brother again. Poor Georgiana, having always sought the approval of a brother or a husband for almost everything she did, she has never equipped herself for the day when she must make her own decisions."

Caroline's eyes filled with tears as she recalled her husband's advice to her in the months after they had come to understand the seriousness of his condition. "Dearest Caroline," he had said, " though I love you dearly and would hate to go and leave you to carry on alone, you know too well that it must happen, do you not?" and when she had nodded, unable to speak for her grief, he had taken her hand and said, "All through our days together, I have sought to teach you everything I know so that when I am gone you will have all the knowledge you need to do whatever you decide is right for you and the children."

She recalled how she had been too afraid to think it then, but she knew now he had been preparing her for the solitary life that was to come. And when it came, despite the anguish of her loss, she had learned to cope, only because he had taught her so well.

Elizabeth saw her tears and embraced her cousin. "Dear Caroline, I am sorry. I did not mean to wound you, but seeing how you have borne your grief and striven to overcome your difficulties, I grow impatient with Georgiana; I fear she cannot succeed because she will not make the effort."

Caroline fought back her tears and urged Lizzie not to be too harsh with her sister-in-law. "Her sole dependence upon Dr Grantley must make it difficult for her, and unlike my Rachel, Virginia is no help at all. If only Mr Darcy can persuade her that she must treat Mr Fraser with some caution, it will be a great relief. Georgiana seems unwilling to listen to any other advice," she said, and Elizabeth promised to do her best as well.

When she left Pemberley, Caroline was feeling less apprehensive. Talking to the Darcys always had that effect upon her. Her cousin Elizabeth had been her confidante since childhood, and the strong bonds of trust and affection that had developed between Mr Darcy and Caroline's own parents, Mr and Mrs Gardiner, had served to enhance her confidence in him. Her late husband Colonel Fitzwilliam had rarely made a significant decision without consulting his cousin, whose judgment he rated above any others. If Mr Darcy intended to speak with Georgiana, Caroline was convinced all would be well.

Rachel and Daniel Faulkner had made their way to Riversleigh without mishap, arriving at the water's edge around midmorning. A bridge spanned the river before its confluence with the stream whose flow had been constrained and directed over a weir to form a small lake. It was a crisp Autumn day, with hardly a breath of wind to ruffle the surface of the water.

The old church stood on the other side of the stream, situated in the green meadows between the lake and the foothills of the mountains to the north. With its rough old exterior and oddly crooked tower, it gave no hint of the treasure it contained.

Rachel had the advantage over her companion in her familiarity with the district, and when he asked a little apprehensively how they were supposed to get over to the other side, she giggled and said, "Now, if you were a true saint, you might have tried walking across," and was astonished when he looked at her quite sharply, with a frown on his countenance like she had not seen before.

"That sounds a little presumptuous, don't you think?" he asked, and she could not tell if he was being lighthearted or serious. She bit her lip; clearly he had not appreciated the joke. It was the sort of thing her father would have said, and she would have laughed with him. But this time, she didn't laugh; instead, she said, in a serious voice, "If we walk downstream for a bit, there's an old crossing place, which brings us out behind the rectory garden. The stream is fordable in this weather, although with the Spring thaw, it would swell to almost double its size and one would be advised to use the bridge. Shall we walk down?"

The change in her tone alerted him; he turned to her and said, "Rachel, I am sorry, I haven't been very good company, have I?" Before she could say anything, he continued, "I have been distracted and anxious and discourteous, have I not?"

"No, not discourteous," she said quietly. "Anxious and distracted perhaps, but I suppose you are concerned about Mr Fraser and Virginia? I know my mother is; she was going to Pemberley to see Mr and Mrs Darcy today. If anyone can help, they can." She saw a sudden smile light up his countenance, and he sighed with relief.

"Thank God, I have been trying all morning to think how I could approach Mrs Grantley to beg her not to trust Fraser. I have known for some time that he has been seeking to marry a young woman of some wealth and consequence, and I was very afraid that he may persuade Mrs Grantley that he is an appropriate suitor for her daughter. He is very persuasive and charming when he wants to be, and ladies like Mrs Grantley, whose lives have been largely sheltered from men like Fraser, may be easily convinced. But if, as you say, your mama has gone to Pemberley today with the intention of revealing what she knows to Mr and Mrs Darcy, then she has done far more than I could hope to do. We must pray that she will be successful," he said.

Rachel explained, "Mama did not tell me in so many words, but I cannot imagine that she would have any other reason for visiting them again today, especially with Virginia away at Ashford Park. Do you not agree?"

He supposed she was right and said so. Then, with a complete change of tone, he said, "Well, with that problem in such good hands, shall we find this ford and try to get across to the church?"

She nodded, smiling, and led the way.

When they reached the old ford, she was disappointed, for instead of the clear water rippling over the flat stepping stones on the bed of the stream, there were great fronds of fern and water hyacinth smothering its path.

"Oh dear, I haven't been here in a while, and the poor stream's choking," she said, trying to clear some of it away, but he stopped her.

"Let me do it," he said and, bending down, pulled aside the vegetation; then, standing on the stones in the middle of the stream, he held out his hands to her and, urging her to mind and not slip on the mossy pebbles, helped her across and supported her up the bank onto the other side.

It was all accomplished so easily, with so little fuss, that Rachel was quite surprised to find herself standing on dry ground with hardly a drop of water on her boots.

She looked up at him and said, "Thank you," adding lightly, "You did that so well, I suppose you must have forded many such streams on the goldfields."

He laughed then, a very agreeable laugh, and said, "Indeed I have, but there were no ladies there needing to be helped across." Rachel laughed too, and as they struck out across the overgrown meadows, towards the rectory gate, he took her hand in his and said, "Watch where you put your feet, Rachel; I had no idea this place was so neglected, although Cassy did tell me there had been no incumbent for over a year."

"Indeed, no one wants it; it's a very small parish."

They reached the gate and passed through it into the rectory garden, which showed some signs of being cared for. The fruit was ready for picking, and the rose bushes heavy with scented blooms; the grass had been recently scythed and tied into bundles and the kitchen garden carefully tended.

The rectory itself was locked, and since he had only asked Cassandra for the key to the church, they went round to the front door, opened it, and went within.

The church was cool and filled with light from the two high windows above the choir loft, which streamed down into the nave. Rachel stood back and let Daniel walk up the aisle. He approached the altar and lifted the rough red cloth that covered it, and she heard him catch his breath as he saw the precious, carved marble panel depicting a young Madonna and child. He knelt to look at it closely, and for one moment, Rachel thought he was going to pray, but then, he sat on the chancel steps and gazed at it as if entranced.

She remained seated quietly in one of the pews at the back of the church, until many minutes later, Daniel rose to his feet, bowed before the altar, replaced the covering cloth, and moved away, still seemingly stunned by what he had seen.

He stood silently looking around the old building; nothing else in the church, except perhaps the baptismal font, came even close to matching the exquisite beauty of the altarpiece.

Looking at Daniel, his tall figure caught in the beam of light from the high windows, Rachel found it difficult to associate him with the man who had stood in the middle of the stream and held out his hands to her. Then, it was his laughter that had caught her attention; now, in the quiet church, she was struck by the almost reverent expression on his face.

When they went outside, she stood quietly while he locked the door and placed the key in his pocket before saying, "Rachel, I have no words to thank you for this wonderful experience, which I owe entirely to you. I had no idea what a profoundly beautiful treasure was concealed within the old church, and I am quite enthralled by it. Thank you again, from the bottom of my heart, for bringing me here." He sounded completely sincere, and there was very little Rachel could say in response. She smiled and said simply that she was very happy he had got so much pleasure from it and she always enjoyed coming to Riversleigh, anyway. It was one of her father's favourite places.

As they passed through the gate into the meadow, he reached out and took her hand in his, ostensibly to help her through the rough, overgrown grass, before saying, "It is a great pleasure indeed, Rachel, to find something so beautiful and rare, and it will forever be associated in my mind with you and this very lovely place."

She coloured and said nothing, biting her lips to avoid smiling too readily, but wanting in her heart to say how deeply she appreciated his gracious words. Never before had anyone said anything as sweetly pleasurable to her, and she wanted to hold it very close to her heart. Sufficiently sensible not to allow herself to exaggerate the significance of his words, yet susceptible enough to want to believe that they must mean he held her in some special regard, Rachel wanted only to return home and retreat to the warm comfort of her room, where she could relive the day's events alone.

Daniel, too, seemed preoccupied and thoughtful as they walked back to the pony cart, but she could not know that his thoughts were somewhat similar to her own. The last young woman he had taken an interest in, some eighteen years or more ago, had been the girl who became his wife. They had both been young; she was not quite seventeen and very pretty when they met, and he, unaccustomed to encountering such beauty in the rough and ready environment of the goldfields of Victoria, had thought she was the loveliest and gentlest person he had ever seen.

Rachel, though older and not conventionally beautiful, had attracted his attention because she retained a similar quality of innocent freshness that he recalled with so much pleasure even after many years. Besides, she was well read and intelligent and sensitive with the kind of quick wit that had delighted him, and he had begun to wonder about the depth of the feelings she seemed to arouse in him, feelings of tenderness and affection that he had not known for years.

Driving home, they spoke only occasionally, and then it was of commonplace things like the way the wind had changed and how much longer it would take to use the road that ran across the bridge. Yet their reticence was comfortable and seemed to suit them well.

When they reached the house, he helped her out and, as she thanked him, said, "It was entirely my pleasure, Rachel, thank you."

She asked him in to take tea, and as he appeared to hesitate, Caroline came into the hall, a letter in her hand.

"Rachel, Mr Faulkner, I am so glad you are back; do come in. I have just had a note from Mrs Higgins, Rosie's mother, which is most worrying." They went into the parlour, and Caroline ordered tea. While they waited for the maid to bring in the tea tray, she handed Daniel the note, which he read and passed to Rachel.

Mrs Higgins wrote to say that she had quizzed Rosie about Mr Fraser the previous night and discovered that she had indeed been "walking out" with the gentleman for about a week, but he had quite suddenly declared that he had business in Leicester and would be gone for a few days.

On being cautioned about him by her mother, Rosie had revealed that he had declared that he loved her and wanted her to come away with him to his farm in New South Wales, which poor Rosie, not being educated in geography, had assumed was a place somewhere near Cornwall, where her aunty Ethel lived by the sea.

Daniel shook his head, unable to believe it, as Rachel read on.

Mrs Higgins wrote that as far as she could make out, her daughter, "being a good, well-brought-up, God-fearing girl," had not succumbed to Fraser's blandishments and had replied that she must ask her parents first. For which Mrs Higgins gave praise to the Almighty, and thanked Mrs Fitzwilliam for her kindness in warning her of the danger in which her child might have unwittingly placed herself.

Rachel sighed. "You must be so relieved, Mama, and so must Rosie's mother be," she said. Caroline was strangely unwilling to declare her relief at the news. "Yes, of course as far as Rosie is concerned, she is safe, but is Virginia? I am concerned that Fraser claimed to have had business in Leicester because that is where Virginia is, at Ashford Park."

"Good God! So it is," Daniel exclaimed, but Rachel was less concerned. "Surely, Mama, he will not be able to appear uninvited at Ashford Park and continue his advances to Virginia in Mr Bingley's house?"

"I am sorry to have to say, Miss Rachel, that he is quite capable of doing exactly that. He will use his charm to get himself invited, and if Virginia wishes to see him, Mr and Mrs Bingley may not have any reason to object, since they know nothing that discredits him," said Daniel.

Caroline agreed. "And we must remember that Mr Bingley is not in the best of health and Jane is unlikely to have a great deal of time to be entertaining visitors, so Fraser will spend most of his time with Virginia. It is most unsatisfactory, and yet there is very little we can do about it. I have already sent a note with this information to Lizzie, and we can only hope that they can intervene in some way to thwart his schemes."

The arrival of the maid with tea and scones, and the eagerness with which Daniel and Rachel, who'd eaten nothing since breakfast, reached for the food brought an abrupt end to the discussion and a concentration upon more pleasurable pursuits. Caroline was especially happy to hear Daniel's praise for the little church at Riversleigh.

"I was enthralled. Never have I seen such a treasure in a small parish church, nor have I seen a church so happily situated in its environment," he said, and Caroline was keen to agree.

"Riversleigh is a beautiful old church, even without its superb altarpiece; I am so very sorry to see it neglected. I cannot think why; the rectory is very comfortable, too. I believe Mr Darcy had it refurbished some years ago for the last incumbent. It's a great pity that it has remained unoccupied for almost two years because the congregation is too small to support a clergyman with a family if he has no other income."

"Cassy did say the living was not very valuable, but having seen Riversleigh, I would have to disagree. I would say with that church, in its exquisite setting, it should be one of the most sought after parishes in the county," replied Daniel.

Caroline laughed and said, "What a pity you are not a clergyman, Daniel. I am sure Mr Darcy would have been delighted to appoint you to the living."

At this, Daniel laughed too, but not as much as he might have been expected to in the circumstances. Indeed he had reddened and looked rather embarrassed. Perhaps, thought Rachel, as she went to get more tea and scones, he was not very amused by ecclesiastical banter. She recalled his rather stern reaction to her remark about walking on water. Surely it wasn't possible that Daniel Faulkner was stuffy about religion? She pondered the question as she poured out his tea, and when he smiled and thanked her so nicely, she discarded the thought right away.

~❧~

Meanwhile at Pemberley, the evening brought an unexpected and far more intractable development. Georgiana had received a letter, delivered to the door by a rider come from Ashford Park. On opening it, she found within a note from her daughter, Virginia, announcing her engagement to Mr Adam Fraser.

At first, Georgiana was so surprised that she stood in the hall, the note in her hand, unable to say a word, until Elizabeth called to her, "Georgiana my dear, what is it?"

When she returned to the drawing room, Georgiana, walking as if in a dream, brought the note to her sister-in-law and said, "There, I always knew Mr Fraser was not as bad as everyone said he might be. He is an honourable man after all. I should have wished, however, that he had approached me first; I am Virginia's mother, even though she is nearly thirty years old. I should have been asked first."

Completely bewildered by her words, Elizabeth reached for her glasses to read the note.

My dear Mama, wrote Virginia in a bold hand.

> *Earlier this afternoon, Mr Adam Fraser, who had called on us yesterday and again this morning, made me an offer of marriage, and I have accepted him.*
>
> *We are engaged, and I hope you will wish us happiness.*
>
> *I am writing this now, and Mr Fraser will arrange to have it carried to Pemberley tonight, because I shall have to tell Mr and Mrs Bingley tomorrow morning, before Mr Fraser arrives to take me to Derby to choose a ring. I do hope they will not make a great fuss and refuse to let me go with him. I do believe that I am well able to look after myself and shall say so, if need be.*
>
> *Mr Fraser wishes to apologise for not having applied to you first, but as he said, he wanted to assure himself that I would accept him and so asked*

me first. After that, there was little more to be said, except to inform you
of our engagement.

Please convey the news to my uncle and aunt Darcy; I know they
will both wish me happy. Do you suppose we ought be married at
Pemberley? Would that not be a good thing, since Papa and you were
also married there?

Your loving daughter, Virginia.

Elizabeth was not just struck by the sheer insouciance of Virginia's note and the sentiments it conveyed; she was almost as astonished by the coolness with which Georgiana appeared to receive the news.

When having read it through twice, she handed it to her husband, and she wondered how he would respond, when only that morning he had listened to a recital of Fraser's misdemeanours and reached the conclusion that he needed to persuade his sister to treat this man with a greater degree of caution and urge her daughter to do likewise.

Mr Darcy's countenance gave little away while he perused Virginia's note; he was not entirely surprised by her news, but he had been astonished by his sister's ready acceptance of it.

When Elizabeth asked, "What can we do?" he replied, "Nothing, my dear. Fraser has proposed to Virginia, and she has accepted him. Not only is she thirty years old and well able to make such a decision, it would appear that her mother has no objection to it. Am I not right, Georgiana?"

With the question addressed directly to her, Georgiana appeared uncomfortable and took a while to answer. When she did, her response included an explanation which Elizabeth found to be puerile. "I know that you do not all approve of Mr Fraser, but I do not believe that anyone can understand, who has not been in my position, the anxiety that I feel about Virginia's situation. Whilst ever I am here to ensure that she is provided for, she will be all right, but there is no certainty in life, and if I were to die and Virginia were still unwed, who would care for her?"

Elizabeth was about to ask why Virginia, who was thirty years old and would surely inherit a good portion of Georgiana's considerable fortune, would need someone to care for her, but seeing Mr Darcy's sceptical expression, she held back and let Georgiana continue. "Perhaps I have not been as strict with Virginia as I was with my older children; it may be that Francis and I both indulged her a little, being our youngest child; whatever it was, I know that she has not the capacity for discrimination and judgment that I would have hoped for. She needs the guiding hand of a husband, and if she has chosen to accept Mr Fraser's offer of marriage, I do not see how I can countermand it."

Mr Darcy's voice was grave when he asked, "And you are content to trust Mr Fraser to provide that guiding hand for your daughter?"

Georgiana looked somewhat discomposed. "I do not know that I do, but if Virginia does, how should I object?"

To her amazement, Elizabeth then heard her husband say, "Very well then, if that is what you and Virginia both want, you may tell her that if she wishes to marry at the Pemberley Church, she may do so. You will need to ask her brother Frank to marry them."

Georgiana was overjoyed. She had expected much more in the way of objections to the match and had been quite surprised that her brother had agreed to the wedding at the Pemberley Church. She could not quite understand how it had come about, but was glad it had turned out as it had. She was not going to ask any questions.

Elizabeth, on the other hand, had to know and later that night, when they were alone, she asked her husband the question that he had known all evening was coming. "Darcy, am I mistaken or did you decide not to tell Georgiana all that Caroline and Daniel have revealed about Fraser, because you believed it was too late?"

His expression was quite serious when he answered, "You are partly right, my love; I had intended to speak to Georgiana and reveal all we had learned about Fraser, but when I saw Virginia's letter, I realised not only that we were too late, but that I should only be making my sister even more miserable than she is, with all those dreadful tales about the man who is to marry her daughter. What good would it do? Virginia is old enough to make her own decisions and she has just made what I consider to be a bad one. Why should I make her mother suffer for it, eh, Lizzie?"

Elizabeth asked, "Have you no concern for Virginia? If she marries this man and he is in truth such a man as he is reputed to be, what hope has she of happiness?"

"Very little, I would have to say, but, Lizzie, there are times when people do things that are impossible to unravel. At the risk of arousing memories painful to you, my dear, may I remind you of the debacle of the elopement of your sister Lydia and Wickham? I would have given anything to undo what had happened, but the fatal step had been taken by them, and all that was left for me to do was to ensure they did not, by their rash behaviour, destroy your happiness and mine as well. To that end, I did all I could to get them to the altar, although I knew there was no certainty of happiness in their marriage. Your uncle Mr Gardiner agreed with me, and we were both to be proved right. But what alternative was there? Let us at least be thankful that Fraser has not persuaded Virginia to elope!"

Elizabeth understood, but was no less depressed by the situation. "I still cannot help thinking this is a dreadful result. If Virginia were our daughter, how should we feel?"

"I thank God she is not, Lizzie, but sadly, I think her father's illness in the last few years and Georgiana's concentration upon her husband has deprived Virginia of the guidance she needed, making her rely upon her own judgment," said Darcy.

Elizabeth was scathing. "Which is clearly deficient, as has been amply demonstrated by her actions and that letter! I fear I can see nothing but misery flowing from this decision."

Her husband was more hopeful. Putting an arm around her, he advised, "Do not upset yourself, my love. Since it is not a matter that we can influence, it is best left to run its course. Sleep on it, Lizzie; it may not look quite so bad in the morning. Better still, either Virginia or Mr Fraser may have suffered a change of mind," he said.

"You cannot be serious," said Lizzie. "I do not doubt that Mr Fraser has calculated that he will benefit considerably from this match and is unlikely to change his mind."

Mr Darcy's voice had a hint of laughter. "No, but Virginia might, when she discovers she will be moving to live in New South Wales. He has no home here; all his prospects, such as they are, lie on the other side of the globe!"

But, on the morrow, no such redeeming change appeared. Instead a note was received from Jane.

Dearest Lizzie,

I have the most extraordinary news. Virginia and Mr Fraser are engaged and gone to Derby to purchase a ring. Virginia told us this morning at breakfast that she had accepted an offer of marriage from Mr Fraser and they hoped to be married in the very near future.

She says she has already written to her mother to give her the news.

Jane was clearly discomfited and Lizzie felt for her sister, since Virginia had been the Bingleys' guest when this engagement had come about. She was sure Jane would feel responsible and miserable with it, fearful that Georgiana would blame her for what had happened at Ashford Park. "Should I go to Jane and reassure her?" Elizabeth asked. "She is plainly unhappy and probably feels she will be blamed for this mess."

Her husband was not certain that the situation called for Elizabeth, who had been recently unwell, to travel twenty miles to comfort her sister about a decision made by her guest, but he did not wish to sound uncaring. Besides, he was genuinely concerned that Mr and Mrs Bingley, for whom he had a great deal of affection, should not be put upon by Virginia and Mr Fraser. So he offered to go himself.

"It is I who should go, or rather it is Georgiana who should go, and I shall accompany her. This mess, as you call it, Lizzie, is nothing to do with you or Jane or Bingley. It is Virginia who has decided to marry Fraser, and her mother should go to Ashford Park, meet the couple, and give them her blessing, if she so desires. I shall send for the carriage, Lizzie, if you would please inform Georgiana that we shall be leaving at half past ten."

After they had left, Elizabeth sat at her writing desk in the morning room and wrote to Caroline.

> *My dearest Caroline,*
>
> *There is no easy way for me to give you the bad news, for despite the best efforts of yourself and Daniel Faulkner and the avowed intention of Mr Darcy to reveal to his sister the truth about Mr Fraser, we learned last night that Virginia has already accepted his offer of marriage. Indeed, at this very moment we believe the pair have gone to Derby to purchase an engagement ring.*
>
> *Incredible as it may seem, Georgiana, who learned of the engagement from a note sent by Virginia from Ashford Park, will accept him as her son-in-law, and in view of this, Mr Darcy has agreed to let them marry at the Pemberley Church.*
>
> *He and Georgiana have only just left to travel to Ashford Park to meet the pair and reassure poor Jane that she is not to blame for this, although it does appear that Fraser has cunningly managed to invite himself to Ashford House in order to propose to Virginia.*

It is, to my mind, the worst of all possible outcomes, for we know nothing good about the man, and yet Mr Darcy seems to believe that since Virginia is thirty years old and has an independent mind, she should be permitted to make her own decision even if it is unarguably the wrong one. It is an assertion that is quite incomprehensible to me, but there is nothing I can do.

I am sorry, Caroline, I find it difficult to say more at this time except to apologise to you and to Mr Faulkner for failing to accomplish what I promised I would do when you visited us yesterday. It seems that, on this occasion, we have been defeated. Our good intentions have been trumped by Stupidity! Please be so kind as to convey my regrets to Daniel Faulkner also.

I trust you and Rachel are well; how thankful you must be that she is such a sweet, sensible young woman. She must be a real comfort to you.

Your loving cousin,

Lizzie

Caroline's discomposure on reading Lizzie's letter was immeasurable. It was, to her, beyond belief that Georgiana Grantley could have accepted, without objection or any attempt to disabuse her daughter about his character and reputation, the man she had decided to marry. That Virginia's own disposition was so contrary made no difference; she was not much older than Rachel, and Caroline could not imagine that she could have been half as sanguine had her daughter done something similar.

In the absence of anyone else, Caroline expressed her sense of frustration to Daniel Faulkner, who had arrived that morning to take tea with them and view Colonel Fitzwilliam's collection of artifacts from the Asian colonies.

While Rachel had gone to order tea, Caroline complained of Georgiana's inaction.

"Could she not have, at the very least, sat her daughter down and talked to her about the risks implicit in marrying such a man and moving to the other side of the world? I am not certain that Virginia understands what she will face if she marries Fraser and goes with him to New South Wales."

Daniel agreed. "If one were to hazard a guess on the basis of Fraser's past conduct, he is unlikely to have troubled her with any details of life in the colony. The young lady is probably unaware that life can be exceedingly hard for women, most particularly those who are unaccustomed to doing their own housework. Unless they have a good deal of money to spend on hiring trained servants, who are not easy to come by, Miss Grantley will find life on a sheep station very different to her present situation," he explained, and his words did nothing to alleviate Caroline's melancholy mood.

Unused to admitting failure, she suffered badly from the knowledge that nothing she could do or say would change what was about to happen at Pemberley.

Reading Lizzie's letter again, she drew some comfort from her reference to Rachel. Caroline had never been concerned about Rachel, only because Rachel had always been a model child who, except for being somewhat accident prone, had given her parents no anxiety whatsoever. So much so, they had assumed she would always be there and for almost thirty years she had been: reliable, steady, always predictable.

Since the colonel's death, Caroline had come to depend upon Rachel for company, and Rachel, who had been something of a solitary soul, had responded warmly to her mother's need. Those who knew them well understood the closeness of their relationship had been born of their mutual desire for companionship and comfort since the death of a beloved husband and father.

In the last few days, Caroline had noticed an almost imperceptible change in her daughter. Concerned with Virginia and Mr Fraser, it had slipped past her unnoticed until last evening, when Daniel Faulkner was bidding them good night.

Rachel had agreed earlier to show him her father's collection, and for a brief moment, as he turned to Rachel and told her he was looking forward to seeing her on the morrow, Caroline noticed an expression on her daughter's face that she recognised, because she knew exactly what it meant, and Caroline's romantic heart was riven, unable to decide if she should rejoice or weep. It was quite clear to her then that Rachel, whether she knew it not, was falling in love.

Chapter Ten

THE NEWS OF VIRGINIA'S engagement to Fraser, though it did
disturb Rachel, did not distract her from her mission, which was to
lay out and explain some of her father's amazing collection of exotic
artifacts to the only person who had expressed any interest in them in years.

Of all their family, in the past only Mr and Mrs Darcy and her grandfather Mr Gardiner had spent any time studying the collection and listening
to the remarkable tales that the colonel could tell about his time in India
and Ceylon. Some ladies had gazed with envy at the gemstones—rubies,
sapphires, and tourmalines—while others had exclaimed at the intricacy
of the carvings and statues, but none had evinced more than an ephemeral
interest. Only Rachel, growing up in the days when her father, having retired
from politics, had time to spend at home, had wanted to know more about
every piece in his glass-fronted cabinet, and he had enjoyed taking them out
and answering her questions, telling her stories about each one, their history
and provenance.

Now, here was Daniel Faulkner, who quite by chance had heard the story
of Shiva, the Hindu god, from a traveller in Victoria, and when he mentioned
it, Rachel had revealed that there was a small brass statue of Shiva in her father's
collection. His curiosity, once aroused, had to be satisfied; hence the invitation
to tea that morning.

Rachel had picked out a few pieces that she thought might be of particular interest to him. Among them, the statue of the god Shiva, a few exquisitely painted miniatures, which had been highly prized by her father, and a tiny set of chess pieces, each intricately carved in creamy white ivory and polished ebony. She knew Daniel played chess and had taken them out especially to let him appreciate the perfection of their detail and balance. She was right. He was fascinated, as much by her knowledge as she explained the provenance and significance of each item, as he was by the artifacts themselves. Many were old and valuable, and he held them almost reverently, handing them back with great care.

"This must be very old indeed," he said, holding the dancing god Shiva in his hands, as she related the story of the great Lord of the Dance, Creator, Preserver, and Destroyer of the Universe, just as her father had told it.

Daniel seemed entranced by the tale and the beautiful statue he held. When he handed it back to her, he said in a very quiet, serious voice, "It is truly remarkable, their belief in a kind of primordial trinity of creation, preservation, and destruction all embodied in the one god. Not very different to our doctrine of the Holy Trinity, is it?"

Rachel was struck by the expression on his face; she had seen it once before as he stood in the old church at Riversleigh, when he first saw the carved marble altarpiece. "I must admit I had not thought of it that way, but you are right, it is a similar concept and yet theirs is a very ancient faith," she said.

"Indeed it is, but that is what makes it even more significant," he said, then setting down a piece he had just picked up, he asked, "Rachel, I should like very much to see the altar at Riversleigh again. I wish to make a sketch of the carved panel. Would you mind accompanying me there, one more time, perhaps on Wednesday?"

She was surprised but did not let him see it. "Of course not, I should be happy to go with you," she replied. "I love the old church and am very sorry it has been closed up for so long without an incumbent. Papa used to say it is the prettiest parish on the Pemberley estate, situated as it is between the mountains and the lake," and when he smiled and thanked her, she knew he was pleased she had agreed to go.

As she put the pieces back in the cabinet, he watched her, and when she had finished and they were leaving the room, she asked, apropos of nothing at all, "Daniel, when do you return to Australia?"

His reply astonished her. "I was to have sailed at the end of this week; indeed I should have been back in London by now, but I have delayed my departure. There are some matters I must attend to, and I have also had a letter from my sister Anna to say that my father is unwell. She urges me to visit him again before I leave England."

"And if you miss your ship, does that mean you will have to wait awhile for another?" she asked, almost too eagerly, but unable to conceal her keenness to know.

He nodded, but did not appear too concerned at the prospect of an extended delay. "I do; unless I apply almost immediately for another berth, I may not get on a ship that will take me there before Christmas, and who wants to spend Christmas on board a ship on the southern ocean?"

"Will it be very cold and wet?" she asked, and he laughed that very agreeable laugh again and said, "Oh no, quite the contrary, it will be dreadfully hot; it will be Summer in the southern hemisphere, remember?"

Rachel looked appalled. "A hot Christmas? Oh no! I cannot imagine it," she cried, and he smiled and said, "That was exactly what I said the first time I stood in the hotel at Ballarat on Christmas Day, drinking cold ale and eating my hot dinner, with a merciless sun beating down outside. I hated it."

"Then, do you mean to spend Christmas in England this year?" she asked as they went out into the hall, and when he replied, "I do not appear to have any alternative," Rachel smiled, but said nothing. She did not trust herself to speak or look up at him, lest she betray her pleasure at the news.

Caroline, coming downstairs, saw them together smiling, happy, quite unaware of her, and could not hold back her tears. She went into the kitchen to give instructions to the cook and came out again, blowing her nose, pretending it was the pepper in the air. When she returned to the parlour, she found them talking about a place in Victoria called Eureka; Daniel was telling Rachel of the political struggle which had taken place there, involving a group of gold miners led by an Irishman called Peter Lalor.

It had started to rain heavily, and Caroline asked Daniel if he would take a light luncheon with them, which he accepted with obvious pleasure, before resuming his story. "There was considerable discontent among the miners and their families, who felt they were being oppressed both by the government, which levied licence fees on miners whether or not they found any gold on their claims, and by the militia, who were sent to enforce the licensing laws. Some of them were corrupt, and this made for even more vexation. To make matters infinitely worse, a miner was murdered, supposedly by a hotelier, and when the man was charged and acquitted, there was outrage and widespread rioting."

"Did not the militia do anything about it?" asked Rachel.

"Oh they did, all the wrong things," Daniel replied. "They bullied and badgered the miners, who then burnt down the hotel!"

Rachel listened, utterly absorbed, and soon Caroline's interest was captured too, for the history of the Eureka Stockade seemed to her to run a very close parallel to what had happened in Manchester at Petersfield in 1819, when she was but a girl. She had vivid memories of Colonel Fitzwilliam relating shocking accounts of the killing of ordinary people by the cavalry, a blunder that was soon ironically dubbed "The Peterloo Massacre."

It was all she could do to keep silent as Daniel described how the miners had formed the Ballarat Reform League to demand the abolition of the oppressive administration and its punitive taxes on the goldfields, as well as full and fair representation by universal suffrage.

Daniel told the story well. "The governor and his officials panicked when the miners began to build a stockade at this place called Eureka, where they had hoisted a rebel flag. Not the Union flag, but a great blue flag emblazoned with the stars of the Southern Cross. It was a beautiful sight, but to the governor, it spelt only treason. Well, inevitably, he called for reinforcements, and just before dawn, they attacked the stockade. The miners were hopelessly outnumbered and outgunned; many were killed by the troopers and many more injured in a stupid attack that lasted less than half an hour! It was outrageous and wholly unnecessary, and it changed my mind about how I wanted to live."

"Did you leave the goldfields after that?" Rachel asked.

"I did, but not immediately," he said. "I had to stay and help the only chaplain comfort the families who'd lost fathers and sons at the stockade. They were absolutely bereft and had no one to turn to for help. And of course, at the time, I was engaged to a young lady in Ballarat. So I stayed on for a while and made my plans."

"What happened to the men who led the rebellion?" asked Caroline, almost afraid to ask, and to her great surprise, Daniel smiled and said, "They were charged, but they were all acquitted, and a year later their leader Peter Lalor was appointed to the Parliament."

"So at least their struggle was not in vain?" Rachel asked tentatively.

"No indeed, I am quite certain it will in the future be regarded as an historic stand for freedom in the colony," Daniel replied.

Both Rachel and Caroline, whose knowledge of the far country was understandably minimal, had been struck by the passion with which he had spoken. It was, to them, a clear indication of his attachment to the colony, and they did not doubt that he intended to return there.

Later, once Daniel had left, Caroline, looking out of her bedroom window, saw Rachel walking across the grounds towards the river. It was where she always went when she wanted to be alone. She had said nothing to her mother, and to Caroline that was proof enough that she was going to lose her. She could not know if Daniel had said anything to Rachel or if he knew how she felt, but Caroline knew in her heart what it would mean to her. Without Rachel, her life would be lonely indeed, yet she wished only for her daughter to find the kind of happiness she had enjoyed in many years of marriage to her beloved colonel.

On Wednesday, Rachel, having told her mother of her errand to Riversleigh, made her way down to the lake, where she had arranged to meet Daniel, who would come direct from Pemberley. He had told her he had an appointment to see Mr Darcy that morning, but had said nothing of the reason for their meeting, and she had not asked either.

As she waited for him to arrive, it was hard to ignore the beauty around her, with the sun bright on the water and glinting off the windows of the old church. It was a scene she could quite easily contemplate for hours. But she forced herself to think of the question that had troubled her all week, the question she did not wish to think about. It had not impinged upon her significantly until a few days ago when she had sensed Daniel's interest for the first time.

She was not yet certain that it was anything deeper than a friendly concern, but if it was, if he did care enough for her to want to marry her, she faced the possibility that she would have to leave her home, her family, and travel across the world to a country of which she knew nothing. It was a daunting prospect; Rachel had never left her parents' home before, nor wanted to, and yet, she had to admit that never before had there been anyone who had given her a good reason for doing so.

She had occasionally known the kind of feelings every young woman has, for young men she had met in her parents' circle of acquaintances; some had shown an interest in her; they had mostly been the sons of local businessmen or politicians, but none had aroused in her even the smallest desire to change her very comfortable life for the dull domesticity that marriage to them offered. Growing up in a home with parents whose values were wholly divergent from the grasping materialism of many of the people around them, she had not found it easy to make friends, let alone consider marriage to one of them.

Yet, with Daniel Faulkner, it had been completely different. From the very first occasion on which they had met and spoken, she had been impressed by his openness, his complete lack of condescension, his genuine interest in her questions, which he always answered quite seriously. Rachel had been surprised and touched.

Her own feelings for him, springing from these simple roots, had seemed to flourish in the fertile ground of their continuing friendship, but without any promise of deepening, until their visit to the church at Riversleigh. On that day she had realised the feelings Daniel had aroused in her were like nothing she had known before.

That morning, dressing in front of her mirror, Rachel had looked at herself critically, examining her slender figure and delicate face, frowning at herself, trying to pierce the surface calm of her features and reach into the place where those new feelings had begun. She dressed with care, choosing a simple blue gown and a white hat with blue ribbons that shaded her face. The colours suited her well; she hoped Daniel would like them.

While she had no indication of his intentions, she wished very much to be certain of her own. Rachel, by nature a cautious young woman, needed to know if what she felt was deep enough to outlast the toil and tribulation that would inevitably follow, should they sail off to Australia. She wondered how she would know and was afraid that if she did not know and made the wrong decision, catastrophe would follow; for what would one do with an unhappy marriage if one was twelve thousand miles from home? It was a cruel conundrum, and despite the brilliance of the day, she frowned again as she pondered the prospect and worried lest she was mistaken and it should all come to naught.

Sudden footsteps pulled her back to the present, and turning round, she saw Daniel standing there with such a pleasing smile on his face as to remove instantly all her concerns and fears. She could not possibly be unhappy with him, she thought in that instant.

"Rachel, on such a glorious morning as this, whatever makes you frown so?" he asked in an accusing voice and then suddenly, anxious that she may have been troubled by some quite legitimate concern, added, "I am sorry; has there been some bad news?"

She shook her head and smiled, rising from the bench on which she had been seated to face him, before saying, "No worse than we heard two days ago. Virginia and Mr Fraser are to marry at Pemberley and leave almost at once for London and thence to New South Wales. Her mother is deeply distressed and believes she will not see her daughter again ever."

"I can understand her concern," he said, "but if I were Mrs Grantley that would be the least of my worries. I am astonished that Mrs Grantley is not more concerned about the character of her prospective son-in-law." Then, seeing her frown deepen, he held out his hand to her and said, "But come, Rachel, let us not waste any more time on matters that are outside our control. I have keys to the church and the rectory as well today, so we have much to see." And she took his hand as though it was the most natural thing to do.

When they got across the stream, more easily this time than before, and reached the church, he opened the door, and as they stepped within, she said, pointing to her satchel, "I did bring my sketchbook and pencils; will you do it or shall I?"

He looked at her and said, "I am sure you would do it much better than I could, but there is no hurry to do it today."

"No? Is that because you are not going until after Christmas?" she asked.

"Hmmm."

His answer didn't help much, and she was unsure what she should do. He did not immediately move to go and look at the carvings as she had expected him to. Instead, he stood just inside the door in the cool interior of the church and asked, "Have you seen inside the rectory?"

Rachel was surprised but answered casually, "Not recently; the last rector was ill for quite some time."

"Shall we take a look then?" he asked, taking the keys out of his pocket.

She nodded, and they went around the church and through a somewhat overgrown cottage garden to the front door, for which he produced the key.

As they stepped inside the door, it was obvious the place had been cleaned and aired. Rachel was puzzled; she couldn't think who could have done it or for what reason. There had been nothing said about a new incumbent. The house was built of the same stone as the church, but clearly of a more recent construction. The hall was wide and light, with a parlour to the left and a dining room to the right, looking out into the orchard, while the kitchen at the back of the house looked towards the weir. Upstairs, they found a large bedroom with windows overlooking the water and a much smaller room, which may have been a nursery, admitting plenty of light and the soothing sound of running water.

They had been through the rooms, making few comments, and had reached the hallway again, when Daniel stopped, turned to her, and asked, "What do you think, Rachel? Do you like it?"

A little flustered by the unexpected question, Rachel stopped and took a moment to compose her thoughts before saying, "It's rather small, but it is so prettily situated..." but he did not let her continue, breaking in to say, "Forgive me, Rachel, I have given you no intimation at all of this, only because there were practical reasons why I could not do so until today, so I shall not complain if you refuse to give me an immediate answer. But if I were to tell you how much I respect and admire you and how dearly I have come to love you, will you marry me?"

Considering that she had recently spent a good deal of time pondering how she would respond to just such a proposition, Rachel was surprised to find that she was literally at a loss for words. She could only think of all the ridiculous heroines in "penny dreadfuls" who, faced with a similar proposal, invariably cried, "But, sir, this is so sudden," and at that moment, Rachel sympathised with them all.

Misunderstanding her silence for discomposure, he asked softly, "Have I been too presumptuous in asking, in assuming that you might have some similar feelings for me? If that be the case, please let me apologise; perhaps I should not have spoken today, maybe it was too soon... or maybe I should have applied to your mother first? Rachel, my dear, I am so sorry if I have offended you."

At this point, realising that he had misconstrued her silence, she suddenly found her voice and said, "No, no, please don't apologise... I am not offended at all; quite the contrary. Indeed, I am sorry to have been so awkward; I hadn't expected you to…"

As she struggled to find words to answer him, he took her hand. "Of course, I understand, you need time to think about it?"

This time her answer came very quickly. "No, I do not, but I do have a problem."

"A problem?" he asked gravely. She nodded without looking at him, concentrating her eyes upon a brass door knob, and then she heard him say, "Is it because I was married before and have a son? I can appreciate your concern, but let me assure you…"

"No, it isn't to do with that at all," she said hurriedly.

"What then? Rachel, let me make it simpler for us both. I love you very much; do you think you could love me?" to which she replied, "I do, of course I do. Oh Daniel… I do love you, but…" and he, determined that this answer was not to go unrewarded, took her in his arms and kissed her, gently at first, but then, when she did not resist, more deeply, after which she was very quiet, until he asked gently, "And what was your problem?"

"It's Mama, leaving her so soon after Papa's death. If I marry you, I may never see her again," and she could not conceal her tears.

"Why?" he asked, and she looked at him in bewilderment.

"Because if we are to settle in Victoria, it is unlikely that Mama will travel across the globe to visit me."

"I see," he said in a very reasonable sort of voice, then asked, "What if she had to travel just a few miles? Would that make a difference?"

She frowned. "What do you mean by a few miles?"

"What if, for example, she had to come down to Riversleigh?" he asked, and his voice was matter-of-fact, giving nothing away.

"To Riversleigh?"

"Hmmm."

"But I don't understand. Why would she come down to Riversleigh to see me?" she asked, looking even more confused.

He smiled then and touched her face gently, as if to wipe away the frown from her forehead and cheeks, and kissed her again, before saying, "Because, my dearest Rachel, I have just come from Pemberley, where Mr Darcy has this morning appointed me rector to the living of Riversleigh."

"What?" she shook her head, unable to take in what he had just said; it made no sense to her.

"Perhaps I should have told you first; then your astonishment would not have been so great. I am sorry, but I had my reasons for not discussing it openly. I needed to be sure of my situation before I approached you."

"But since when have you…" she began, and he put a finger to her lips,

"Let me explain. During the last five years in Australia, I took Holy Orders and have been a deacon and a rector of a country parish in Victoria. I have told very few people, just my sister, Anna, and Cassy and Mr Darcy, of course. Cassy had to know because I had to attend chapel daily while I was at Camden Park, and it was Cassy who suggested that I take a look at the church in the village when I hinted that I was not entirely committed to returning to the colony. However, after I had seen Riversleigh, she also mentioned it to her father, who then sent for me to discuss the possibility of my appointment." Seeing the astonishment on her face, he said, "I am sorry if I have surprised you, my love, but I did not wish to say anything to you or your mother, until those matters were finally settled."

"I understand," said Rachel and then asked, "Does Cassy know about me?"

"No, not yet; I did tell Mr Darcy, however, that I had an intention to marry, but had not made the lady an offer until I was certain of my prospects, a position of which he was very supportive. I said nothing more, but I mentioned it because I was given to understand that his preference is for a married man at the rectory," he explained. "Mr Darcy had said that the parish has been serviced by Reverend Frank Grantley from Kympton, but they badly need their own rector with a wife who could help with his parish duties."

"And do you believe I would make a good rector's wife?" she asked, with a smile, and he took her in his arms and assured her in the fondest possible words that he was confident no rector in the land would have a more perfect wife. Though unaccustomed to such extravagant expressions of affection, Rachel was delighted with the warmth of his words and the tenderness of his manner. She was certain now that nothing, not even the need to travel to the other side of the planet, would have kept her from accepting him. Of all the men she had met in her life, only Daniel Faulkner had made her admit to such feelings.

Once he had assured himself that she had quite understood the depth of his affection for her, he wished to consult her considered opinion. "And what is your opinion, Rachel? Do you think I would make a good rector for the parish of Riversleigh?" he asked.

Her answer delighted him. "I think the people of Riversleigh are very fortunate indeed to have you as their rector, as I shall be to have you for my husband."

"And you do not mind being a clergyman's wife?"

"Why should I? It is your faith and your wish, and it is you I love; I have no reason to object. I do not love you more or less for it."

"And how do you like the rectory?" he asked rather tentatively.

"I like it very well; I think it's charming; it will need some refurbishment, of course, but Mama will help me with it," she replied.

"No need for that," he said with a smile. "Mr Darcy has undertaken to have it completely refurbished. All you need do is instruct his steward what work you wish to have done. You may want to consult your mama about fabrics and colours, perhaps, but everything will be made ready for us."

"That is very generous of Mr Darcy; I have always loved this place; it is so tranquil and unspoilt, I could quite happily spend the rest of my life here with you," said Rachel, and he drew her arm through his, kissed her hand, and looking at his watch, said, "I suppose we had better be getting back, my love; we should tell your mama first. Will you tell her? Or do you wish me to ask her for your hand?"

Rachel laughed. "I think I would like to tell Mama myself; I will let you explain to her how it is that we are to live at Riversleigh and not in Victoria. I shall enjoy that."

They locked the rectory door and returned to the church, and in the stillness she felt bold enough to ask, "Shall we be married here, do you think?"

"Of course, my love," he replied. "With that wonderful altarpiece, why would we go elsewhere? Besides, it was here I first realised that I loved you too well to leave England and all this. But is it what you wish?"

"Oh yes, I cannot imagine a better place," she replied softly, and they left, happy and content in the certainty of their love, and as they stepped outside and looked across the river at the village and the hills beyond, confident too of their future in the community they hoped to serve.

Caroline had spent the morning clearing out cupboards and putting together a basket of items for next Saturday's charity fair. She saw them arrive and went out into the hall to greet them and knew before a word was said that they were engaged. As tears filled her eyes, Rachel embraced her mother and took her upstairs directly, while Daniel waited in the parlour. Knowing the reason for her tears, Rachel wanted to tell her everything as fast as she could, just so she could set her mother's heart at rest.

As she heard it, Caroline, at first amazed by the news about Daniel, wept with relief. "Oh my darling girl, I am so happy. I never wanted to push you into anything, but I will confess I was sad that you might never know the kind of happiness your papa and I enjoyed. Then, just last week I thought you and Daniel looked as though you were falling in love, and while I wanted it to be true for you, I was so desperately afraid that it would mean you would go away to the ends of the earth and I would never see you again. But this, oh Rachel, this is wonderful news!"

"Mama, tell me, do you really like him? I mean for himself? Do you respect and love him for what he is, not just because I love him?"

There was no equivocation in Caroline's response. "Of course, my dear, everything about him, every opinion we hear of him is good and agreeable. He is clearly an honest man with sound principles and such a gentle, amiable disposition, and yes, I did respect and like him well before I thought he showed some partiality for you. So set your mind at rest," she said, and Rachel embraced her mother.

"Thank you, Mama, that makes me very happy," she said.

"I am very happy for you, my dear," said her mother, "and to think we owe it all to Mr Darcy."

"Indeed, even though Daniel did not mention me at the time."

"Just think, my dear, how pleased Mr Darcy and Lizzie will be when they discover that you are to marry Daniel," said Caroline. "I cannot believe this has worked out in this happy way. If there is one thing I regret, it is that your papa will not be there to see you married."

At that, both mother and daughter wept again, before going down to the sitting room, where Caroline greeted her future son-in-law warmly. "Mr Faulkner—if I may call you Daniel—let me say how happy I am, Daniel, to welcome you into our family."

Daniel responded with all the correctitude of a man who was conscious of the need to explain his circumstances, and while Rachel went upstairs to change, he told Caroline in some detail the manner in which he had come to a decision to enter the church.

"It was chiefly born of my experiences in the colony, where it was plain to see how those men and even some women, who lacked faith and sound principles, could so easily be drawn into a morass of corruption, where money was all that mattered. People holding high office, no less than ordinary men, were equally guilty of unscrupulous conduct themselves or turned a blind eye to it in others in return for favours or money. I knew I could not survive long in such a society, and when my wife died, I became very dejected, lacking any hope.

"I took the opportunity offered by the chaplain to assist him in his parish as a lay worker. He opened up a door to a new life for me. I gave some of the money I had made on the goldfields to my wife's parents for the upbringing of my son and invested the rest in a small wool scouring business in Victoria. I have to say I did not expect it to do particularly well, but some years later, they went into partnership with an exporter of wool and thereafter were exceedingly successful, and I was also a beneficiary of their success. It brings me a reasonable and regular income, which is the extent of my so-called fortune, Mrs Fitzwilliam. For the rest, I shall depend upon my stipend as rector at Riversleigh," he explained and then continued, "After working for some time with the chaplain at Ballarat, during which time my view of life improved considerably, I became more interested in the idea of entering the church myself. With his help and recommendation, I was accepted. As I have told Mr Darcy and Rachel, I have served as a deacon and a rector of a small rural parish in Victoria. I said nothing to you and Rachel because I was unsure of obtaining a living in England."

Caroline waited until he had finished and said, "My dear Daniel, please do not feel you have to apologise or explain yourself to me any further. If Mr Darcy is sufficiently confident to appoint you to Riversleigh and my dear daughter loves you as she says she does and you love and care for her, then I am perfectly content. If you can make her happy, that is all I ask; it is what her father and I wanted for Rachel and all our children."

Rachel returned in time to hear Daniel tell her mother that since he had lost his young wife sixteen years ago, he had met no other woman for whom he had felt the same esteem and affection until he met her daughter.

"I am honoured that she has accepted me, and I give you my promise to love and care for her and secure her happiness to the very best of my ability," he said, and as Rachel came to his side and took his hand in hers, Caroline rose and embraced them both. It seemed to her there was no longer any concern about her daughter's future felicity.

❧

Writing to her son David and her daughter Isabella, Caroline expressed her happiness at the engagement of their sister in the warmest terms.

I am sure, David, that you will find Daniel Faulkner both intelligent and amiable and will agree that your sister is fortunate indeed. As to his background and prospects, they must be considered to be excellent, since he is Anna Bingley's brother and the rector of the parish of Riversleigh, to which Mr Darcy has appointed him. You will not doubt that this last piece of news is a matter of great joy to me, as it means my dear Rachel will be no more than twenty minutes' distance from me by pony cart.

We hope you and Lucy will come to dinner to meet Daniel three weeks from today and that young James may be allowed away from school to accompany you. I am sure if you were to see the headmaster and explain the circumstances, there will be no objection.

Meanwhile, I am to go with the happy pair to Hertfordshire, to see Daniel's parents. You may recall Charlotte Collins' sister Maria—she is Daniel's mother and her husband, Doctor Faulkner, is unwell, and Daniel must visit him and take Rachel, too. We shall travel by train and expect to be away for a week or ten days at the most. Give my fondest love to Lucy and my dear granddaughter, and do not forget to give young James the good news about his sister.

We look forward to seeing you.

Your loving mother etc

Her letter to Isabella, though fundamentally similar, contained more of the sort of information that a woman would insist upon knowing.

My dearest Isabella,

I cannot tell you with what pleasure I write to confirm my suspicion, expressed in my last letter to you, of a possible attachment between your sister Rachel and Mr Daniel Faulkner, soon to be known as Rev Daniel Faulkner. He must be one of the most pleasing and discerning men I have met in years, and Rachel is clearly deeply in love with him and he with her.

Dear Isabella, when one compares him to that awful fraud Adam Fraser, to whom Virginia Grantley is engaged, one has to give thanks to the Almighty, for there is no comparison between the two men.

I hope I have not surprised you too much with this news, but they are in fact engaged, and he is to be the new rector of Riversleigh parish, which you may recall is not above half an hour's walk from home or half that time were I to take the pony cart.

That he was already a clergyman was not revealed except to Cassandra and Mr Darcy until he could be certain that the position would be his. But now it is all settled and they are to be married after Christmas.

Mr Darcy has generously agreed to refurbish the rectory for them, and better still, Rachel says he has told Daniel he will increase the rector's stipend once they are married. Of course, Rachel has her own income too, thanks to your dear papa's good sense and excellent management, so they should be quite comfortable.

I hope that Philip and you will come to dinner with us to meet Daniel, three weeks from today, and when you are here, you may be able to help Rachel choose her wedding clothes. She is so engrossed with the whole idea of being in love with Daniel that she gives no thought at all to the practicalities of getting married. I am able to attend to matters of linen and household things, but she will need some help with her wedding gown. Your advice will be invaluable.

They broke the news to Mr Darcy and Lizzie the day after they became engaged, and tomorrow we are all invited to a small celebration at Pemberley. I have to say, Isabella my love, that while I have always enjoyed the Darcys' dinner parties, I am not looking forward to this one because Virginia and that dreadful Adam Fraser will probably be there, too. As for poor Georgiana, I cannot imagine how she must feel.

Meanwhile, we are to leave for Hertfordshire, where we are invited to stay at Netherfield with Jonathan and Anna Bingley and call on Daniel's parents.

I know you will remember Lizzie's friend Charlotte Collins, who passed away last year; well, her sister Maria is Daniel's mother. I am looking forward very much to the visit and will tell you all about it when we meet.

Do give my fondest love to your dear husband and to my darling grandchildren.

Your loving mother etc

PS, I have just had some wonderful news: Rachel has returned from visiting Cassy and it appears that we will not have the dubious pleasure of the company of Virginia and Mr Fraser, for they are gone with Georgiana to London to purchase Virginia's wedding clothes and trousseau. Such a relief! I can now say with absolute certainty that I shall definitely enjoy the dinner party at Pemberley tomorrow. In fact, I am looking forward to it.

Chapter Eleven

THEIR VISIT TO HERTFORDSHIRE was rendered even happier by the good news that Daniel's father Doctor Faulkner was said to be on the mend and unlikely to require the hazardous surgical procedure that they had all feared could leave him a permanent invalid.

Instead, the man from Harley Street had returned to London, and Doctor Charles Bingley of the Bell's Field cottage hospital had recommended rest, a light diet, and some moderate exercise, which Dr Faulkner declared after just two weeks had given him a whole new lease on life.

"These young fellows seem to know a whole lot more about our bodies than we did, and what's more, they are not afraid to experiment with new remedies. Dr Bingley was very frank with me, though. 'Either you will feel very much better very soon, or you will collapse and probably die of a heart attack,' he said, and though I confess I was somewhat shaken by his words and your mother was ready to order her mourning gowns, I did appreciate his honesty," he told his family.

Anna and Daniel both laughed, but Maria Faulkner could not see the humour in it, she said, berating her husband for making fun of such a serious matter. "It is so like your father to make light of such things," she complained. "Why, I have been a nervous wreck these past few months."

Daniel's reunion with his parents and their meeting with Rachel seemed to imbue their visit with true heartfelt delight. There could be no doubt that seeing their son again and finding him not only in good spirits, but engaged to be married as well, had brought real joy and comfort to his parents. That the young woman he was to marry was intelligent and charming, with an excellent background and a modest income of her own, and that Daniel, having entered the church, had just been appointed by Mr Darcy to a living on the Pemberley estate had the Faulkners almost believing in miracles.

That they knew little of the hardship and privation he had endured while in Australia, and the distress he had suffered at losing his young wife and having to surrender his infant son, was due in no small part to Daniel's genuine desire to protect his parents from his afflictions. It made it easier for them to enjoy his present good fortune.

But Anna Bingley was not deceived. She had, with Jonathan's help, gathered sufficient information from various sources about her brother, which had frequently left her in tears, despairing of his ever returning safely to England. For her, the reunion was infinitely more poignant, and when they returned later to Netherfield, the tears she had fought back all evening flowed freely as she and Daniel talked together.

"My dear brother, I cannot tell you how glad I am that you are to remain in England. For so long we were fearful of what might have befallen you in a country of which we know so little and so much of what we hear is truly dreadful. The accounts of brutality of the penal colonies, the crime, the terrible tales told by those who return, gave us little hope; it has been a nightmare!" she cried, and her husband attested to the truth of her words.

"Anna is right, Daniel," said Jonathan gravely, "she has been very concerned, and it has been exceedingly painful for your parents; your mother has been worried recently with your father's illness, and though Anna has been with them daily, trying to comfort them, it has not been easy."

Daniel, who had been deeply moved by all the emotions that had been aroused once again, was genuinely contrite. He put his arms around his sister and apologised for having caused her and their parents so much anguish. "I am sorry, truly sorry for all this, Anna, it is part of the unreality of being so far from every familiar person and thing that one cannot comprehend what effect it is having upon those left behind many thousands of miles away. Mired in my own misery and that of the many wretched people I saw around me, my concentration was upon the present. I never realised how much pain my long silences were causing my family back in England. Forgive me, Anna, I can do no more than say how very sorry I am, and now I am back here, I promise never to leave this land again."

At this extravagant claim even Anna laughed, and Jonathan said, "I don't think we would wish to make a prisoner of you, Daniel; you must travel if you wish, but we are all relieved I am sure to learn that you do not intend to return to the antipodean colonies."

"I think I can give you that promise very easily, Jonathan. It is a wonderful land of opportunity; many hardworking men and some desperate ones have made good there, but it is still a hard, cruel place with few of the gentler features that make for a happy and peaceful life. I have seen things done there, outrages that I cannot account for, by men who are considered to be upright human beings. I do believe I have given enough of my life to the Great South Land and have no wish to return. My dear Rachel and I have determined that Riversleigh will be our world for a while. Mr Darcy tells me there is a great deal of work to be done in the parish for the poor and their children; we are both looking forward to it very much."

So saying, he drew Rachel to his side, and both Anna and Caroline smiled; their relief was obvious. Caroline had but one regret. "If only," she thought, "if only dear Fitzy were here with us, it would be perfect." However, unwilling to spoil the happiness of all those around her, she said nothing.

⚜

Meanwhile at Pemberley, at a ceremony attended only by a few relations and even fewer friends, Virginia Grantley was married to Mr Adam Fraser.

Although they hosted the wedding and the breakfast that followed, neither Mr Darcy nor his wife could, with any degree of honesty, express much pleasure at the marriage, but it seemed the bride and groom were sufficiently pleased with themselves and each other to behave as though they expected to live happily ever after.

Mr Fraser had expressed his confidence that his bride would find life in their new home interesting, and Virginia had already declared that she was looking forward to an exciting voyage to New South Wales. It suited them well that there was no one present to contradict them.

They had left for London soon afterwards, in one of the Pemberley carriages, thereafter to embark upon a ship that would sail on the first of

November for New South Wales. Apparently, Fraser had not had enough of the colony; he had been heard singing its praises to anyone who would listen, boasting of the money there was to be made and the ease with which he could get things done by men who would risk life and limb to carry out his orders. He claimed to be keen to return to the sheep station, where he expected his wife would discover the delights of life in the Australian "outback."

Georgiana Grantley tried very hard to smile as she bade them goodbye, but her tears were not long in coming. Her initial relief at the prospect of having her daughter married to a man of respectable family and good prospects, as she believed Adam Fraser to be, had been somewhat diluted by the realisation of the enormous distance there would be between them; twelve thousand miles or more and a voyage of many months, her brother had told her.

There had also been certain rumours about Fraser and his activities that had disturbed her: his habit of borrowing large sums of money against the value of a forthcoming wool clip or the way he boasted of winning at cards. They had caused her some anxiety, but not sufficient to warrant an appeal to Virginia to reconsider her decision. Georgiana was unsure that any such request would have been taken seriously, for Virginia, at thirty, with the security of her own income, was far too pleased with her acquisition of a handsome and personable husband to worry about such trifling matters.

Back at Netherfield, while Daniel Faulkner and Rachel combined delight with duty, spending time together and with his family, Caroline had the particular pleasure of the company of Jonathan and Anna Bingley. They had always been close friends, with Jonathan having been one of Colonel Fitzwilliam's most successful political protégés.

They had shared some basic principles of social justice as well as the honours of many a victorious campaign, and though the colonel had retired from the political fray many years before his death, Jonathan had retained an active interest, as had Caroline.

That his daughter Anne-Marie had married Colin Elliott, a Member of Parliament and of Mr Gladstone's government, had served to enhance rather than impair Jonathan's philosophical commitment. Although his wife, Anna, was less involved, she nevertheless believed implicitly in her husband's reasoning and confessed also to a profound admiration for Caroline's work, which Anna acknowledged whenever they met.

"I wish I had grown up with the kind of knowledge Jonathan and you had; I might then have devoted more of my time to my fellow human beings; sadly my youth was spent in much less inspiring pursuits: learning to draw and paint, embroider linen, and play the harp," Anna complained, but her husband would not permit her to continue.

"You shall not devalue your accomplishments, my darling; Caroline knows as well as I do that your painting and music are of a very high standard and give great pleasure to all those who see and hear your work, including myself. There are not many young women I know who have mastered the harp as you have done or captured the beauty of a landscape on canvas as you do, while someone may always be found to carry a placard or organise a meeting. I know Caroline will agree with me," he said, and Caroline did.

"Oh my dear Anna, your husband is quite right. I never did master either of the instruments I studied because I married Fitzy at sixteen and became deeply involved in his work," said she, adding, "But the struggle to get things done is quite daunting, and often one feels betrayed by leaders who promise to do things, then change their minds after an election. It can break your heart; both Jonathan and Colin Elliott have said so often," she claimed.

"I certainly have, and Anne-Marie will tell you that Colin Elliott feels the same; he has told me of the anger he felt when Mr Gladstone abandoned significant sections of the Education Bill to placate the churches," said Jonathan, putting an arm around his wife's waist. "Believe me, Anna, involvement in political causes does bring satisfaction, if one succeeds in achieving a useful goal, but it can also be a most disagreeable experience, and I doubt that you would have enjoyed it, my dear. Caroline has been one of our most intrepid supporters, and I am sure even she will agree."

In the days that followed, Caroline and Anna spent some time alone together, and for the first time in many months, Caroline found she was able to speak openly of the loss of her husband. Anna was a solicitous and understanding listener to whom she could reveal her feelings.

"I always knew, because he was several years older, that it was possible I would be left a widow, but I never thought it would be this soon. I used to tell myself that he was fit and healthy and showed no sign of disease of any kind; there was no reason to suppose that he would die any earlier than Bingley or Mr Darcy. When he suffered the first attack, with no warning, I was so shocked; I refused to believe that it was happening. When Richard told us, Fitzy did try to make me accept it; he had no fear of death, but worried that I would not be able to deal with it when it came. Oh, it was not the practical matters he was concerned about—I was always good at those things. It was losing him, it was the loneliness after all these years that I could not cope with. Oh Anna, I cannot help it, I do miss him... I am sorry..." she said and wept.

Anna put her arms around Caroline, and as she did so, tears spilled down her cheeks, for though Caroline had probably not been aware of it as she spoke, Anna's own situation mirrored hers. The thought that Jonathan, several years her senior, could die just like Colonel Fitzwilliam had done, leaving her to endure the same loneliness, was heart wrenching. How could she hope to alleviate Caroline's grief when she could see in it a reflection of her own future?

But, determined not to surrender to melancholy, Anna dried her eyes and let Caroline think her tears were shed in sympathy. Trying to reinforce Caroline's resilience, she subdued her own concerns and spoke gently of the children and grandchildren, who she was certain would be a source of comfort, and was astonished by Caroline's response. "I had thought so too, but they no longer belong to me, except young James, who is still a child. In the end, they each belong to their own wives and husbands, mothers, fathers, and siblings; even Rachel is no longer mine. She was until a few weeks ago, but she is Daniel's now. Only Fitzy was mine, and now that he is gone, while I can borrow some time from the lives of my children or grandchildren, mine is now truly a solitary life. I am grateful indeed for the company of my friends and the affection of my family, but I cannot let myself depend upon them. I must learn to live my life as best I can," she said, drying her eyes.

On their return to Derbyshire, while Daniel had much to do with matters pertaining to his new parish, the ladies had other things on their mind. There were decisions to be made about the wedding breakfast, and although it had been suggested that they be married at Kympton, both Daniel and Rachel had a strong preference for Riversleigh, which meant persuading Frank Grantley to marry them there instead of in his own church.

Then there was Rachel's request that there should no extravagant celebration, asking instead for the family to gather for a quiet wedding breakfast at her mother's home. "I should very much like the money that would have been spent to go to the orphans," she said and was immediately supported by Daniel, who claimed that he had always thought far too much money was spent on feeding people who were already pretty well fed. "I agree with Rachel, the money would be better spent giving the orphans a good, hot meal; let them enjoy our wedding breakfast, too," he said, and that settled the question to everyone's satisfaction.

There was also the matter of the refurbishment of the rectory, which involved both Rachel and her mother spending not money but more time than they could afford at Riversleigh. Nevertheless, they did get it all done by the time the families arrived, as invited, to meet Daniel Faulkner and congratulate their sister.

Her older brother and sister, who had almost given up on seeing Rachel married, were truly delighted, especially after meeting Mr Faulkner, whose exemplary character and pleasing manners could not fail to impress them.

Later, when they went upstairs to talk about wedding gowns and flowers for the church, Isabella, who had been close to Rachel before her own marriage to Mr Bentley some years previously, embraced her young sister.

"My dear Rachel, I have no words to tell you how very happy I was to receive Mama's letter with the news of your engagement. You have always been in my thoughts, and I have hoped that one day you too would be as happy as I am. I know that it was not important to you, but as the years passed, I will confess that I did occasionally complain to Mama. She was never as anxious as I was, and it seems she was right, for I think that your wait was worthwhile. Your Mr Faulkner seems to be a fine man and I am sure you will be very happy together."

Rachel smiled with the confidence of one who is certain of her situation. "Thank you, Bella, I believe I shall; you were a good example to me. I recall the difficult times when your Mr Bentley returned after many years and we were not sure if he would propose. You were uncertain, but I always knew he would. I was quite sure he loved you."

Isabella smiled, recalling well those harrowing times. "I know you were, and I was grateful for your optimism then, because I had very little hope myself, having turned him down without giving him a proper reason for doing so. Philip said later that he had always loved me and wondered how I could fail to see it. Tell me, how was it with you and Daniel Faulkner? How soon did you know?"

"Not immediately, I think I knew quite soon after we met that I liked him, certainly more than any other man I had met; however, we believed he was committed to returning to the colonies, so it seemed sensible not to allow myself to fall in love with him. But he was so amiable and kind, so unlike anyone else I had met, it was not easy."

"And did you?"

"I'm afraid I did," she admitted, "but as it turned out, he had been contemplating his own future unbeknownst to me. He had made a decision to stay in England and with Mr Darcy being willing to appoint him to the living of Riversleigh, he felt able to make me an offer."

This time her sister felt able to tease her a little. "And when he did, how much time did you take to give him your answer?" she asked, with an unmistakable twinkle in her eye.

Rachel laughed a little nervously. "Not a great deal I'm afraid; not very much at all really," she confessed, and Isabella feigned outrage.

"Rachel, you are not going to tell me that you accepted him at once?"

"Oh dear, I am afraid I am, at least almost at once. I was so taken aback when he asked me to marry him that I couldn't say anything for a few minutes, and then, to my horror, he seemed to think it meant I was refusing him, and he started to apologise, whereupon I had to rush in and say no, he was not to apologise, and yes, I did love him and I would marry him, which pleased him very much, I think."

At this admission, Isabella laughed and embraced her sister. "Oh Rachel my dear, is that not just like you! I am delighted for you both. My dear Philip liked him almost immediately upon meeting him, and you seem so well suited to each other. I know you are going to be very happy."

They went downstairs to find the rest of the family gathered in the parlour for tea, listening to Daniel's tales of the antipodes, of which he had a great collection. There was no doubting his ability to keep his listeners interested, which Isabella said was an exceedingly useful gift for a clergyman, and Rachel giggled, recalling the many occasions on which they had fallen asleep in church during a boring sermon.

⚜

Caroline, meanwhile, had also acted upon a plan she had fashioned, in consultation with Jonathan Bingley, about which she had as yet spoken to no one else. She had particular concerns about the inheritance she would one day leave to her children and wished to use the opportunity of having her entire family together, on such a felicitous occasion as this, to settle the matter, so there would be no possibility of disputes and bitterness poisoning their relationships after her death. To this end, she had invited her husband's friend and lawyer, the attorney Mr Jennings, to attend the family reunion on Saturday evening.

On his arrival, he had been ushered in to Colonel Fitzwilliam's study, where Caroline thanked him for his attendance and then placed a sheaf of papers including her own will on her husband's desk, ready for his perusal. She had written down very clear instructions and requested that he read them and advise her on their suitability for incorporation into her will.

When he appeared somewhat confused by her request and asked why she was taking this course of action, she replied quite frankly, "My dear Mr Jennings, I do not intend to die and leave my family to squabble over the estate, which my dear husband and I have put together so carefully and over so many years. Colonel Fitzwilliam would never forgive me. So I have decided that instead of being surprised on the morning after my funeral, they will all be forewarned of my decisions and the reasons for them. I should very much like for you to be present to reassure any of my children of the legitimacy of my actions. I do not wish any one of them to feel hard done by after I am gone," she explained.

The attorney, himself a widower, whose wife had died some five years ago, expressed some disquiet. "Forgive my asking, Mrs Fitzwilliam, but have you any reason to suppose that... what I mean is... have you experienced any problems regarding your health recently?"

Caroline laughed. "Certainly not, I am in excellent health, Mr Jennings. I am not doing this because I am about to die, far from it; I merely want this whole business settled, so we can all go on enjoying the rest of our lives, however long or short they may be. I want my children to know what they will inherit and there's an end of it. I need you to assure me that what I wish to do is fair and legal."

Mr Jennings was unequivocal in his response. "My dear Mrs Fitzwilliam, there could be no doubt of that at all; the property is yours as is the business, and you may dispose of them as you wish. No one, not even one of your own children, can gainsay your right to do it. The colonel was very clear and quite determined when he said to me, 'Mr Jennings, I want you to ensure that Caroline has complete control over everything; she must decide how she wishes to divide up the estate among our children, according to their circumstances,'" he said.

At this she laughed and then bit her lip as though she could hear Fitzwilliam's voice in his words. "Well, now I have decided, and I need your help to present my plan to my children and make them understand why I have done this." So saying, she left him to work in the study and went to join her family, having ensured that he had plenty of refreshments to keep him happy while he toiled over the task she had set him on.

After they had all finished tea and were in good spirits, she shepherded them into the drawing room and, having settled them down with very little preliminary explanation, brought in Mr Jennings, whom everyone except Daniel knew well, but no one was expecting to see at this time.

There was a general murmur in the room, of mild surprise perhaps, before Caroline said, "I know you are all wondering what I am about to do and why Mr Jennings is here; well, I am going to tell you. I have done this because I do not wish to leave you with any nasty surprises when I am gone, and before you ask, no, I am not unwell, but this is as good a time as any.

"We are about to celebrate Rachel's engagement to Daniel Faulkner and two days after Christmas, we will meet again to see them married. Today, I wish you to know what I have decided to do about the family estate, which, in your father's will, was left entirely in my hands. I asked Mr Jennings to join us, so you can ask him any questions you wish to and he can set your minds at rest about what I have done. I thought it would be best, so we need have no anxiety or squabbling after I am gone."

Both Isabella and David protested that she was talking about dying as though it was imminent.

Caroline, anticipating their objections, held up a hand. "I may not look as though I am about to leave you, and I assure you I am in very good health, but we never can tell when we are to be called away, so please bear with me, my dears. Here is what I have decided. I intend to leave the home farm and this house to James, on condition that if any of his sisters is widowed and needs a home, they will have a place here."

At this, young James, who was cuddled up close to his eldest sister, Isabella, smiled without much understanding and rested his head on her shoulder. Isabella shivered and put her arms around him. The decision did not affect either Isabella or David; they had homes of their own and had no interest in the farm, but the thought of her mother's death was chilling.

Caroline went on, "David will continue to run the family business, and he will get all of his father's shareholding to add to his own, while my shares, which make up almost a third of the total, will be divided between my three daughters, Bella, Amy, and Rachel, who will also receive a third each of the interest from my investments as regular income."

All three young women looked quite pleased with this announcement, but there was more to come.

"Finally, there is your father's annuity. It is not large and will not add much to your own incomes if it were to be divided amongst you. So I am asking you to agree to let me use it to help perhaps one of the most needy groups in our community: women, usually but not always widows, with young children, who have no one to support them and nowhere but the workhouse to go for shelter.

"I propose to purchase the old manor house at Arrowfield and have it made ready to be used as a refuge for these women and their children. If you agree and we make an immediate start, we may well be able to take in a few of them this Winter. I should like Amy and Rachel to help me with organising it. Your dear husbands will minister to their spiritual needs, no doubt, but I think we must ensure they are fed and sheltered as well."

Both her daughters looked a little surprised but neither demurred. They were both aware that in the parishes of Kympton and Riversleigh there would be many such women, with nowhere to go but the workhouse.

Caroline continued, "I shall set the place up and run it for now, but when I am gone, I shall expect you to continue with the work. Your father and I often discussed the need for such a place, and I am quite sure he would approve of it. Now, are we all agreed?"

Amy and Rachel agreed immediately, and not a single voice was raised in dissent. Caroline looked around the room at her children, their husbands and wives, and smiled. If any of them had been shocked by her extraordinary plans, they were very good at concealing their feelings, she thought.

"Bless you," she said and then turned to the attorney at her side. "Now, Mr Jennings will answer any of your questions," she offered, and the gentleman looked ready and willing to oblige, but apart from a couple of formalities, no one troubled him for advice that evening.

"I shall prepare a formal document incorporating all these matters and provide each of you with a copy," he explained. "The original document will of course be lodged in my safe."

When it was done, Caroline said to Mr Jennings with a bright smile, "Well, that wasn't at all difficult, was it, Mr Jennings?" to which he replied, "Not at all, Mrs Fitzwilliam, I could wish that all my clients managed their business with the same ease and civility as you and your family have just done."

Later that night, following a splendid celebratory dinner and after all their guests had either departed or retired to bed, Caroline wrote to Anna and Jonathan Bingley, expressing her thanks especially to Jonathan for his advice, which she had sought while at Netherfield.

I believe I owe it to you, Jonathan, that everything was so well accepted by all of my children; your advice that I should explain my reasons to them surprised my attorney, Mr Jennings, but later even he was impressed by the civility with which the business was done.

Inviting them to attend the wedding of her daughter Rachel to the Reverend Daniel Faulkner in December at the parish church at Riversleigh, she wrote:

My dear Anna, it gives me such joy to tell you that your dear brother Daniel has been received with such affection and warmth by everyone in the family that Rachel claims he will soon be their favourite in-law! My eldest girl, Isabella, had occasionally complained that I wasn't doing enough to find

Rachel a good husband; well, she now admits that left to her own devices,
Rachel has done very well indeed. His kind and considerate nature together
with his undoubted intelligence and excellent judgment will ensure he will
be both a good husband and an exemplary rector of the parish.
I am confident my dear husband would have approved of him.

There could be no higher praise from Caroline.

As the year drew to a close, with light snow falling on the mountains and
a little sunlight struggling through the high windows of the church, Rachel
was married to Daniel Faulkner in the presence not only of their families and
friends, but almost all the people of the parish of Riversleigh, who had come to
welcome their new rector and his wife.

Transformed by the hard work of several parishioners who had provided
their labour, the church and its superb altarpiece glowed as Frank Grantley led
the congregation in the marriage service and blessed the pair who had chosen
to serve this small community together.

After a somewhat grander than expected wedding breakfast, for Caroline
had not the heart to do otherwise for Rachel, the couple left, not to speed to
some stately hotel but to return secretly to the warmth and intimacy of the
rectory that was their new home.

It had been Daniel's idea, put rather tentatively at first, for he had feared
she may be disappointed, but Rachel had agreed enthusiastically, convincing
him that she wanted nothing more. Daniel had been concerned that she may
have been disappointed, for they had spoken once or twice of visiting the
Lake District; Daniel had heard a great deal about its beauty but had never
been there.

But Rachel had reassured him, "The Lakes can wait until we have some
time to spare, perhaps next Summer. Besides, Mrs Darcy has invited us to stay
at her farm on the Albury Downs, where we will be a good deal warmer than
in Cumbria!" she'd said.

"And have you accepted?" Daniel asked, to which she replied softly, "I
have indeed, but I shall have to confess that we will be spending a few days
at Riversleigh first, before travelling south to Woodlands. But have no fear,

Mrs Darcy is the very soul of discretion, she will not say a word to anyone, I can promise you that."

"And are you certain it is what you want, my love?" he asked, still anxious to please her, and Rachel had put her arms around him as she said, "More certain than I am of anything else, Daniel, except that I love you and want to be your wife," which brought a predictable fond response.

As Rachel wrote in her diary that night:

I believe Daniel was very surprised when I told him I could think of nothing I should like better than to spend our wedding night at the rectory at Riversleigh. But truly, I cannot, for what could be sweeter than to fall asleep with the sound of the river rushing over the stones and awake at dawn beside my dear husband, hearing the birds calling in the wood behind the church, and look out upon the clear water with the mountains in the distance, knowing that this is indeed our home. Where better to affirm our love?

Chapter Twelve

THE ROSES THAT COLONEL Fitzwilliam had planted in a garden bed beside the windows of his study had long finished their blooming, and Caroline was pruning them hard, recalling as she did so that it was a task her late husband had carried out with great energy at the end of each year, declaring that the deeper the cuts in Winter, the more vigorous would be the new growth in Spring and the more beautiful blooms she would have. The memory was vivid and it hurt; it was with some difficulty that she held back the tears.

She had decided it was the day to prune the colonel's roses. Concentrating upon her task, she had not heard the arrival of a vehicle at the front door, and it was not until she heard the crunch of footsteps on gravel that she looked up and saw Mr Jennings, her attorney, standing a few feet from her as she gathered up the pruned debris into a wheelbarrow.

Surprised, she smiled and got to her feet. She knew he was due to deliver some documents relating to the changes to her will, but had not expected that he would be around this early in the New Year. "Mr Jennings, how very nice to see you. Are you here on business or is this a social call?" she asked and was surprised to hear him say, "I have brought your copy of the document, as promised, but I had hoped to convey my best wishes for the New Year as well. We have not met since Miss Rachel's wedding," he reminded her.

"That is true," said Caroline, and she thanked him, then seeing it was almost eleven o'clock, invited him to take tea. As they walked around to the entrance, she saw the large basket of exquisite hothouse blooms standing beside the front door.

Mr Jennings, like his father before him, was an enthusiastic grower of exotic orchids; she remembered her husband having long conversations with both men about their collection. "Are these from your conservatory? They are beautiful, Mr Jennings, thank you; I do hope you haven't completely denuded your orchids; oh what glorious colours, and they do last forever, unlike my roses, which though beautiful, are often blown too soon, for all the effort we put into them."

"Yes indeed," he said, "it was the reason my father preferred to grow orchids. He said they gave a better return for the effort."

Caroline laughed and said, "That is a very utilitarian argument to use about something as beautiful as flowers, Mr Jennings, but he was right. My husband loved roses above all other flowers; he spent hours tending them. But I do know he admired your father's orchids very much, and who would not? They are quite superb." Mr Jennings, clearly pleased, helped her carry the basket indoors and waited in the hall until she had divested herself of gloves and hat before entering the parlour.

Once they were seated, Mr Jennings extracted the document he had prepared from his briefcase and presented it to her, watching her as she read it through. When she had done so, she said simply, "That looks exactly right, Mr Jennings, thank you. But there was no need for you to bring it with such haste."

Jennings smiled, indicating that it had been no trouble to do so. He had known Caroline and Colonel Fitzwilliam for most of his life, since his father had been the colonel's attorney while he was still at college studying the law. He remembered being struck by her beauty and vivacity when she and the colonel were married, and the energy with which she would take on and pursue each of the causes her husband espoused. She was still a remarkably attractive woman, he thought, and she had lost none of her vitality or humour.

During the next hour, they took tea and refreshments and talked of many things, mostly inconsequential matters. Occasionally she mentioned the colonel, and Mr Jennings looked rather uncomfortable, as if he wished she hadn't, and Caroline wondered at his discomposure.

Noticing that Mr Jennings had suddenly gone very quiet, Caroline, trying to make conversation, asked if he was returning to Derby that evening.

"No, I am not," he replied. "I expect to stay in the area for a day or two; I have taken rooms at the Matlock Arms," but he gave no reason. Thereafter, it seemed there was very little else to talk about, except for Caroline to offer Mr Jennings more tea. His revelation that he was staying at the Matlock Arms indicated to her that he would not be in a great hurry to leave. Perhaps, she thought, he may even expect to be asked to stay to dinner. After her exertions in the garden, Caroline was beginning to feel rather tired, and as the afternoon wore on, she wondered how she could, politely and without offending him, send her unexpected guest on his way.

Suddenly and fortuitously, there was a disturbance outside the window, and looking out, she saw Sarah, one of the maids, running out of the farm gate in a clearly distressed state. Glad of the distraction, Caroline rose and moved quickly to the door, making as if to leave the room.

It was then that Mr Jennings stood up and, barring her way, said in a rather strange formal voice, "Mrs Fitzwilliam, would you spare me a little time, please? There is an important matter I wish to bring to your attention."

Surprised, Caroline stepped back, but pointed out that she wished to discover what had caused her maid to run out of the farm gate.

"If you will pardon me, Mr Jennings, I am concerned about Sarah, she is obviously in some distress; I will return as soon as I am satisfied that she is safe and all is well." She spoke so firmly, he knew he had to move aside.

When Caroline returned, having settled the matter of Sarah's temporary anguish, she found the attorney sitting somewhat disconsolately beside the fire, which had almost died out in the grate. The room was cold, and Caroline apologised before she set about swiftly stoking it up to a reasonable blaze.

She noted as she did so that he had not offered to do the job himself, presumably expecting her to summon a servant, but Caroline was keen to be rid of him and did not wish to prolong the process. She was about to order more tea, when he said, "I think I have had sufficient tea, thank you, Mrs Fitzwilliam. There is a matter that I particularly wish to speak to you about."

More than a little surprised, Caroline sat down in the chair across from him, wondering what it could be that was so urgent, since he had assured her that everything concerning her will had been carefully checked and was quite in order and there appeared to be no problem with the new arrangements she had put in place.

When he began to speak however, her surprise turned to amazement, for it appeared Mr Jennings had nothing to say about her will. Instead, it seemed he wished to make her an offer of marriage. Caroline, who was aware that Mr Jennings was some years her junior, could scarcely believe what she was hearing.

He spoke in much the same kind of voice and used very similar language to that which he used when giving her legal advice, and made no pretence of being in love with her, for which Caroline was grateful.

"At least it means I need feel no remorse at refusing him," she thought as she heard him declare that he had always respected her and her family and hoped that the long association that existed between his firm and her family would help strengthen her trust in him.

As she listened, her astonishment increasing with every sentence, he reminded her that his father and he had served her family for many years with unswerving loyalty and placed on record his admiration for the manner in which she had supported her husband Colonel Fitzwilliam in all his endeavours. But he proceeded to point out that as a woman alone she may not have the same advantages that she enjoyed as the colonel's wife and would probably value the protection and favour of a husband.

Having pointed out the potential hazards of her present situation, he then stated his hope that she would consider his proposal favourably because, he said, they had always got on well together and he had decided that they could be excellent companions for each other in the future. He assured her gravely that he would ask for no changes to be made in her will, since he respected her desire to provide for her children, as he had for his, and added that if she did not wish to move to Derby, he would not press her to do so, understanding her desire to remain in the home she had made for her family over many years.

"Which means," thought Caroline, "he intends to move in here!" It was not a prospect that appealed to her at all.

Finally, almost as an afterthought, he added that he thought he should assure her that, although it had been five years since the death of his late wife, he had made no approaches to any other lady because, he claimed, none of them would have been a worthy successor nor did he believe they could have made him happy. "That I have done today what I have avoided these five years is proof of the admiration and respect I feel for you, and I hope most fervently that it will convince you to accept my suit, " he concluded a little breathlessly, leaving Caroline feeling exceedingly discomfited.

When she said nothing at first, Mr Jennings seemed to realise that she had been surprised by his approach and waited a while before saying, "I understand that you may need some time to consider my proposal, perhaps to consult your family, which is why I have arranged to remain in the district until Tuesday afternoon. With your permission, I will call on you again on Tuesday morning…"

At this moment, Caroline realised that she had to speak now. It was impossible to let him leave and return in two days' time for her answer. With great discipline, she spoke quickly, but not so fast as to give offence. "No, Mr Jennings, that will not be necessary," she said, and her heart sank as she saw relief and some satisfaction reflected in his expression. Clearly, he expected her to accept him. She went on, nevertheless. "Acknowledging the time and thought that must surely have been expended upon your decision to make such an offer, I would not wish to prolong the uncertainty; indeed I am very conscious of the sincere concern and solicitude that have motivated you and I thank you for it. However, I must say with regret that I am unable to accept your kind offer, not because I have any doubts about your character or the sincerity of your sentiments, but because, Mr Jennings, as anyone who knows me will tell you, I have not the slightest desire to marry again."

The look of complete disbelief that crossed his face surprised her. It seemed he doubted her word; it was as though he thought she was waiting to be convinced and was preparing to launch into another justification for his proposal and the wisdom of accepting it.

Before he could begin, Caroline decided that more candour was called for. "Mr Jennings, as you have stated, our families have a long association and we have known one another for many years. Yet, I doubt there has ever been an occasion on which you could have supposed that I was the sort of wife you would have chosen for yourself, nor have I ever imagined that I would have been happy with you for a husband."

Seeing the astonishment reflected on his face, she added quickly, "This is no criticism of you; you are a good man and one of the most reliable I have known, and I have often enjoyed your company. But, having been so happily married to my dear husband for so many years, I should never want to risk losing that sense of perfect contentment by entering into any other association, however advantageous it may promise to be."

Caroline continued, "Besides, as you know, I have set in train certain plans for my own life, which will not fit comfortably with marriage to anyone. I shall be far too busy with other things, including the purchase and running of Arrowfield House."

Clearly crestfallen, Mr Jennings could not conceal his disappointment but accepted her explanation with dignity and, to Caroline's immense relief, left soon afterwards. Before he entered his vehicle, he turned around and said, "In view of your decision, I think I shall return to Derby tomorrow afternoon. Should you wish to make any amendments to the document, please do send me word to the Matlock Arms."

Caroline thanked him again for his work, closed the door, and went upstairs to her room. The effort of maintaining her composure had left her exhausted. She would never know for certain what had prompted Mr Jennings to make his offer. It was improbable that it was based on mercenary motives alone, though he did know her financial situation well, but neither could she credit him with any depth of feeling for her, so dry and passionless had been his performance.

That he should think she, after being married to her beloved Fitzy for almost a lifetime, would within a few months of his death consider marriage to his attorney, who had decided they could be "excellent companions," had affronted and dispirited her. She had neither the inclination nor the energy to do anything more than fall into bed.

Since her husband's death, Caroline had moved from the large bedroom they had shared for all the years of their marriage to a smaller room, which looked out across the grounds to the river. It was pretty, cosy, and held no memories for her, having once been Isabella's room. Lying on the narrow bed, Caroline wept, and this time, there was no Rachel to comfort her.

A romantic at heart, she had been teased often by family and friends for her inclination towards sentiment; yet with a husband who loved her dearly, Caroline had sublimated her youthful romanticism in a passionate marriage that had brought them both great happiness and contentment. Like her cousin Lizzie, she had vowed never to marry without the deepest love and had found Mr Jennings's proposition to her to make a second marriage based chiefly upon convenience quite abhorrent. It was all she could do not to shudder with distaste as he spoke. It had raked up the sources of her grief, and she wept alone.

It was late evening and quite dark in the room, when her maid came to call her and prepare her bath. She remembered to ask Sarah if she was feeling better; the girl had been upset by a teasing remark from one of the grooms concerning her appearance. She was young and volatile, and had not quite recovered her composure. Catherine comforted her and assured her that there had been no harm meant, promising to speak sternly to the young man on the morrow.

Afterwards, she sent the maid away and returned to bed, claiming she had a headache and would need no dinner. Sarah persuaded her to take a cup of hot chocolate—it had been her husband's favourite cure for insomnia, and it always worked. She fell into a deep sleep but awoke earlier than usual. The sun had not risen, nor had the birds, but Caroline, clear-headed and in better spirits, rose and wrote to Anna Bingley.

My dearest Anna, she wrote:

> *I trust this finds you, Jonathan, and the children well and happy. It must be such a delight to have them with you. Mine are gone now to make their own lives; even Rachel, the last of the fledglings, has her own nest.*
>
> *Daniel and Rachel are back from their honeymoon at Lizzie's farm on the Albury Downs, where they claim the servants had strict instructions to spoil them. They are now in residence at Riversleigh.*
>
> *Mr Darcy was as good as his word and had the rectory completely refurbished for them, even to new plumbing and heating. It is very comfortable now. It is a special joy for me to see my Rachel, who I once believed had forsworn matrimony altogether, so much in love and contentedly married.*
>
> *As for your dear brother Daniel, he makes no effort to conceal his deep affection for her, and he seems to have taken very well to being the rector of Riversleigh. I attended church there on Sunday and was most impressed with his fine voice and excellent sermon. Judging from the faces of his parishioners, they were too.*
>
> *Anna my dear, I write also to acquaint you and Jonathan with my plans for the property at Arrowfield, which I have decided to purchase and refurbish as a place of refuge for widowed and deserted women and their children.*

My children are all agreed that it is a worthy cause on which to spend their father's annuity, and I know he would approve absolutely of our project.

Amy and Rachel will assist me (with the blessing of their husbands, naturally) in running the place, and I hope we will take in our first guests very soon.

When you are next in Derbyshire, I look forward to showing you and Jonathan how we are getting on…

Concluding her letter with the usual felicitations, Caroline rose, and hearing the chorus of birds starting up in the orchard, she went to the window, drew back the curtains, and looked out upon the sun rising on a new day.

Later that morning, having breakfasted and taken her usual walk around the garden, Caroline decided that she would go to Riversleigh and visit Rachel and Daniel. Since rising that morning, she had felt an overwhelming desire to see her daughter, enfold her in her arms, and be sure in her heart that she was truly happy. She had tried to tell herself that it was only a silly response to the extraordinary behaviour of Mr Jennings, which had so unsettled her, but it would not do. She had to go.

Sending for the steward, she asked for the carriage to be brought round, went upstairs to get her wrap and bonnet, and informed the housekeeper that she would be back in time for dinner.

It was almost midday when she reached the rectory at Riversleigh, having used the longer route through the village and over the bridge. Approaching the church, Caroline could see both Daniel and Rachel in the garden, and they came to greet her as she alighted from the vehicle. It was quite clear that they were delighted not only to see her, but had also some further cause for satisfaction, which they were keen to communicate to her. Caroline was aware of this as they embraced her most affectionately, before ushering her indoors with some haste.

Once they were within, Rachel was quick to reveal that they had just been preparing to set out to visit her mother, to bring her some wonderful news. Caroline could not imagine what this could be, and was about to ask, when Daniel Faulkner, taking out a letter from the inside pocket of his coat, handed it to her, saying, "That letter had arrived for me a few days before we returned from Woodlands; it comes from Victoria, from the father of my late wife. He writes that my son, Martin, who is now almost seventeen years old, has been awarded a scholarship to study at a college in Scotland. He will be embarking onboard a vessel; indeed, he should be on his way already, which will bring him to England early in the Spring."

Caroline could scarcely believe it. "That is wonderful news! Daniel, you must be delighted!" she cried, and he replied, unable to contain the emotion in his voice, "Indeed I am, we both are. It is almost two years since I last saw my son, and when I decided to settle in England, my one regret was that I may not have the opportunity to see him for an even longer period. This letter has changed all that and brought us such joy; we have spoken of little else since receiving the news."

"I can well believe it, and I am delighted too, for your sake and for your son. It must be a most valuable opportunity for him. Do you know at which college he is to study?" Caroline asked and was told that it was at a very prestigious college in Edinburgh.

"I am assured that it is an excellent institution with a fine academic reputation; Martin is very fortunate indeed," said Daniel.

Tea had been brought in, and Rachel, handing her mother a cup, said quietly, "We do have one little problem, Mama, we were wondering how we might accommodate Martin during his vacations, because there is but one tiny spare room here and..." at which Caroline put down her cup and declared, "But, Rachel my dear, surely that is not a problem; young Martin can stay with me; he can have David's room, which has been empty since your brother moved to Manchester." And seeing the surprise on Daniel Faulkner's face, she added quickly, "That is, if you have no objection, Daniel, I should be perfectly happy to have him to stay when he is home from college, and of course you can visit each other whenever you wish."

Both Daniel and Rachel could not contain their pleasure at this offer, and once they had assured themselves that it would not inconvenience her in any way, they embraced Caroline and thanked her for her generosity.

Caroline was quick to assure them that she would look forward to having young Martin Faulkner to stay. The arrival of a parishioner sent Daniel to the front door, leaving mother and daughter alone, and affording Rachel the opportunity to ask, "Are you quite sure, Mama? After all, Martin will be a complete stranger…" but Caroline would have none of it.

"Of course I am sure, what's more, I cannot imagine anything better for my James, who will also be home on holidays, than a young man, just a few years older than he is, who can tell him all about the great colonies on the other side of the world and that long sea voyage. It will be quite wonderful, and they will be excellent company for each other."

She did not add that her own heart had leapt at the thought of a young boy, a few years older than her own Edward had been when she had lost him, living in her home. If Martin was anything like his father, Caroline was confident that they would get on very well indeed, and perhaps, her solitary life might be enlivened from time to time by his bright presence.

Looking out of the parlour window, they saw Daniel walking around to the vestry with his visitor, and Caroline, seeing the expression on her daughter's face, said, "Besides, my darling, Daniel and you need to spend time on your own; I can see he is going to be busy in the parish, but he loves you dearly, and I want you to be very happy together."

Rachel put her arms around her mother and said quietly, "Thank you, Mama; I am quite sure we will; indeed, I must confess I have never been happier in my life. There, are you content?" she asked, and Caroline smiled and said, "I am, perfectly content."

END OF PART TWO

THE LEGACY OF PEMBERLEY

Part Three

The Inheritance

Chapter One

I T WAS THE WEEK after Laura Ann Gardiner's birthday. She was nineteen and quite beautiful, but because of a childhood tendency to suffer from respiratory disorders, her beauty was of a rather fragile kind, making her appear much younger than her years. She was a great favourite in the family on account of her gentle nature and engaging disposition, which was probably why her grandparents, Mr and Mrs Darcy, had insisted that her birthday would be celebrated with a rare event: a ball at Pemberley.

No one had any doubt that this was a tribute to his granddaughter, because the Master of Pemberley was not fond of dancing. Despite this, Mrs Darcy and he had hosted the celebrations with great style, to the satisfaction of a large party of family and friends. Laura Ann's happiness had been almost inexpressible, and the Darcys were well pleased.

Sadly missing from the occasion had been Mr and Mrs Bingley on account of Mr Bingley's continuing indisposition. Indeed, plans were afoot for them to travel to southern France and Italy in the Autumn, where they would remain until the following Spring. Mrs Darcy, whose affection for her sister Jane would not let her consider such a long separation with any degree of equanimity, had spent much of the previous month attempting to persuade her husband that he too could benefit from such a vacation, and in this she had been supported by her daughter and son-in-law.

While Mr Darcy had insisted that he was in perfectly good health and had no need of such an excursion, Doctor Richard Gardiner, who had recently attended upon both Mr Bingley and Mr Darcy, was convinced that time away from Pemberley, in a climate as salubrious as was proposed by the Bingleys and in such unarguably congenial company, could only improve his health and would afford Mrs Darcy an opportunity to avail herself of the benefits, too. He had not as yet suggested this to his father-in-law, but had made the point to his wife.

A casual observation from Cassandra that her mother was looking rather weary after the exertion and excitement of Laura Ann's birthday ball brought an immediate response from Mr Darcy. Looking across at his wife, who for once was disinclined to contradict her daughter's remarks on her health, he asked, "Is this true, my dear?" to which Elizabeth replied with some care, "Oh I think Cassy is making much of a very little matter; I did mention that I had been lacking in energy of late, and Jenny has been preparing a herbal tonic for me, which I have to say is not the pleasantest potion I have taken, but she assures me it will do me good..."

Her husband interrupted her, clearly concerned. "Lizzie, why have you not spoken of this condition before? Does Richard know of this?" he asked.

As Richard and Cassy exchanged glances, Elizabeth, seeing an opportunity, decided to take advantage of it. "No, I did not think it sufficiently serious to trouble Richard with it," she began, "it is not a constant condition, it is intermittent..."

"But persistent?" Mr Darcy probed, as though he and not Richard were the physician.

"Yes, but it is not as though I am in pain. It is only a general feeling of malaise, as though I had become overtired..." Elizabeth explained.

"Which you probably have, Mama," said Cassy, butting in, as she began to comprehend the drift of the conversation, "indeed I have noticed that you seemed paler and more fatigued than usual after Laura Ann's birthday celebrations."

Elizabeth made as though to dismiss her concerns, but Darcy would have none of it. Turning to his son-in-law, he demanded to know if his wife's condition was serious, to which Richard replied, "It is not at the moment, sir. I would say that Mrs Darcy has become rather exhausted over the Summer. She has been very busy, and it has been an unusually warm season. However, if nothing is done to ameliorate it, the condition could worsen as Winter approaches, and she could be stricken down with influenza or bronchitis, but a good long rest, a change of scene, sunshine, good company, and some wholesome, nourishing food would quickly see her recover her natural energy."

It took Mr Darcy only a few minutes to decide that what he had been resisting on his own behalf was absolutely imperative to the restoration of his wife's health. "As you know, Richard, Charles and Jane Bingley leave for Europe next week. Bingley has leased a villa in the south of Italy where they will spend the Winter, and he has on more than one occasion invited us to join them. Would it help Mrs Darcy, too? Would you recommend it?" he asked.

Cassy smiled as her husband nodded, endorsing the idea wholeheartedly. "Without any reservation, sir; it would be the very thing, since it would provide all those essential ingredients I have just mentioned. In the company of Mr and Mrs Bingley, you would enjoy the benefits of travelling overseas without any of the aggravation of being with a party of strangers. I would say it is the ideal opportunity, sir," he concluded, and Cassy could not help noting the expression on her mother's face.

Mr Darcy's mind was made up. "Thank you, Richard, I will send a note to Bingley this afternoon, and Lizzie, my dear, we can begin preparations for the journey right away," he said.

Richard had one more suggestion, calculated to set the seal upon his father-in-law's decision. "I am expected at Ashford Park this afternoon, sir; I can take the note and bring you a response directly," he said, and while Darcy rose and went to his study, Cassy and her mother embraced.

"Richard, I cannot thank you enough; not for myself, my fatigue is probably temporary and will disappear in time, but for Mr Darcy. I have been concerned that he will not stop working, and if he does not take some rest away from Pemberley, he, like Colonel Fitzwilliam, may suffer a sudden breakdown. Yet I have not been able to persuade him," said Elizabeth.

Richard sought to reassure her that her husband was unlikely to suffer the fate of his cousin Colonel Fitzwilliam, whose constitution had been weakened considerably through his years in the military and later in the south Asian colonies.

"Mr Darcy is in much better health than the colonel was, but I agree that he does work ceaselessly and could do with time away from Pemberley. I am sure you will both benefit from this journey. It is an excellent decision," he said.

A week later, Darcy and Elizabeth, with a couple of trusted personal servants, left to join the Bingleys and travel first to London and thence to France and Italy, leaving Julian and Jessica resident at Pemberley, with Cassandra and her son Darcy Gardiner in charge of the estate.

Anthony Darcy, the young heir to Pemberley, and his cousin James were both delighted to have the run of the grounds while their grandparents were away. Both boys, though too young to fully comprehend the responsibility that would one day lie upon young Anthony's shoulders, were, nevertheless, well schooled in the importance of the work done on the estate. James' mother, Cassandra, had had the care of her young nephew since the death of his mother, Josie, and though his father, Julian, had since married again, Anthony had remained by his own choice with the Gardiners, and the two boys were as close as brothers.

Cassy, who for many years had assisted her father in the running of the Pemberley estate, had at all times insisted that the boys knew the significance of the duties that had to be performed, and furthermore, she had, by taking them with her on many occasions, ensured that they knew and often became friends with many of the people who lived and worked on the estate.

After her son Darcy was appointed to the position of manager, Cassy had played less of a role in the supervision of activities on the estate, but had spent more time on the ancillary organisations like the school, the library, and the hospital, which her parents had set up for their tenants and workers as well as the people of the district. Both James and Anthony took an interest in her work and often travelled around the district with her.

On a fine morning, some days after the Darcys had left for Europe, Cassandra was driving in her curricle with Laura Ann and the two boys. They had a basket of groceries for the hospital and were making their way to Littleford, where Cassy had arranged to meet with her son Darcy's wife, Kate, who was uncharacteristically late that morning.

When she did arrive, Kate had news for them. Cassy had been concerned that their little boy may have been taken ill, but Kate assured her that little Michael was quite well. "But," she added, "we have new neighbours; they've just moved in at Willowdale Farm, and of course, we had to stop and say welcome to the district."

Cassy was eager to know who they were. Willowdale Farm was an old freehold property left vacant after its owner had died some years ago. Lying across the river from the home she and Richard had shared before they had moved to Camden Park, the main dwelling was a Georgian-style cottage, sitting atop a terraced garden filled with a myriad of flowers and a broad meadow and orchard behind it.

But Cassy's happiest recollection was of three ancient beech trees that stood like sentinels in the grounds of Willowdale Farm. Her children had loved the trees; both Edward and Darcy had spent hours in their spreading branches, while their grandmother Mrs Gardiner watched, terrified that they would fall, but they never did. The memory brought tears to her eyes.

"Who are they?" she asked, and Kate replied that the family were called O'Connor.

"They are recently come over from Ireland, I believe," she said. "I met the mother, her son, and two daughters. I did not see Mr O'Connor."

"Perhaps he works in town or at the mills," Laura Ann suggested, and Kate said she thought because Mrs O'Connor was wearing black that perhaps he was dead and she was a widow.

"Oh, poor woman, and with three children too," said Cassy. "Perhaps we should call on her later and take a basket?"

Kate laughed and said, "We could, but they are not very little children," she explained. "The son seems somewhat older than the girls, in his mid-twenties maybe. The older girl is very tall, and the younger one is tiny and very pretty; she cannot be more than eight or nine years old. I've asked them all to tea on Saturday."

Returning from the hospital, they passed by Willowdale Farm and noted that the O'Connor family were nowhere in sight, which made Laura Ann curious, and Cassy said she could go to tea with Kate on Saturday and meet the O'Connors, if she wished.

"Will Elena be there?" asked Laura Ann, and on being assured that Kate's younger sister would indeed be present, she agreed that she would come to tea on Saturday. The two had become firm friends since Kate had married Laura's brother Darcy, and there was the added attraction of the Darcys' little son to play with.

Elena, recently engaged to a young gentleman from the neighbouring county of Staffordshire, had provided Laura with the sisterly companionship she had missed since her own sister, Lizzie, had married Mr Michael Carr and moved to live at Rushmore Farm.

"May I stay over, Mama?" she asked, and Cassy made no objection.

"Certainly, if your brother and Kate have room for you, and you are not in the way," she replied.

Before Laura Ann could ask, Kate assured her that she was very welcome to come to tea on Saturday and stay overnight. "Of course you may, Laura; I'm sure Elena will enjoy having you to help with the ladies from Willowdale Farm. Besides, you should have a lot to talk about. I understand from her last letter that Elena and Mr Featherstone have decided to be married next Easter."

"So soon?" Laura Ann expressed her astonishment, and even Cassy looked surprised.

"Yes indeed, it appears Mr Featherstone's mother is unwell, and since Simon is her only son, she is keen to see him settled," Kate explained. The information added a whole new reason for Laura Ann's desire to see Elena again, and so it was settled that she would go.

By the time Mrs O'Connor and her daughters came to tea on Saturday, Kate had learned much more about the family. Mr O'Connor had indeed died several months ago, leaving his wife and family with a small inheritance. He had had a clothing business, which had accrued many debts that had to be settled before the family could leave Ireland. Kate's housekeeper had gathered a good deal of information whenever she had met Mrs O'Connor's cook at the market in Matlock.

They were not poor; Mrs O'Connor continued to receive a regular annuity from her father's estate, and she was a very good manager of money, but with little capital left, the somewhat run-down farm at Willowdale was all they could afford. They had no experience of farming, and when Kate mentioned this to her husband, Darcy wondered how they would get on running the place with no men around to organise the farm labour. "I understand the son is a writer; he has taken clerical work with a firm in Derby, probably to help the family, so he is unlikely to have much time or inclination for farming," he said, surprising his wife with the information.

"It's a firm we use for some of the supplies we order for Pemberley. I was there yesterday, and I met young Mr O'Connor, who is in charge of inventories.

He seemed efficient and obliging, but it must be a deeply frustrating situation for a writer," Darcy remarked.

"He certainly looks the part; he is very handsome and wears his hair a little longer than most," said his wife with a twinkle in her eye. "I confess I thought it was a pity Elena was already engaged."

Darcy laughed and scolded her gently, "You ladies are all the same; you will not cease matchmaking. Tom O'Connor is handsome enough, I grant you, but Elena is much better off with Simon Featherstone. He is the only son of a respectable middle-class family, whose fortune comes mainly from commerce, which I assure you is much more secure than farming."

"Or writing," said his wife, agreeing, but adding that the young man was unlikely to remain an inventory clerk. "I did see some inspirational fire in his eyes, and when his mother introduced him to me as Tom, he said very firmly, 'Thomas, please, Mother.'"

"Did he indeed? Well, Thomas O'Connor would certainly look better on the cover of a book, would it not?" Kate agreed, and as they retired to bed, she continued to speculate about young Mr O'Connor and his literary career, until her husband muttered sleepily that he was unlikely to become another Charles Dickens and he supposed they could let the tenant farmer tend the cows if they had no other help on the farm.

On Saturday, Laura Ann arrived early to see Elena, whose engagement to Mr Featherstone had been the high point of the Summer. That there was going to be a wedding at Easter added new excitement, and the two young women retired upstairs. Duly warned by Kate, they were ready to greet the visitors when their little pony carriage came up the drive and Mrs O'Connor and her two daughters alighted.

Mrs O'Connor apologised that her son, Tom, would be delayed by a few minutes, since there was not enough room for him to sit in their carriage without crushing his sisters' gowns and he had offered to walk up to the house, which it was generally agreed was very considerate of him.

The ladies were ushered into the sitting room where tea was laid out in front of the fire, and presently Darcy came down to join them. Introductions were made by Kate, and Mrs O'Connor, who had been shown to the best seat, took to admiring the room and the lovely aspect it commanded of the garden. "This is such a sweet room, Mrs Gardiner; it must surely be your favourite spot," she declared in a somewhat theatrical voice, as Kate handed her a cup of tea and acknowledged that it was indeed one of her favourite places in the house.

The elder Miss O'Connor, though only seventeen, was very tall, indeed taller by several inches than her mother, and Mrs O'Connor informed them that Marguerite was trained to give singing lessons, while she herself could teach the pianoforte. They had hoped, she said, to find some pupils in the area and wondered if Mrs Gardiner knew of any young ladies in the neighbourhood who might be in need of lessons.

There were footsteps on the gravel drive, and young Elvira O'Connor, who had been standing beside the window, cried out that it was her brother arriving and ran out of the room into the hall as the door opened to admit him. Laura Ann, who had followed Elvira, was the first person he saw as he entered the house and surrendered his coat and umbrella to the servant.

Not having met before, they both stood silently looking at one another until Kate arrived and said, "Please do come right in, Mr O'Connor."

He apologised, then, for being late and explained that he had gone back to fetch an umbrella because it had looked like rain. "And since I must not crush my sisters' gowns by crowding into the carriage, I thought I had better bring an umbrella; although I must say I felt rather foolish when the sun came out just as I was walking out again."

His lighthearted remark allowed him to conceal any awkwardness he might have felt at being late and provided Kate with the opportunity to introduce her husband, Mr Darcy Gardiner, her sister Miss Elena O'Hare, and her young sister-in-law, Miss Laura Ann Gardiner, all of whom he greeted with grace and courtesy before taking a seat beside the fire and accepting tea and cake. Thereafter, while Darcy attempted with only limited success to engage him in conversation about his work or the cricket season just finished, the ladies took over the general discourse for the next hour.

Since Mrs O'Connor and Marguerite kept both Kate and Elena occupied answering questions about the neighbourhood, it fell to Laura Ann to ensure that their guests were fed, which she did with her usual gentle charm, succeeding where others did not in persuading Mr O'Connor to surrender his plate and tea cup and have them replenished. She recommended that he try the apple tea cake, which he did, and when he told her the cake was delicious and asked if she had made it, she agreed with him that it was, but being by nature both modest and truthful, said she had not. "It was Elena; she makes wonderful cakes. My brother declares that Mr Featherstone will have to be watchful or he will become very fat!" and when Mr O'Connor looked puzzled, she laughed softly and explained. "Oh, I am sorry, of course you do not know Mr Featherstone; he is the gentleman who is engaged to Elena, and he is very slim and tall."

"And does he love cake?" asked Mr O'Connor, to which Laura Ann replied, "Indeed he does; we think almost as much as he loves Elena."

At this artless response, Mr O'Connor laughed out loud, and everyone in the room turned and regarded him with surprise, for he had sat so quietly for almost an hour. Darcy Gardiner, returning to the room, was quite astonished to see the man he had found rather reticent engaged in an affable and lively conversation with his young sister.

Presently, Laura moved away to where her sister-in-law appeared trapped between her two inquisitors, and Tom O'Connor smiled as he watched her gently extricate Kate and let her herself in between them, continuing to answer their enquiries and press more cake upon them as she did so.

When almost all of the refreshments had been consumed together with several pots of tea, Mrs O'Connor seemed ready to take her leave, but little Elvira, who had been doing some exploring, came in and announced that there was a beautiful pianoforte in the room across the hall.

Mrs O'Connor and Marguerite both expressed a desire to see the instrument, and so the entire party trooped into the formal drawing room, which drew even more admiration from the visitors.

Mother and daughter, both musicians, could not say enough about the very superior pianoforte, which had once been Cassandra's and upon which all her children including Laura Ann had learned to play. They begged to be allowed to hear it played, and when Kate, unwilling to set herself up for the task, turned to Laura, she, quite unselfconsciously, seated herself at the instrument and obliged.

As her little audience stood around her enjoying the performance, Elena noticed that Mr Tom O'Connor had moved over to the far side of the room, from where he was gazing across at Laura Ann as she played.

Whether it was the glow of the late afternoon sun filtering in at the windows and gilding the young performer's hair, the sweet music, or her own romantic imagination, she could not tell, but Elena began to suspect that Tom

O'Connor was clearly beguiled by Laura Ann. While Kate had been satisfying the curiosity of his mother and sister, Elena had noticed the ease with which Laura had drawn Tom into conversation, where previously he had sat almost silent for the best part of an hour, and now, here he was, apparently entranced by her playing. She wondered whether Laura Ann had been at all aware of his interest, but knowing her well, thought not; it was not the sort of idle pastime Laura Ann indulged in.

Not long afterwards, the visitors, having declared they had rarely heard such exquisite playing, thanked Laura Ann and their hosts and left. As the servants cleared away the remains of the tea, Kate and Darcy went upstairs. Elena, dawdling deliberately, meaning to get Laura alone and tease her, heard footsteps rushing up the drive. She went to the door and opened it to find Tom O'Connor outside.

Coming out of the drawing room, Laura Ann saw him too and before he could speak, said, "You forgot your umbrella!" She rushed away to fetch it as he stood at the door, and when she returned, he took it and thanked her profusely, apologising again for having troubled them, all the time never taking his eyes from her face. Elena was completely convinced that he was already smitten.

"Thank you, and may I say again how much I have enjoyed this afternoon and, most particularly, your performance on the pianoforte, Miss Gardiner. I do hope we shall meet again soon," he said and left almost reluctantly, leaving Laura Ann standing in the doorway, smiling.

Elena was certain that they would meet again. The gentleman was so plainly fascinated, he would surely ensure that they met again, as soon as he could possibly arrange it.

Chapter Two

THE FOLLOWING DAY BEING Sunday, Laura Ann and Elena went to church. Although Elena had changed her mind the previous evening about teasing her young sister-in-law about Tom O'Connor, believing that something of a more serious nature may well eventuate, she could not resist asking one seemingly innocuous question.

"And what did you think of our new neighbours, Laura?"

Laura's reply, characteristically artless, gave her no scope for speculation at all. "I think they are exceedingly interesting; each one is so different from the other, they appear completely unrelated. Would you not say so?"

Elena, somewhat disconcerted by this opinion, asked, "How do you mean?"

"Why, simply that they appear so unlike one another; Mrs O'Connor is loquacious and dramatic, Miss Marguerite O'Connor is elegant and accomplished but not so animated as her mother, and little Elvira is so sweet and dainty, they are all quite different," Laura explained.

"And Tom, Mr O'Connor, how do you judge him?" asked Elena, taking great care not to imply anything unusual at all in the tone of her voice.

She need not have been concerned, for her companion certainly was not; answering the question with her usual ingenuousness, she said, "He is different again to all the others of his family, though perhaps he may be like his late father; we cannot tell. I would say his disposition is rather more thoughtful, but open, all the same."

"Open?" Elena protested. "Your brother Darcy claims he hardly got two sentences from him when he attempted to draw him into conversation."

"Ah, but then my brother talked to him about cricket, which Darcy loves but Mr O'Connor, having come lately from Ireland, would know nothing about. I am surprised he succeeded in getting two sentences out of him on the subject," said Laura, smiling. "No, I think he is a little reserved as one expects a newcomer to the district to be; Mama always says it is not pleasing to see all these boisterous young men from Birmingham and London gassing about trying to impress us. I think his manners are very pleasing, and though he is rather quiet, he appears to have a good sense of humour."

"And of course, he is quite handsome, would you not say?" Elena was keen to get a response, and she did. "Yes, he is, but not as handsome or as tall as your Mr Featherstone."

Both girls laughed then, and Elena was left with the distinct impression that Laura Ann had no intention of saying any more about young Tom O'Connor than she had done so far. Indeed her next question was clearly framed to change the topic of conversation. "Elena, if you are to be married soon, shall you still want me to be your bridesmaid?"

"Of course," said Elena, "why would I not?"

Before either could say anything, they heard voices, and around the corner came Mrs O'Connor and her two daughters, followed at some distance by Tom O'Connor. They were walking home from church, too. As the parties met, they stopped and greeted each other beside the road, and when they proceeded on again, Elena found herself between Marguerite and her mother, and walking behind them, Mr O'Connor offered Laura Ann his arm, while Elvira insisted on skipping along beside them.

They talked of one thing and another, and Mr O'Connor mentioned again Laura's performance on the pianoforte, which, he declared, was without any doubt the best he had heard. Unused to such extravagant praise, she thanked him but said her elder sister, Lizzie, and her sister-in-law, Kate, were both much more proficient than she was, "because they have had very distinguished teachers and practice much more often than I do." Her companion would not accept this and insisted that as far as he was concerned, her playing had been perfect.

They walked on until they reached Willowdale Farm, and although Mrs O'Connor pressed them to come in and take tea, both Elena and Laura resisted, explaining that the Gardiners would worry if they were late back from church. Which left it open for them to be invited to come on another day, which they promised they would. Once again, Elena was absolutely certain that day would not be long in coming, especially when Mr O'Connor insisted on accompanying the two ladies for the rest of their walk home and, as he left them, expressed the hope they would soon meet again.

Laura Ann was taken home to Camden Park by her brother Darcy that evening, and she had a great deal to tell her mother about the new family at Willowdale Farm.

"The two girls are not at all alike," she said. "Marguerite is tall and elegant, while Elvira is full of energy and their brother is different again. He seems modest and amiable, but a little more reserved than the rest. But Mrs O'Connor is like no one I have ever met. She speaks as if she were in a play. Every word is carefully articulated and every feeling dramatised."

Cassy laughed. "What do you mean, Laura Ann? You have obviously had an entertaining afternoon," she said, and then her daughter wished immediately to correct any misapprehension.

"No, Mama, I do not mean to suggest that Mrs O'Connor was strange or behaved oddly. She was perfectly well mannered, indeed they all are; it was just that she does have a most extraordinary manner of speaking, as though she was on stage."

Cassandra was amused and surprised. "Perhaps she has been—on the stage, I mean. It is not uncommon, especially in Ireland, that young women seek employment in the theatre. I do not believe it is regarded, as it is here, as worthy of censure or suspicion," she said.

Later in the week, they were to learn from Kate that Mrs O'Connor had indeed been an actress in Dublin for many years, which could account for the rather theatrical manner of her delivery, as well as the elaborate form of the invitation that had arrived, asking them to dine at Willowdale Farm in a fort-night. Inscribed in perfect copperplate upon a piece of handmade note paper, it was a work of art, almost, said Kate, like a handbill for a play.

Kate had brought it over to Camden House because Laura Ann had been included in the invitation, and when her mother was applied to, Cassy said, "Of course she can go; I would like her to get out and about and meet more young people. She misses Lizzie very much, and the two O'Connor girls may be just what she needs, being somewhat closer to her age at least. I believe you had a rather entertaining afternoon last Saturday."

"We certainly did, and yes, they are a very interesting family. Both girls are friendly and pleasant; young Elvira is charming, but the mother is quite a different proposition altogether. It must be her time on the stage that makes her dramatise everything and speak as though she is addressing an audience even if she is only admiring the view," said Kate.

Cassy revealed that Laura had had much the same impression of the lady, but had given a generally favourable account of the family. "And young Mr O'Connor?" she prompted.

"Ah, young Thomas, he is a grave and serious fellow, though he cannot be more than twenty-four or five," said Kate. "Darcy found him rather dull, but then he tried to interest him in joining the cricket team! Elena and Laura were much kinder to him. He is certainly very well spoken, and I understand he plays the pianoforte, too. Marguerite says he wishes to be a writer, but has taken clerical work in order to help his family following the death of their father."

Cassy was impressed. "That must say something for his character and his affection for his mother and sisters, at the very least. There are not too many young men who have talent but will sacrifice such an ambition."

"Yes indeed," said her daughter-in-law, "and he must have a fair knowledge of music too; he was most appreciative of Laura Ann's performance on the pianoforte."

"Was he? Well, she did not mention that little matter at all," said Cassy, looking quite surprised.

Kate smiled and said nothing to Cassy, but when she returned home, she did tell her young sister of it, only to be apprised of Elena's suspicions regarding Tom O'Connor's feelings towards young Miss Gardiner. "I have no doubt that he is already very taken with Laura Ann, and she must feel it and so did not wish to say anything to her mother. Mark my words, Kate, and observe them when we dine at Willowdale Farm," she urged, and Kate, though rather more sceptical than Elena, decided she would do just that.

Meanwhile, Laura Ann, quite oblivious of the interest she had aroused among her in-laws, expressed her pleasure at being included in the invitation to Willowdale Farm. "I was not really expecting to be asked, Mama," she said. "After all they have not met you and Papa; I was only another visitor. It is kind of them to invite me, too."

Cassy pointed out that most people did not stand on strict ceremony these days, especially in the country. "The family must want to make as many friends as possible in the neighbourhood. It is always hard to settle into a new place, and they have moved from Ireland, which must be very different," she explained.

When Laura Ann admitted that indeed it must be difficult for newcomers to make friends, her mother added, "Perhaps we should call on them; after all, they are our neighbours, too—Willowdale Farm is not three miles from here and lies across the river from our old family home. I think I shall suggest to your papa that we call on Mrs O'Connor," she said and was interested to note that Laura Ann seemed very pleased.

"I think that would be very nice, Mama; they must be rather lonely out there and I am, sure they would appreciate it if you did call on them. Would you like me to mention it to Mrs O'Connor when I dine with them? She may appreciate some warning, seeing they have just moved in," she asked, and Cassy was quite touched by her consideration of the O'Connors.

"Yes, they may well like some notice; people here don't leave cards like they do in London. I will ask your papa, and then you can mention it to Mrs O'Connor when you go to dinner. Don't make too much of it, mind; I don't want her going to a lot of trouble. If I can get your papa away, we might call after church on the Sunday following your little dinner party. I wouldn't want to call before, they may feel obliged to invite us too, which would be far too much trouble for them, and I wouldn't want that," said Cassy.

When the day of the dinner party arrived, Laura Ann took rather more care than usual, dressing for the occasion; yet she did not wish to appear overdressed and was careful to select a simple blue silk gown and wore very little jewellery.

Cassy tried to persuade her to borrow some of her own. "Do you not wish to wear my sapphire necklace, my dear? It would look perfect with that gown, and it matches your pretty earrings."

But Laura Ann would not be tempted. "Oh no, Mama, that would be far too much for a small family dinner party. I think my little pendant is quite sufficient."

Cassy did not press her, and when her brother called to collect her, Laura Ann asked his opinion. "Darcy, do you think this gown suitable? Do I look all right?" she asked, to which he expressed his approval in no uncertain terms.

"You look perfectly lovely, Laura. I've just left Kate and Elena arguing over the amount of jewellery they are to wear as though they were attending a grand ball at Chatsworth, not dining at Willowdale Farm," he declared.

When they finally reached Willowdale Farm, however, it was plain that Mrs O'Connor and her daughters had not been inhibited by the modest scale of the function. They were dressed in the height of fashion; even little Elvira wore a beautifully embroidered gown of taffeta and lace, while Miss Marguerite O'Connor wore dark blue velvet with flowers in her hair. As for Mrs O'Connor, her black taffeta gown must have had several petticoats that rustled as she walked and made her appear even more like a stage queen in some tragic melodrama.

Indeed, when she greeted the visitors and welcomed them into her home, she did so with such an air of gracious condescension, she may well have been the Duchess of Devonshire in the great hall at Chatsworth.

Her son was perhaps the only one of the family who did not appear to have dressed up for the occasion, being simply attired, with a soft cravat at the neck, in the style affected by some Irish poets, instead of a stiff collar and tied bow, but, as Kate pointed out to Elena, "as handsome and amiable as ever."

There was, fortunately, much more to talk about on this occasion, since it was the first time they had been at Willowdale Farm. The ladies were particularly keen to admire the room and the accessories, including several paintings of landscapes in Ireland, which hung upon the walls.

"They are the work of my dear late husband, who was a wonderful painter," said Mrs O'Connor with sincere enthusiasm, standing before a pretty if somewhat unremarkable painting of the Wicklow Hills. "He taught both my daughters to paint, but neither are as good as he was, and sadly Tom was not keen at all."

When Tom made some remark about not having sufficient talent, she appeared to chide him, saying accusingly, "He prefers to spend his time writing."

Seeing the young man's embarrassment, Kate asked, "Do you write prose or poetry, Mr O'Connor?" at which he became quite tongue-tied and stuttered that he was only a scribbler and did not rate his work so highly as to describe it in such literary terms. "It is only a hobby of mine, I enjoy playing with words," he said quietly.

Darcy tried to change the subject and asked how he found his work, but he looked even more dejected, and it was Laura Ann who rescued the conversation by saying, "But you do like music, do you not, Mr O'Connor?" and when he enthusiastically agreed that he did, she asked, "And do you play?"

Before he could answer, both his sisters piped in, announcing that he did indeed and he played the pianoforte better than either of them. Despite their brother's protestations, the girls and especially little Elvira seemed determined to ensure that their visitors adequately appreciated his talents, and a promise was extracted from him that he would play for them after dinner.

When they went in to dinner, Tom O'Connor was placed at the head of the table with his mother to his right and Kate Gardiner to his left, while the rest of the diners sat as they pleased, leaving Laura Ann sitting opposite him with Elena and Elvira on either side of her. As Marguerite O'Connor chatted on to Elena, Elvira said very little during the meal, affording Laura plenty of time to observe their hosts, and on more than one occasion she caught Tom O'Connor looking at her, and once, when their eyes met, she smiled and saw his face crease into a smile that altered completely its usually serious expression.

It left Laura thinking about this extraordinary young man who was unlike anyone she had known before and wondering about him in a way that she had never needed to with any other gentleman she had met. When they withdrew to the drawing room, Laura's attention was held by the manner in which Tom helped his sisters, in the absence of a manservant, to ensure that their visitors were all provided for, before opening the very elegant instrument that stood in an alcove and inviting first Kate and then Laura Ann to play. Kate, who obliged with a delightful nocturne by John Field, an Irish composer, was applauded as much for her choice as for her performance, and when Laura followed with a nocturne by her favourite, Chopin, Tom had to ask about the similarity in their styles, leading to a conversation about the two composers, which revealed to Laura and Kate the extent of his interest and knowledge of music.

He was then urged to play for them, but only after both his sisters had amply demonstrated their talents and received plenty of praise for their skill, did he finally take his place at the instrument.

Choosing a composition he had committed to memory, he played with such warmth and feeling that compelled attention, even Darcy, whose knowledge of music was not extensive, was drawn in, and Laura Ann was captivated.

When they applauded, Tom was clearly pleased, though he reddened with embarrassment when she said, "You play so well, with so much expression, I should have thought you could be a concert pianist rather than a writer. I wish I could play with as much feeling as you do."

The others, who had gone to refill their cups, did not hear his reply, as he spoke softly and quite directly addressing her, "You will, eventually, when you have lived for longer in the world and known deep emotions. I play only for my own pleasure and have not the patience to practice as I should. I would never make a good concert pianist. But you, Miss Gardiner, play like an angel already; your touch is delicate and perfectly suits Chopin. Never before have I heard his music as sweetly played."

"Thank you, it's very kind of you to say so; I also love to play for my own pleasure rather than for an audience," said Laura Ann. She had been touched by his words, and as she met his eyes, she had no doubt that they were spoken sincerely and not merely to flatter her. She thanked him again, not trusting herself to say much more; glad too that other members of her family had not heard the exchange. For a young girl experiencing the first stirrings of a new emotion, it was a very special moment. She feared that if Elena had heard it, she would have been teased about Tom O'Connor, and Laura Ann was not ready for that.

Before leaving, she found time to convey the message from her mother to Mrs O'Connor, who was genuinely delighted that Sir Richard and Lady Gardiner were to call on them. "Thank you, Miss Gardiner, please convey my appreciation to your parents. I shall look forward very much indeed to receiving them on Sunday. Will you come too?" she asked, and when Laura Ann said she could not be certain, because she had promised to visit her sister at Rushmore Farm, both Mrs O'Connor and Tom seemed disappointed.

"But you will come to the church fair next Saturday, will you not?" she asked, explaining that they were trying to raise money for the Irish orphans, and when Elvira jumped in to ask if she would help her with the doll stall, Laura could not possibly refuse.

"Yes, of course. I should love to help," she said and saw Mrs O'Connor and her family regard her with obvious appreciation.

Later that night, as she contemplated the events of the evening, Laura Ann could not avoid the conclusion that her estimation of their new neighbours had undergone a subtle change since their first meeting.

While she still regarded Mrs O'Connor with some amusement, mostly on account of her manner of speaking, she had begun to see that behind the image of a drama queen, there was a kind woman with a generous heart, and both her daughters had been nothing if not courteous and amiable towards her.

But it was Tom O'Connor who had made the most singular impression upon her. His comments upon her performance at the pianoforte, with the assurance that she would, as she experienced deeper feelings, learn to express them in her playing, had fascinated and engaged her thoughts.

Laura Ann had to acknowledge that he was without any doubt at all the most intriguing young man of her acquaintance. It was a quite unexpected but completely pleasurable consequence of the O'Connors' dinner party, which she decided she would keep to herself for a while.

Chapter Three

WHILE HER PARENTS CALLED on the O'Connors at Willowdale the following Sunday, Laura Ann went to visit her sister, Lizzie Carr. The two sisters embraced warmly, always happy to see each other, for they had been very close and missed one another keenly since Lizzie's marriage to Mr Carr. Lizzie and Laura Ann enjoyed nothing better than a good tête à tête.

Lizzie had a secret to tell her sister; she was expecting another child next Spring. After the delight this piece of information caused had been well expended, there was even more, for it seemed Lizzie's husband had decided that they were to travel to the United States to visit his family. Lizzie, excited beyond words, was a little disappointed that her sister did not appear to match her degree of elation at the news.

"Laura Ann, are you not happy for me? I have wanted to travel to the United States for years, and now at last, my wish is about to come true. You do not look at all pleased," she said, genuinely puzzled by her sister's lukewarm response.

When Laura said simply, "Of course I am pleased for you, but I am unhappy for myself, for I shall miss you, Lizzie; we shall probably not see each other again for ever so long."

"But I expect we shall only be gone for some months, and I shall write, of course," Lizzie said, trying to console her, but Laura remained disconsolate.

"I had hoped very much that you would be here, so I could see you more often. When do you expect to travel?"

"Oh, it will not be until after the baby is born, and then we shall have to wait for good weather. Mr Carr will not have us travel with the children if the seas are too rough," Lizzie explained.

Her sister seemed to brighten up immediately. "Oh, that will not be so bad then; I thought you would be gone before Christmas!"

"Oh no, I would not wish to have my baby born anywhere else; besides, Mama would not permit it," Lizzie said and then asked, "Where is Mama today?"

"Calling on our new neighbours, the O'Connors," said Laura Ann, and when her sister heard of the new neighbours at Willowdale Farm, she wanted to know everything about them.

"I did hear that the old place had been taken, but no one seemed to know the family at all. Who are they and what are they like?" Lizzie asked.

Laura tried to sound casual as she responded to the questions. "They're an interesting family. Mrs O'Connor is a widow; she was an actress once, in Dublin many years ago, and still retains some of that dramatic style in her speech and gestures, which is rather funny."

"And has she any children?"

"She has three, and two of them are grown up. There's Marguerite, who must be at least seventeen—she's very elegant; little Elvira is nine and very sweet, and then there's Thomas."

"Thomas," Lizzie repeated the name, then asked, "And how old is Thomas?"

At this seemingly innocuous question, Laura Ann became rather tongue-tied before saying, "I don't know how old he is. He is the eldest in the family, so he may be twenty-four or -five. I cannot really tell. But he is very well mannered and a most accomplished person, Lizzie; he writes poetry and plays the pianoforte most beautifully."

Lizzie was very surprised. "Indeed? And when did you hear him play?" she asked.

When Laura explained, she could not keep the enthusiasm out of her voice, especially as she described that part of the evening when the ladies had been invited to play and finally Mr Tom O'Connor was persuaded to take his place at the instrument.

"Lizzie, I have never heard a young man play so well nor with such a fine touch before," she said, and there was no doubting the warmth of her praise. Looking at her young sister, Lizzie noted the flush on her cheeks and her bright eyes and decided not to ask too many more questions for the moment.

Later, after they had taken lunch and were playing with her son in the garden, Lizzie asked another, more pointed question. "And what does Mr Thomas O'Connor do, when he isn't writing poetry or playing the pianoforte?"

Once again Laura Ann blushed and seemed unable to answer immediately, except to say that she thought he worked in a store in Matlock and had heard their brother, Darcy, mention a clerical position. "But he would like to be a writer, I think," she added, and Lizzie stopped playing with her little boy and said, "A writer? Like Mr Dickens or Miss Brontë?"

"I don't really know, Lizzie; he is quite modest and does not rate himself so. He says he just enjoys playing with words, but I think he should be a musician. I told him so, but he says he has not the patience to practise and will never make a concert pianist," Laura replied.

"He's right, of course; there are many hundreds of persons who might play well, but unless they have the discipline and persistence, they will never succeed. Mr O'Connor must be a wise and sensible young man if he can make such a judgment about himself," said Lizzie.

"Indeed he is; at least I think he is. He is a very unassuming person, not at all vain or arrogant like some young men."

"And how does he look? Is he plain or handsome?" Her sister pressed her advantage.

"Elena says he is handsome, though he is not as tall as her beloved Mr Featherstone," Laura said.

Lizzie, noting that her sister had taken refuge in quoting their sister-in-law, asked, "And you? Do you not think Mr Thomas O'Connor is handsome?"

This time, Laura Ann could evade the questions no longer and responded with a degree of warmth that her sister found interesting. "I do; he is quite handsome, but that is not the important matter. Lizzie, he is a very agreeable person with the most pleasing manners. He is easy to converse with too and has so many ideas; I must confess that I have never before met anyone as interesting as Mr O'Connor."

Lizzie Carr could recognise the signs of an incipient romance when she saw them and smiled, before asking much more gently, "I think you rather like Tom O'Connor; am I right, Laurie dear?" she used the diminutive that their brothers had used when as children the two girls were known to their family and friends as Lizzie and Laurie.

Perhaps disarmed by the intimacy of the childhood pet name, Laura could pretend no longer and confessed in a rush, "I do, Lizzie; I think I like him very much."

"And Thomas? Do you know how he feels?" asked Lizzie.

Laura shrugged her shoulders; she was more diffident now. "I wish I knew. He is very charming and kind; I think perhaps he does like me a little, but I cannot be sure. Oh Lizzie, I wish I was like you. I remember how certain you were about Mr Carr, almost from the start."

Lizzie laughed, remembering well. "I was not as certain as you might have thought, but I knew soon enough."

"How does one know, Lizzie?" Laura asked, and Lizzie said with the confidence of the happily married young woman, "Oh, Laurie my dear, you will know when it's right, I can promise you that."

Her sister looked a little downcast, and Lizzie resisted teasing her. "Don't look so dejected, Laurie; just enjoy his company while you can, and when it happens, you will know."

Laura Ann made her sister promise that she would tell no one what they had spoken of and in return assured her that she would be the first to know if and when "it happened," and they embraced one another.

Laura Ann left to return home, taking the route through the village and, passing the haberdashers, saw the two O'Connor girls outside, looking at something in the window. They did not see her, and Laura, reluctant to delay her return home, walked on and came face-to-face with Tom O'Connor in the street outside the book shop.

He seemed surprised to see her and greeted her as though it had been weeks since their last meeting, when in fact it had been but a few days. "My sisters are visiting their dressmaker, who lives behind the haberdasher's shop. While waiting for them, I have been using my time studying the books in the shop window," he explained, adding, "I see there is a new novel by Mrs Gaskell. Do you know her work?"

Laura had to admit that she was unfamiliar with the novels of Mrs Gaskell. "I believe my sister Lizzie favours her, but I must confess my preference for the Brontë sisters."

Tom O'Connor smiled and said, "Ah yes, of course, the strange sisters who lived on the Yorkshire moors and published under the names of gentlemen. I regret to say I have not read them at all, although I have read of them. It must have been a great scandal at the time. Which of the sisters is your favourite?" he asked, and before she could answer, the two Misses O'Connor appeared, and Elvira cried out with pleasure at seeing Laura and ran to embrace her in the street, while her elder sister seemed no less happy, though not quite so demonstrative in her greeting.

After a few more minutes of small talk, Laura was about to take her leave of them when Tom O'Connor declared that she should not be walking home alone at that hour and they would walk with her as far as the crossroads. It was of no use to protest that she would be quite safe, she had done this often; his sisters agreed with him, and they walked on together.

When they reached the crossroads and parted, Laura thanked them for accompanying her, while Marguerite and Elvira reminded her that they looked forward to seeing her at the church fair on Saturday.

Reaching Camden House, Laura, finding her mother in the sitting room, began to tell her Lizzie's good news. The excitement of the Carrs' new baby and their plans to travel to the United States next year so absorbed their time and interest that it didn't seem necessary, Laura thought, to tell her mother about her meeting with the O'Connors, until later, when Cassy mentioned the family herself. Speaking of their visit to Willowdale Farm that morning, she said, "We met Mrs O'Connor and all her children. They are certainly an interesting family. Miss Marguerite O'Connor and her brother, Tom, seem intelligent young people, and little Elvira will be a beauty when she grows up, but the mother—dear Laura, I must say even with your warning, I was unprepared for the oddness of her manner. It is not that she is snobbish or pretentious, because clearly she is not, but she must dramatise every utterance. When she offers an opinion on a painting or a piece of tapestry, she makes it sound like the last judgment! Your papa was hard-pressed to conceal his amusement, especially since he had not the advantage of hearing your account of her. Indeed, at one stage, he was compelled to excuse himself, while she was in full flight, and go outside to look at the view from the terrace. Tom O'Connor accompanied him, and it seems your papa was quite favourably impressed with him."

Laura, genuinely pleased with all this information, tried hard to conceal her interest as her mother continued, "Did not Darcy say he had taken some clerical work in the town in order to help the family?"

Laura nodded. "He did, but my brother thought it must be very frustrating work for someone who wishes to be a writer…"

Cassy was quite sympathetic. "I can understand that very well, especially if he has some talent. Perhaps if your papa refers him to Walter Tate, he might have some work for him at the printery. He is clearly well educated and could be quite useful to Walter."

"Do you think that's possible, Mama? If that were possible, I am sure Mr O'Connor would be most gratified," said Laura, hoping not to betray her own pleasure at the prospect.

"Well, I might mention it to your papa, but I would suggest that we say nothing of this to young Tom O'Connor until there is something definite. It would not do to raise his hopes in vain."

Laura agreed and let the conversation return to her sister Lizzie's prospective journey to America. Cassy was concerned. "I wonder how difficult it would be travelling to America with two young children; I suppose they will take their nurses with them, but it will not be easy. I daresay Mr Carr wants them to meet his family."

"And Lizzie says she has been longing to travel to the United States," said Laura, and Cassy agreed. "I know, she was always keen to travel, even when she was a little girl. But I shall miss her and the little ones."

On the following Saturday, Laura Ann came down to breakfast dressed and ready to go to the church fair, and when her father offered to drive her there on his way to the hospital, she accepted gladly.

They were halfway there when he said suddenly, " Laura, I don't suppose young Tom O'Connor will be at the fair, but if you do see him, would you ask him to go round to see Walter Tate at the offices of the *Matlock Review* next week? He may need to make an appointment—Walter can be quite busy—but it is important that he sees him as soon as possible."

She had to ask, "Is this about a job, Papa?" She spoke as casually as she could.

"Hmmm, yes," her father was careful not to raise expectations, "your brother said he was working as a clerk for a builder in Matlock; your mama thinks he would be better suited for work at the printery. He's an educated young fellow, and he told me of his interest in writing. I have spoken to Walter Tate, and he is happy to see him. If he has something suitable, he may make him an offer. It may not be much, but at least it will be in the right industry. So if you do see Tom, tell him; if you don't, we shall have to send him a note. But Laura, whatever you do, do not tell Mrs O'Connor; she will probably feel the need to announce it to the neighbourhood, and that would not do," he said, laughing, and Laura, glad of the distraction, laughed with him. She did not want her father to know that Tom O'Connor would definitely be at the fair; indeed he had told her so himself before they had parted at the crossroads on Sunday evening.

The grounds around the church seemed quite busy when Laura arrived. There was a small marquee and several stalls set up, and some of the ladies of the parish were bustling around already. Her father asked if he should call for her on his way home, but Laura said she would probably walk home with the O'Connors. As she made her way in, she saw Mrs O'Connor and Marguerite carrying two baskets and Elvira holding up a large sunshade. Clearly they were not expecting rain. Laura went directly to help them and was disappointed not to see Tom anywhere in sight.

As they covered the tables and unpacked their wares, she kept looking, but he did not appear. An hour later, she had almost given up hope of seeing him and was wondering if she should send her father's message through Marguerite, who was likely to be more discreet than her mother, when she saw him walking through the crowds towards their stall.

Mrs O'Connor, who had been very active all morning, spruiking and selling and swapping stories with all and sundry, had repaired to the marquee with Marguerite to rest her feet and take a cup of tea, leaving Elvira and Laura Ann to mind the stall. Since it was early afternoon and custom was slow, Laura had agreed to let the little girl go and watch the clowns performing on the lawn in front of the church. She was glad now that she had done so.

As Tom approached, she was surprised to see his usually pleasant countenance darkened by an uncharacteristic frown and thought perhaps he was unwell or out of sorts. She smiled, and in spite of his polite greeting, Laura could not help feeling he was rather preoccupied. She did not ask about nor did he give any reason for his absence earlier in the day.

Laura decided she would take the opportunity to pass on her father's message at once, before the ladies returned. "I have a message for you from my father," she said in a rush.

"A message from Doctor Gardiner?" He seemed surprised.

"Yes, he said would you go to the offices of the *Matlock Review* and ask to see Mr Walter Tate. My father thinks he may have some work that may suit you. He is a very busy man, and you may need to make an appointment," she explained, "but you should do so without delay."

When she looked at him, his expression had changed completely. "Some work at the *Review*?" he asked, in a tone that suggested he had not fully comprehended the message.

"Yes, my father knows the Tates well. I understand he has mentioned your name to Walter Tate and he wishes to meet you."

"Miss Gardiner, I am astonished and delighted. I don't know what to say. It is very kind of your father to mention me. It was only last Sunday, when your parents called on my mother, that I told him how very much I would like to be a writer... I had no idea he knew the owner of the biggest publishing house in the county," he said, and when Laura asked, "Will you go?" his reply left her in no doubt. "Will I? Of course I will; first thing on Monday morning. I should love to get work with the *Review*, any kind of work. Please convey my heartfelt thanks to your father, and thank you too, Miss Gardiner, for bringing me this wonderful news."

Laura Ann, seeing his increasing enthusiasm, felt the need to add a word of caution. "My father doesn't know for certain what work Mr Tate may have for you; it may not be much, and my brother Darcy says Walter Tate is a very hard-nosed businessman, unlike his father who was also a philanthropist. If he does take you on, he is likely to work you quite hard," she warned.

Tom O'Connor did not seem at all daunted. "Hard work does not scare me, Miss Gardiner; the lack of it does. I must help support my mother and sisters, which is why I have taken the work I do now, even though I have no enthusiasm for it. But if Mr Tate will give me work at the *Review*, I shall work twice as hard, if need be, to satisfy him."

"My father thought it was best that you do not mention this to anyone else, until after you have met with Mr Tate and come to some agreement," Laura advised, and Tom concurred.

"Of course, I shall not speak of it to anyone," he said, just as they saw his mother and sister returning from the marquee. Mrs O'Connor and Marguerite greeted him with questions as to why he had not arrived earlier. "We were lucky that Miss Gardiner kept her promise, or we would have had no help at all," they complained.

Tom explained that he had been on his way to the church when he had noticed two men with measuring tapes and instruments in the grounds of the old workhouse and had tried to discover what was going on. "One of the men said the property had been acquired by a Mr Barwick, a hardware manufacturer from Birmingham, who was going to pull the old place down and build his family a mansion," he said.

"A mansion in the grounds of the old workhouse? Now there's a turn up for you," exclaimed Mrs O'Connor, dramatically turning her eyes to the heavens. "Fancy having a mansion in the neighbourhood! Who would have thought it? Barwick! I wonder who they are, and will they be good neighbours, do you think?"

Marguerite was sceptical. "I doubt they will have much time for us, Mother, if they are building themselves a mansion," and despite her mother's apparent excitement, she pulled a face and said, "I don't think I like the idea of a mansion in the neighbourhood; especially not if it's occupied by a hardware merchant from Birmingham!"

"Manufacturer, not merchant," her mother corrected her and scolded, "That is not worthy of you, Marguerite; it makes you sound snobbish, as though you thought you were better than them. What is wrong with a hardware manufacturer, pray?" As mother and daughter bickered about the prospect of having the Barwicks as neighbours, Laura Ann, who had finished packing up the baskets, decided it was time to leave. Claiming she had promised to be home by five, Laura asked to be excused. Having thanked her profusely for her help, Mrs O'Connor sent her regards to her parents and returned to squabbling with her daughters.

Tom O'Connor stepped out and, producing his trusty umbrella, declared that he would see Laura safely home. It was the least he could do, he said, since she had been so kind as to spend most of her Saturday helping at the fair, and neither his mother nor his sister could disagree.

As they walked, Laura pointed to the cloudless skies and asked, "Do you always expect it to rain without warning?" at which her companion laughed and said, "So would you if you had lived most of your life in Ireland, Miss Gardiner. But I must confess that today I was not thinking only of the rain."

"What then?"

"I had intended to accompany you if you decided to walk home this evening and felt the umbrella would provide me with an appropriate accessory," he replied, and when she laughed, he abandoned the pretence of seriousness and laughed with her.

"Well, thank you for your kind intention. No doubt the accessory would prove quite useful as a weapon were we to meet with footpads or villains on the way," she quipped, whereupon he exclaimed, "Footpads and villains! Good God, I had not thought we would be in danger from them in these parts, but I assure you, Miss Gardiner, if they do dare to appear, I shall protect you not just with my umbrella but with my life."

As she laughed again, he stopped and asked in a more serious voice, "May I call you Laura Ann?" to which she replied lightly, "Only if I may call you Tom."

"Of course you may," he said, and there was no mistaking the expression of delight that transformed his grave countenance. Here was a young man clearly very pleased with the unexpected way things had turned out that afternoon.

They were not far from Camden Park, and as they walked on, speaking of many matters, trivial and serious, Laura decided that she was going to tease her companion a little. Curious as to why he had looked so irate when he had arrived at the fair, she asked if anything had happened to displease him.

"Displease me?" He seemed not to understand.

"Indeed, because you did look as though something very disagreeable had occurred," she said. "I wondered at your being so upset."

"Perhaps I was. I will admit that I am more concerned than my mother and sister about the appearance in the district of this man Barwick from Birmingham. I have heard some bad stories of the things such men do."

"Why? If he means to build a mansion for his family, why should that disturb you?" Laura asked.

His handsome face darkened, and she was surprised by the passion in his voice as he explained, "Because, Laura Ann, they are capable of ruthless exploitation and destruction of small communities. All over the north of England, and indeed even in some parts of Ireland, these men have turned poor people into slaves working in the mills and factories; men and women and even young children who used to live and work on farms have been herded into squalid slums, working long hours in vile conditions to earn a pittance. That is how they make the money that enables them to buy up land and build their mansions."

Laura Ann, who had led a somewhat sheltered life at Camden Park, had heard of the factory towns in places like West Yorkshire and the Midlands, but had never seen one, nor had she had the misfortune to meet anyone who had endured the conditions that Tom O'Connor described.

As she listened in silence, he told her of his experiences trying to find work in two of the textile towns and the appalling, insanitary conditions in which many men and women lived and worked. "It was too horrible; I could not, even if I had to starve, I could not do it, nor could I subject my mother and sisters to that dreadful environment."

"And do you believe Mr Barwick is one of these men?" Laura asked quietly.

"I cannot say for certain; he may be an exception, but I doubt it. If he were, he would not make sufficient money to build a mansion for his family. No, Laura Ann, they are all intent upon making more and more money, and the only way is to take advantage of the poor, who have no alternative but to work for them."

He spoke with great seriousness, then suddenly stopped and, seeing tears in her eyes, said, "But I am sorry; I must be boring you with all this, forgive me," and though she protested that she was certainly not bored, he determinedly changed the subject and asked about her interest in music, saying again how much he had enjoyed her playing and looked forward to hearing her play again. "Will you?" he asked, and she promised that when next they were together and there was an instrument available, she would gladly oblige, although, she added, "I shall want you do the same, because as I told my sister, Lizzie, I have never heard a gentleman play with such a fine touch as you."

At this artless compliment he blushed and protested that she must not be so extravagant with her praise. "It will make your sister think I am some kind of a show-off who performs in order to be praised."

This time it was her turn to protest. "Indeed she will not; Lizzie knows you are not a show-off, because I told her that your sisters had mentioned that you played, else we would not have known at all. Besides, Lizzie plays very well herself and appreciates anyone who can. She would never think ill of you for playing the pianoforte."

Her spirited response surprised and delighted him, and he spoke very gently. "Thank you, Laura Ann; it was very kind of you to speak so well of me, and I apologise for upsetting you. I should love to meet your sister, Lizzie, and hear her play. Please forgive me."

Clearly delighted, Laura Ann forgave him without delay, so their conversation could proceed as amicably as before. As they walked through the grounds of Camden Park, Laura wondered how much of this evening's happenings she was going to reveal to her sister, Lizzie. She could not recall any other gentleman with whom she had maintained a conversation with so much ease, nor a companion she had found so interesting and agreeable as Mr Tom O'Connor.

Arriving at Camden House, they found a carriage at the entrance. Laura did not immediately recognise the vehicle, which was smart and new, but as they went to the door, she heard her Aunt Caroline's voice in the hall.

She had been visiting her brother Richard and his wife and was about to leave when Laura Ann and her companion came up the steps into the hall.

Tom O'Connor surrendered his umbrella to a servant and was introduced to Mrs Fitzwilliam, who had been complaining about the arrival in the district of a certain Mr Barwick. "The hardware manufacturer from Birmingham?" asked Tom.

"The very one, do you know him?" Caroline demanded accusingly.

"No, but I do know he means to build a mansion in the grounds of the old workhouse," said Tom, proceeding to reveal what he had learnt that morning. Caroline seemed not in the least surprised, but added ominously, "That is not all he means to build. I am informed reliably by a friend in the council that Mr Barwick intends to buy up several of the older properties in the district and build a series of Roman villas for other rich businessmen who may wish to own a county residence in Derbyshire. Doubtless he hopes to turn a very nice profit in the process."

"Roman villas! That would be horrible!" said Laura Ann, and Tom O'Connor stood shaking his head. "One mansion was bad enough, but a series of villas…?"

"Indeed, set among the foothills of the Peak district! Can you imagine?" Caroline was furious. "I intend to see the council on Monday, and if I get no satisfaction there, I shall approach Walter Tate and ask him to begin a campaign in the *Review* and the *Pioneer*. It is unthinkable that these men can ruin our peaceful villages with their hideous, opulent buildings. Oh, how I miss my Fitzy; he would have known exactly what to do. When he purchased our little farm, it was precisely because there was nothing that could despoil the surrounding countryside. This dreadful scheme would have broken his heart," she declared.

After fulminating for a little longer, Caroline rose to leave, and as she did so, so did Tom O'Connor, retrieving his umbrella from the hall. Light rain was falling as he bade them good night. "Are you intending to walk home, Mr O'Connor?" Caroline asked, and when he said he was, said, "Well, if you would wait a few more minutes, I can take you. There is no sense in your walking three miles in the rain when there are empty seats in my carriage," she said.

Tom thanked her, and having given Cassy further instructions for her husband, Caroline said her farewells and left, taking young Mr O'Connor with her, leaving Cassy and Laura Ann to ponder at the strange coincidence of their meeting.

"I wonder what Mr O'Connor will make of Caroline. She is exceedingly angry about this Barwick person's plans for Roman villas," said Cassy.

"I am not surprised, Mama," said Laura. "Tom saw Barwick's men at the old workhouse, and he was angry too. So it is quite possible Aunt Caroline may find in him an ally in her battle against the hardware merchant, which would be useful, especially if he gets work with the *Review*."

"You may well be right. Things have been quiet here recently; they may get quite interesting, especially if Caroline gets a campaign going against this man Barwick," said her mother as they went upstairs to dress for dinner.

That night, at dinner, Laura Ann asked her father about the mills and factory towns in the Midlands and West Yorkshire, relating a little of what Tom O'Connor had told her. "Is this true, Papa?" she asked and was surprised when he replied that it was.

"Indeed," he said, "there were parts of the north country where things were much worse, because the mill owners joined forces to push down the wages of the workers by refusing to compete with each other. It means a man accepts what his employer offers or starves, because no one will pay him any better, and if he makes too much of a fuss, he gets branded a troublemaker and will not be hired at all."

Laura was appalled. "Will not the law protect them?" she asked, to which her father replied that the men who made the laws were the representatives of the men who ran the mills, and they were unlikely to concern themselves with protecting the workers.

"It seems so unfair. I am not surprised now that Mr O'Connor is so angry about it," she said. "He said he would rather starve than work for them."

Her father smiled and said quietly, "Well, he is fortunate that he has an education and is not a man with a family of young children to feed, clothe, and keep warm. Most of the men do, and they have not the luxury of refusing work, however menial or poorly paid; often their wives and children must work too, in equally horrible conditions."

Cassy saw tears in Laura's eyes and said gently, "It is a hard, unfair system, Laura dear, and at least Mr O'Connor is sufficiently compassionate to be concerned. Many young men, especially wealthy or educated ones, are too busy pursuing their own ambitions to care."

Laura was somewhat comforted by her mother's words, but hoping desperately that Walter Tate would offer Tom O'Connor work, knowing how much it would mean to him, she said no more and went quietly to her room.

There, she curled up in her favourite chair beside the window, and gazing out at the darkening park, she wondered again about Tom O'Connor. The more she turned over in her mind his words and ideas, the more she felt he was a man she had never imagined she would meet—inspiring yet modest, compassionate and angered by injustice yet gentle and softly spoken; poetic too and, yes, very handsome. Laura Ann had to accept that she liked him a good deal more than she had admitted even to herself.

Chapter Four

CAROLINE'S VISIT TO THE council chambers coincided with the arrival at Willowdale Farm of a messenger from the legal firm representing Mr Barwick. A rather cocky young man, very well attired and with an attitude to match, introduced himself and handed Marguerite a letter.

"What is it about?" she asked, somewhat bemused, but he told her in a patronising tone of voice that she need not worry her pretty head about it.

"Just hand it to your father, my dear," he said and departed before she could explain, leaving poor Marguerite in tears, recalling that she had no father to whom she could hand it over. With her brother away in town, Marguerite decided to open the letter. After all, she argued to herself, it would make no difference either way.

When she had it open and had read part of the way down the page, her bewilderment increased considerably, for the letter contained an offer to purchase Willowdale Farm and its adjacent meadows, orchard, and pastures, at a sum even she knew was considerably less than what they had paid for it. Despite the turgid legal jargon in which it was couched, Marguerite could make out that the offer was being made by the firm acting on behalf of their client, who intended to purchase several properties in the area in order to "improve" them and claimed they were offering to pay "above the market price" for the land. Clearly, Marguerite thought, they did only want the land, for if this client was the same one their brother had mentioned on Saturday, the hardware merchant from Birmingham, who was building a mansion on the site of the old workhouse down the road, it seemed unlikely that he would spend any time or money on "improving" an old Georgian residence. Rather, he would most likely pull it down and build another mansion in its place.

Knowing her mother's propensity for overdramatisation, Marguerite decided that she would keep the letter and show it to her brother first. She therefore concealed it in her pocketbook, which she took with her when she went into the village. It would not signify at all, she thought, if her mother knew nothing of their predicament for a few more hours.

In the village, she went into the haberdashers and bought some thread and some buttons, and was walking past the book shop when she saw Laura Ann emerge with a small parcel in her hand.

The thought occurred to Marguerite that Miss Gardiner, having been born and bred in the area and whose family owned much property here, may well know something more about the situation. At least, she may know whom they could consult, Marguerite thought, and on an impulse, she approached her and, after they had exchanged greetings, said in a confidential whisper, "Dear Miss Gardiner, I am afraid we have had some very worrying news, and I wonder if I may ask your advice."

Laura, though quite surprised at being asked for advice, could easily discern that Miss O'Connor was very upset. Despite her apparent composure, she was pale and her voice trembled when she spoke. "Marguerite, of course you may, but what is this bad news? I hope it does not concern any member of your family—your mother and sister are well?" she asked, very concerned.

"Oh yes, they are all well, though I doubt they will be for much longer when they have read this letter," she said, extracting it from her pocketbook and handing it to Laura, adding, "It was delivered to our house this morning."

Noticing that her companion was clearly nervous and looked more than once over her shoulder, Laura suggested that they should walk down to the park, instead of trying to read the letter in the main street, and Marguerite agreed immediately.

Taking a seat in a secluded part of the park, where they could not be over-looked, Laura read the letter and was horrified by its significance. Purporting to be a benign offer to purchase, it contained the veiled threat that a refusal of this offer might seriously disadvantage the present owner of the property. There was even an implication that the client would get his way by means of council acquisition, and in such an eventuality, the recalcitrant owner may be the ultimate loser, since the price paid may well be far lower than the present offer.

While Laura read, Marguerite watched her and, as she reached the end of the letter, asked, "Can you understand why I did not wish to show this to Mama?"

"Yes indeed, I can. It would have frightened and worried her. But what I cannot understand is how they are able to do this. By what authority do they make such offers and such implied threats?" Laura knew she was out of her depth, but she knew also that her aunt Caroline would not be. Many years of dealing with councillors and their minions had given her the experience and courage to question just about anyone in authority. "I think we should let my aunt Caroline see this letter. She is already aware of people who are trying to buy old properties and build mansions on them for the newly rich; several Roman villas are planned."

"Roman villas!" Marguerite was incredulous. "Where?"

"Presumably, wherever they can persuade or compel people to sell their land," Laura replied, "including at Willowdale Farm."

"I cannot believe it, Laura; my family put all the money we could gather together after my father's death, every penny from his old business and all our savings went into Willowdale Farm. We were led to believe that nobody wanted this property, it had been abandoned, and now a few months later, we are being asked to sell it for less than we paid for it."

Laura tried to comfort her. "I am quite sure they cannot legally do any such thing, but either Aunt Caroline or my brother Darcy, who lives across the river from Willowdale Farm, will be able to tell us more. If you come with me, we could find Darcy and ask him."

Marguerite, who had few other options, agreed, but needed to stop at home first. "I must take these things to my mother; she will want to be getting on with her work and will worry if I am delayed. But what shall I tell her?"

"I shall come with you, and we will tell her that we are going across the bridge to take tea with Kate and see how well her roses are doing. We could bring some back for your mama," Laura suggested, and Marguerite was grateful indeed.

"Thank you, I'm sure Mama will like that," she said.

Darcy and Kate Gardiner were not surprised to see Laura Ann; she was a frequent and welcome visitor to their home. They were, however, unprepared for the appearance of Miss Marguerite O'Connor, particularly in a state of some discomposure.

When, after their initial greetings and an invitation to take tea or lemonade, she sat quietly while Laura explained the reason for their visit, it soon became apparent to the Gardiners that Marguerite and her family had a very real problem on their hands.

Darcy put it succinctly. "It seems from what you say, Miss O'Connor, that if your family accepts the offer put by Barwick's attorney, you would have to sell Willowdale Farm, but then, you would have no home and inadequate funds to purchase another. And if you refused, there are these indeterminate threats that you could lose your home anyway and be even worse off."

"And either way, Willowdale Farm would be destroyed, and they'd build a lot of dreadful villas in its place," cried Laura Ann. "What can we do, Darcy?"

Darcy looked unsure. "I wish my grandfather were here or Colonel Fitzwilliam, they'd know what to do."

"Why don't we talk to Papa?" his sister asked.

"We could do that, but Papa is not really interested in matters of property and is unlikely to know how one can legally thwart the plans of a developer."

With Marguerite looking increasingly more anxious, Laura said, "Well, there's Aunt Caroline; she was very concerned about Barwick's plans, even though she was unaware of the problem with Willowdale. I know she was going to the council again this morning."

It was Darcy who suggested that they meet at Pemberley and talk about the problem together.

"Why Pemberley?" asked Laura Ann. "Mr and Mrs Darcy are away, and Anthony is not able to help us solve the problem, is he? He is ten years old."

"But Julian might, and it is right that we ask him," said Darcy.

Marguerite was puzzled; she knew little of the complex relationships that existed within the Pemberley families. "What has Pemberley to do with Willowdale Farm?" she asked.

"Everything," said Darcy. "Pemberley has everything to do with the manner in which land is bought and sold and developed in this district, because in the end, it will reflect upon the estate itself and the people who live and work here. My grandfather has always believed that and has taught me to look not at the prosperity of the estate alone, but of all the villages and farms that depend upon it. If the properties around Pemberley are chopped up into little parcels of land and sold off to buyers from outside the county, who have no particular interest in or love of the land, Pemberley itself will decline in value and stature. Mr Darcy certainly believed that, and I am sure Julian understands that as well as his father does. He may not have wanted the responsibility of the daily management of the estate, but I am quite certain he loves Pemberley and will do what he can to protect its interest."

Laura Ann agreed. "Mama has always believed that. Uncle Julian is much younger than her, and she knows his first love was his scientific work, but she is convinced of his loyalty to Pemberley. In fact, after his marriage to Jessica, he seems to have settled into life at Pemberley very easily."

Kate laughed a little wry laugh. "That would not be difficult, especially when Darcy and his mother do all the hard work," she said, but did not deny that Julian appeared to have more time for the family estate. She supported also the suggestion that Caroline Fitzwilliam be consulted. "I agree with Laura Ann that Caroline should be asked; I do not believe there is one other person I know who is so well versed in the detail of council matters, and her advice will be invaluable."

Darcy was charged with taking the message to his parents and his uncle Julian, while Kate would visit Caroline. Meanwhile, Laura and Marguerite were to tell no one but Tom O'Connor of the letter that had been received from Barwick's attorney and persuade him to come to Pemberley on the morrow.

"Your brother, being the eldest in the family, must attend the meeting at Pemberley tomorrow, but were your mama to find out about the letter, she may well be so upset, she could talk to the neighbours, and if a rumour starts running, we will have little hope of doing anything at all to avert this disaster," Darcy warned, adding, with deep sincerity, "And let us give thanks that Mr and Mrs Robert Gardiner are in London and unable to intervene; that at least is in our favour."

Returning to Willowdale Farm, they found Tom in a state of high euphoria. His meeting with Mr Walter Tate had resulted in an offer of a position at the printery, initially as an under-manager who would oversee and direct the printing of the *Review*, but with the prospect after some months of a position in which he could occasionally write for the paper.

"I cannot yet believe it myself," he said, unable to stop smiling as he spoke, "and Laura Ann, I shall be forever in your father's debt. Please, Miss Gardiner, do tell him and say that I thank him from the bottom of my heart. I shall write to him too, of course." Both Laura and Marguerite were so pleased for him, they regretted having to curtail his happiness with the news of the threat to Willowdale.

On the pretext of hearing more about his new job, they took him out into the garden, and there, while Mrs O'Connor revelled in the scent of Kate's roses, which she was arranging in a bowl, Marguerite revealed the letter, begging him not to let their mother discover the truth.

Upon reading it, Tom was so stricken that he was speechless for fully five minutes. He walked about the terrace, clearly confounded. He had feared for the neighbourhood on hearing about Barwick's plans for mansions and villas for the wealthy, but had never dreamed it could affect his own home. "But what is to be done? Who will help us?" he asked and was told of the plans they had made to meet with Julian Darcy and Caroline Fitzwilliam at Pemberley.

"Why at Pemberley?" he asked; like his sister, he was unaware of the ramification of interests in the district. When it was explained, he agreed and added that he had talked with Mrs Fitzwilliam when she had offered him a ride in her carriage and found her to be a most knowledgeable and determined lady. "If anyone can help us, she can," he said, and turning to Laura Ann he said, "I have written a letter to Doctor Gardiner giving him my good news and thanking him for his kind recommendation, all the more valuable since it was unsolicited. I intended to post it tomorrow, but if you would take to him tonight, Miss Gardiner, I should be most grateful."

She indicated that she would be more than happy to do so, but invited him to call on her father and thank him personally, whenever he wished. "He will be very happy to see you I am sure," she said, adding as an afterthought, "and so will Mama and I."

He smiled, and though he said nothing, she knew he was pleased. Laura Ann was glad that something good had come of his meeting with Walter Tate to alleviate the shock and anxiety caused by the attorney's letter.

What Laura could not have known was the incipient fear that many Irish families had of being thrown off their land and left destitute. Having been treated with scant respect in their own country for centuries, they had little faith in the systems of administration and justice. Consequently, they placed a far greater value on the kindness and support of friends.

~v~

When it was time for Laura Ann to leave, Tom walked with her to the gates of Camden Park and, as they parted, said again, "I shall never forget the kindness of your father; it has given me so much hope. It has opened up a whole new horizon for me, as indeed have you, Laura Ann. May I say that I enjoy and value your friendship like no other I have known in all my life. It is very special to me."

Taken aback by the extravagance of his words and the intensity of feeling they implied, Laura recalled something Elena O'Hare had once said about her fellow countrymen. "One must beware of the Irish, Laura Ann; they have a dangerous streak of poetry in their speech. They will use words to create ecstasy out of simple pleasures and make great tragedy out of tiny wounds," she had said.

At the time, Laura had laughed and said surely that could not be such a bad thing, if one could make much of little, especially if life only gave one small servings of happiness. Perhaps, she thought now, that streak of poetic exaggeration may come through in other situations as well.

Nevertheless, she appreciated the sincerity with which he spoke and responded with characteristic honesty, "And so do I value and enjoy your company, Tom; I have never had so many interesting conversations before with anyone," she said, watching with some amusement as his eyes lit up with deep pleasure and a smile transformed his countenance. He kissed her hand, saying softly, "Thank you, Laura Ann. I did say you played Chopin like an angel, did I not? But I now believe you really are an angel; God bless you."

Truly, Laura thought, never before had she known such a fascinating young man.

Chapter Five

WHEN THEY MET AT Pemberley, none of the members of the family had any notion of how they would deal with the situation that confronted the O'Connor family. At the time Darcy Gardiner had approached his mother and then his uncle Julian Darcy about the plan, they had been somewhat cautious in their support. Cassandra had expressed sympathy for the O'Connors and suggested that perhaps they could be offered the services of Mr Darcy's lawyers to contest Barwick's approach, but Darcy and Laura had convinced her that it would be useless to take the matter into the courts; everyone knew that developers had the money to litigate forever, and the O'Connors could not afford it.

While Julian and Jessica were so incensed by the prospect of having Pemberley surrounded by a patchwork of subdivisions, each with its own mansion or Roman villa, that they offered wholehearted support to any campaign against the men who would perpetrate this atrocity, they were unsure as to what more they could do.

"My father has long predicted that if these people are permitted to do as they wish, much of the best land in these parts would soon be destroyed," said Julian gloomily.

His nephew agreed. "That is unarguable. They will fell the woods, subdivide and fence the commons, and dam the streams as they have done elsewhere in England. The rural scene will disappear beneath a tide of development."

"And," Laura Ann added, "they will build these hideous Roman villas all over the countryside."

"I think Aunt Caroline will be best able to advise us," said Jessica, and since Julian agreed, it was settled that they would meet for a council of war on the morrow.

When they did gather around midmorning in the saloon, Caroline had both good and bad news for them. The good news concerned the imminent arrival in England of Martin Faulkner—a young man not yet seventeen years old, son of Daniel Faulkner, who had recently married Caroline's daughter Rachel. Not everyone in the party knew of Martin, and Caroline took much pleasure in enlightening them, explaining that he had won a scholarship to study at an excellent college in Edinburgh, adding with genuine delight, "And during school holidays, he is to stay with me. I have very good reports of him, and if he is anything like his father, I expect we will get on very well. You must all come over and meet him when he arrives."

Knowing how much Caroline missed having her family around her, especially since the death of her beloved colonel, the rest of the family agreed that the arrival of young Martin Faulkner was very definitely happy news for her as well as Daniel and Rachel.

But, on the question of the developer Mr Barwick, Caroline had no good tidings for them; indeed, the situation was quite the reverse, and the news was worse than they had first thought.

On her visit to the council, Caroline had discovered that Barwick proposed to purchase three large properties, and there was nothing that anyone could do to prevent him from building any number of Roman villas or any other dwelling so long as his plan had the approval of the council.

"In addition to the old workhouse site, on which he is building a residence for his own family, he has also bought up a farm just outside of Matlock and is in the process of negotiating with the Clarke family to buy Trantford Manor," she said, and the gasps this information elicited from Cassy and Jessica were proof of their outrage.

Trantford Manor was a large property situated at Birchgrove some miles from Pemberley, boasting an old historic manor house in a picturesque setting, with a large mixed farm, stables, and several tenants' cottages all screened from the road by a grove of graceful old birch trees that gave the district its name.

The Darcys and Gardiners knew the Clarke family that had lived at Trantford Manor for several generations. The death of their father a few years ago had resulted in some financial embarrassment for his wife and daughters, and it was generally known that they lived now in somewhat straitened circumstances.

"I cannot believe they would sell to a developer who would destroy the place and throw their tenants out on the street," said Jessica, who was a friend of the younger Miss Clarke. "It is their family home."

Caroline was not so sure. "Well, Mrs Clarke is probably too old to care, and her eldest daughter is married to an ambitious man, who will probably prefer to have the money rather than an historic manor house," she said and proceeded to reveal that she had seen the plans submitted by Barwick for the development at Birchgrove and they included seven Italian-style villas and other smaller dwellings, each in their own enclosed subdivision of a few acres.

"As for the birches, they would be the first to go. What would be the point of Roman villas if they are hidden from view by a grove of trees?" she asked dramatically.

"Good God!" said Julian, "that would be a tragedy. How on earth can he be stopped?"

"Well he cannot, not at Birchgrove if the family agrees to sell," said Caroline, "because if he acquires the property and the council approves his plans, he is quite entitled to go ahead and build them."

Jessica spoke a little tentatively, conscious of her situation as Julian's wife. They were guests at Pemberley since Julian had relinquished his right to inherit the estate, and she had no wish to force her opinions upon any of them, but she did have an idea she wished to explore. "I wonder what price they have offered the Clarkes for Trantford," she said, and Tom O'Connor, who had been sitting with Darcy and Kate Gardiner, transfixed by the scale and elegance of Pemberley and reluctant to intrude with an opinion on what was clearly a family conference, spoke for the first time. "If it is anything like the offer they have made for Willowdale Farm, it will not be a fair price," he said, producing the letter and passing it round.

Having read the letter, Jessica said, "I think I should like to visit the Clarkes; I knew the younger Miss Clarke well and I am sure I could find out."

"And if you did, what would we do?" asked Cassy.

"If we could suggest to them that it is not a fair price, that they are about to be cheated, they may not wish to sell, or at the very least, they may agree to delay the decision to sell."

"And how would that affect Willowdale?" asked Laura Ann, whose chief concern had been to help the O'Connors save their home.

Jessica explained that any delay in acquiring the properties, and the possibility that he may not get them as cheaply as he had hoped, would disrupt Barwick's plans and buy more time for the O'Connors and Willowdale.

"It would certainly allow us time to work on the council, not all of whom are in favour of Barwick buying up parcels of land all over the county. Some of them are concerned about outsiders coming in, manipulating the market, and cheating the landholders of their rights," said Caroline.

She then paused, took a deep breath, and said, "Now, I do have another suggestion, which, if all else fails, could be used to protect Mrs O'Connor and her family from being harassed into selling Willowdale, but we shall have to act very quickly."

Caroline's skill and her many successes in dealing with such matters were well known; everyone turned to listen. Addressing Tom O'Connor, she said, "Mr O'Connor, forgive me, but I have to ask you a few questions before I can tell if this plan will succeed. You will need to reveal exactly the price your family paid for Willowdale and produce your title deed. Would you be willing to do that?"

Tom looked a little surprised, but made no objection. "The title deeds and other papers relating to the purchase are with the lawyers in Derby. I would be quite happy for you or Mr Darcy Gardiner to see them, and I doubt that my mother would have any objection," he said.

"Very good," said Caroline and then proceeded to outline her plan. "Cassy and Julian, this is where you come in. We shall have to get Mr Darcy's attorney out here to advise on the details and draw up the documents, but, in a nutshell, the plan is to have you lend the O'Connors a sum of money from the Pemberley Trust; it need not be large, an inconsequential but credible sum is all that is required, but they must lodge with your lawyers the title deed to Willowdale Farm as security for the loan. Consequently, Willowdale Farm will be legally under mortgage and the O'Connors will no longer be free to sell their property to Barwick or anyone else."

"Is that all?" asked Cassy.

"Yes," said Caroline, smiling.

"That is a brilliant scheme," said Darcy, but Tom asked, "What if they offered to pay off the loan and so release the property?"

"They may offer, but if Cassy and Julian, representing the interests of the Pemberley Trust, refuse, they are stymied and can go no further. No one can compel the Pemberley Trust to accept any offer from Barwick in repayment of a loan for which the O'Connors are responsible."

Julian shook his head. "Caroline, how on earth did you think up such a perfect scheme?"

"And so simple, too," said Laura Ann.

Caroline smiled and said modestly, "My father did something similar once, when a competitor tried to force his hand over a couple of our properties in Liverpool. It worked then, Mr Darcy was the lender on that occasion, and I just thought it might work again. It does depend on Cassy and Julian agreeing to the deal and Mr O'Connor, of course."

"There would be no time to consult my father," warned Julian.

"There would be no need," said his sister. "We are joint trustees, Papa has authorised us to act in Anthony's interest, and anything that affects Pemberley is certainly in Anthony's interest."

"Of course it is," said Laura Ann. "Well done, Aunt Caroline; your plan may save Willowdale for the O'Connors."

Caroline was cautious. "If you are willing to participate, Tom?" she said.

Tom O'Connor was beaming, clearly overjoyed. "I can see no objection at all, Mrs Fitzwilliam; it is such a simple device and perfectly legal, too," he said.

Laura Ann could not help smiling at his joy. She had seated herself beside her mother, keen to observe her responses to the discussion, and she had not been disappointed. Cassandra had been clearly impressed with Caroline's plan.

"I cannot see anything wrong with the scheme; we shall ask the attorneys to draw up the documents for signing, and I think after that, you need no longer worry about Mr Barwick," she said, and Tom O'Connor, delighted with this new plan, shook hands with everyone, thanking them for their help, while his sister Marguerite had tears in her eyes and had to leave the room in order to compose herself. She had borne the weight of their fears ever since the letter had arrived, but Tom spoke for all of them. "I have no words to tell you how grateful I am; my sister Marguerite and I were terrified at having to tell my mother of the predicament in which we were placed. We had no idea how we could extricate ourselves from this dreadful situation."

"It is in our interest too, Mr O'Connor," said Julian. "I think, had my father been here today, he would have approved of this action totally. We are happy to help you, of course, but the prevention of this type of piecemeal development is very much to the advantage of the Pemberley Estate."

"It is kind of you to say so, Mr Darcy, and I accept what you say, but I know it has been the means of saving our family from certain ruin."

As they were dispersing to take tea and refreshments, which had been brought in and laid upon the table by the window, Jessica said quietly, "I think I shall still visit Miss Clarke at Trantford tomorrow. I cannot bear the thought of all those Roman villas dotted around the dales, and even less can I contemplate the felling of those beautiful birches."

A few days later, they met again, with Julian, Cassy, and Darcy Gardiner representing the Pemberley Estate, and Tom O'Connor and his sister Marguerite acting for their mother. In the presence of their lawyers, a cheque for one hundred pounds was passed to Tom and his sister and immediately deposited with their attorney for safe keeping, while the title deeds for Willowdale Farm were placed in the hands of Mr Darcy's attorney. Confidential letters were exchanged which set out the reasons for the arrangement.

Subsequently, a letter sent from the lawyers representing the Pemberley Trust to the Barwick's agents made it clear that Willowdale Farm was not available for sale. Whether this alone was sufficient to discourage Mr Barwick would never be known, for some weeks later, his agents were informed by attorneys for the Clarke family that Trantford Manor was no longer available for sale to Mr Barwick. In fact, they claimed that they had had a better offer, which they were inclined to accept, although they did not reveal from whom the offer had been received.

At the site of the old workhouse, however, demolition and construction went on apace, and as the weeks passed, a strange dwelling, more suited to accommodate an ancient Roman dignitary and his entourage than the family of a hardware manufacturer from Birmingham, rose higher every day. As it neared completion, assisted by a veritable army of workmen, the Barwick family were seen visiting the site, and the ladies, all fashionably attired and coiffured, as described by their neighbours, seemed almost as grotesque as the building they expected to inhabit.

Tom O'Connor saw and loathed every brick and stone in the wretched edifice and thanked Laura Ann, God, and Caroline, in that order, every day that Willowdale Farm had been spared a similar fate.

Freed from the dullness of his job as an inventory clerk and admitted to the hallowed offices of the *Matlock Review*, Tom O'Connor seemed to gain a new sense of confidence and appeared altogether more cheerful than before, which pleased Laura Ann.

Their friendship deepened quickly, as each admitted their interest, first to themselves and then to each other. By the end of Autumn, it was becoming increasingly obvious to those who knew and saw them together often that their feelings were deeply engaged.

He was clearly enchanted by her, never having known a young woman of such thoughtfulness and charm, who was blessed also with a delicate beauty that quite belied her determination and strength. As he became better acquainted with her family, most particularly her mother, Tom O'Connor saw that these were attributes they shared. Cassandra Gardiner was without any doubt one of the most remarkable women he had ever had the good fortune to meet, and her delightful daughter had clearly inherited many of her qualities, together with a disarming openness of disposition that he had never encountered in a young lady before.

When his sister Marguerite teased him about Laura Ann, he had admitted that he loved her, but when she had asked whether he intended to propose to her, he had replied, "If only I had been in Ireland and Laura Ann had been the girl next door, I should have proposed already. But, my dear sister, I am sure you will agree that I have far too little to offer her at this time. Can you imagine what her family will say to an offer from me? I shall have to earn myself a reasonable promotion at the *Review* before I can even contemplate such a possibility."

Marguerite O'Connor urged her brother not to undervalue himself. "You do realise, do you not, Tom, that many girls do not regard money as the most important requirement for happiness? I believe Laura Ann would agree with me that love and nobility of character are of much greater consequence. While she may make her own judgment regarding your character, she cannot know that you love her unless you tell her so. Have you told her yet that you love her?" she asked.

Her brother coloured and replied, "I have not, but I am quite sure she must know how I feel. She is so exceptional, so enchanting, I doubt that I have been able to conceal my feelings for her, even though I have not told her in so many words."

Marguerite's counsel was succinct. "My dear brother," she said, "I would strongly advise you to do so at the earliest opportunity, even if you must explain that for practical reasons, you feel unable to make an offer of marriage now. A lady likes to know she is loved and will make allowance for the fact that a man must sometimes delay a formal offer until his financial circumstances permit him to do so. If she knows how you feel, she may be willing to wait, but not if she has no notion at all of your feelings for her."

"Do you really think so?" asked Tom, not entirely convinced.

She nodded. "I do, and what is more, I believe that there is a good chance that Laura Ann may well return your affection. I have observed her closely when we are all together, and I think I have seen the signs," she said, and placing a hand upon his arm, she wished him luck in his quest.

Miss O'Connor was almost correct in her assessment of Miss Gardiner's state of mind, for Laura Ann was so completely fascinated by everything about Tom O'Connor, she had already confessed to her sister, Lizzie, that she did not think anyone else would ever measure up to him in her estimation.

"Lizzie, I think I have not met any other person, neither man nor woman, who can so utterly and delightfully hold my attention. When he speaks, it is clear that he has the eyes and soul of a poet, which is apparent even if he is only talking about the most ordinary things," she declared, and when her sister asked for an illustration of this extraordinary quality, she'd said, "Just the other day, we were discussing clouds."

"Clouds?" Lizzie repeated, wishing to be clear she had heard right.

"Hmmm. I said I had always thought of clouds as great mounds of cotton wool filled with rain, being pushed around the sky by the wind."

"And what did Tom say?"

"He agreed; he said they might look like that sometimes, perhaps before a shower of rain, but he said that was just a perception and we ought not see them only in that light. He said clouds could also be light and fanciful and full of sunlight; wisps of cloud could often be seen on a Summer's day, flying like flocks of white birds or floating like butterflies across the sky, and before a storm, great towering clouds might look like mountains rising above an angry sea. Clouds, he said, could do all sorts of amazing things. It was only a matter of catching them when they were doing it, he said."

"And have you? Caught them looking like that, I mean," asked Lizzie, quite astonished at this poetic streak in her young sister.

Laura Ann laughed. "Indeed I have, I went out very early one morning before breakfast and lay on the little lawn behind the conservatory so the maids could not see me and think I was mad! I looked up at the sky and there, exactly as Tom had said, were flocks of little light clouds, floating very gently across the sky. They could quite easily have been white birds or butterflies. It was beautiful, Lizzie. I had never thought to look at clouds that way before. When I told Tom about it, I thought he would laugh and tease me, but he smiled and said, 'You must do more such observing, Laura Ann; if you do, you will see many more wonderful things that are often hidden from us as we walk upright, never noticing what flies above us or lies below at our feet.'

Lizzie laughed and said she would look out for her sister next time she went into the woods. "I expect to see you, lying prone in the grass, looking at the ladybirds and caterpillars as well as the clouds." Then in a more serious voice she looked directly at Laura Ann and asked, "And when you have had your fill of lying in the meadows and looking at clouds and butterflies and birds, Laurie dear, what do you think you are going to do about Mr Tom O'Connor?"

She was teasing her young sister and did not expect the response she received. "I believe I am going to marry him, Lizzie," she said.

Lizzie was speechless, not so much at the content of her answer but the calm insouciance of her manner. "Are you sure?" she asked.

Laura Ann answered candidly, "I am."

"And has he proposed to you?"

"Not yet, but he will, I think, when he is ready."

"And do you know if he loves you, Laurie?" Lizzie persisted, a little concerned at her young sister's absolute certainty.

"I know he does, but I don't know if he knows it yet. But I am sure he will quite soon," Laura Ann replied.

Lizzie knew better than to probe further, but it was quite clear to her that young Laura Ann had made her decision and it was unlikely that anything anyone could say would change her mind.

Richard Gardiner had travelled to London to attend a conference of physicians when Caroline came to visit Cassandra, ostensibly to report the glad tidings that the council had refused approval for the Barwicks to build three more mansions at the farm he had acquired outside of Matlock. "I received the information just last afternoon; I understand that the councillor who originally promised to ensure that it would all be approved is assisting the constabulary with their enquiries," she declared, clearly gloating.

"Oh Caroline, that is such good news! Laura Ann will be so pleased," said Cassy.

They moved into the sitting room where tea was served, and as the maid departed, Caroline said, "Speaking of Laura Ann, Cassy, you cannot be unaware that she and young Tom O'Connor are..."

"Falling in love?" Cassy completed her question.

"Yes, or at least are very close to it. I am not putting this to you as something that must cause consternation, Cassy; in truth, they are both such attractive young persons that I take some delight in seeing them together, knowing they will inevitably fall in love. Nor am I attempting to interfere in matters concerning your family; I accept it is entirely something that you and Richard must resolve," she said.

Cassandra smiled, knowing how well Caroline loved her young niece. "But I could not help wondering how you would both respond to a proposal of marriage from Mr O'Connor. You see, Cassy, if you are not well disposed towards it, I fear that permitting Laura Ann to continue the association with Tom is likely to result in a great deal of unhappiness."

Cassandra was silent for a few minutes, as though composing her thoughts before she spoke. "I must thank you, Caroline, for your concern, especially since I know that it stems from your affection for Laura Ann. I have, for some weeks now, been contemplating the same question. Like you, I have observed them together and concluded that they are well on the way to being in love. Considering that Laura Ann is nineteen and has never shown an interest in any young man before, it is quite delightful to see how spontaneously and honestly she expresses her feelings; it is as though she cannot hide them, nor does she wish to do so," she said.

"And how do Richard and you feel about it?" asked Caroline.

"While I cannot say for certain how Richard would feel about an offer from Mr O'Connor, particularly in view of his lack of any fortune or profession, I know he likes him well enough and I know also that Richard would never do or say anything that would hurt Laura Ann in any way and neither would I. By that I do not mean to imply that he would readily agree to a marriage between them, but if she were to ask her father, it is inconceivable that he would refuse her permission to become engaged."

Caroline, uncertain as to the reason for this categorical statement, asked, "Are you saying she is his favourite child and so will not be refused?"

Cassy shook her head. "No, not at all, Richard has no favourites. He has always treated all the children alike, even though it has been a little difficult recently with Edward's wife being rather tiresome," she explained.

"What then?" asked Caroline.

"Well, there is with Laura Ann another matter that must affect the way we deal with this situation. As you would know, Caroline, she does not have a very strong constitution. As a child, she was always falling ill with respiratory infections and bronchitis, which have left her with a weakened heart and lungs. While I have been concerned with her day-to-day health, my husband has made investigations, studied the condition, and consulted colleagues who have specialised in treating such conditions. It seems Laura Ann has developed a weakness of the heart that is common among young children who suffer from such illnesses at an early age. It has left her with a serious infirmity of both the heart and lungs. Consequently, he is of the opinion that Laura, while she is in no immediate danger, is unlikely to live beyond her thirties."

Caroline gasped. "Oh my God, Cassy, what are you saying?" she cried.

Cassandra's voice was very low and near to breaking, and Caroline moved to sit beside her on the sofa and hold her hand. "I am saying that Laura Ann may not live into middle age, unless her condition improves considerably or some new treatment is discovered to treat and strengthen her heart. In view of this, were Tom O'Connor to propose and Laura to accept him, neither Richard nor I will refuse them permission to marry," she said. "If it is going to make her happy, what right have we to prevent it when she may have so little time left to enjoy that happiness?"

Caroline held her hands tight as tears filled Cassy's eyes. "Does Laura Ann know?" she asked.

Cassy shook her head. "She does not, nor do we intend to tell her. Richard believes it would impose an unconscionable strain upon her and probably destroy any prospect of her leading a normal life. Only my parents know and now you do too. If Tom O'Connor does propose and asks her father for her hand, then Richard will take him into our confidence, because he would have a right to know."

Caroline was thoroughly contrite, feeling she had intruded cruelly upon the agony her brother's family had borne alone for years.

"Cassy, I am sorry I questioned you and needlessly caused you the pain of telling me all of this. I would have understood if you had told me to mind my own business."

"Why should I have done that, Caroline? All you did was to express a very genuine concern for Laura Ann; you were not to know the circumstances. We have chosen not to speak more generally of it. But I am happy that I have told you; it will help you understand what we have had to live with for some years now. We felt it would have been unfair to cripple her with the knowledge and even worse to have others know and pity her when she is such a bright spirit and enjoys life so much," Cassandra explained. "Oh Caroline, when I look at her, she is lovelier than Lizzie was at her age; there is something quite remarkable about her delicacy and freshness, and yet I know that she may not be with us very long. Richard says there is always hope; medical science is developing new cures, and if we are very fortunate, she may well live a lot longer, but it is very much in the lap of the gods and the scientists, I fear."

Caroline embraced her as she wept. Having known the agony of losing a son, a loss the passage of years had done nothing to assuage, Caroline could feel Cassy's pain, exacerbated as it was by her inability to share it with all but a few members of her family. By sheer mischance, Caroline had become one of those.

Unbeknownst to either of them, Laura Ann and Tom had met that afternoon in a quiet part of the woods around Camden Park, and among other things, they had admitted to one another what they had both known and could no longer pretend to ignore.

Following Marguerite's wise counsel, Tom had told Laura in the warmest, most tender words he could conjure up that he loved her, but before he had reached the point at which he intended to confess that he was as yet unable to make an offer for her hand, being only a lowly under-manager at the *Matlock Review*, Laura had smiled like an angel and said, "Now, that is so very agreeable, Tom, because I do believe I love you too."

Surprised and delighted by her openness and honesty, he had added, "Then will you marry me, Laura Ann, not right away, but soon?"

Her response that she would certainly marry him whenever he wished it had left him speechless, but speech was not a necessity, as they fondly embraced and confirmed their love.

Laura Ann had observed her sister, Lizzie, fall in love and seen her blossom into womanhood after her marriage to Mr Carr. Recalling her promise that when it was right, she would know, Laura Ann knew, with the sunlight falling on their faces as they kissed, that what she was feeling now was right.

"May I tell Mama?" she asked softly, and he replied, "Of course, but I think we should wait until I ask your papa's permission. I shall ask Marguerite to help me write a letter to him tonight."

"May I tell Lizzie then, please?" she pleaded. "I cannot hold it all inside; I must tell someone, else I shall explode with happiness."

He laughed then and said, "We cannot have that, my darling! Of course you want to tell your sister; will she approve, do you think?"

Laura Ann eyes suddenly filled with tears, as she declared, "I know she will, and I know she wants me to be as happy as she is."

At this he looked quite serious and said softly, "And I promise you will."

As he kissed her again, she closed her eyes and thought, "It is just as Lizzie said, I know it's right, and Lizzie will be pleased when I tell her there were heaps of fluffy white clouds floating like birds overhead."

Meanwhile, Caroline had risen and prepared to leave; her vehicle waited at the entrance and Cassy accompanied her to the door.

It was one of those still, late Autumn evenings when it seems a hush has fallen upon the earth as though it is waiting for something special to happen. The sun had slipped below the mountains, leaving a deep rose-gold glow in the sky, making a spectacular backdrop for the park and woods of this beautiful estate.

"Of all this, Cassy is mistress," thought Caroline, "yet her heart must surely be riven with sorrow for her child." The irony was excruciatingly painful, especially for one who knew both Cassy and Richard intimately, as she did.

They stood together awhile, and Caroline was about to step out into the porch when two persons appeared at the far end of the avenue, walking arm in arm. Laura Ann and Tom O'Connor walked slowly towards them through the grounds of Camden Park, talking together, oblivious of anyone else. They stopped in the shadow of one of the great old oaks that graced the park and kissed, first fleetingly, tenderly, like butterflies on the wing, then more ardently, reluctant to break apart.

Caroline and Cassy looked at one another and stepped back indoors, unwilling to spy, however unwittingly, on their love, and though neither spoke, there were tears in their eyes.

Presently, the pair emerged from the trees and returned to the gravel walk. As they neared the house, Tom caught sight of the vehicle and drew Laura Ann's attention to it. Recognising Caroline's carriage, Laura ran the rest of the way, the ribbons of her hat flying, her face alight with pleasure. As she reached the steps, her mother and Caroline came out and heard her calling out to them breathlessly, "Mama, Aunt Caroline, have you heard? Mr Barwick is not going to build any more Roman villas anywhere in the district. The council will not permit it, and the land he has already purchased is to be resold. Tom says all the news will be in the *Review* tomorrow—he wrote it himself!" Caroline did not have the heart to tell her that she did know already; Cassy and she both pretended they had heard it for the first time and expressed immense satisfaction at the news.

By the time Tom O'Connor had reached the steps, Laura was excitedly telling her mother and Caroline the story as it would be reported in the *Review*. "Mr Tate asked Tom to write the story—is it not wonderful? And it's mainly down to your clever scheme to outwit Mr Barwick! Aunt Caroline, thank you," she said and impulsively embraced her as they stood there on the steps of Camden House.

Turning to her mother, she added, "When Papa returns from London, we must tell him all about it; he will be pleased that Mr Tate has said that Tom is to write a regular column for the *Review* every week and he will be paid extra for the work. Isn't that wonderful, Mama?"

There was no mistaking either the sheer exhilaration and delight reflected in her face or the warmth of the affection with which Tom O'Connor regarded her, quite unable to conceal his feelings. Cassandra congratulated him and invited him in to take tea with them as Caroline embraced her young niece and bade them all goodbye.

As she drove away, she turned and saw the three figures pass through the entrance and into the house together, and despite the sadness of what Cassy had revealed, she resisted the temptation to be melancholy.

Caroline, who was no stranger to the heights of happiness as well as the abyss of misery, felt deeply for her brother's family. Yet, her heart was filled with a deep sense of joy at seeing the love that clearly absorbed both Laura Ann and Tom. The future, she thought, was not in their hands, but of Laura Ann's present happiness she had no doubt at all.

END OF PART THREE

An Epilogue...

As THE YEAR DREW to a close, those members of the Pemberley families who remained in Derbyshire were acutely aware that this Christmas would be like no other. Mr and Mrs Darcy were not in residence at Pemberley; together with the Bingleys, they were wintering in the south of Italy, a journey undertaken chiefly on account of the indisposition of Mr Bingley and in the hope that both Mr and Mrs Darcy might benefit from the opportunity it afforded for rest and relaxation.

Letters received through the Autumn had assured their families that it had been a prudent decision. Mr Bingley's health had improved; he was looking and feeling very much better, and so, it seemed, was Mr Darcy. Rest and recreation in the salubrious climate of southern Europe had certainly brought their reward. Consequently, both Jane and Elizabeth claimed they were happier and more content as well. But they missed their families and friends, and begged them to write with all the news, to help allay their longing for home.

In the weeks and months that followed, the Darcys and Bingleys, enjoying the warm hospitality and mild Winter that their villa on the Mediterranean offered, received in response many letters, of which a few should suffice to draw together the threads of this narrative. Cassandra, Darcy, and Caroline were their chief correspondents, but letters had arrived from many other members of the family, too.

Two letters, one from Jessica and the other from Kate, arrived one sunny morning, bringing both good and bad news, which Elizabeth read out to the others around the breakfast table.

Jessica, having first given a description of her little daughter Marianne's progress for the benefit of her doting grandparents, proceeded to write:

I know you will be happy to hear that we have had some success with regard to the Irish children from the village who are, at long last, to be permitted to attend school. You will recall that my brother Jude has spent many months trying to persuade the parish priest at Matlock to let them in, but because they are of the Roman Catholic faith and also because they were unable to pay anything towards their education, he would not.

Now Jude and Julian have spoken with Frank Grantley, and, I must add, with the very persuasive efforts of dear Amy, it has been agreed that the Irish children will be permitted to attend the Kympton parish school from next Spring. Julian has offered to assist with any additional expense that the school may incur. I need not tell you how happy Jude is; he feels it is his duty to carry on the work of our dear mother and father, helping these unfortunate people, who, having fled the famine in their own land, have found so little comfort in England.

Julian and I have given Jude our word that we will support his efforts, for he does not have much money to spare, to ensure that the children, at least, will be given some chance of a better life.

I know Mama will have approved, and I hope you and Mr Darcy will also be pleased.

As Elizabeth read, Mr Darcy had listened keenly. When she concluded that part of the letter, he said, "That is excellent news, Lizzie; I am glad that Frank has been persuaded to take the children in at Kympton. I suppose I could have asked him to, but it was much better that he came to the right decision himself. There is nothing worse than allowing a group of children, already damaged by gross poverty, to grow up without any learning or hope of improving their lot. Such exclusion from the community sows the seeds of dissension and conflict, and I am sure both Jude and Julian have understood that well. I confess I am quite proud of them," he said, and Elizabeth, noting the look of satisfaction on his face, smiled and agreed, "Indeed, so am I."

Turning over the page, she said, "Oh look, here's a postscript," and she read:

I cannot close without adding this happy news, which we have just received.

I am sure you will be delighted to know that my dear brother and his wife, Teresa, are expecting a child and look forward to a birth next Summer, by which time we all hope you will be back at Pemberley.

Needless to say both Jane and Lizzie responded with expressions of delight that made both their husbands smile. However, Mr Bingley did warn that he would not be persuaded to rush back to England on account of a new baby unless the weather improved, and Mr Darcy remarked that he was quite sure young Jude Courtney and his wife would manage very well with the help of all their aunts and uncles, provoking an argument with their wives, which delayed the reading of Elizabeth's next piece of correspondence, which came from Kate Gardiner.

When she did get it open and ran her eye over the pages, Lizzie began first to smile, then to chuckle, and finally to laugh out loud as she put the letter down on the breakfast table and proceeded to take off her glasses.

Jane, eager to know what it was that had so diverted her sister, picked up the letter and began to read.

After the first two lines of familial greetings, Kate launched into a vivid description of the discomfiture of the family of Robert and Rose Gardiner.

The tale concerned their daughter Miranda, who had but recently married a certain Mr Croker. Kate wrote:

It would seem that Miranda and Mr Croker, having spent their honeymoon in London and Paris, seem too enamoured of the high life in these cities to want to return to Derbyshire. They have taken an expensive apartment in a fashionable part of London and are enjoying themselves, largely at the expense of Mr and Mrs Robert Gardiner, to whom Miranda has already applied for an increase in her allowance and for assistance with paying her bills.

Miranda also receives, we understand, a regular income from the estate of her late grandfather, which must greatly annoy her brothers, who have not been so lucky. It would seem her mama is very distressed at not having her favourite child close at hand and together with Lady Fitzwilliam complains bitterly of their misfortune to anyone who visits and cares to listen.

Darcy met one of the brothers at his club in Derby and was informed that everyone in the family, except his mother and grandmother, was heartily sick of Miranda and her Mr Croker.

At this point, Jane stopped reading and said in a voice that clearly reflected her feelings, "Oh dear, is that not a great shame, Lizzie? Robert and Rose must be dreadfully disappointed."

Elizabeth, who had by now recovered her composure sufficiently to take up the letter again, responded, "My dear Jane, it can only be disappointing to one who had high expectations of this marriage. None of us did; it was quite clearly an ill-considered and unwise match, and for my part, it has completely fulfilled my expectations."

Jane refused to be cynical. "Oh Lizzie, that is not true, surely?"

"It certainly is, and unless I am very much mistaken, I believe Robert could not have expected much better himself. Croker was clearly a fortune hunter, who saw an opportunity to do well for himself by marrying Miranda and getting his hands on some of her grandparents' money," said Elizabeth.

"Well, if that was his intention, he is bound to be disappointed himself," said Mr Darcy quietly as he peeled an orange and proceeded to take its segments apart. The others looked at him, curious to discover what he meant. Miranda's grandfather James Fitzwilliam was Darcy's cousin. "Miranda's grandfather may have left her a generous allowance, but I am aware that he has ensured that the estate is very well protected from the kind of stupidity that may afflict his sons or anyone else who may think to raid the coffers. James did not trust either his sons or Rose to administer the estate; he has put in place a trust arrangement that compels them to live within their means or go out and earn more money. So I doubt that Mr and Mrs Croker will be able to finance their extravagant lifestyle by applying to the family for very much longer."

Elizabeth could not help laughing, but she also turned accusingly to her husband and said, "Why did you not tell us of this before?"

Mr Darcy smiled, making it plain that he was enjoying this. "It did not seem to matter until now. After all, we have only just heard of the Crokers' demands upon Robert and Rose. Besides, James swore me to secrecy; he knew if either his wife or his daughter discovered the truth, they would have pestered him to change his will."

"Oh dear, poor Miranda and Mr Croker; how very dismayed they are going to be," said Lizzie, not bothering to hide her glee.

"They will certainly be both dismayed and poor, if they continue as they have done," said her husband, still smiling, "and I cannot say that I will be at all surprised at the consequences."

Some days later, returning from their morning walk, Jane and Lizzie found more letters awaiting them. Jane's were from her daughter Emma and her son Jonathan, and she retired to read them in the privacy of her room.

Emma's was full of family news and, apart from conveying their general well-being and happiness, contained nothing that was of significance to anyone other than her parents.

When she opened Jonathan's, however, Jane was surprised to read that he had met with Robert Gardiner, while on a visit to London. He wrote:

Coming away from Whitehall, where I had met with Colin Elliott, I was walking across the park when I happened to bump into Robert Gardiner, and I must confess, Mama, if he had not stopped and greeted me, I should not have known him, he was so changed from when we last met.

But he was clearly keen to continue the conversation, and not wishing to stand out in the cold, I invited him to lunch with me at my club. There, I was even more astonished to discover that Mr Gardiner was seriously depressed.

Unsolicited and without any prompting from me, he poured out a tale that left me quite miserable having heard it. It would seem his daughter Miranda, whose elopement and marriage to a certain Mr Croker caused something of a stir, is determined to live in London, with occasional forays to Paris. Not only is her husband unwilling to support this lavish lifestyle, Robert Gardiner claims he is incapable of doing so, since his pretence of affluence has proved to be just that, a sham. Sadly, Mr Gardiner, who clearly misses his daughter terribly, travelled to London to see her, only to find himself embroiled in a contretemps between Miranda and her husband on the question of their finances.

While there was little I could do for him, he clearly needed to unburden himself, and it seemed to alleviate his gloomy mood somewhat.

I have not spoken of this to anyone but my wife, but, recalling some previous history involving the Gardiners, I did think you and Aunt Lizzie would appreciate the information.

Jane, having read the letter through, took it immediately to her sister, who was enjoying hers from Cassy, with news of young Lizzie Carr's expectation of another child and their planned visit to the United States.

I know I ought be pleased for her because Lizzie has always wanted to travel overseas, but, Mama, I shall miss her and the babies so much; it is selfish of me, I am sure, but I cannot help it, wrote Cassy, and Elizabeth knew exactly how she must feel. Mother and daughter were especially close, and Lizzie resolved to write very soon to offer some comfort.

When Jane entered her room, Jonathan's letter in hand, the sisters exchanged letters, and as Lizzie read Jonathan's account, she almost found it in her heart to feel some sympathy for their cousin Robert Gardiner, but aware of his past callous conduct towards Emily and Jude, Lizzie hardened her heart and said, "Well, Jane, I think it must be quite clear, at least to Robert, that inordinate pride almost always precedes desolation. It is a hard lesson, but one both he and Rose needed to learn."

Jane, tenderhearted and forgiving, was less censorious.

"But, Lizzie," she said, "do you not suppose that Robert will find some way to help Miranda? It does appear that she is in dire distress, and I am sure he loves her dearly and would wish to help her."

"I do not doubt it, Jane," her sister replied, "nor do I doubt her capacity to wheedle some funds out of her father or her grandmother. No, I cannot feel sorry for either of them. Robert is selfish and weak, and Miranda is thoroughly spoilt, as was her mother. They will use each other and Robert or anyone else who will believe them, without any compunction at all."

Jane sighed and continued reading Cassandra's letter to her mother. "Well, at least Cassy sends us good news," she said as they went downstairs together, and Lizzie agreed, recalling even as she did that there were matters even Jane did not know, which Cassy and Richard had bravely endured.

─❧─

They had been several months in Italy, and it was almost Spring by the Mediterranean, when Mr Darcy received a letter from his sister.

Lizzie had been to the shops with Jane and arrived in time to find her husband preparing to drive out to the post office in the town. In his hand he held a letter addressed to Georgiana, who had been spending Christmas with her elder daughter in Hampshire.

Mr Darcy seemed anxious, and Elizabeth was concerned, but he reassured her. "I have had a letter from Georgiana, which required an immediate response; I am taking it to the post office myself to ensure that it gets away in time for the boat to England. You may read her letter if you wish, Lizzie; it is in the top drawer of my bureau," he said as he entered the carriage and was driven away.

Lizzie was puzzled; it seemed odd that Mr Darcy would need to send an urgent response to a letter from his sister. As Mr Bingley was dozing by the fire in the sitting room, Jane and Lizzie went directly upstairs and found Georgiana's letter. It had been hastily written in a troubled hand, quite unlike Georgiana's usual neat copperplate, and it was filled with her anxiety and concern about her daughter Virginia. Appealing to her brother, to whom she had always turned for advice, Georgiana wrote:

My dear brother,

I am sorry to write you such distressing news. I cannot believe it myself, but I have had a letter from Virginia in New South Wales, in which she claims to be totally miserable. She complains about the conditions, the house, the weather, the flies, and much more. Everything she had been led to expect is turned upon its head.

I enclose hers herewith, so you may see how it is with her. Indeed, she threatens to abandon her home and husband and return to England on the next ship leaving New South Wales, unless I agree to travel to Australia myself to help her cope with her problems. I am unsure how my presence will affect their situation, if it is likely to help or hinder them, nor do I know if Mr Fraser will welcome my arrival. He may well regard it as an intrusion into their lives, since there is no hint in Virginia's letter that he is a party to the invitation to me.

Besides, I know nothing of how such a journey is to be arranged. My dear brother, I am so bewildered, please tell me what I should do. I shall await your advice before writing to Virginia.

Although she had been fairly sanguine about the troubles of her cousin Robert's daughter Miranda, Elizabeth did not receive this news with the same composure. For not only was Georgiana her sister-in-law, for whom both she and Mr Darcy felt a warm and protective affection, there was also the question of what to do with Virginia if she abandoned her marriage and returned to England. Would Virginia assume that she could rejoin her mother, who was a guest at Pemberley, and continue to live there herself, Lizzie wondered. It was not a prospect that Elizabeth regarded with any degree of serenity.

Putting down Georgiana's letter, she picked up Virginia's note enclosed within. Obviously written in haste and probably sent away secretly, so as not to alert her husband, it was a litany of complaint from start to finish.

Plainly Virginia had believed Adam Fraser's exaggerated accounts of the status of his position on the property in New South Wales and had been rudely surprised to discover that he was not the owner nor even the manager of the sheep farm, but merely the overseer or under-manager, whose rank, income, and accommodation were all well below his wife's expectations.

She wrote bitterly of the conditions:

They are uniformly unpleasant and almost impossible to imagine for one who has lived chiefly in England. The weather is hot and the sky mostly cloudless as the sun burns down upon the land, which is baked hard and quite unlike any place I have ever seen. The animals seem depressed as they wait to be shorn of their heavy wool coats, and it seems nothing will do, but they must all be gathered in the one paddock, bleating all the time, and pushed through a narrow race by men on horseback with the help of dogs, to be washed and made ready for the shearers.

As for the domestic arrangements, I think a farm labourer on my Uncle Darcy's estate would have a more comfortable cottage than we have here.

The wind whistles through the walls, and sand comes in under the doors and horrid creatures crawl in with it. The servants, who are mostly ex-felons, are untrained and unwilling to serve, and mostly do so sullenly; if I did not have my maid with me, I think I should have died. The food is plentiful, but that is all one can say, because its preparation is the most primitive, being all done upon a blazing hearth or in a blazing oven. The result is usually inedible, being either burnt or undercooked. Yet, no one else seems to complain, which convinces me that they must all have been so long away from home, they have quite forgotten how life was back in England...

So it continued over two pages, in which Virginia catalogued her grievances, lamented the lack of "civilised accoutrements," claimed she could not continue in such a situation unsupported, and begged her mother to join her.

Elizabeth shook her head in exasperation. "Oh Virginia, stupid girl, what did you expect?" she said almost to herself, and then turning to Jane declared, "It is clear, is it not, that Adam Fraser has completely taken her in? All that talk of his exciting life in Australia had her believing she was going to live the life of a wealthy landowner's wife with servants at her beck and call."

"What advice do you suppose Mr Darcy has sent Georgiana?" Jane asked, and her sister looked dubious.

"I cannot believe his attitude would be very sympathetic, Jane," she replied. "When Virginia announced that she was going to marry Fraser, she was warned about the uncertainty of conditions in the colonies, but she chose to ignore it. Now that she has had a rude awakening, it is unlikely that Darcy would be inclined to support her contention that she is an innocent victim of deception and the harsh climate of the southern colonies."

Jane thought her sister was being a little unsympathetic, but the return of Mr Darcy not long afterwards proved Elizabeth right. On being asked how he had responded to Georgiana's appeal for advice, he explained briefly that he had sent his sister an express communication, advising her not to consider travelling to Australia as her daughter urged her to do, since it was unlikely to do any good at all and may well do much harm.

"I believe that it would not only be of no help to Virginia, being far more likely to exacerbate her situation and any problems she may have with her husband, but it would also be quite inimical to Georgiana's own well-being. I cannot see that transporting herself thousands of miles across the sea, to live in an inhospitable climate without any of the comforts she has been accustomed to all her life, will be of any benefit to her."

"How then have you advised her to respond to Virginia?" asked Elizabeth.

"With sympathy and firmness, my dear," Darcy replied, and Jane and Lizzie both noticed a distinct twinkle in his eye, as he added, "Virginia is too far away to throw a tantrum. When she threatens to abandon her husband and return to England, she has no notion of how or where she will live and by what means. Having married Fraser, she has no longer an independent income, apart from a modest personal allowance, and probably hopes to extract both money and sympathy from her mother. However, I have advised Georgiana to counsel her daughter that she will have no access to any further sums of money, since the rest of her father's fortune is in trust to be shared with her siblings into the future."

Seeing the looks of dismay and alarm upon the faces of his wife and sister-in-law, Darcy smiled and said, "Have no fear, ladies, Virginia will not starve; she is still a very wealthy young woman, and so long as she does nothing stupid, like leaving her husband and returning to England, upon a whim, she will have adequate means to live in reasonable comfort." Noting that they did not appear convinced, he added, "I have assured Georgiana that the very best thing she can do for her daughter is to ignore her grumbling and urge her to make the best of her life. She is young enough and sturdy enough to adapt to conditions in a new country, unlike Georgiana, who would probably become ill and miserable there."

Since Lizzie and Jane had no alternative solution to offer, it seemed that Mr Darcy had had the last word on the matter.

Other letters, from Caroline and Amy, brought more news from Derbyshire, in particular the establishment by Caroline of a home for destitute women and children at Arrowfield House and the imminent arrival in England of Daniel Faulkner's young son, Martin. Two new families had also recently settled in the district, the O'Connors and the Barwicks.

Caroline spoke highly of the O'Connors, and Elizabeth recalled that Kate had mentioned them too, especially two charming and talented young girls in the family. They were pretty and accomplished, and their widowed mother was an actress from Ireland, Lizzie recalled.

Of the Barwicks, there was little said except they were rich and hailed from Birmingham, where they had made their money in hardware.

"Another of those families who arrive out of nowhere and leave as suddenly, no doubt," said Lizzie, recalling the Hendersons, but Mr Darcy, who had also received a letter from their grandson, pointed out that the Barwicks appeared to be keen to buy up land in the district, in order to build mansions for the wealthy. "Mr Barwick is not just rich, Lizzie; he is a developer. This is certainly not welcome news," said Mr Darcy, a deep frown furrowing his brow. "There is no knowing what these men will do, especially if they are able to get the ear of the council. I should hate to think of them buying up parcels of land all over the county and building a string of hideous mansions, as they have done in the south," he said, and Lizzie, understanding his unease, felt rather apprehensive herself.

"Caroline does not seem to like them much either," she said. "She writes that the women are ostentatious and the men brash and boorish; she intends to campaign against their plans to build villas for the rich in the Peak District."

A week or two later, a letter from Jessica brought more news of the Barwicks and related briefly Mr Barwick's attempts to buy up a number of properties in the area, including the recently acquired home of the O'Connor family, Willowdale Farm. Jessica described in detail the steps that had been taken to foil their plans, concluding with some satisfaction:

> *Not only have we succeeded in saving Willowdale Farm for the O'Connors, who are indeed a charming family; we believe we have staved off an attempt to buy up and subdivide Trantford Manor. The family were keen to sell, but Julian and I have persuaded them not to sell to the Barwicks and have offered to buy the place ourselves. Julian believes that it is a fine property, with which opinion Darcy and Aunt Cassy both agree, and since we shall have to make our own home somewhere, it may as well be at Trantford, not twenty minutes' distance from Pemberley. We would very much like our children to grow up within reach of Pemberley, for all that it means to us and the community we live in. It is a decision we have taken for our future, and we hope that you and Mr Darcy will both agree it is a good one.*

So wrote Jessica to her mother-in-law, and Lizzie, on taking the letter to her husband, had the satisfaction of seeing him smile and say, "That is perhaps the most sensible decision Julian has made since he and Jessica were married, and I have no doubt her influence has been significant," and as his wife nodded, he said, "I think, Lizzie my dear, we may safely entrust the future of Pemberley to our children. Do you not agree?"

"I certainly do," said his wife. "I think they have surely proved themselves well able to understand and discharge their responsibilities to Pemberley and our community."

It had been only the previous night that they had discussed their concerns at being away from Pemberley for an extended period of time, longer than ever before. Mr Darcy had been restless; he worried that things may not always be done as they should, and Lizzie had tried to reassure him, pointing out that with Cassy and Richard there, as well as Darcy and Julian, he need not be anxious.

"If there were to be a crisis, there are many wise heads that would help resolve it, surely?" Lizzie had said, and after a while, he had agreed that she was right.

"Besides," he had said, regarding her with some amusement, "being away from the responsibilities of Pemberley has given us time together, and I am very grateful for that."

Elizabeth agreed; it had been an opportunity to enjoy the particular pleasures of their marriage, the rich companionship, their shared interests, the closeness and intimacy they had treasured for many years.

It was while pondering these singular advantages of their present situation that Darcy had, without warning, confided in her something he claimed had haunted him all his adult life. He had, he said, a most melancholy recollection of the unhappiness of his mother, Lady Anne Darcy, whose loneliness had been so obvious to him, yet had escaped the notice of his father, who carried out all his responsibilities to the estate in an exemplary fashion but never seemed to notice the despair of his young wife.

"I made myself a promise, long before I had any notion of marriage myself or met anyone who might be my wife, that I would not make the same mistake; I resolved that I would not marry a woman with whom I could not fully share all aspects of my life, because I had no wish to see her suffer as I saw my dear mother suffer—disconsolate and alone. Not all the pleasures that Pemberley could offer made up for her desolation of spirit," he said, and Elizabeth confessed then that she had read some of the verses composed and copied out in the notebooks his mother had left in the library at Pemberley. Darcy expressed both surprise and pleasure. "Did you like reading them?" he asked, and she, after pausing to consider her response, said, "Yes, they are beautifully composed and express well her feelings, but I will say that I found them sad, deeply sad, and though I knew nothing of what you have just told me, I could not fail to sense her unhappiness. I knew there must have been a reason, but was reluctant to pry." They had never spoken of this before, not in all the years of their long and happy marriage.

When he asked, "Lizzie, why did you not speak to me of it? When you read what my mother had written, did you not want to ask me about her melancholy when it was so clear to you?"

Elizabeth felt tears sting her eyes, and she could not answer him immediately, but slowly she explained, "I did want to ask, but I was afraid that it may have looked like criticism of your father, and I knew how very highly you regarded him. I had no wish to hurt your feelings... I thought you may resent my asking..."

To which Darcy's response was to put his arms around her, to reassure her. "I certainly did esteem and admire him, Lizzie, but I loved my mother dearly, and when I discovered how little attention he paid her, how little he seemed to care that she suffered, even as she carried out all her duties to him and presided over the household at Pemberley without complaint, I confess I did resent it very much. It was what made me more cautious and reserved; I was determined not to repeat my father's mistakes when I chose a wife. When we married, I resolved never to let anything come between us and taint our marriage..."

"And indeed you have not, my love," she responded with warmth and conviction. "I have always known that I could come to you with any of my problems and be assured of your understanding; you were ready to help even before we were married, when it was my most undeserving sister and her feckless lover. Never have you turned away from me or left me feeling abandoned or lonely—especially not in our darkest moments—never have I felt alone, nor have our children."

He smiled then, clearly moved by her words, and said, "And you, my dearest Elizabeth, you have been more to me than I ever dared to hope, much more. We have shared so much."

He held her very close then, knowing that their love had exceeded all their expectations and brought them deep contentment. This mostly carefree interlude in Italy had afforded them an opportunity to reaffirm the depth of those precious shared emotions.

~~

On the following morning, a letter from Cassy brought even greater felicity. *Dearest Mama and Papa*, she wrote:

Having received yours, with so much good news about Mr Bingley's recovery and your own enjoyment of the excellent weather, we are all quite envious because we are moving into a spell of cold weather. But I hasten to say that I have some good news, which has helped warm our hearts after a quiet Christmas without you.

Our dear Laura Ann is engaged. There, is that not a delightful surprise? The young man is a Mr Thomas O'Connor, who with his mother and sisters has recently come to live at Willowdale Farm. The O'Connors are a charming family and, Mama, Tom is indeed a very talented but modest young man, with an ambition to be a writer. He has a position with the Matlock Review, *and Richard tells me Walter Tate is well pleased with his work.*

Laura Ann and he share a love of music and poetry; they have been friends for a while and it became increasingly clear to us that they were falling in love. Mr O'Connor has proposed to and been accepted by Laura Ann, who declares that Tom is the best and most interesting man she has ever met. She is quite transformed since their engagement, and they seem very happy together. Richard and I have given them our blessing.

Dear Mama, you and Papa know well the truth about Laura Ann's heart condition, which has been concealed from her for many years. For this same reason, Richard and I decided, once we were sure that Tom O'Connor was a man worthy of our daughter, a man we could love and trust, that we would not stand in the way of their marriage. Richard has spoken with Tom in confidence, explaining exactly what Laura Ann's condition could mean. Richard says Tom wept when he told him, but declared that it made him all the more determined to ensure her happiness. While he may not be wealthy or have an estate to offer, he loves her dearly, and Laura is happier than we have ever seen her.

They have not the means to make a separate home, but Richard and I feel that for Laura's sake, they should live at Camden House after they are married, and they have both agreed. We think it will suit us all well.

Dearest Mama, we hope you and Papa will be back at Pemberley by Easter, when they will be married. We look forward very much to your return home.

Richard and Laura Ann send their love.

Your loving daughter,

Cassy

When Elizabeth and Darcy had read the letter, they looked at one another, and there was no doubt in their minds what this news meant. Young Laura Ann was a special favourite.

They had enjoyed the time spent in southern Italy, away from the damp northern Winter, significantly improving their health and restoring their spirits. But Spring was here, and though it may not be as temperate in Derbyshire as it was by the blue Mediterranean, if young Laura Ann was in love and preparing to be married, it was definitely time to return to Pemberley.

Postscript

IT IS HARD INDEED for a writer to say farewell to her characters, and mine have been with me for the better part of ten years. As they developed, I have told their stories for the entertainment of many readers who came to love them almost as much as I do. Of that, their letters and messages have left me in no doubt.

The Pemberley characters, of whom the first were borrowed from Jane Austen's *Pride and Prejudice*, and others who appeared on the scene as we travelled through the years, have become part of my family. I shared their joys and sorrows, their tears and laughter and, like many of my readers, always wanted to know more about them.

We have now spanned a period of fifty years together, and it is surely time to bring this series to an appropriate conclusion and leave the rest to the imagination of my readers.

I confess that I have wondered how it would be to revisit Pemberley, twenty years on, with the new generation of owners in charge. I have even dreamed, once or twice, of returning to Pemberley, to walk among its familiar groves and observe how the new master—young Anthony Darcy—plays his role.

Where would life have led Julian and Jessica? What of young Darcy Gardiner and his lovely Kate? And little Laura Ann?

As you can see, it is hard indeed for me to let them go. But, for now, these are just questions, and whether I take up my pen again to find the answers will depend on many things.

Meanwhile, albeit reluctantly, but with the hope that they will continue to bring you pleasure, I must say goodbye and thank you all—my characters, my publishers, and my readers—for the most delightful decade of my life.

Rebecca Ann Collins
2009

Appendix

A list of the main characters in *The Legacy of Pemberley:*

Emily Courtney (nee Gardiner)—cousin of Elizabeth and Jane

Rev James Courtney—her late husband

Emily's children—Elizabeth Harwood, William Courtney, Jessica Darcy, and Jude Courtney (Jessica is married to Julian Darcy, son of Mr and Mrs Darcy)

Mr Mancini—a flower farmer, who leases some land at Oakleigh

Teresa—his granddaughter

Robert and Rose Gardiner—Emily's brother and his wife

Miranda—their daughter

Mr Croker—a business acquaintance of Robert Gardiner

Caroline Fitzwilliam and Colonel Fitzwilliam—Emily's sister and her husband

Isabella, David, Rachel, Amy, and James—their children

Georgiana Grantley—Mr Darcy's sister

Rev Francis Grantley—her husband

Virginia—their youngest daughter

Rev Frank Grantley—their son, the new rector of Kympton

Amy—his wife (daughter of Colonel Fitzwilliam and Caroline)

Jonathan and Anna Bingley—son and daughter-in-law of Mr and Mrs Bingley

Anne-Marie Elliott—Jonathan's daughter and wife of Colin Elliott MP

Daniel Faulkner—brother of Anna Bingley

Adam Fraser—a friend of Daniel Faulkner

Sir Richard Gardiner—a physician, husband of Cassy Darcy

Laura Ann—their youngest daughter

Lizzie Carr—her elder sister, married to Mr Michael Carr

Darcy and Kate Gardiner—son and daughter-in-law of Cassy and Richard Gardiner

Elena O'Hare—Kate's younger sister

The O'Connor family—an Irish family recently settled in Derbyshire

Mrs O'Connor—a widow

Tom, Marguerite, and Elvira—her three children

And from the pages of *Pride and Prejudice:*

Mr and Mrs Darcy of Pemberley

Mr and Mrs Bingley of Ashford Park

Acknowledgments

The author wishes to thank her family and friends for the love, encouragement, and help they have given her in all of the work associated with this series of novels.

Thanks are due also to Ms Claudia Taylor, librarian, for help with research; Marissa O'Donnell for her artwork; Beverly Wong-Kleinjan and Aimee L Fry for their work on the websites; Anthony and Rose for invaluable technical help and moral support over the entire project.

Thank you, too, to all her readers, who have read the Pemberley novels and written to say how much they enjoyed them.

A very special thank you to Miss Jane Austen for her inspiration and example.

—Rebecca Ann Collins
www.rebeccaanncollins.com

About the Author

A lifelong fan of Jane Austen, Rebecca Ann Collins first read *Pride and Prejudice* at the tender age of twelve. She fell in love with the characters and since then has devoted years of research and study to the life and works of her favorite author. As a teacher of literature and a librarian, she has gathered a wealth of information about Miss Austen and the period in which she lived and wrote, which became the basis of her books about the Pemberley families. The popularity of The Pemberley Chronicles series with Jane Austen fans has been her reward.

With a love of reading, music, art, and gardening, Ms. Collins claims she is very comfortable in the period about which she writes, and feels great empathy with the characters she portrays. While she enjoys the convenience of modern life, she finds much to admire in the values and world view of Jane Austen.